S0-BZT-615

THE BABY-SITTERS CLUB

KRISTY AND THE WALKING DISASTER

DON'T MISS THE OTHER
BABY-SITTERS CLUB GRAPHIC NOVELS!

KRISTY'S GREAT IDEA

THE TRUTH ABOUT STACEY

MARY ANNE SAVES THE DAY

CLAUDIA AND MEAN JANINE

DAWN AND THE IMPOSSIBLE THREE

KRISTY'S BIG DAY

BOY-CRAZY STACEY

LOGAN LIKES MARY ANNE!

CLAUDIA AND THE NEW GIRL

KRISTY AND THE SNOBS

GOOD-BYE STACEY, GOOD-BYE

JESSI'S SECRET LANGUAGE

MARY ANNE'S BAD LUCK MYSTERY

STACEY'S MISTAKE

CLAUDIA AND THE BAD JOKE

ANN M. MARTIN

THE BABY-SITTERS CLUB®

KRISTY'S KRUSHERS
COACH

KRISTY AND THE WALKING DISASTER

A GRAPHIC NOVEL BY

ELLEN T. CRENSHAW

WITH COLOR BY BRADEN LAMB AND JASON CAFFOE

graphix
An Imprint of
SCHOLASTIC

Text copyright © 2024 by Ann M. Martin
Art copyright © 2024 by Ellen T. Crenshaw

All rights reserved. Published by Graphix, an imprint of
Scholastic Inc., *Publishers since 1920.* SCHOLASTIC, GRAPHIX,
THE BABY-SITTERS CLUB, and associated logos are trademarks
and/or registered trademarks of Scholastic Inc.

The publisher does not have any control over and does not assume any
responsibility for author or third-party websites or their content.

No part of this publication may be reproduced, stored in a retrieval system,
or transmitted in any form or by any means, electronic, mechanical, photocopying,
recording, or otherwise, without written permission of the publisher. For information
regarding permission, write to Scholastic Inc., Attention: Permissions
Department, 557 Broadway, New York, NY 10012.

This book is a work of fiction. Names, characters, places, and
incidents are either the product of the author's imagination or are used
fictitiously, and any resemblance to actual persons, living or dead, business
establishments, events, or locales is entirely coincidental.

Library of Congress Control Number: 2023947641

ISBN 978-1-338-83556-4 (hardcover)
ISBN 978-1-338-83555-7 (paperback)

10 9 8 7 6 5 4 3 2 1   24 25 26 27 28

Printed in China 62
First edition, September 2024

Edited by Cassandra Pelham Fulton
Color flatting by Preston Do and Lorraine Grate
Creative Director: Phil Falco
Publisher: David Saylor

This book is for the
members of the Lunch Club
A. M. M.

For Mom and Dad. Thank you for evening readings
of the comics pages; for grammar lessons, swing dancing,
sing-alongs, and endless hands of rummy. Most of all, thank you
for enthusiastically supporting my career as an artist.
E. T. C.

KRISTY THOMAS
PRESIDENT

CLAUDIA KISHI
VICE PRESIDENT

MARY ANNE SPIER
SECRETARY

DAWN SCHAFER
TREASURER

JESSI RAMSEY
JUNIOR OFFICER

MALLORY PIKE
JUNIOR OFFICER

STACEY MCGILL
NEW YORK BRANCH

CHAPTER 1

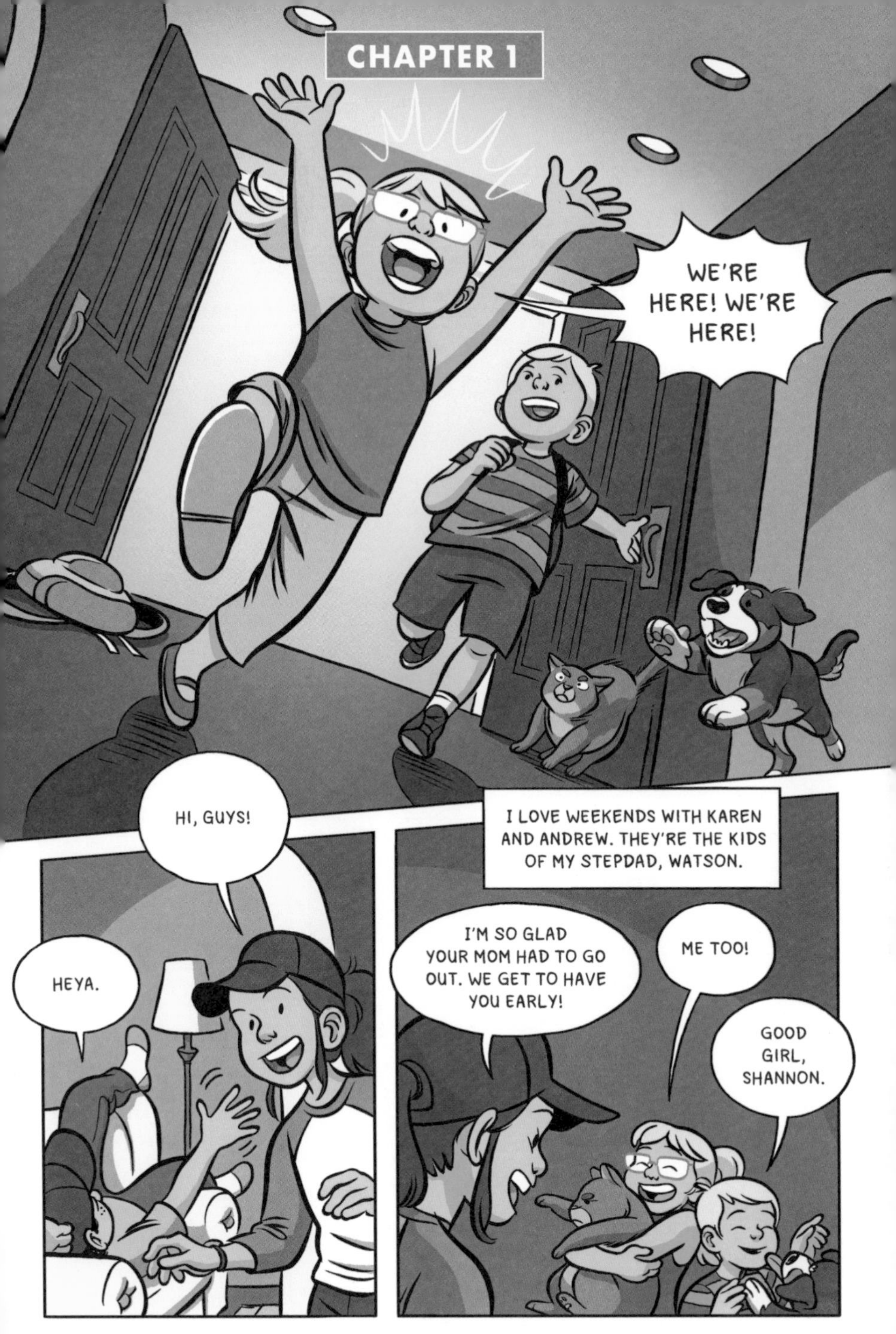
WE'RE HERE! WE'RE HERE!
HI, GUYS!
HEYA.
I LOVE WEEKENDS WITH KAREN AND ANDREW. THEY'RE THE KIDS OF MY STEPDAD, WATSON.
I'M SO GLAD YOUR MOM HAD TO GO OUT. WE GET TO HAVE YOU EARLY!
ME TOO!
GOOD GIRL, SHANNON.

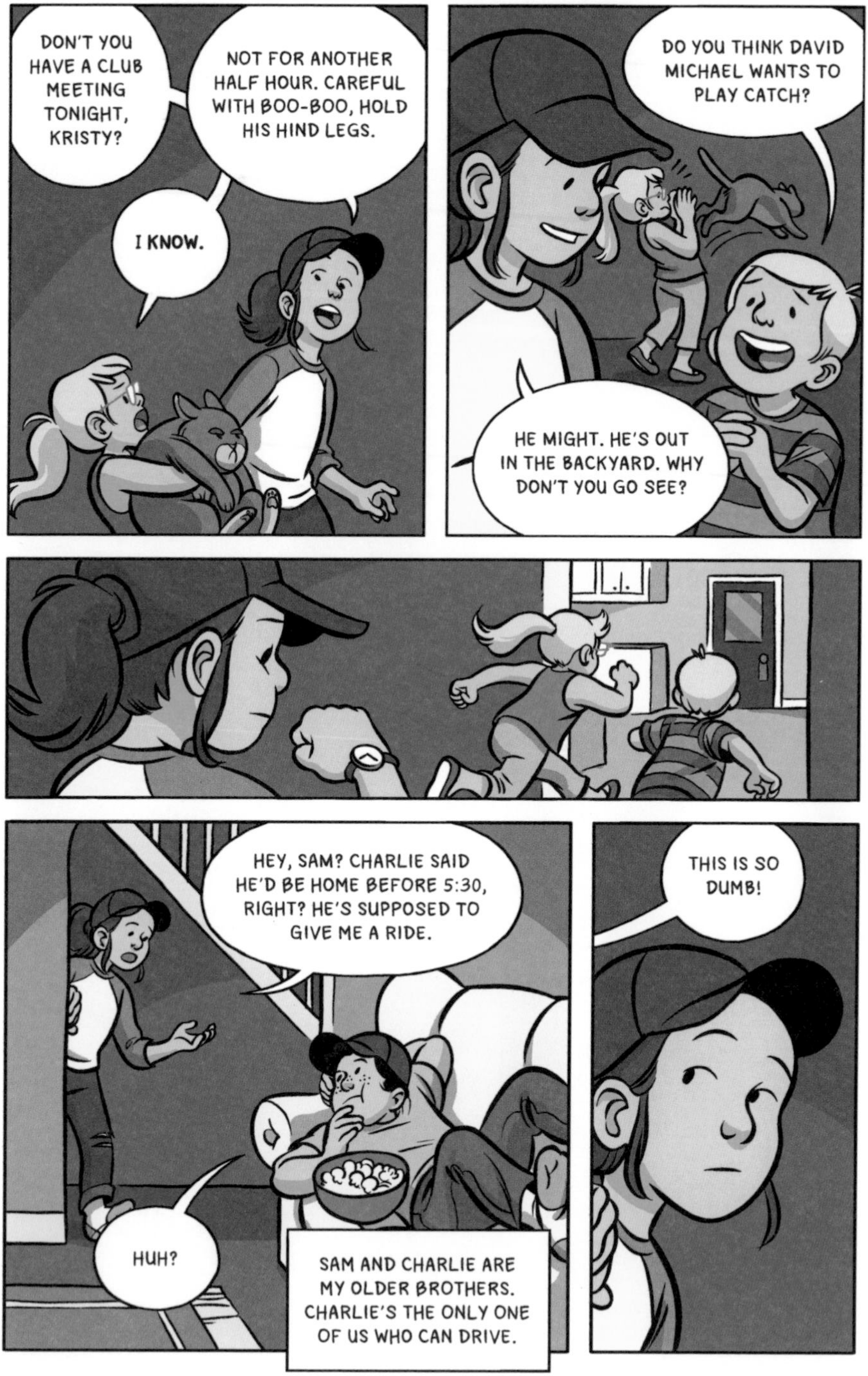
DON'T YOU HAVE A CLUB MEETING TONIGHT, KRISTY?
NOT FOR ANOTHER HALF HOUR. CAREFUL WITH BOO-BOO, HOLD HIS HIND LEGS.
I KNOW.
DO YOU THINK DAVID MICHAEL WANTS TO PLAY CATCH?
HE MIGHT. HE'S OUT IN THE BACKYARD. WHY DON'T YOU GO SEE?
HEY, SAM? CHARLIE SAID HE'D BE HOME BEFORE 5:30, RIGHT? HE'S SUPPOSED TO GIVE ME A RIDE.
HUH?
SAM AND CHARLIE ARE MY OLDER BROTHERS. CHARLIE'S THE ONLY ONE OF US WHO CAN DRIVE.
THIS IS SO DUMB!

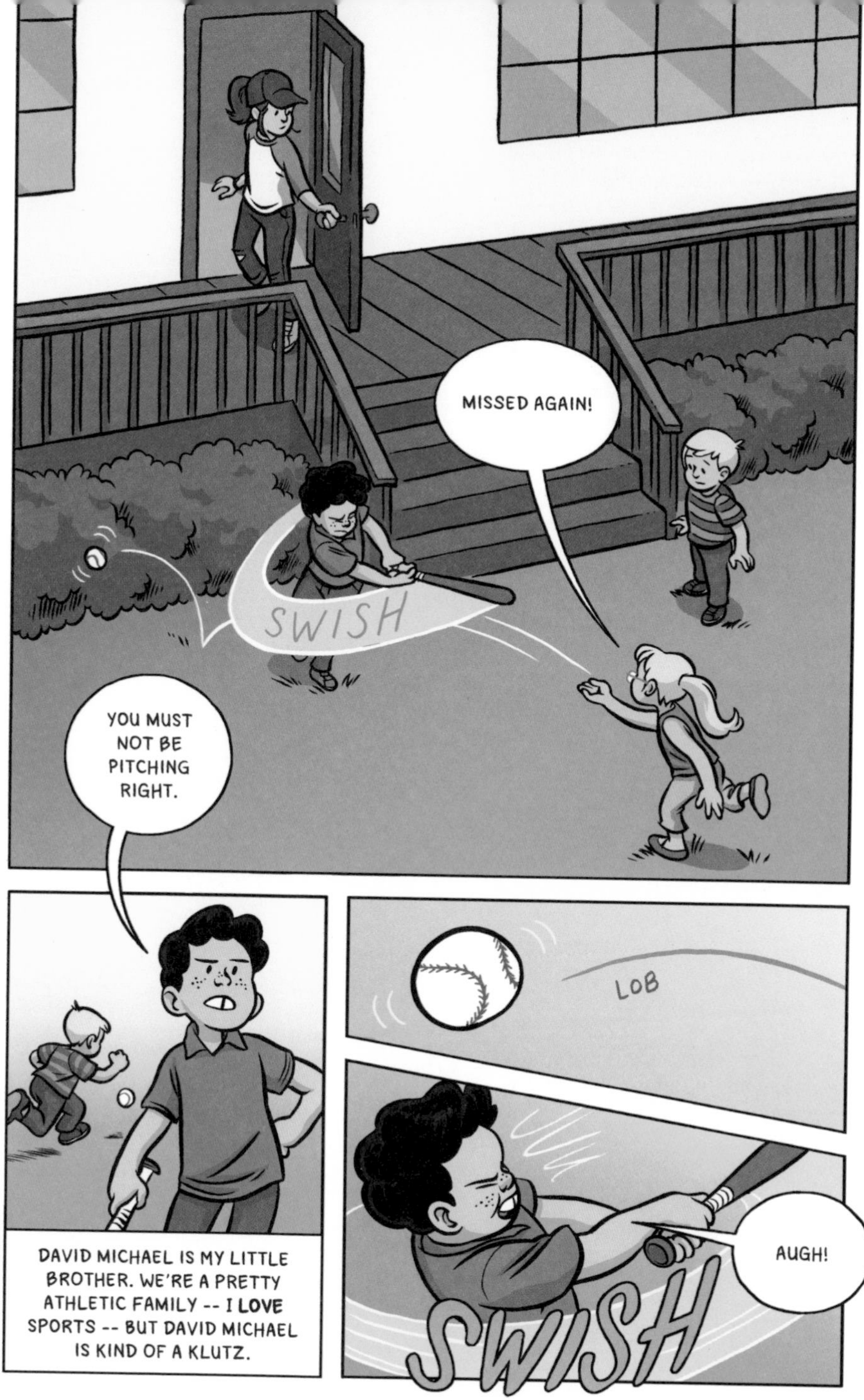
MISSED AGAIN!
SWISH
YOU MUST NOT BE PITCHING RIGHT.
LOB
DAVID MICHAEL IS MY LITTLE BROTHER. WE'RE A PRETTY ATHLETIC FAMILY -- I **LOVE** SPORTS -- BUT DAVID MICHAEL IS KIND OF A KLUTZ.
AUGH!
SWISH

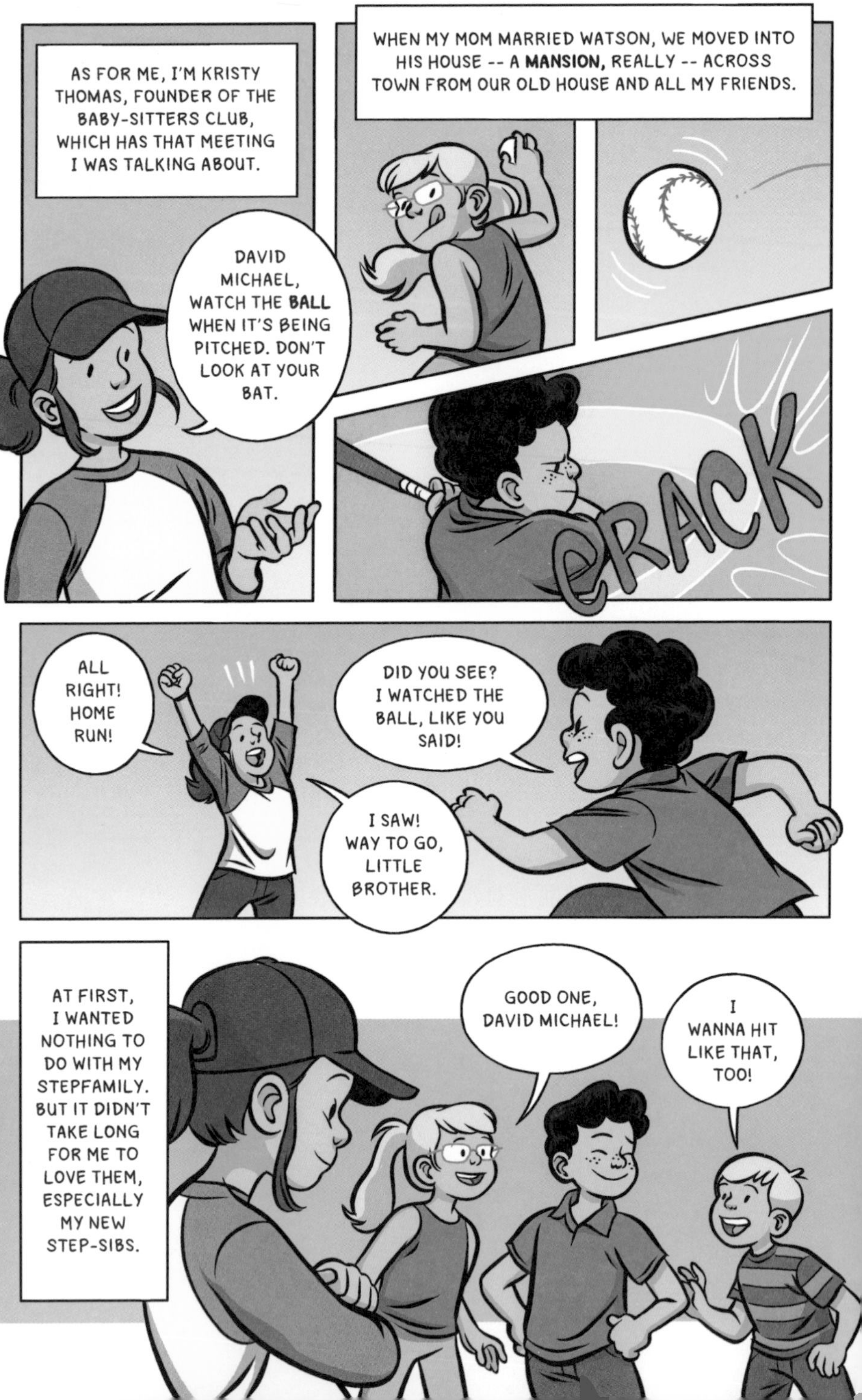
AS FOR ME, I'M KRISTY THOMAS, FOUNDER OF THE BABY-SITTERS CLUB, WHICH HAS THAT MEETING I WAS TALKING ABOUT.
WHEN MY MOM MARRIED WATSON, WE MOVED INTO HIS HOUSE -- A **MANSION,** REALLY -- ACROSS TOWN FROM OUR OLD HOUSE AND ALL MY FRIENDS.
DAVID MICHAEL, WATCH THE **BALL** WHEN IT'S BEING PITCHED. DON'T LOOK AT YOUR BAT.
CRACK
ALL RIGHT! HOME RUN!
DID YOU SEE? I WATCHED THE BALL, LIKE YOU SAID!
I SAW! WAY TO GO, LITTLE BROTHER.
AT FIRST, I WANTED NOTHING TO DO WITH MY STEPFAMILY. BUT IT DIDN'T TAKE LONG FOR ME TO LOVE THEM, ESPECIALLY MY NEW STEP-SIBS.
GOOD ONE, DAVID MICHAEL!
I WANNA HIT LIKE THAT, TOO!

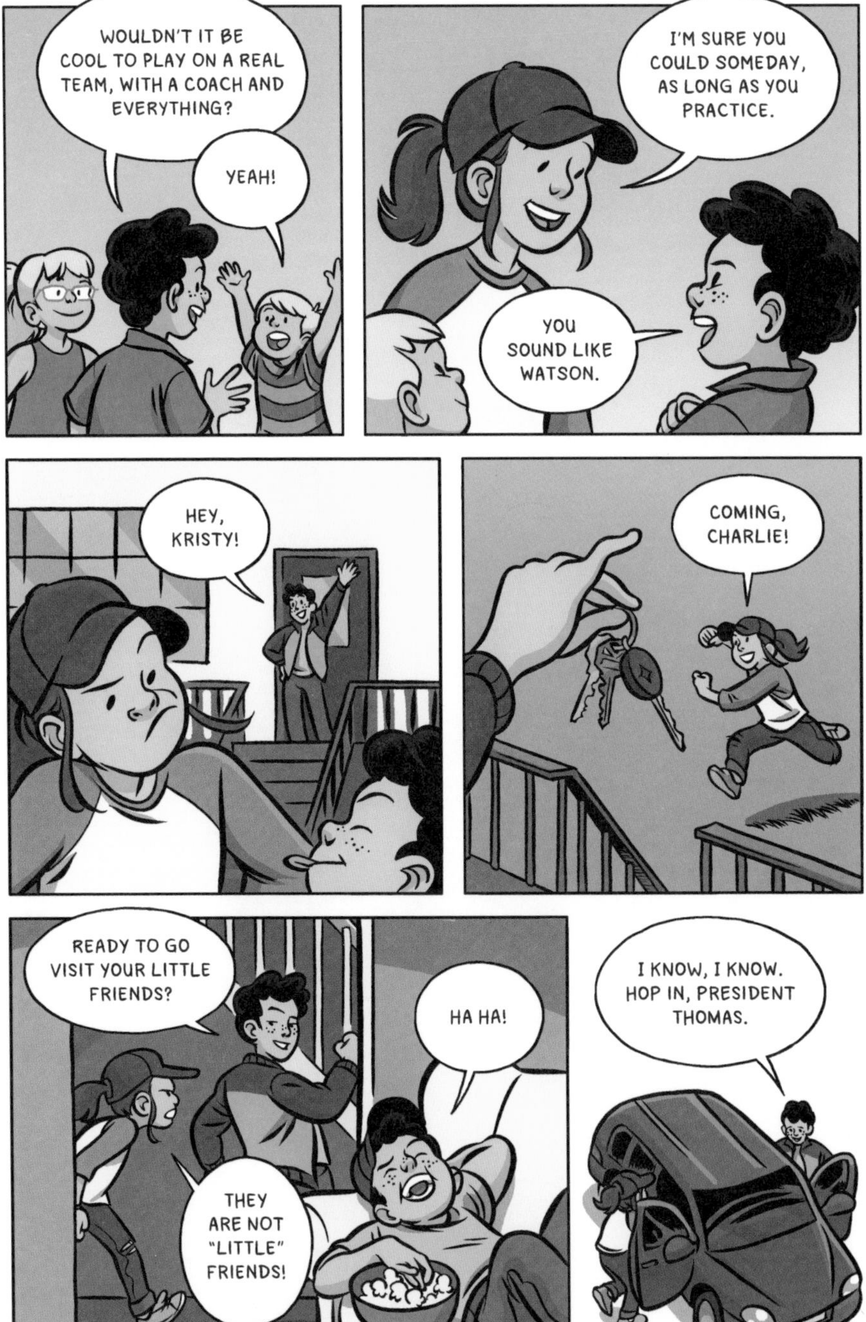
WOULDN'T IT BE COOL TO PLAY ON A REAL TEAM, WITH A COACH AND EVERYTHING?
YEAH!
I'M SURE YOU COULD SOMEDAY, AS LONG AS YOU PRACTICE.
YOU SOUND LIKE WATSON.
HEY, KRISTY!
COMING, CHARLIE!
READY TO GO VISIT YOUR LITTLE FRIENDS?
HA HA!
THEY ARE NOT "LITTLE" FRIENDS!
I KNOW, I KNOW. HOP IN, PRESIDENT THOMAS.

CHAPTER 2

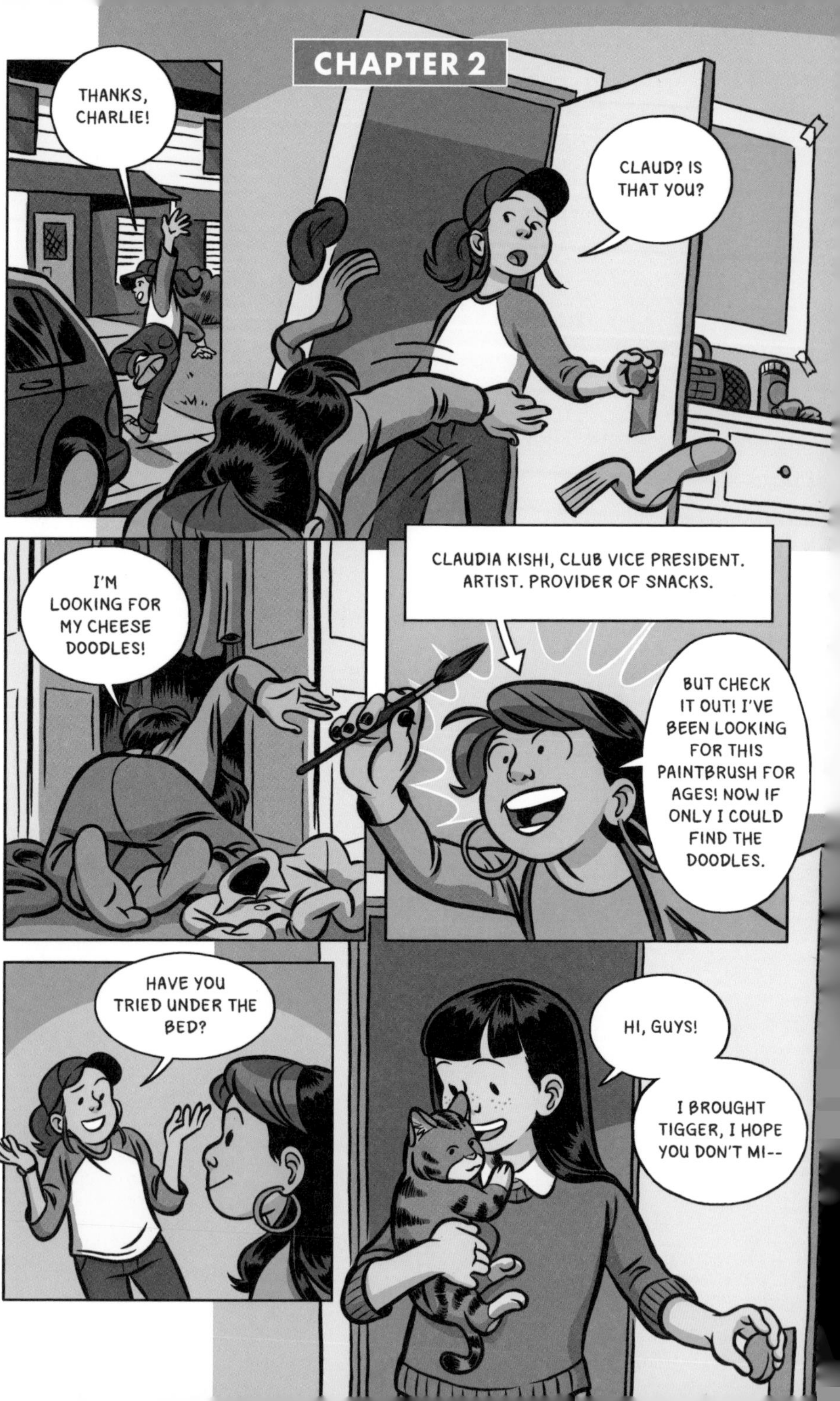
THANKS, CHARLIE!
CLAUD? IS THAT YOU?
I'M LOOKING FOR MY CHEESE DOODLES!
CLAUDIA KISHI, CLUB VICE PRESIDENT. ARTIST. PROVIDER OF SNACKS.
BUT CHECK IT OUT! I'VE BEEN LOOKING FOR THIS PAINTBRUSH FOR AGES! NOW IF ONLY I COULD FIND THE DOODLES.
HAVE YOU TRIED UNDER THE BED?
HI, GUYS!
I BROUGHT TIGGER, I HOPE YOU DON'T MI--

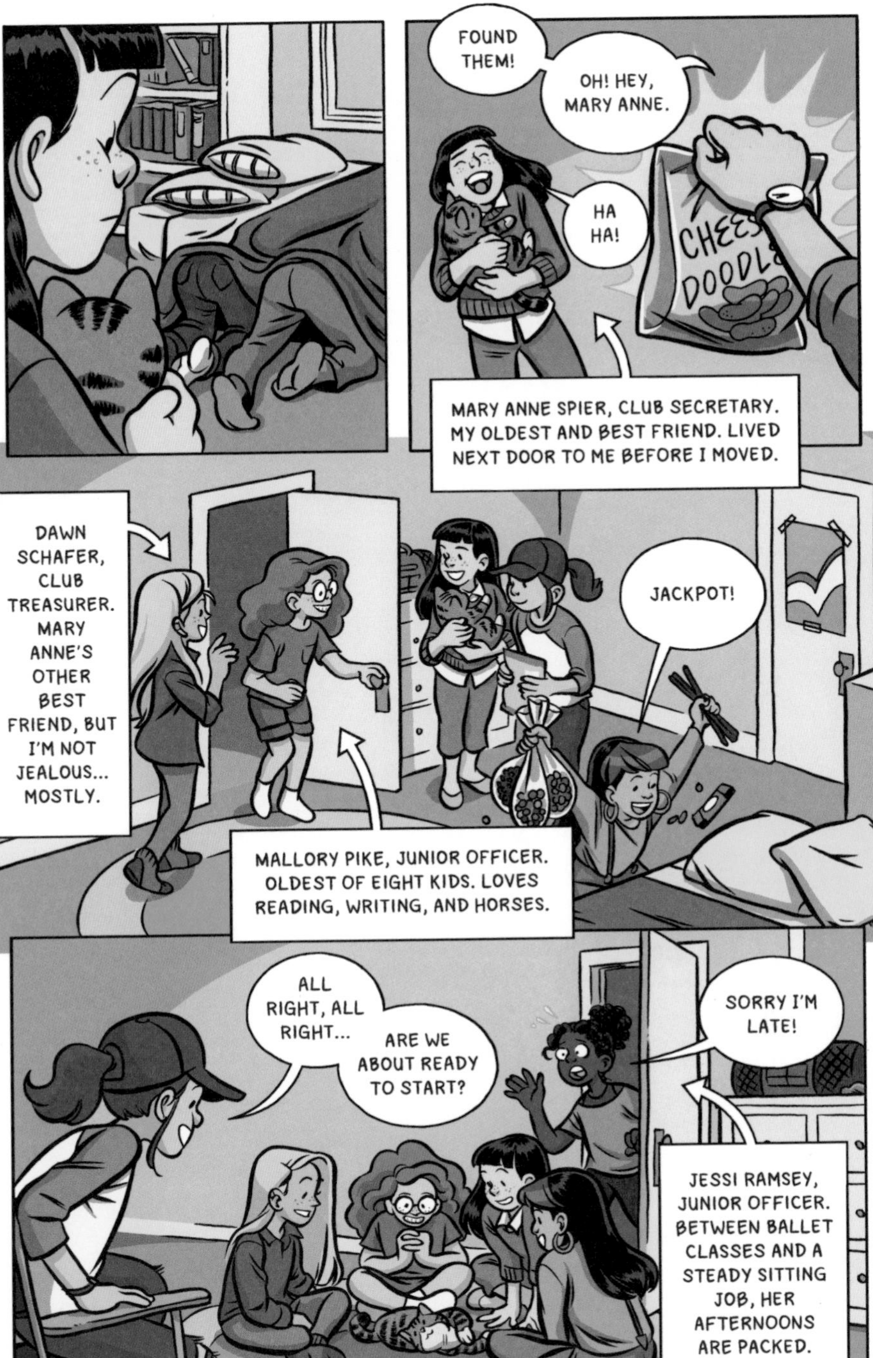
FOUND THEM!
OH! HEY, MARY ANNE.
HA HA!
CHEES DOODLE
MARY ANNE SPIER, CLUB SECRETARY. MY OLDEST AND BEST FRIEND. LIVED NEXT DOOR TO ME BEFORE I MOVED.
DAWN SCHAFER, CLUB TREASURER. MARY ANNE'S OTHER BEST FRIEND, BUT I'M NOT JEALOUS... MOSTLY.
JACKPOT!
MALLORY PIKE, JUNIOR OFFICER. OLDEST OF EIGHT KIDS. LOVES READING, WRITING, AND HORSES.
ALL RIGHT, ALL RIGHT...
ARE WE ABOUT READY TO START?
SORRY I'M LATE!
JESSI RAMSEY, JUNIOR OFFICER. BETWEEN BALLET CLASSES AND A STEADY SITTING JOB, HER AFTERNOONS ARE PACKED.

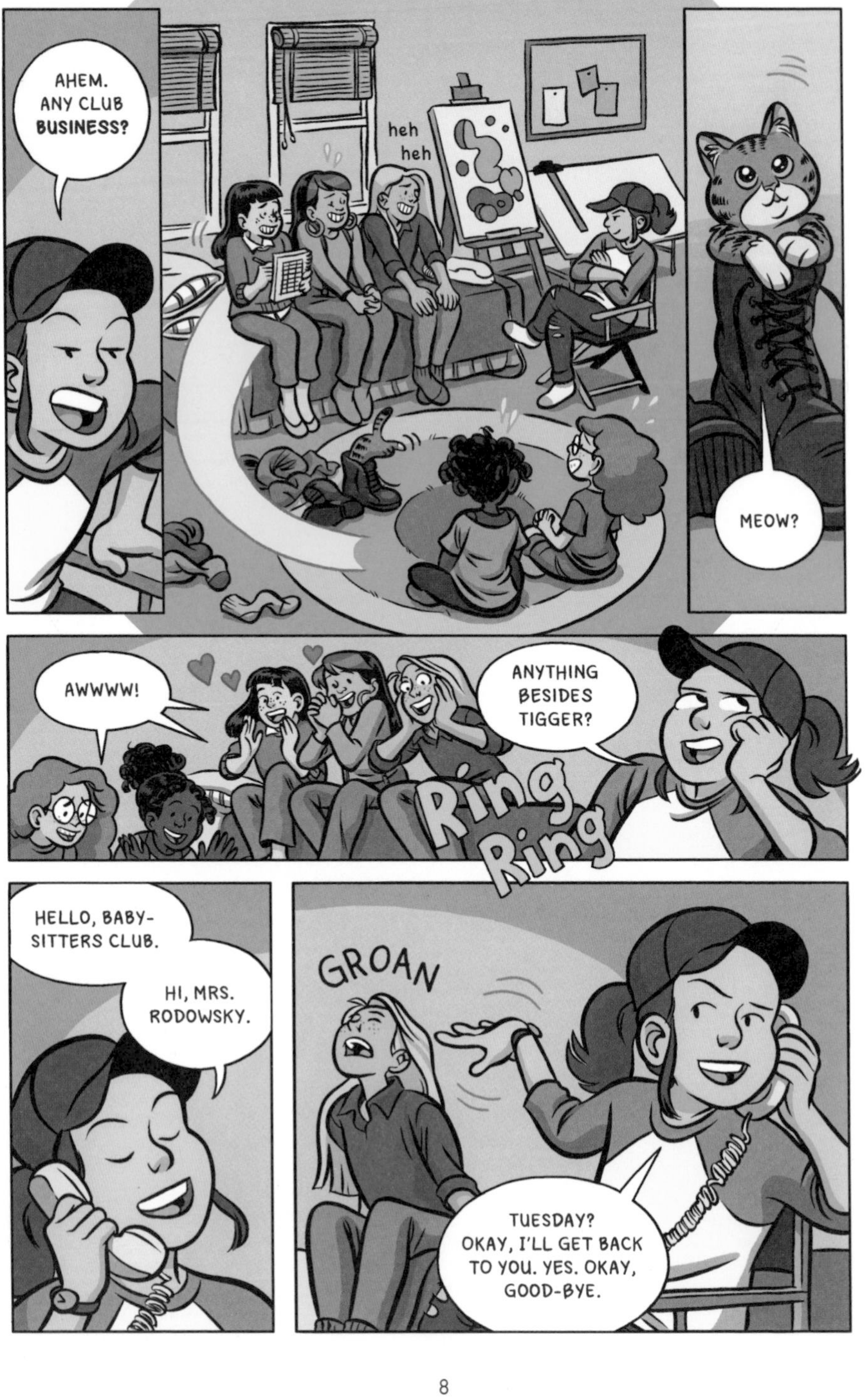
AHEM. ANY CLUB BUSINESS?
heh heh
MEOW?
AWWWW!
ANYTHING BESIDES TIGGER?
Ring Ring
HELLO, BABY-SITTERS CLUB.
HI, MRS. RODOWSKY.
GROAN
TUESDAY? OKAY, I'LL GET BACK TO YOU. YES. OKAY, GOOD-BYE.

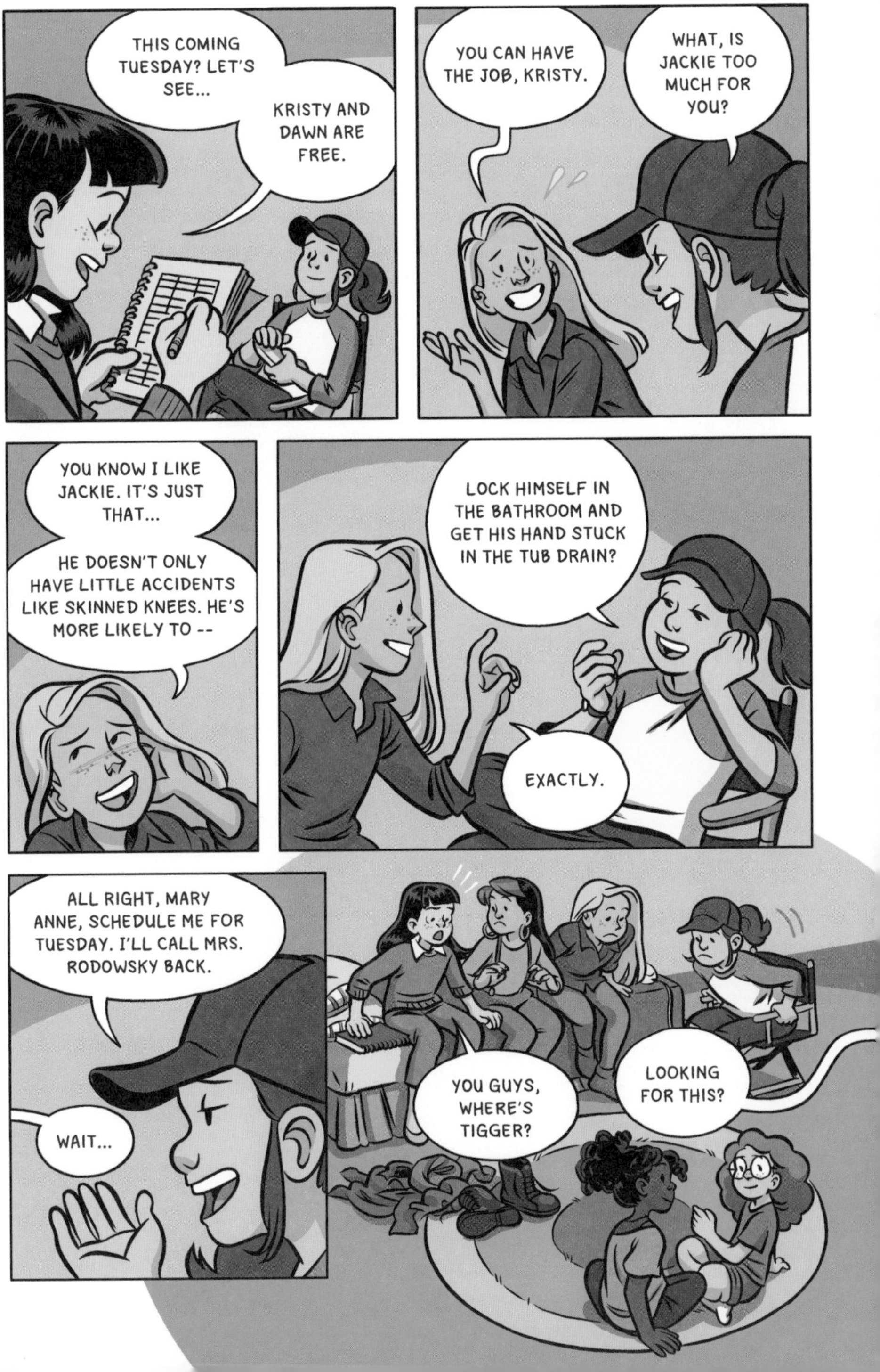
THIS COMING TUESDAY? LET'S SEE...
KRISTY AND DAWN ARE FREE.
YOU CAN HAVE THE JOB, KRISTY.
WHAT, IS JACKIE TOO MUCH FOR YOU?
YOU KNOW I LIKE JACKIE. IT'S JUST THAT...
HE DOESN'T ONLY HAVE LITTLE ACCIDENTS LIKE SKINNED KNEES. HE'S MORE LIKELY TO --
LOCK HIMSELF IN THE BATHROOM AND GET HIS HAND STUCK IN THE TUB DRAIN?
EXACTLY.
ALL RIGHT, MARY ANNE, SCHEDULE ME FOR TUESDAY. I'LL CALL MRS. RODOWSKY BACK.
WAIT...
YOU GUYS, WHERE'S TIGGER?
LOOKING FOR THIS?

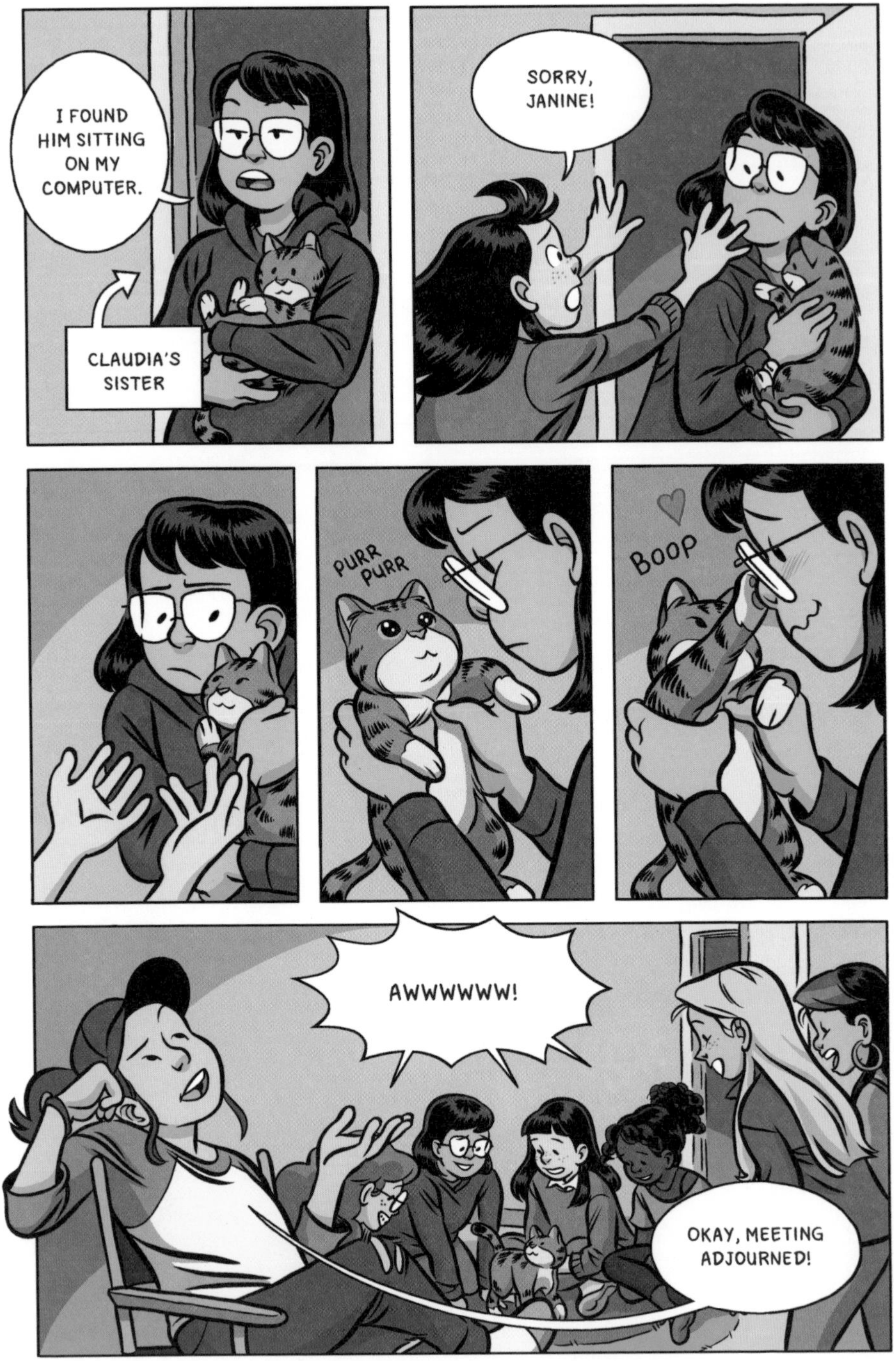
I FOUND HIM SITTING ON MY COMPUTER.
CLAUDIA'S SISTER
SORRY, JANINE!
PURR PURR
BOOP
AWWWWWW!
OKAY, MEETING ADJOURNED!

CHAPTER 3

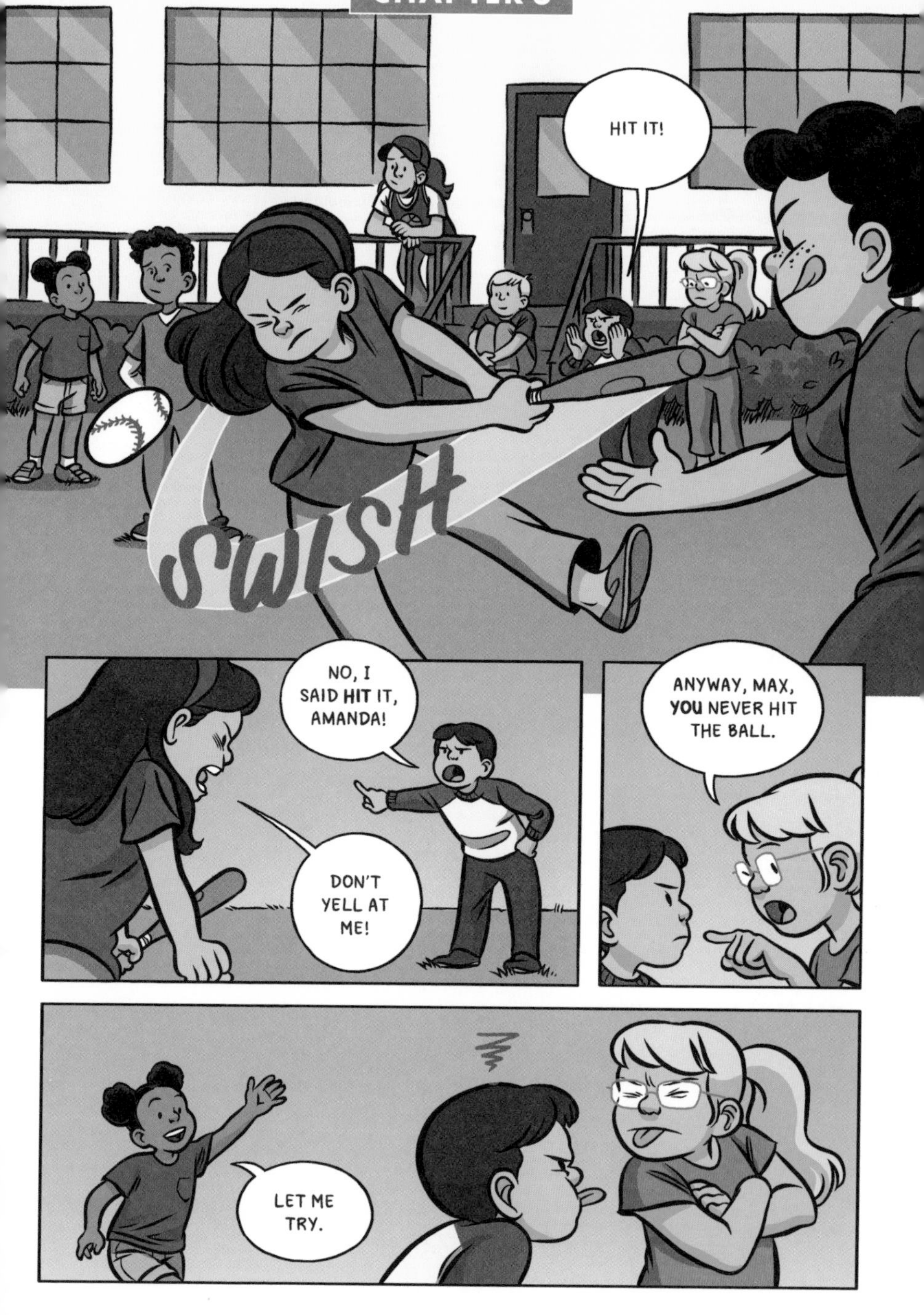

HIT IT!
SWISH
NO, I SAID HIT IT, AMANDA!
DON'T YELL AT ME!
ANYWAY, MAX, YOU NEVER HIT THE BALL.
LET ME TRY.

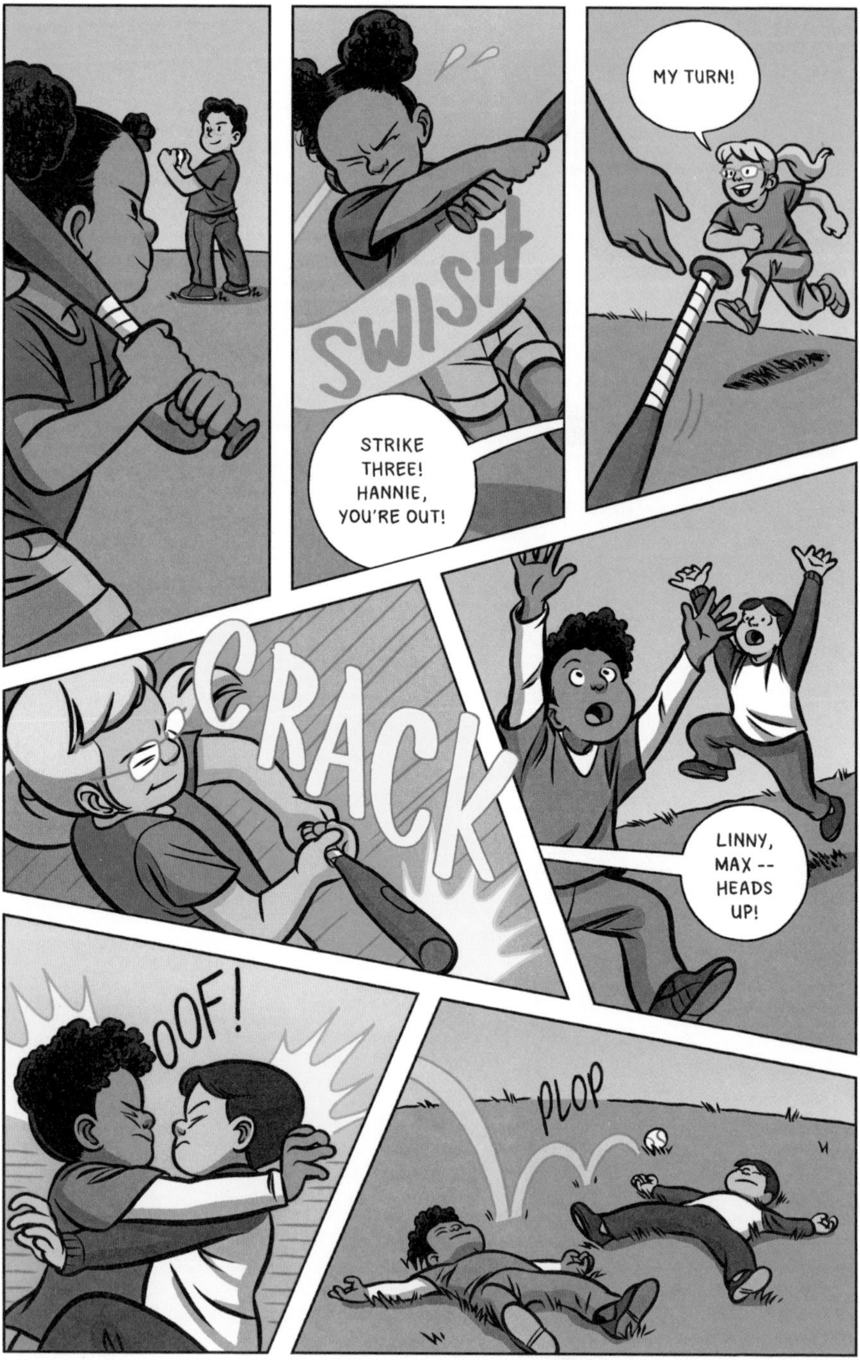
SWISH
STRIKE THREE! HANNIE, YOU'RE OUT!
MY TURN!
CRACK
LINNY, MAX -- HEADS UP!
OOF!
PLOP

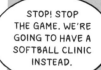

STOP! STOP THE GAME. WE'RE GOING TO HAVE A SOFTBALL CLINIC INSTEAD.

CLINIC? LIKE A HOSPITAL?

NO, IN THIS KIND OF CLINIC, WE'LL WORK ON THINGS THAT WOULD HELP YOUR SOFTBALL GAME. I'LL BE YOUR COACH.

LIKE IN LITTLE LEAGUE!

YOU ALL SHOULD JOIN LITTLE LEAGUE. OR PLAY T-BALL.

I CAN'T. I'M NOT OLD ENOUGH.

NO ONE WOULD WANT ME.

OR ME.

I DON'T **WANT** TO JOIN.

I DON'T LIKE PLAYING BALL **THAT** MUCH.

WELL, THE REST OF US **DO**.

IT WOULD BE NICE TO BE ON A TEAM. I JUST DON'T WANT TO EMBARRASS MYSELF.

OH, DAVID MICHAEL...

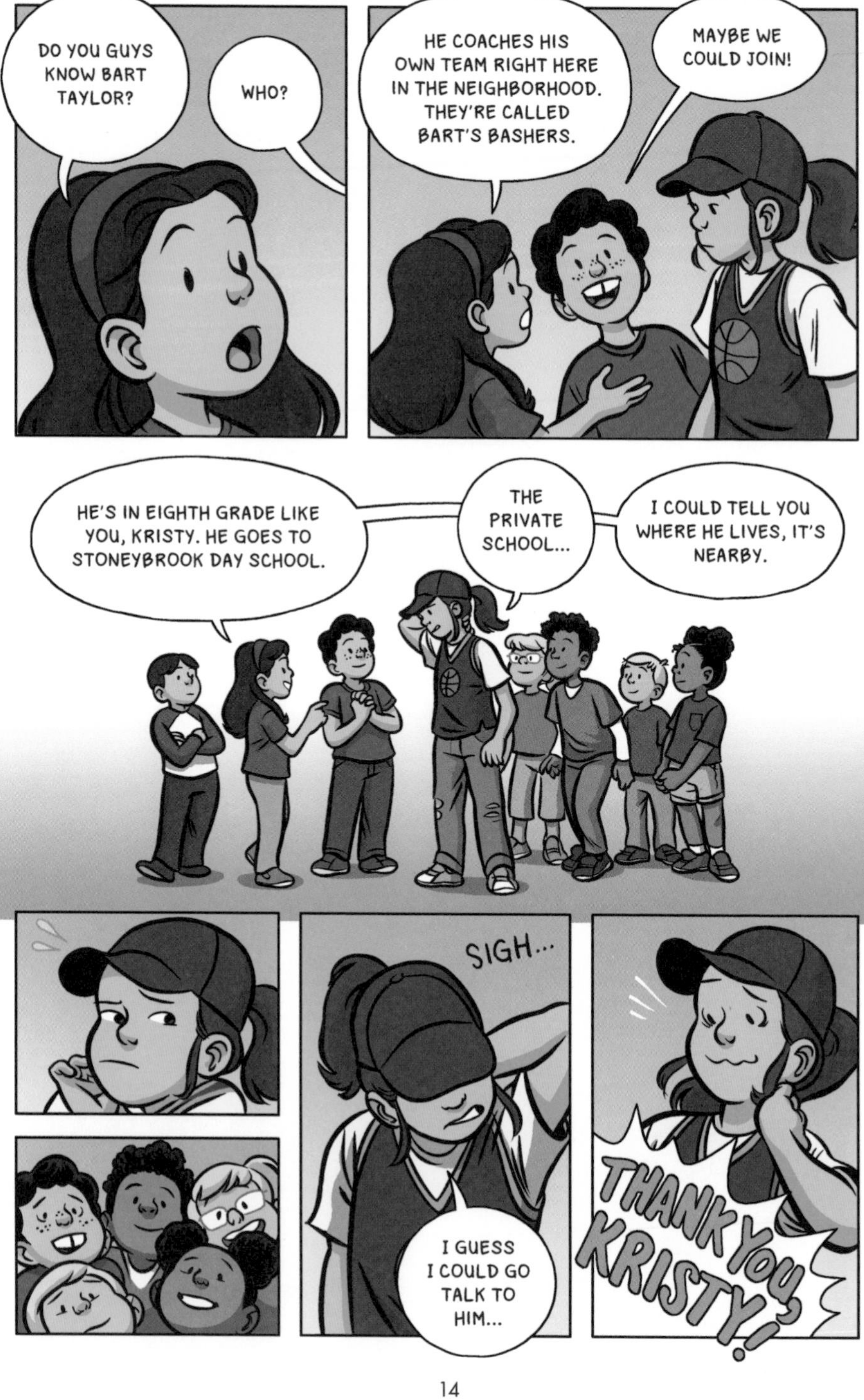
DO YOU GUYS KNOW BART TAYLOR?
WHO?
HE COACHES HIS OWN TEAM RIGHT HERE IN THE NEIGHBORHOOD. THEY'RE CALLED BART'S BASHERS.
MAYBE WE COULD JOIN!
HE'S IN EIGHTH GRADE LIKE YOU, KRISTY. HE GOES TO STONEYBROOK DAY SCHOOL.
THE PRIVATE SCHOOL...
I COULD TELL YOU WHERE HE LIVES, IT'S NEARBY.
SIGH...
I GUESS I COULD GO TALK TO HIM...
THANK YOU, KRISTY!

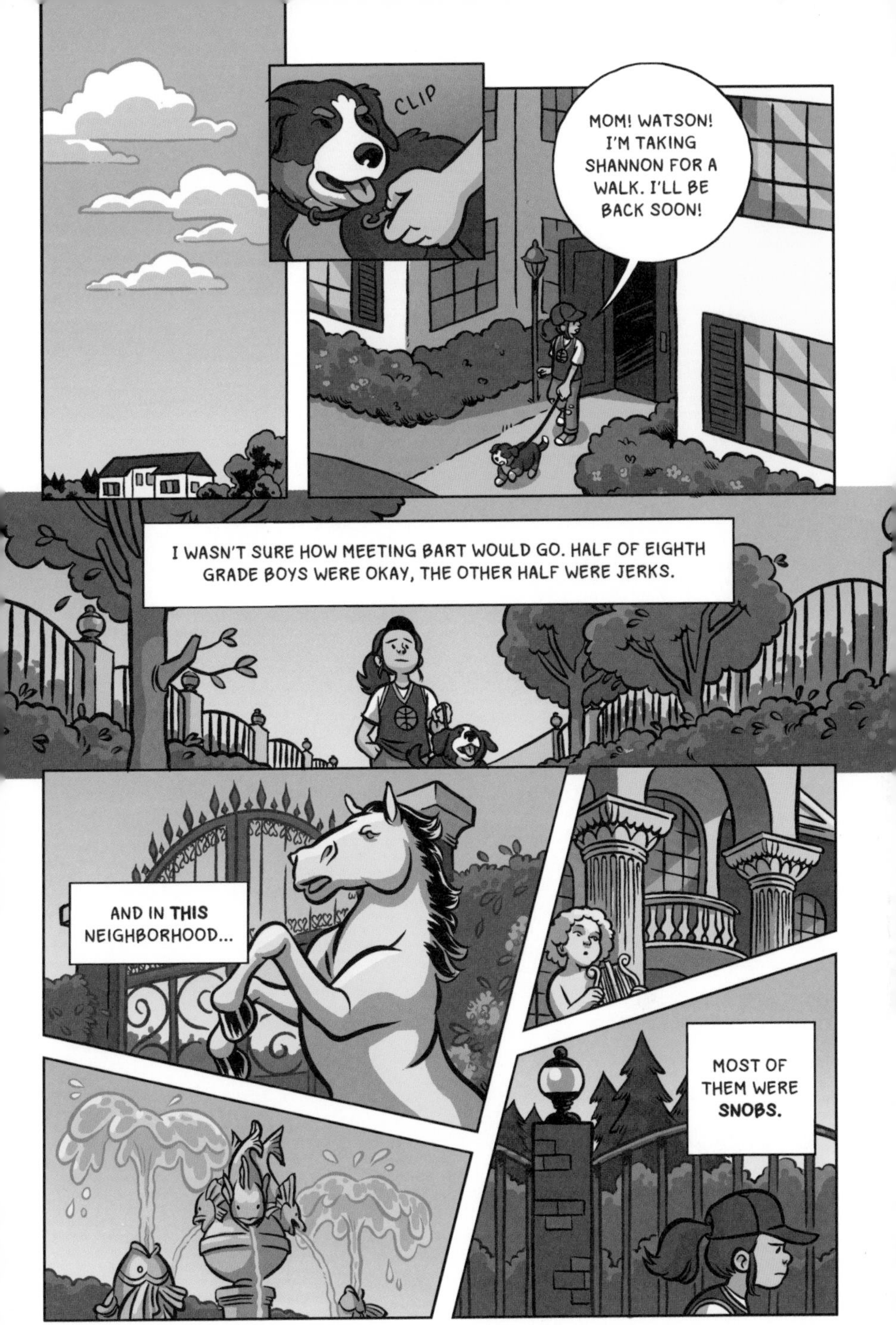
CLIP
MOM! WATSON! I'M TAKING SHANNON FOR A WALK. I'LL BE BACK SOON!
I WASN'T SURE HOW MEETING BART WOULD GO. HALF OF EIGHTH GRADE BOYS WERE OKAY, THE OTHER HALF WERE JERKS.
AND IN THIS NEIGHBORHOOD...
MOST OF THEM WERE SNOBS.

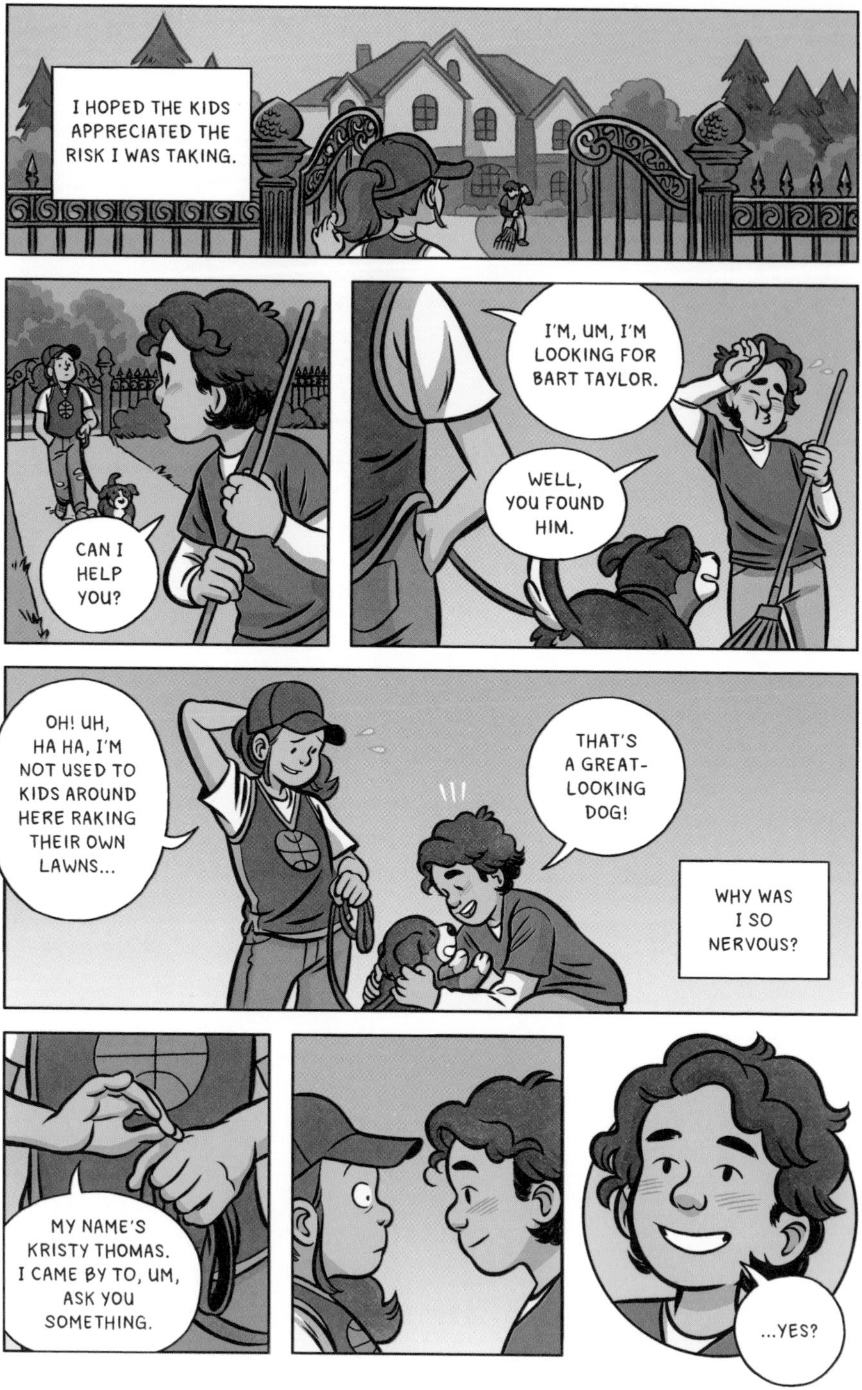
I HOPED THE KIDS APPRECIATED THE RISK I WAS TAKING.
CAN I HELP YOU?
I'M, UM, I'M LOOKING FOR BART TAYLOR.
WELL, YOU FOUND HIM.
OH! UH, HA HA, I'M NOT USED TO KIDS AROUND HERE RAKING THEIR OWN LAWNS...
THAT'S A GREAT-LOOKING DOG!
WHY WAS I SO NERVOUS?
MY NAME'S KRISTY THOMAS. I CAME BY TO, UM, ASK YOU SOMETHING.
...YES?

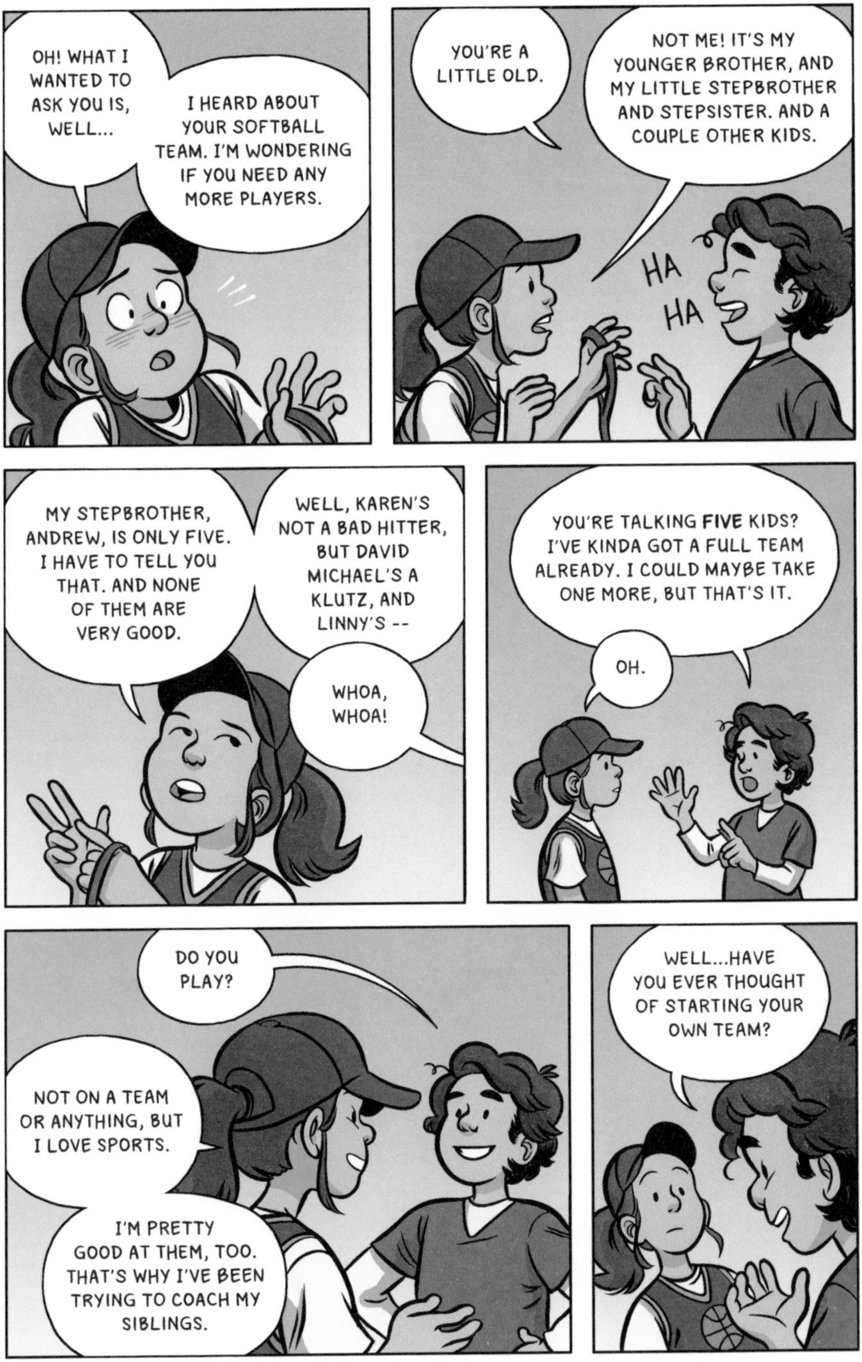
OH! WHAT I WANTED TO ASK YOU IS, WELL...
I HEARD ABOUT YOUR SOFTBALL TEAM. I'M WONDERING IF YOU NEED ANY MORE PLAYERS.
YOU'RE A LITTLE OLD.
NOT ME! IT'S MY YOUNGER BROTHER, AND MY LITTLE STEPBROTHER AND STEPSISTER. AND A COUPLE OTHER KIDS.
HA HA
MY STEPBROTHER, ANDREW, IS ONLY FIVE. I HAVE TO TELL YOU THAT. AND NONE OF THEM ARE VERY GOOD.
WELL, KAREN'S NOT A BAD HITTER, BUT DAVID MICHAEL'S A KLUTZ, AND LINNY'S --
WHOA, WHOA!
YOU'RE TALKING **FIVE** KIDS? I'VE KINDA GOT A FULL TEAM ALREADY. I COULD MAYBE TAKE ONE MORE, BUT THAT'S IT.
OH.
DO YOU PLAY?
NOT ON A TEAM OR ANYTHING, BUT I LOVE SPORTS.
I'M PRETTY GOOD AT THEM, TOO. THAT'S WHY I'VE BEEN TRYING TO COACH MY SIBLINGS.
WELL...HAVE YOU EVER THOUGHT OF STARTING YOUR OWN TEAM?

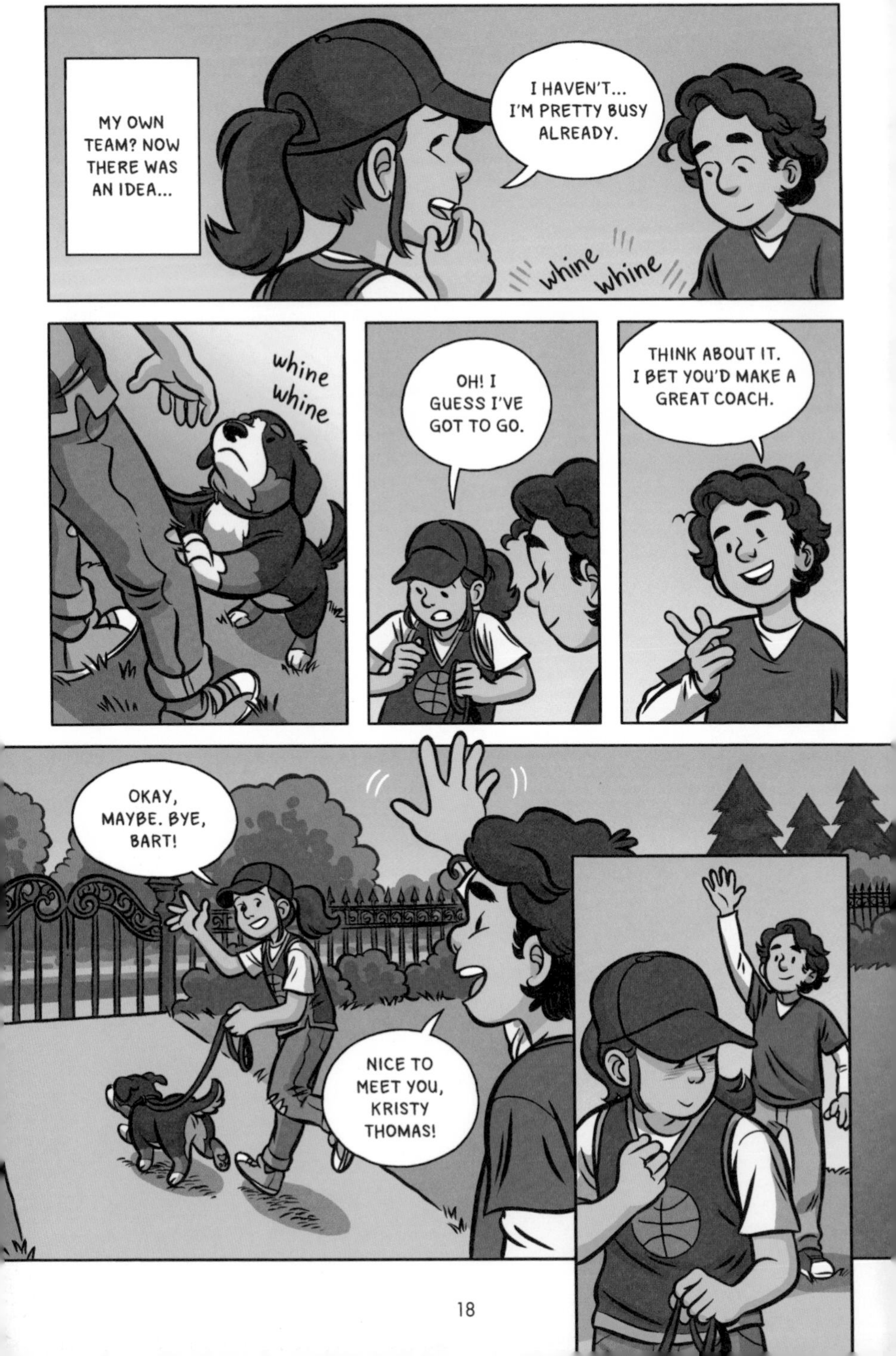
MY OWN TEAM? NOW THERE WAS AN IDEA...
I HAVEN'T... I'M PRETTY BUSY ALREADY.
whine whine
whine whine
OH! I GUESS I'VE GOT TO GO.
THINK ABOUT IT. I BET YOU'D MAKE A GREAT COACH.
OKAY, MAYBE. BYE, BART!
NICE TO MEET YOU, KRISTY THOMAS!

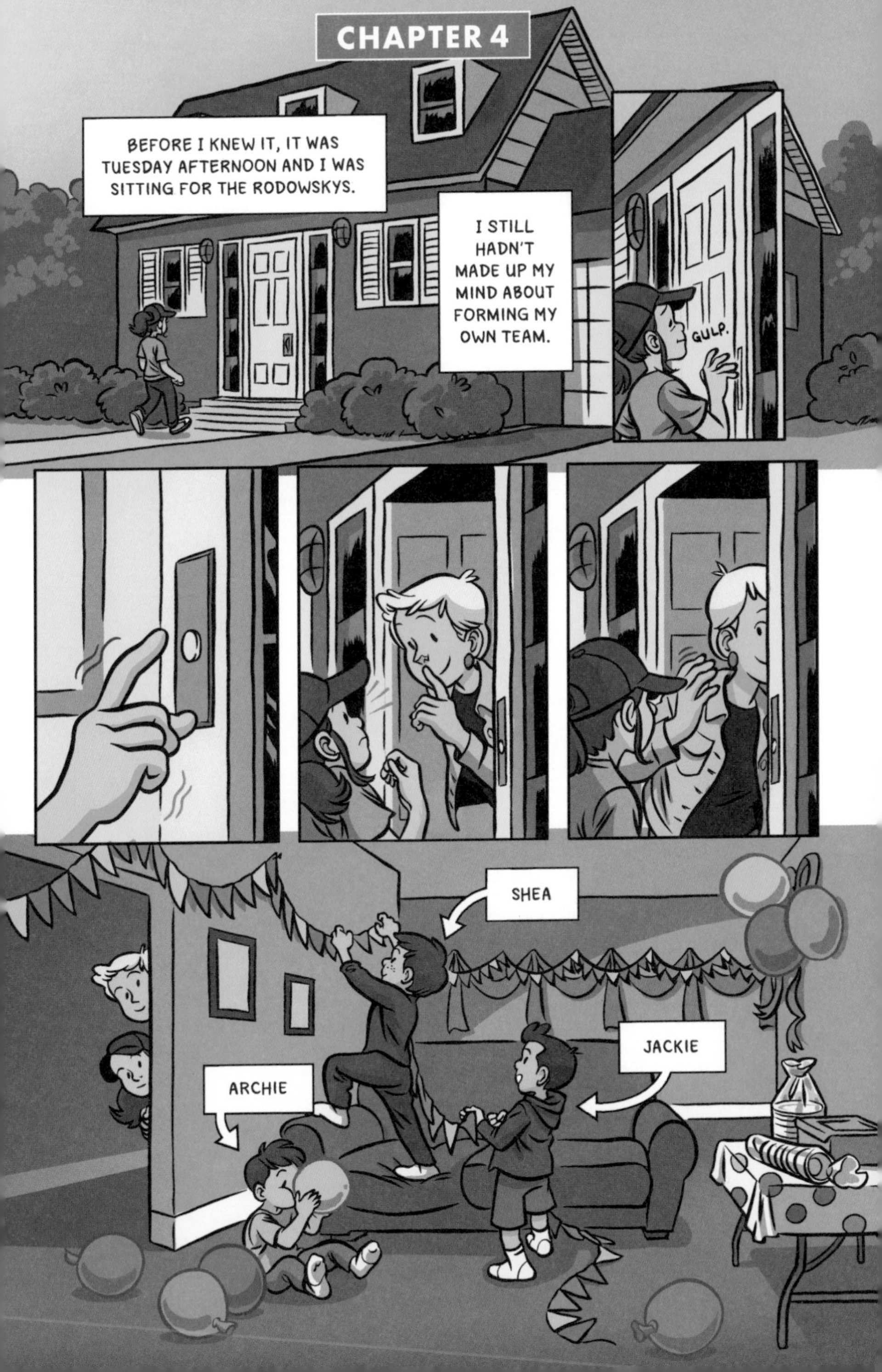
CHAPTER 4
BEFORE I KNEW IT, IT WAS TUESDAY AFTERNOON AND I WAS SITTING FOR THE RODOWSKYS.
I STILL HADN'T MADE UP MY MIND ABOUT FORMING MY OWN TEAM.
GULP.
SHEA
JACKIE
ARCHIE

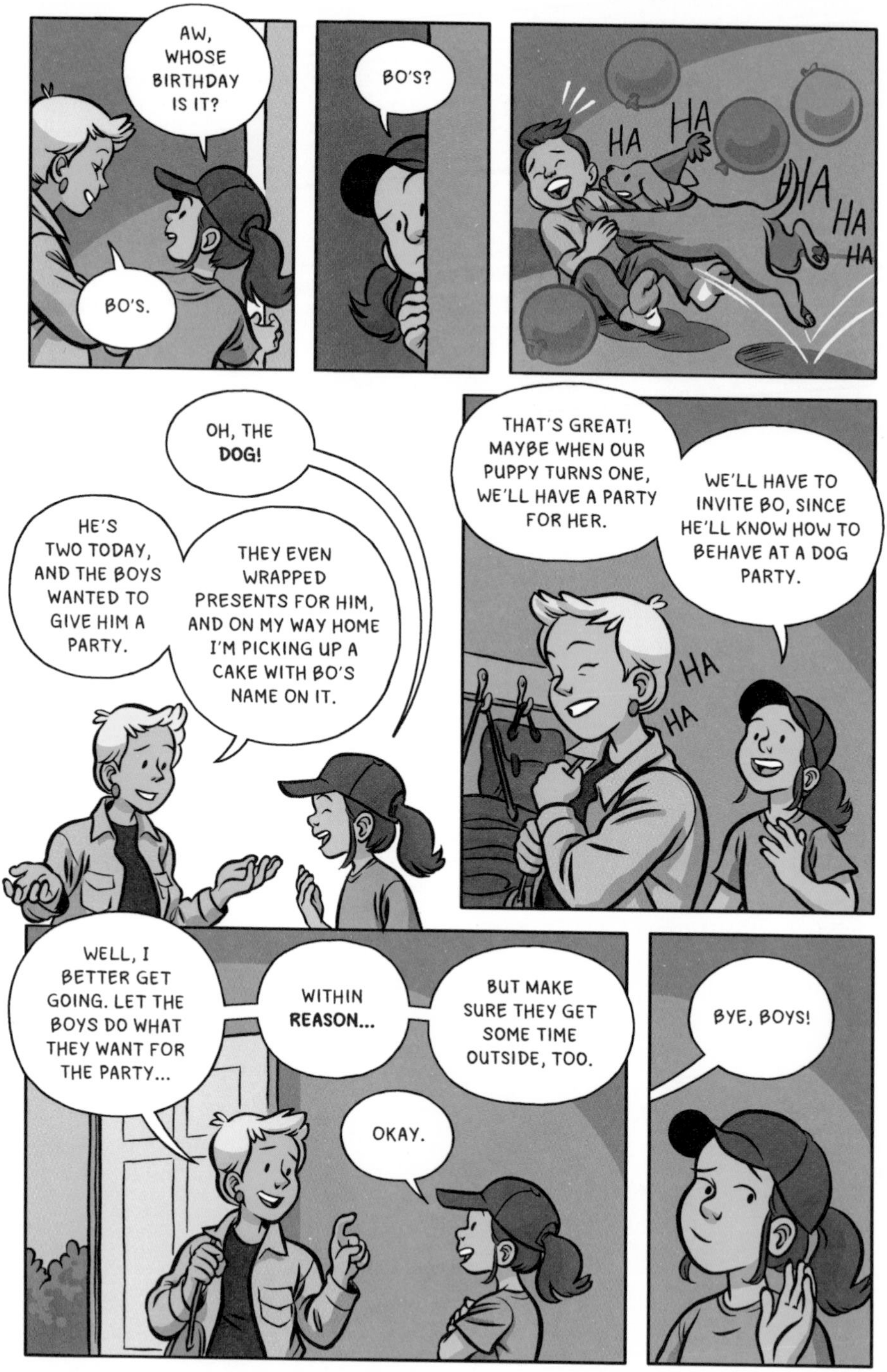
AW, WHOSE BIRTHDAY IS IT?
BO'S.
BO'S?
HA HA HA HA HA HA
OH, THE **DOG!**
HE'S TWO TODAY, AND THE BOYS WANTED TO GIVE HIM A PARTY.
THEY EVEN WRAPPED PRESENTS FOR HIM, AND ON MY WAY HOME I'M PICKING UP A CAKE WITH BO'S NAME ON IT.
THAT'S GREAT! MAYBE WHEN OUR PUPPY TURNS ONE, WE'LL HAVE A PARTY FOR HER.
WE'LL HAVE TO INVITE BO, SINCE HE'LL KNOW HOW TO BEHAVE AT A DOG PARTY.
HA HA
WELL, I BETTER GET GOING. LET THE BOYS DO WHAT THEY WANT FOR THE PARTY...
WITHIN **REASON...**
BUT MAKE SURE THEY GET SOME TIME OUTSIDE, TOO.
OKAY.
BYE, BOYS!

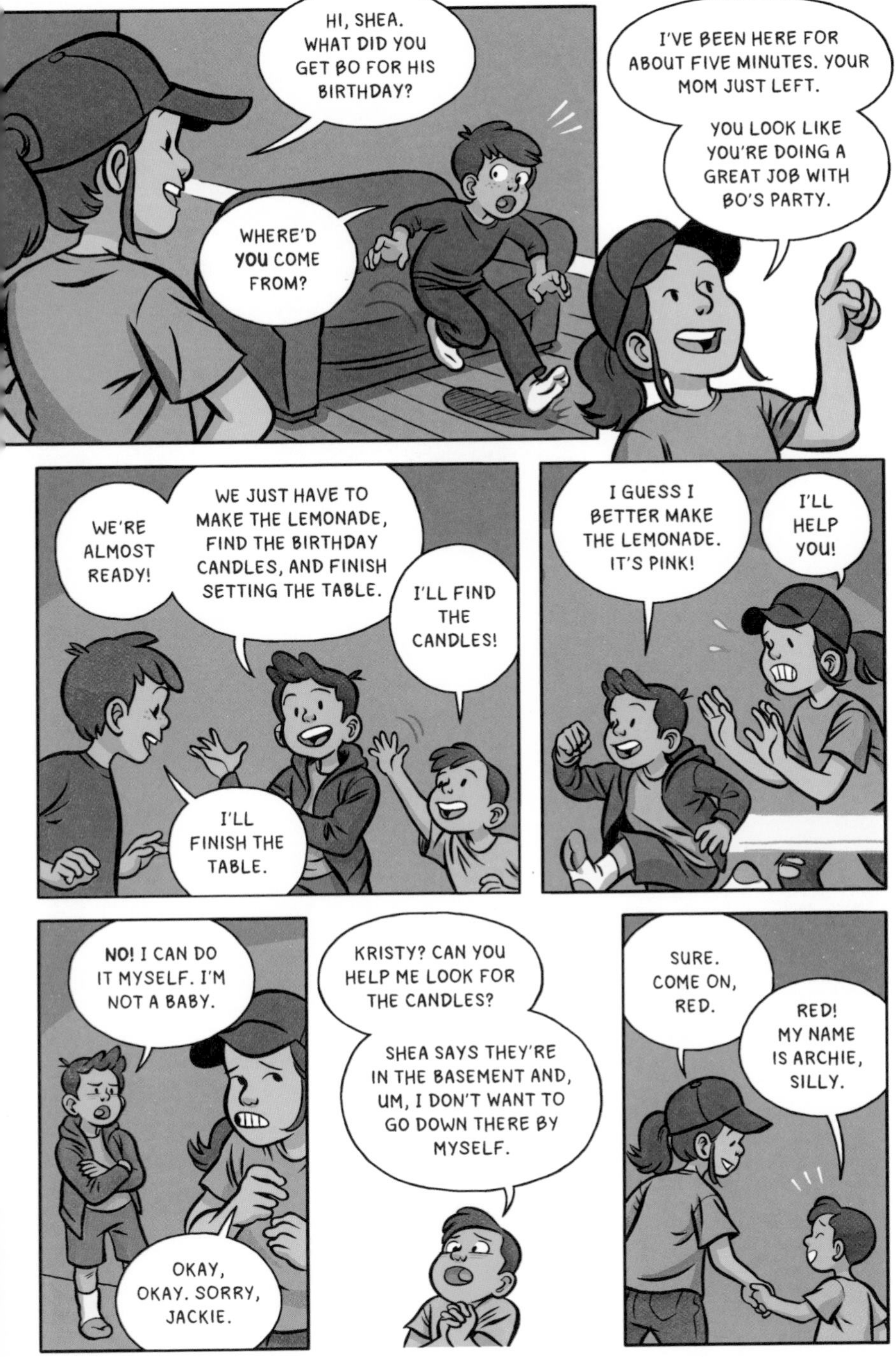

HI, SHEA. WHAT DID YOU GET BO FOR HIS BIRTHDAY?
WHERE'D YOU COME FROM?
I'VE BEEN HERE FOR ABOUT FIVE MINUTES. YOUR MOM JUST LEFT.
YOU LOOK LIKE YOU'RE DOING A GREAT JOB WITH BO'S PARTY.
WE'RE ALMOST READY!
WE JUST HAVE TO MAKE THE LEMONADE, FIND THE BIRTHDAY CANDLES, AND FINISH SETTING THE TABLE.
I'LL FIND THE CANDLES!
I'LL FINISH THE TABLE.
I GUESS I BETTER MAKE THE LEMONADE. IT'S PINK!
I'LL HELP YOU!
NO! I CAN DO IT MYSELF. I'M NOT A BABY.
OKAY, OKAY. SORRY, JACKIE.
KRISTY? CAN YOU HELP ME LOOK FOR THE CANDLES?
SHEA SAYS THEY'RE IN THE BASEMENT AND, UM, I DON'T WANT TO GO DOWN THERE BY MYSELF.
SURE. COME ON, RED.
RED! MY NAME IS ARCHIE, SILLY.

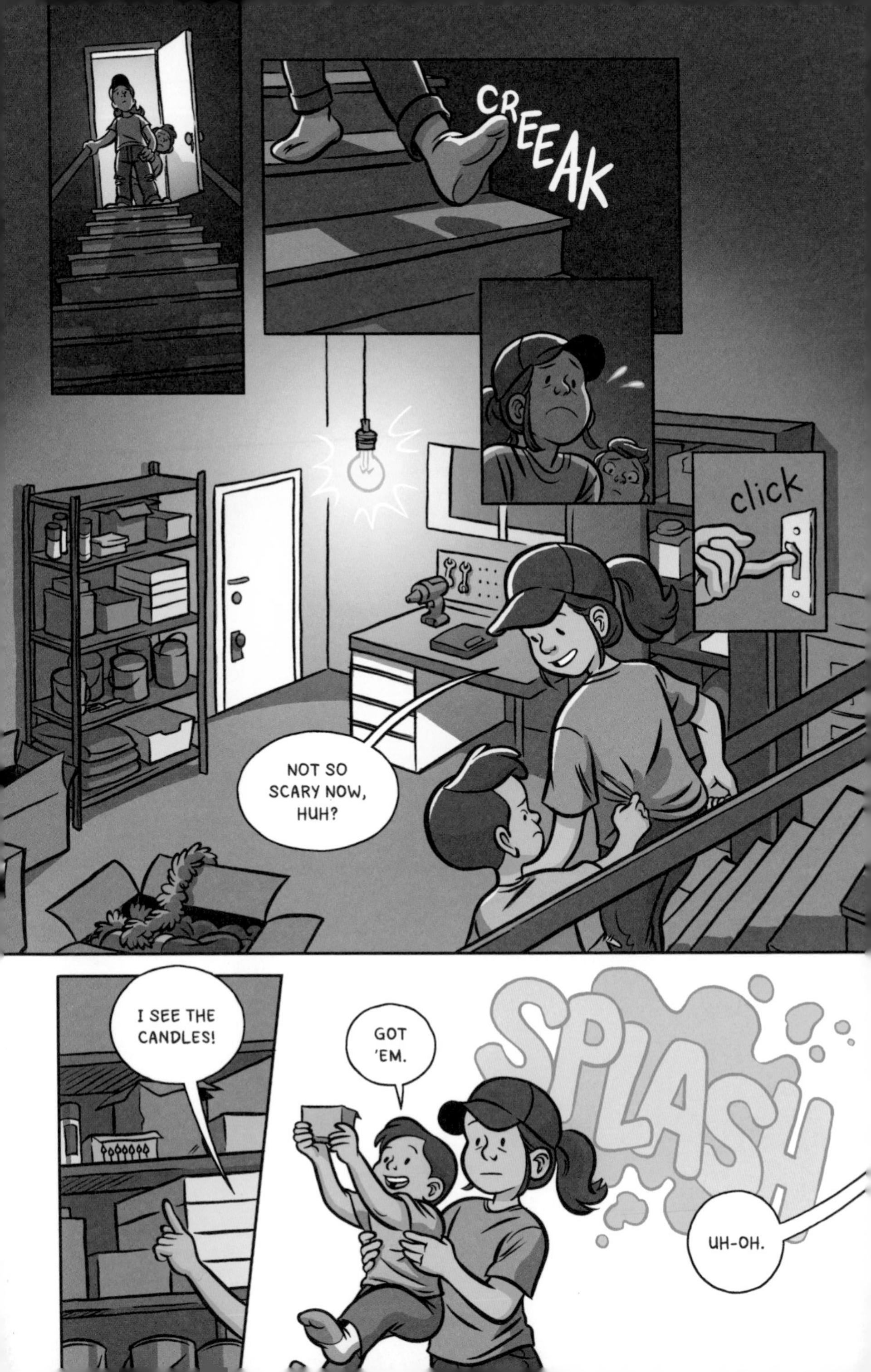
CREEAK
click
NOT SO SCARY NOW, HUH?
I SEE THE CANDLES!
GOT 'EM.
SPLASH
UH-OH.

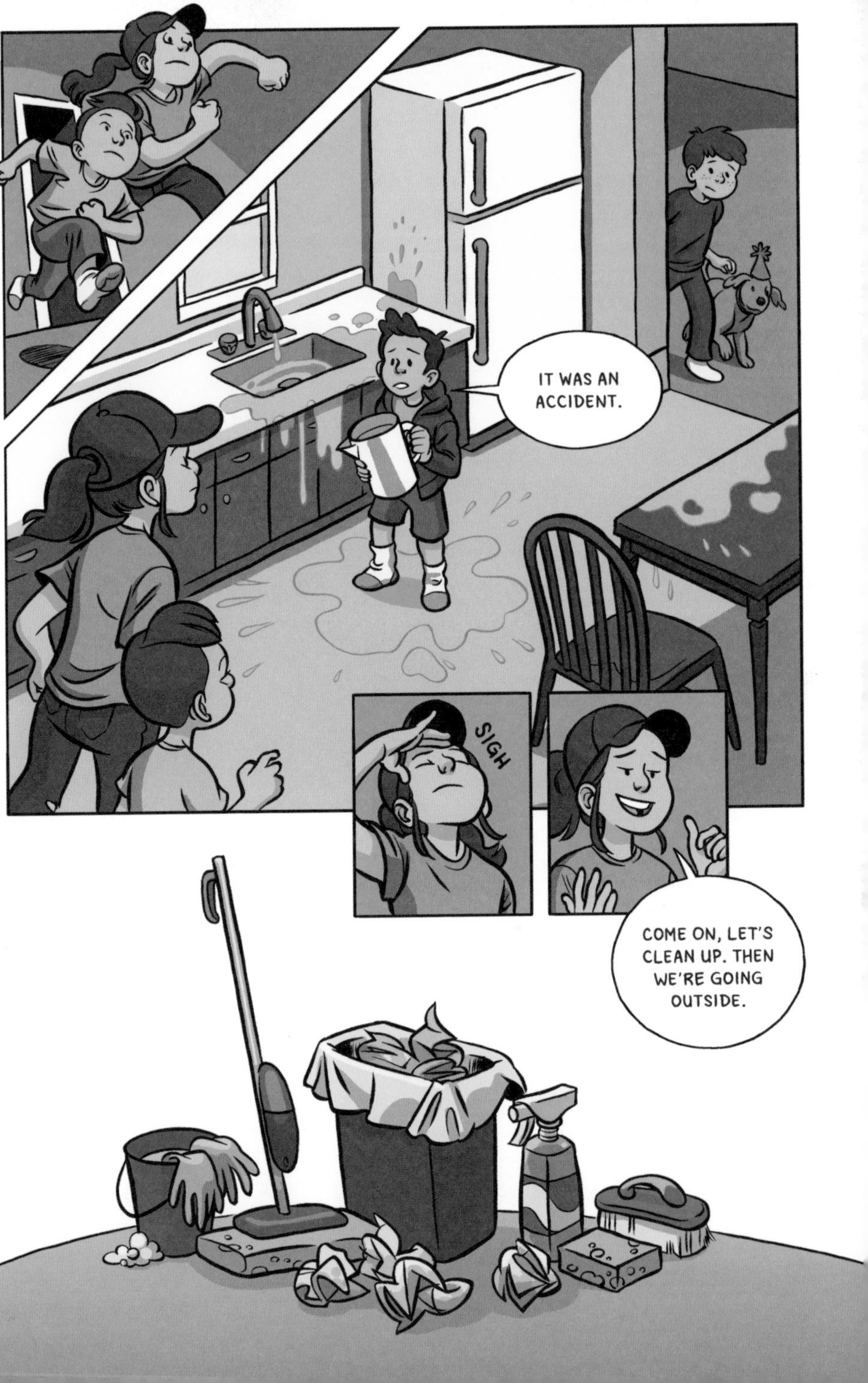
IT WAS AN ACCIDENT.
SIGH
COME ON, LET'S CLEAN UP. THEN WE'RE GOING OUTSIDE.

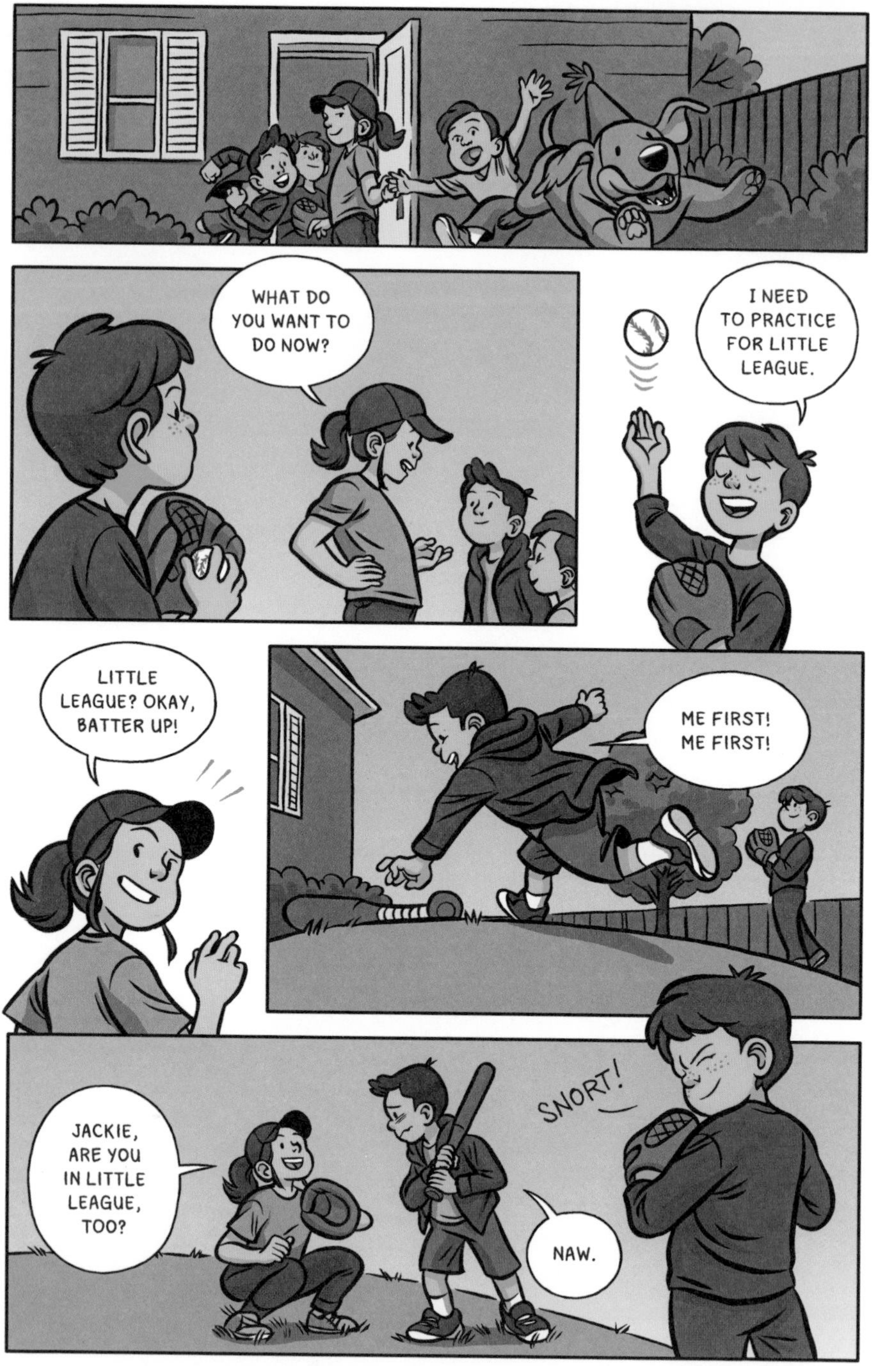
WHAT DO YOU WANT TO DO NOW?
I NEED TO PRACTICE FOR LITTLE LEAGUE.
LITTLE LEAGUE? OKAY, BATTER UP!
ME FIRST! ME FIRST!
JACKIE, ARE YOU IN LITTLE LEAGUE, TOO?
SNORT!
NAW.

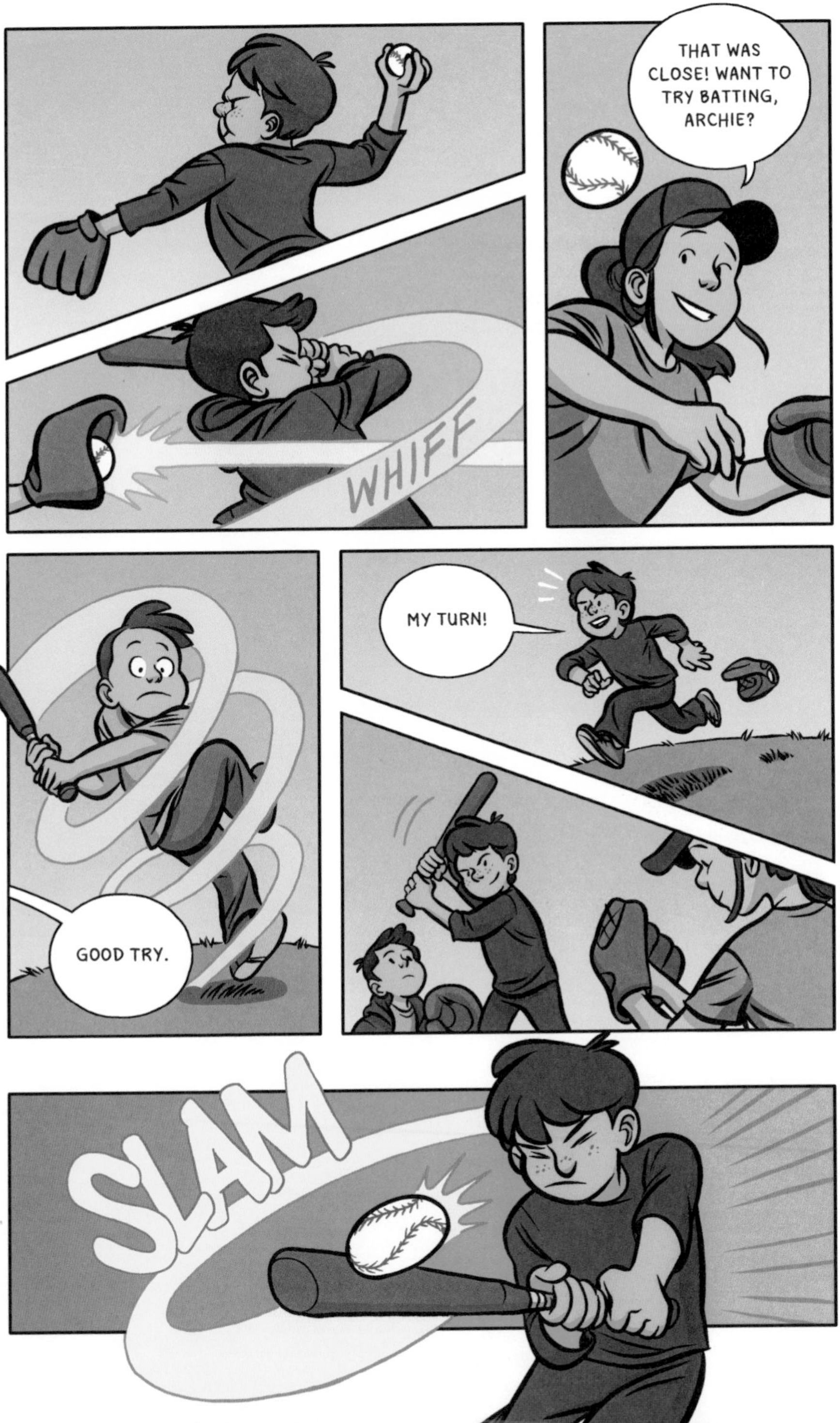
WHIFF
THAT WAS CLOSE! WANT TO TRY BATTING, ARCHIE?
GOOD TRY.
MY TURN!
SLAM

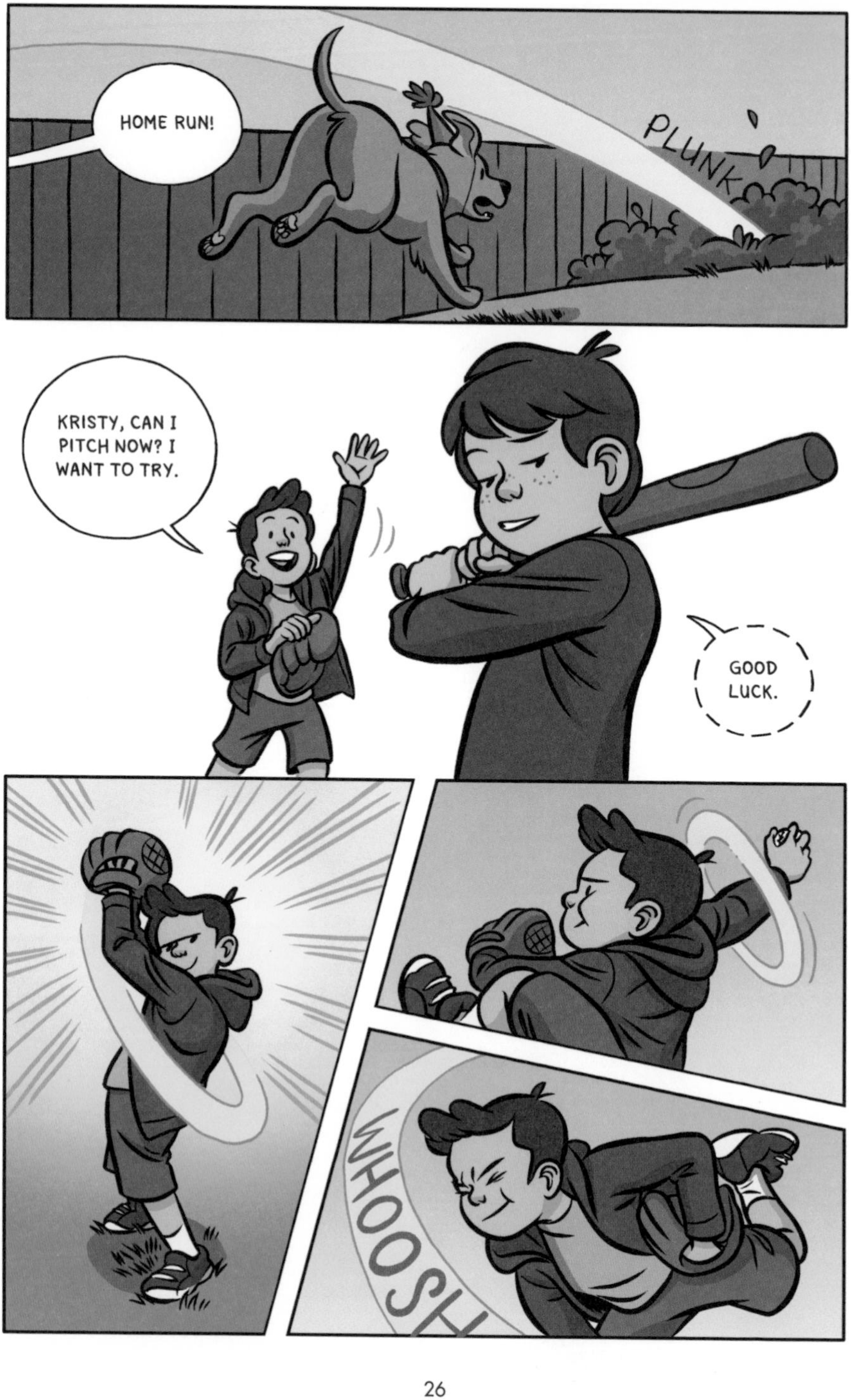
HOME RUN!
PLUNK
KRISTY, CAN I PITCH NOW? I WANT TO TRY.
GOOD LUCK.
WHOOSH

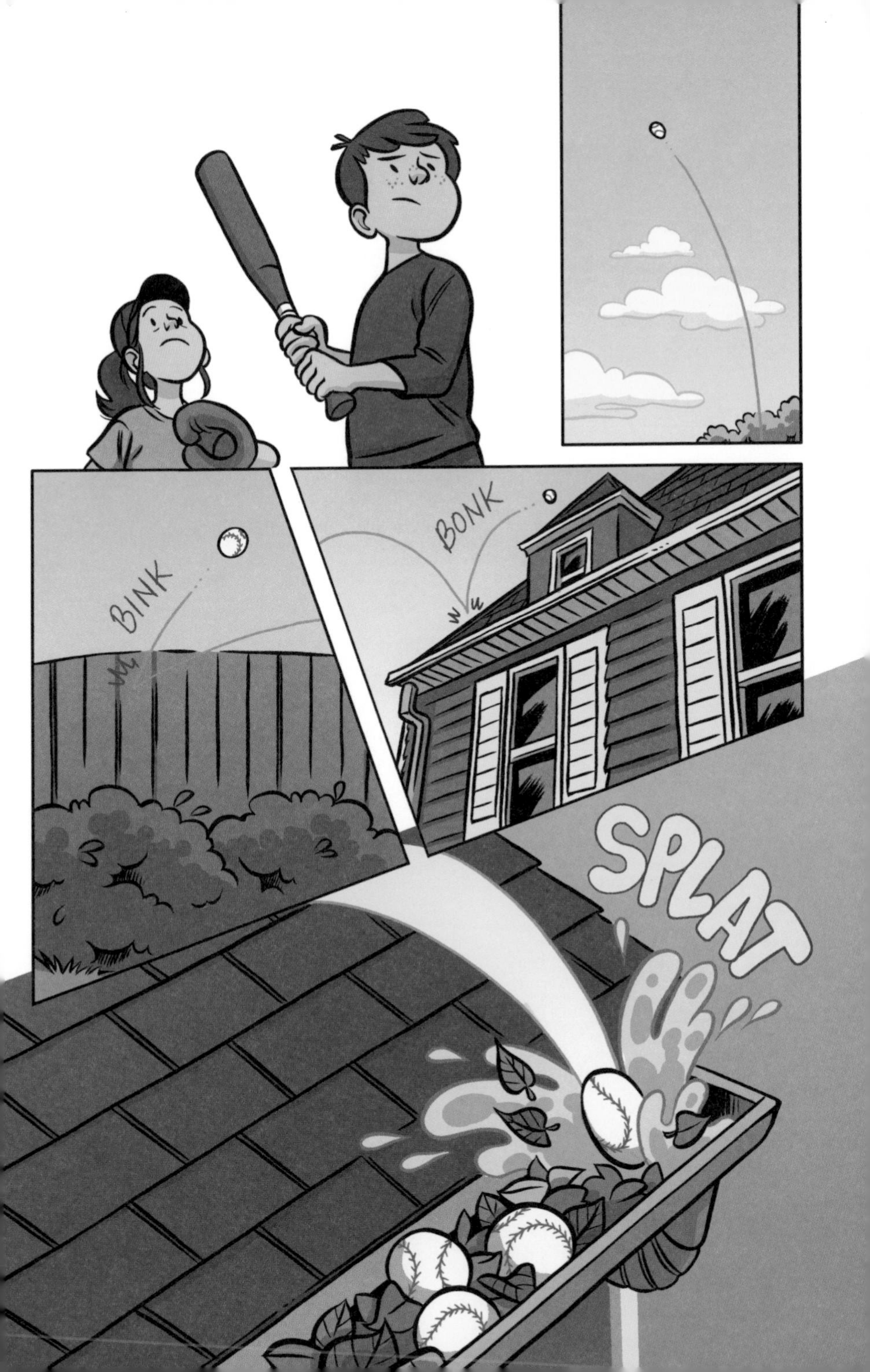
BINK
BONK
SPLAT

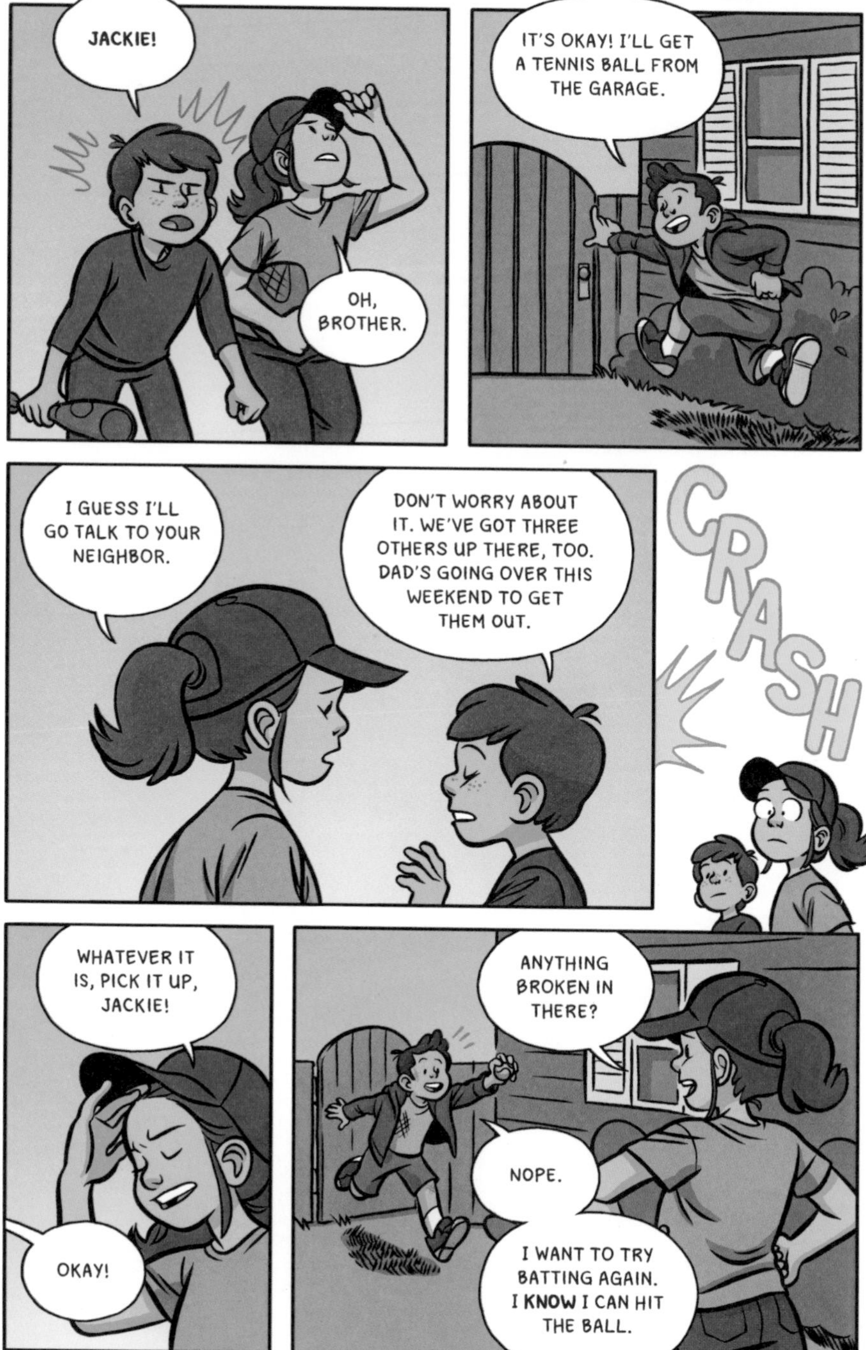
JACKIE!
OH, BROTHER.
IT'S OKAY! I'LL GET A TENNIS BALL FROM THE GARAGE.
I GUESS I'LL GO TALK TO YOUR NEIGHBOR.
DON'T WORRY ABOUT IT. WE'VE GOT THREE OTHERS UP THERE, TOO. DAD'S GOING OVER THIS WEEKEND TO GET THEM OUT.
CRASH
WHATEVER IT IS, PICK IT UP, JACKIE!
OKAY!
ANYTHING BROKEN IN THERE?
NOPE.
I WANT TO TRY BATTING AGAIN. I **KNOW** I CAN HIT THE BALL.

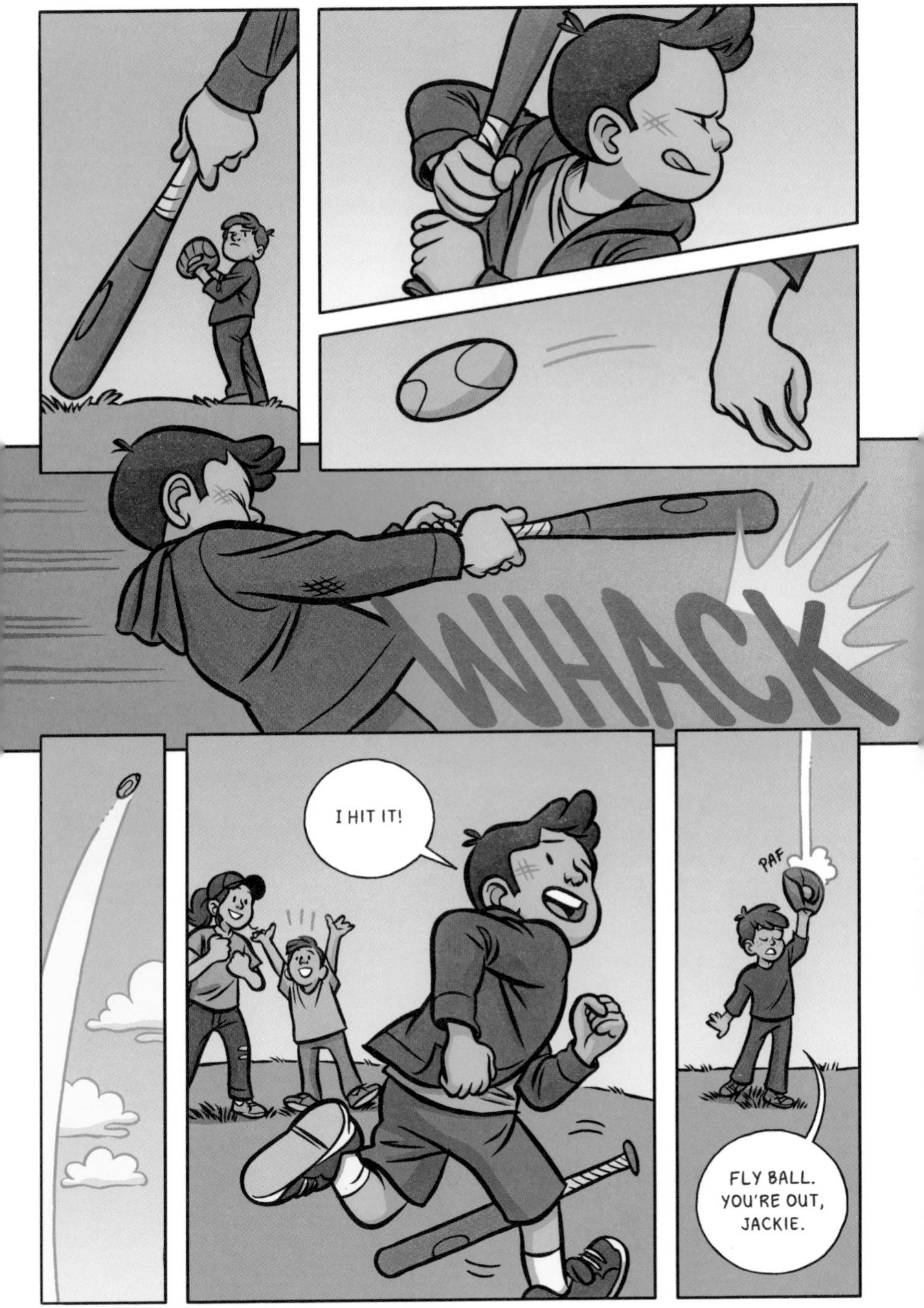
WHACK
I HIT IT!
PAF
FLY BALL. YOU'RE OUT, JACKIE.

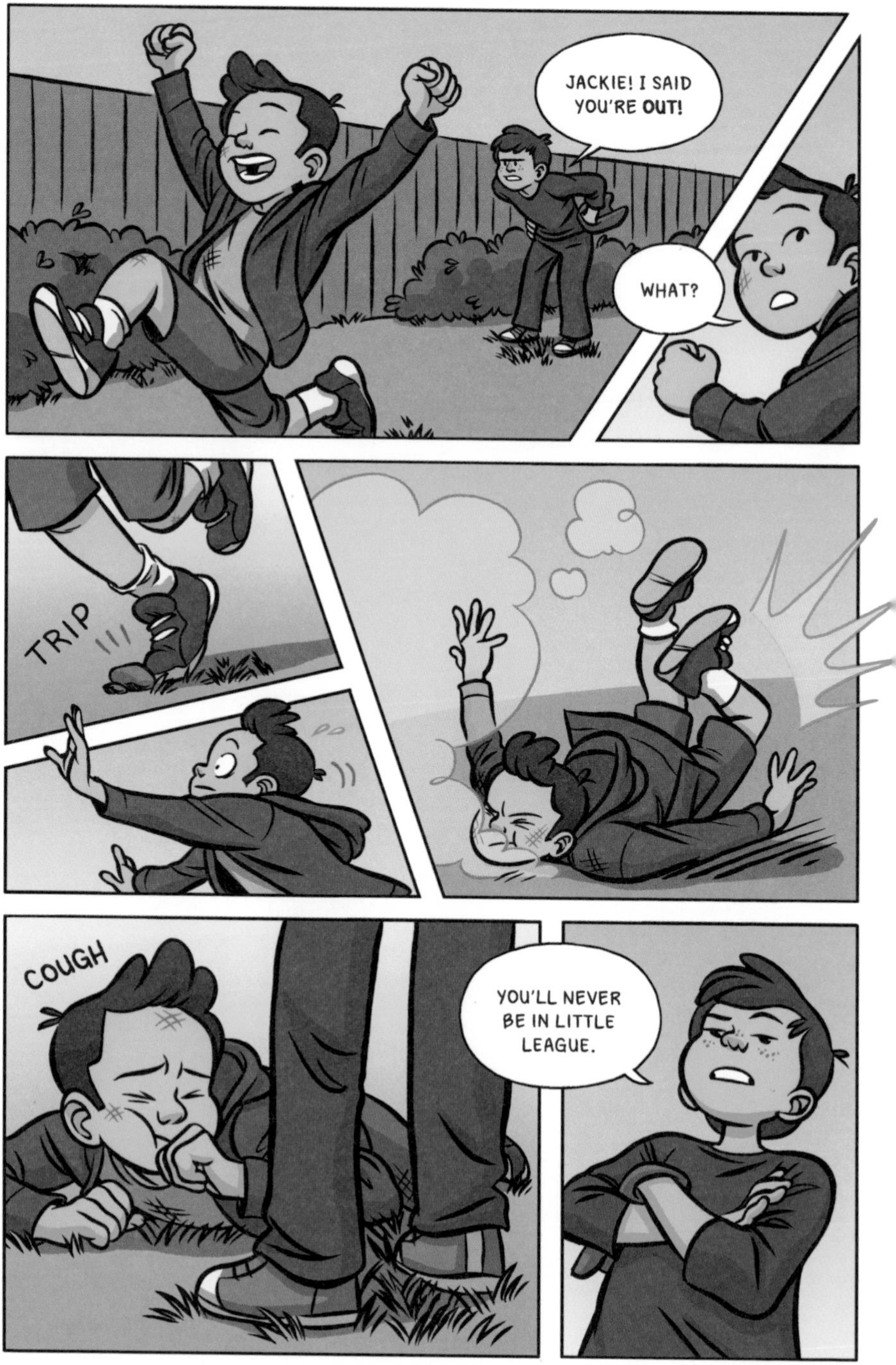

JACKIE! I SAID YOU'RE OUT!
WHAT?
TRIP
COUGH
YOU'LL NEVER BE IN LITTLE LEAGUE.

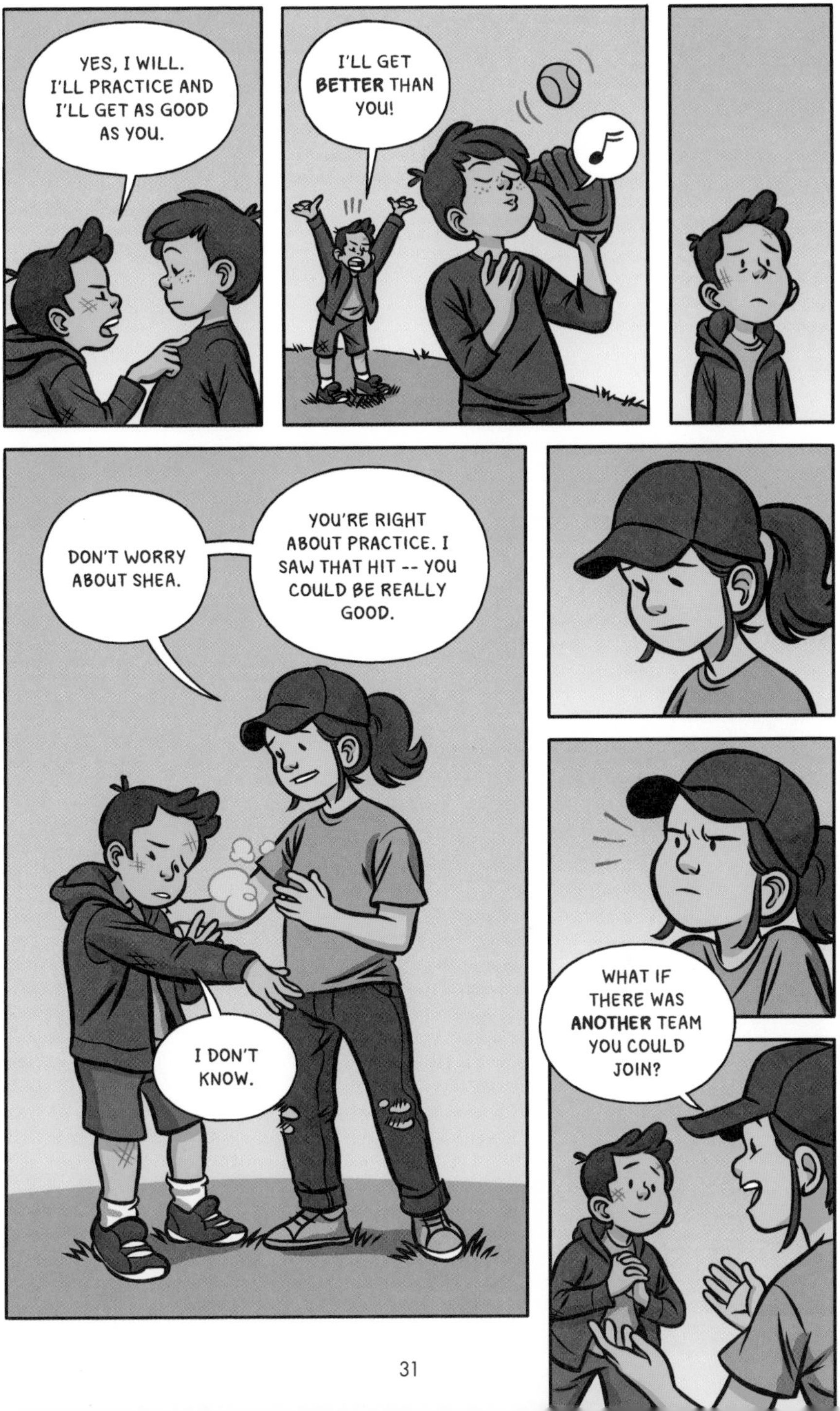
YES, I WILL. I'LL PRACTICE AND I'LL GET AS GOOD AS YOU.
I'LL GET BETTER THAN YOU!
DON'T WORRY ABOUT SHEA.
YOU'RE RIGHT ABOUT PRACTICE. I SAW THAT HIT -- YOU COULD BE REALLY GOOD.
I DON'T KNOW.
WHAT IF THERE WAS ANOTHER TEAM YOU COULD JOIN?

CHAPTER 5

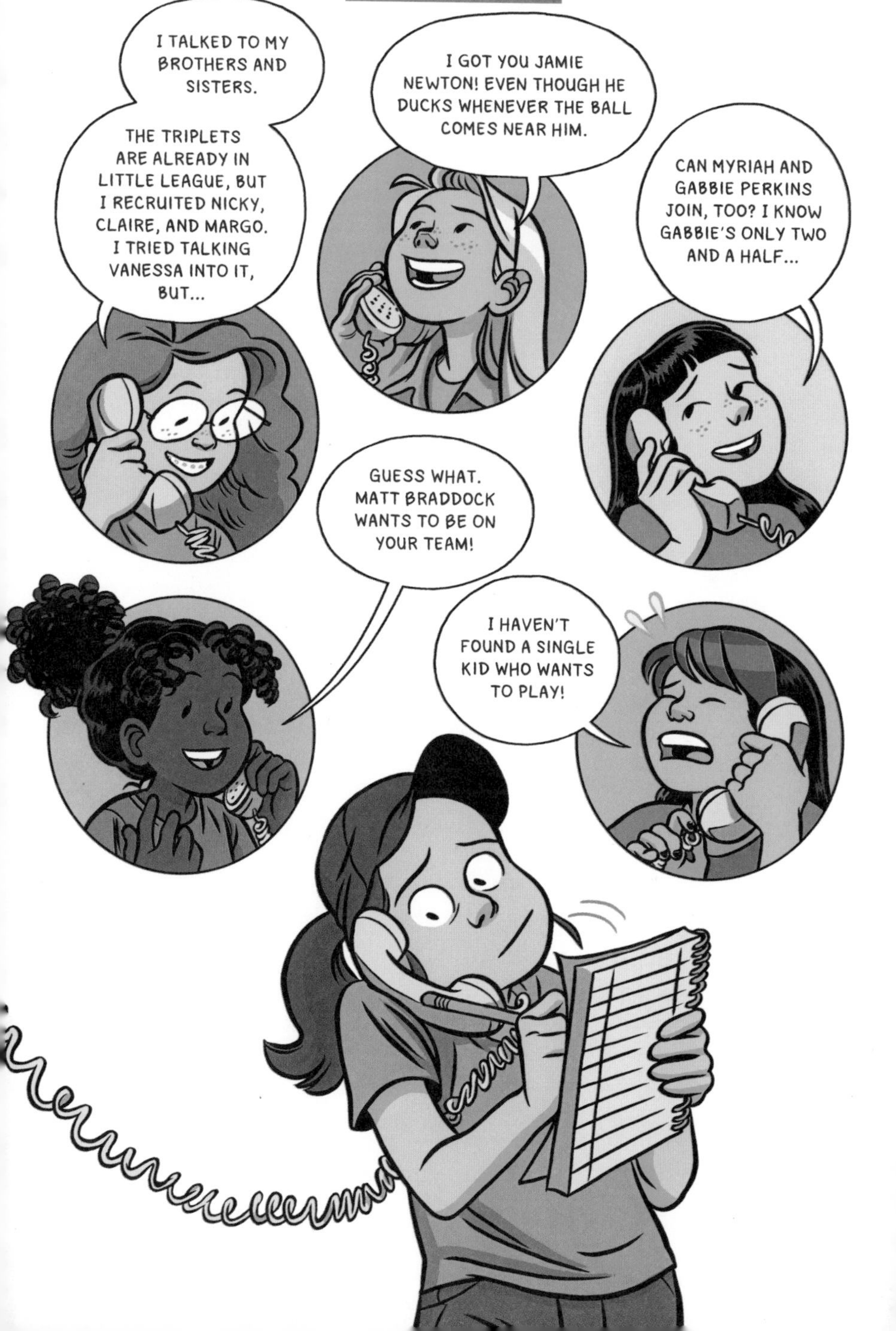
I TALKED TO MY BROTHERS AND SISTERS.
THE TRIPLETS ARE ALREADY IN LITTLE LEAGUE, BUT I RECRUITED NICKY, CLAIRE, AND MARGO. I TRIED TALKING VANESSA INTO IT, BUT...
I GOT YOU JAMIE NEWTON! EVEN THOUGH HE DUCKS WHENEVER THE BALL COMES NEAR HIM.
CAN MYRIAH AND GABBIE PERKINS JOIN, TOO? I KNOW GABBIE'S ONLY TWO AND A HALF...
GUESS WHAT. MATT BRADDOCK WANTS TO BE ON YOUR TEAM!
I HAVEN'T FOUND A SINGLE KID WHO WANTS TO PLAY!

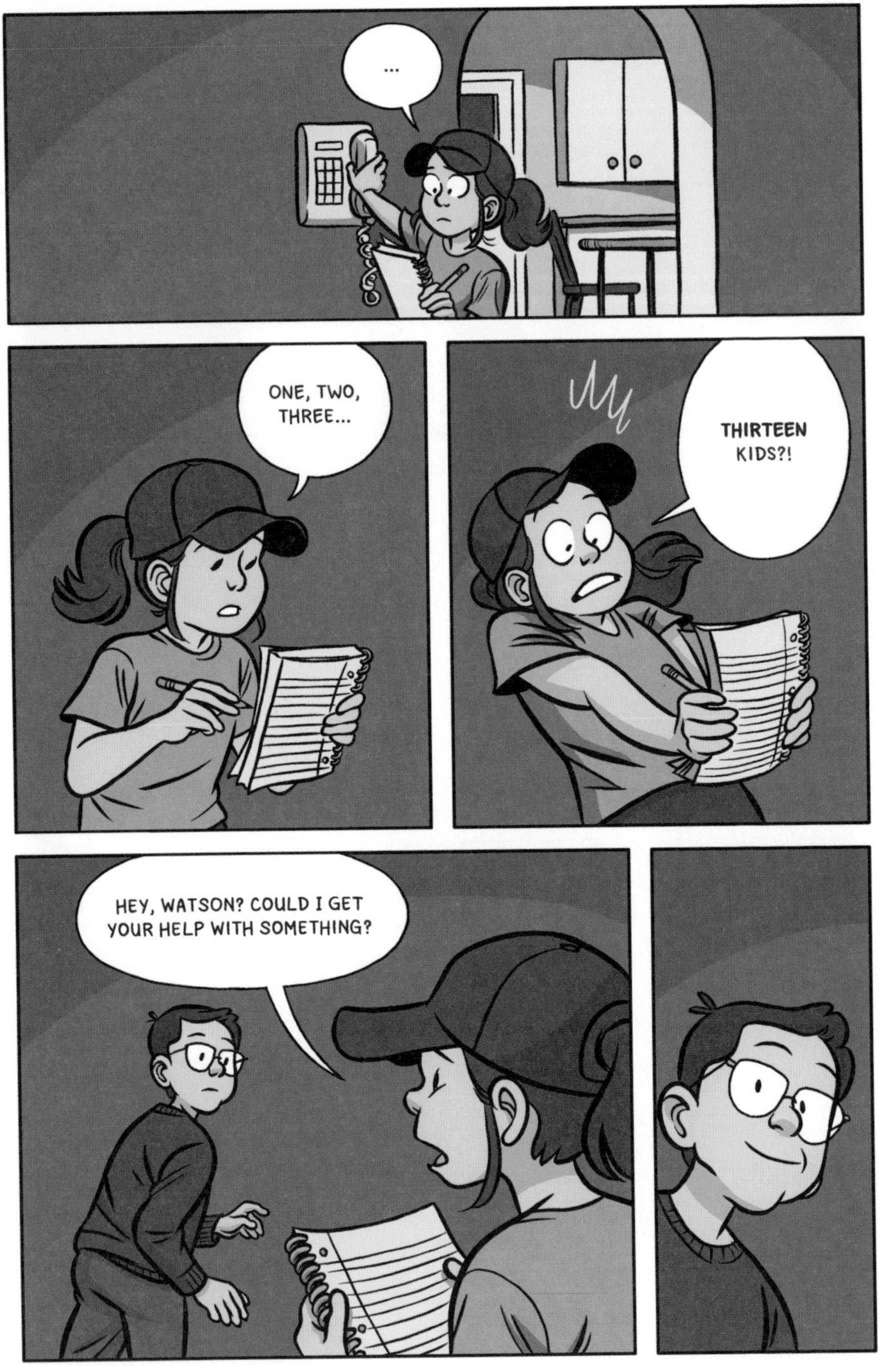
...
ONE, TWO, THREE...
THIRTEEN KIDS?!
HEY, WATSON? COULD I GET YOUR HELP WITH SOMETHING?

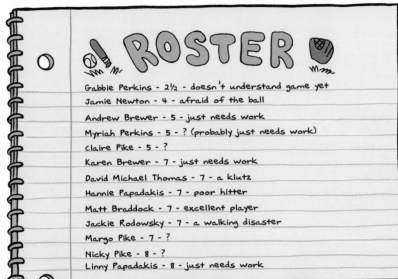

ROSTER

Gabbie Perkins - 2½ - doesn't understand game yet
Jamie Newton - 4 - afraid of the ball
Andrew Brewer - 5 - just needs work
Myriah Perkins - 5 - ? (probably just needs work)
Claire Pike - 5 - ?
Karen Brewer - 7 - just needs work
David Michael Thomas - 7 - a klutz
Hannie Papadakis - 7 - poor hitter
Matt Braddock - 7 - excellent player
Jackie Rodowsky - 7 - a walking disaster
Margo Pike - 7 - ?
Nicky Pike - 8 - ?
Linny Papadakis - 8 - just needs work

LATER

SO, YOUR OWN SOFTBALL TEAM.

I WROTE DOWN WHAT EACH KID NEEDS TO WORK ON. SEE?

MOST OF THEM ARE PRETTY YOUNG.

YEAH, I DID THE MATH. THE AVERAGE AGE IS ABOUT SIX YEARS OLD.

WHAT AM I GETTING MYSELF INTO?

ISN'T THIRTEEN AN UNLUCKY NUMBER? OR, WAIT. MAYBE IT'S A LUCKY NUMBER?

MAYBE IT WOULD HELP IF YOU HAD A MISSION STATEMENT. SOMETHING TO KEEP YOU FOCUSED ON WHAT'S IMPORTANT.

WHY DID YOU WANT TO START A TEAM IN THE FIRST PLACE?

35

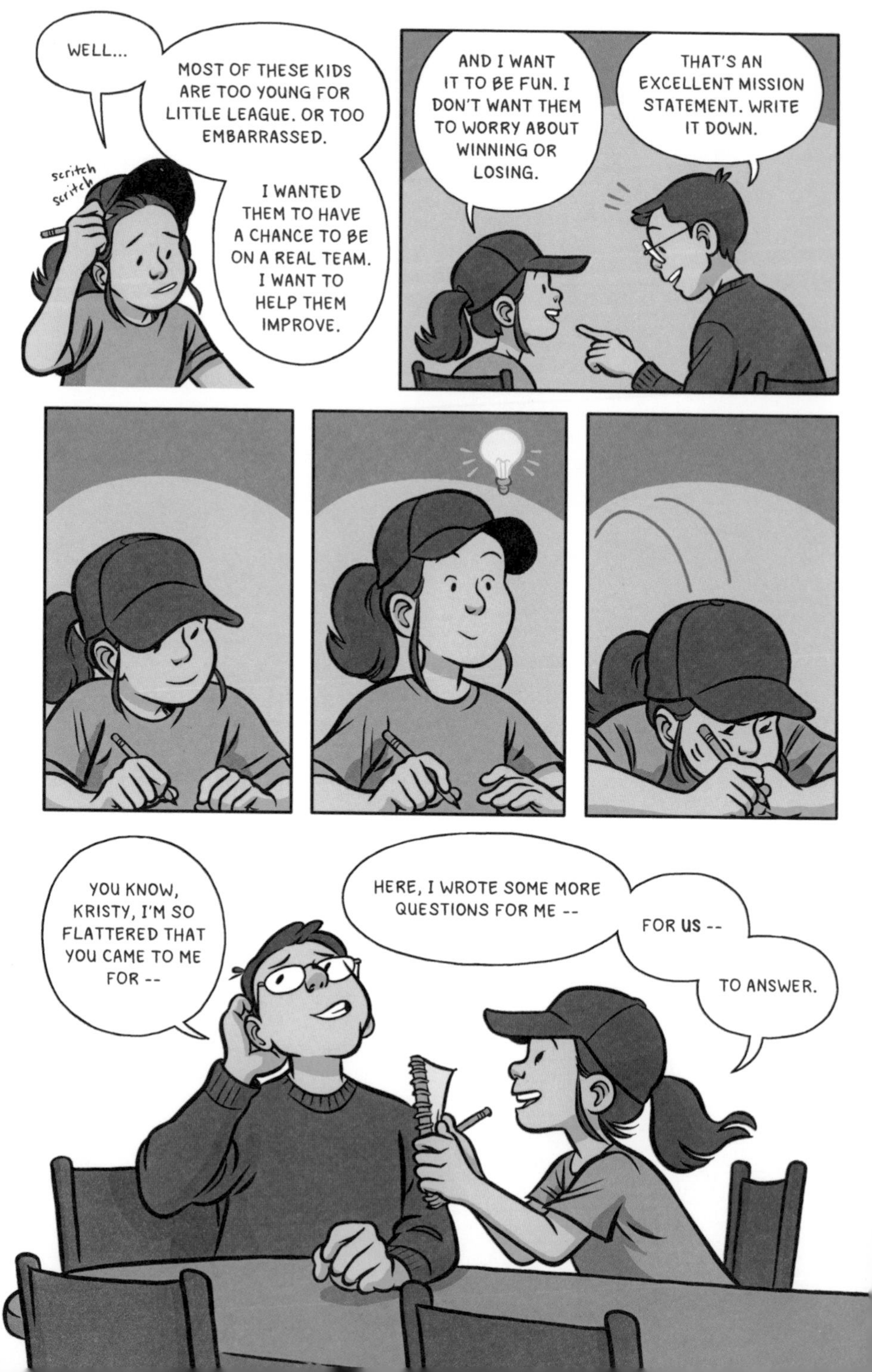
WELL...
MOST OF THESE KIDS ARE TOO YOUNG FOR LITTLE LEAGUE. OR TOO EMBARRASSED.
scritch scritch
I WANTED THEM TO HAVE A CHANCE TO BE ON A REAL TEAM. I WANT TO HELP THEM IMPROVE.
AND I WANT IT TO BE FUN. I DON'T WANT THEM TO WORRY ABOUT WINNING OR LOSING.
THAT'S AN EXCELLENT MISSION STATEMENT. WRITE IT DOWN.
YOU KNOW, KRISTY, I'M SO FLATTERED THAT YOU CAME TO ME FOR --
HERE, I WROTE SOME MORE QUESTIONS FOR ME --
FOR **US** --
TO ANSWER.

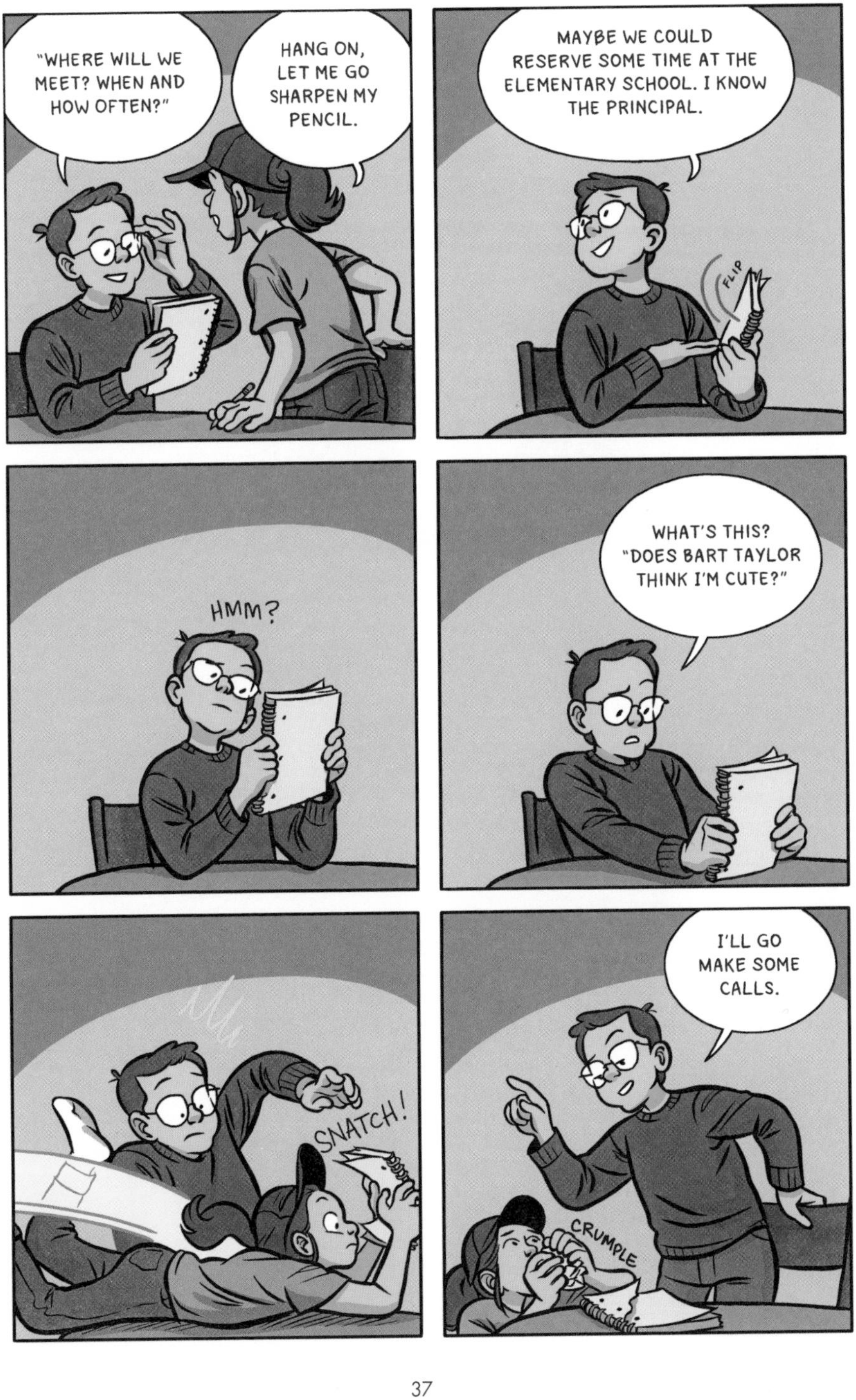
"WHERE WILL WE MEET? WHEN AND HOW OFTEN?"
HANG ON, LET ME GO SHARPEN MY PENCIL.
MAYBE WE COULD RESERVE SOME TIME AT THE ELEMENTARY SCHOOL. I KNOW THE PRINCIPAL.
FLIP
HMM?
WHAT'S THIS? "DOES BART TAYLOR THINK I'M CUTE?"
SNATCH!
I'LL GO MAKE SOME CALLS.
CRUMPLE

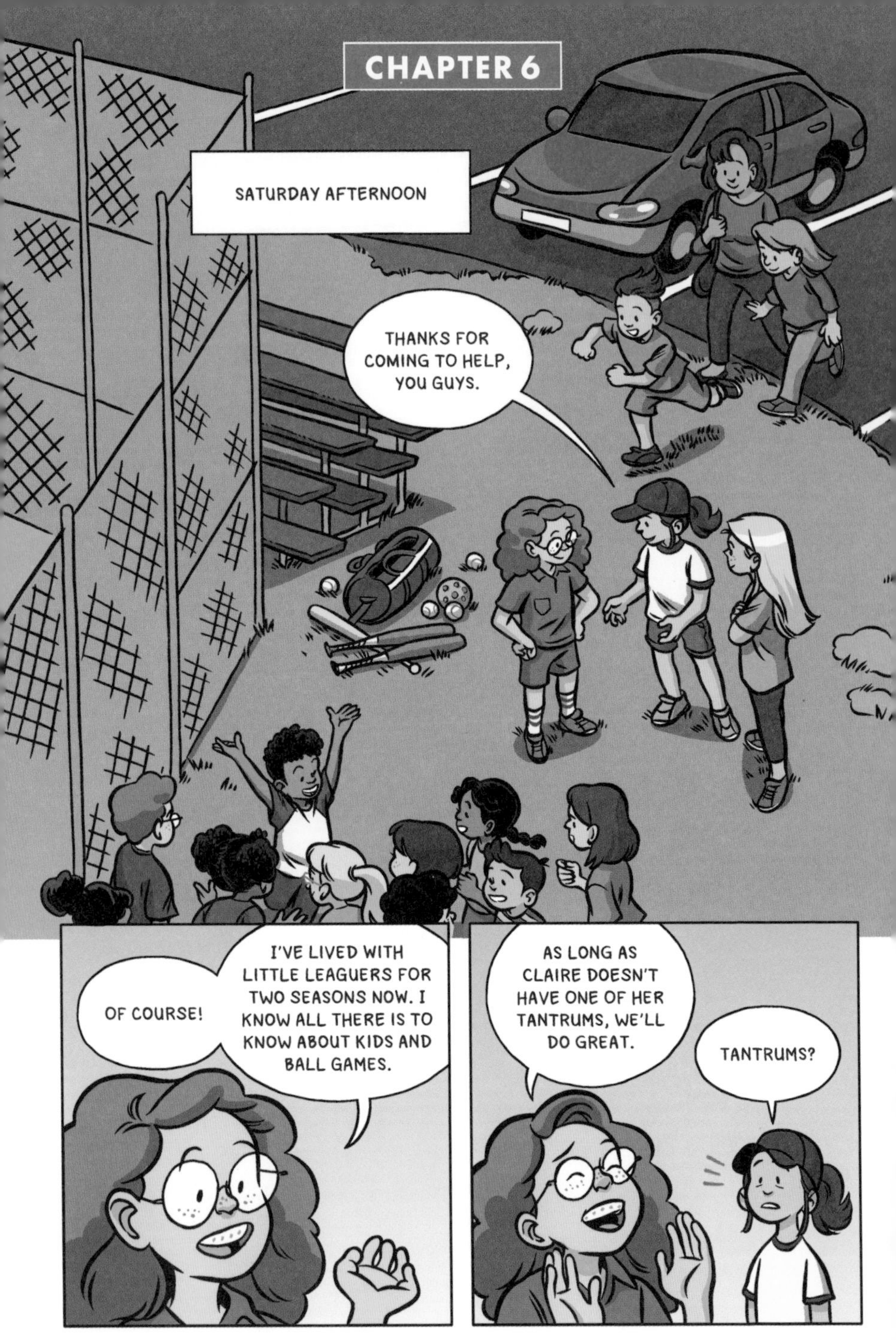
CHAPTER 6
SATURDAY AFTERNOON
THANKS FOR COMING TO HELP, YOU GUYS.
OF COURSE!
I'VE LIVED WITH LITTLE LEAGUERS FOR TWO SEASONS NOW. I KNOW ALL THERE IS TO KNOW ABOUT KIDS AND BALL GAMES.
AS LONG AS CLAIRE DOESN'T HAVE ONE OF HER TANTRUMS, WE'LL DO GREAT.
TANTRUMS?

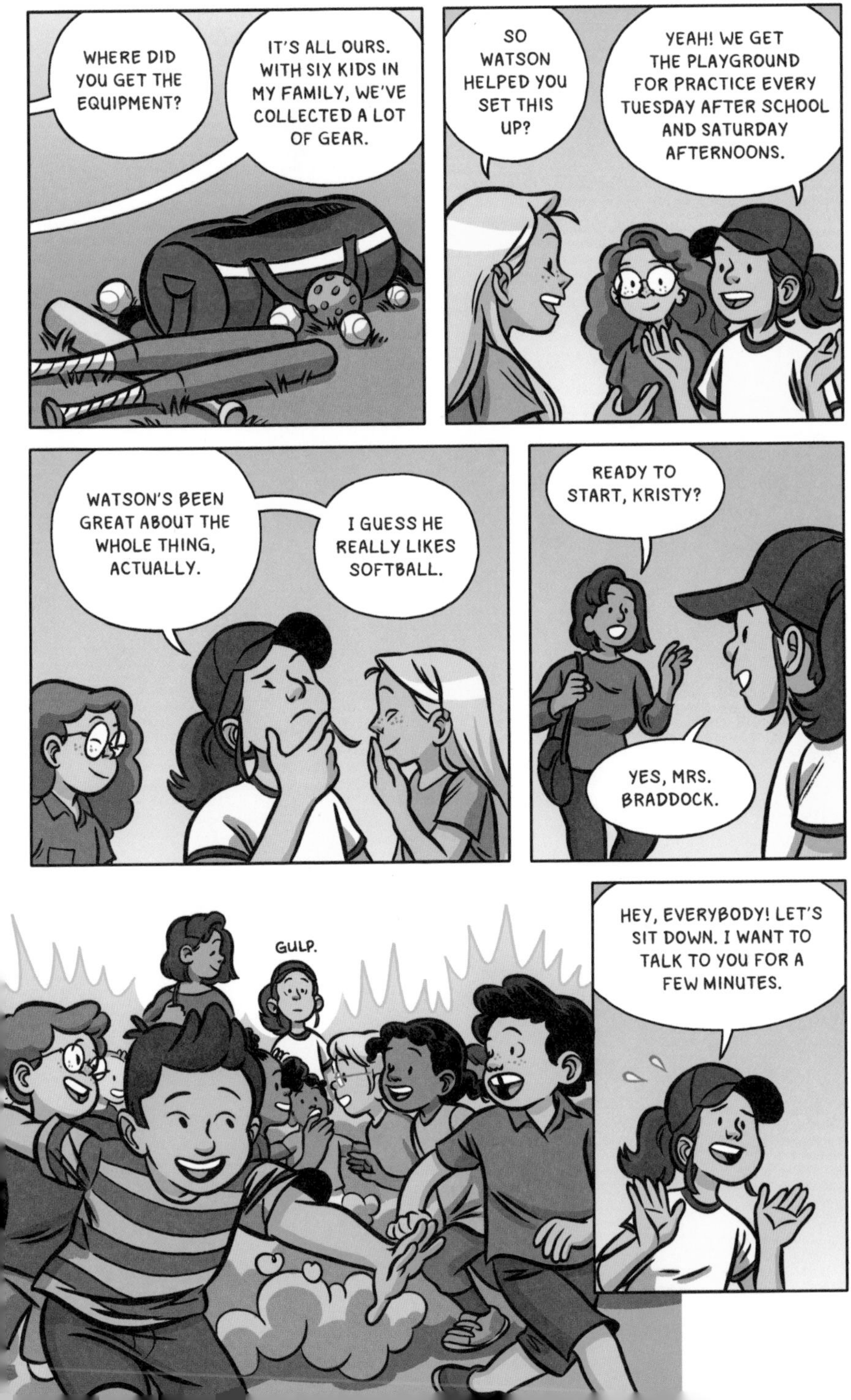
WHERE DID YOU GET THE EQUIPMENT?
IT'S ALL OURS. WITH SIX KIDS IN MY FAMILY, WE'VE COLLECTED A LOT OF GEAR.
SO WATSON HELPED YOU SET THIS UP?
YEAH! WE GET THE PLAYGROUND FOR PRACTICE EVERY TUESDAY AFTER SCHOOL AND SATURDAY AFTERNOONS.
WATSON'S BEEN GREAT ABOUT THE WHOLE THING, ACTUALLY.
I GUESS HE REALLY LIKES SOFTBALL.
READY TO START, KRISTY?
YES, MRS. BRADDOCK.
GULP.
HEY, EVERYBODY! LET'S SIT DOWN. I WANT TO TALK TO YOU FOR A FEW MINUTES.

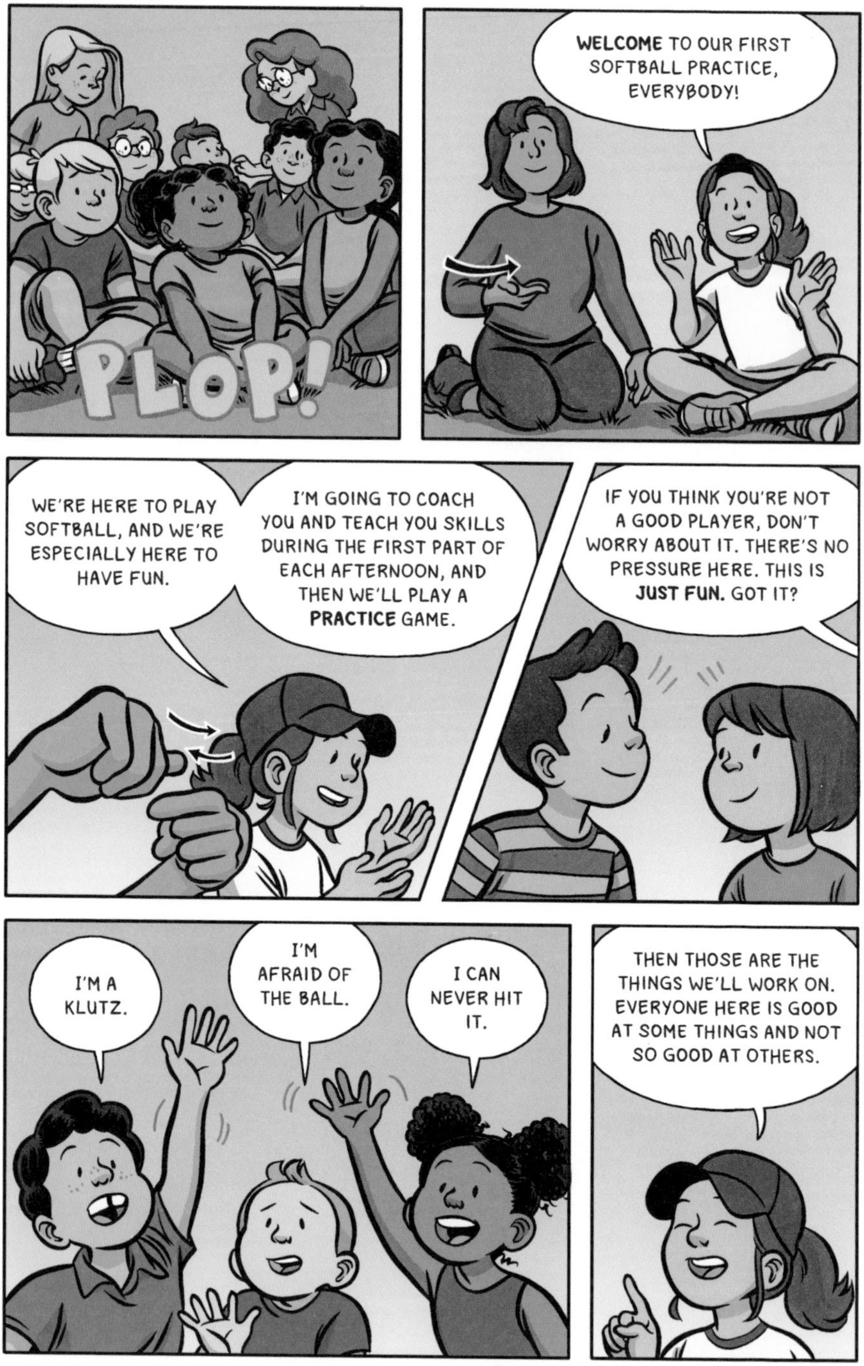
PLOP!
WELCOME TO OUR FIRST SOFTBALL PRACTICE, EVERYBODY!
WE'RE HERE TO PLAY SOFTBALL, AND WE'RE ESPECIALLY HERE TO HAVE FUN.
I'M GOING TO COACH YOU AND TEACH YOU SKILLS DURING THE FIRST PART OF EACH AFTERNOON, AND THEN WE'LL PLAY A PRACTICE GAME.
IF YOU THINK YOU'RE NOT A GOOD PLAYER, DON'T WORRY ABOUT IT. THERE'S NO PRESSURE HERE. THIS IS JUST FUN. GOT IT?
I'M A KLUTZ.
I'M AFRAID OF THE BALL.
I CAN NEVER HIT IT.
THEN THOSE ARE THE THINGS WE'LL WORK ON. EVERYONE HERE IS GOOD AT SOME THINGS AND NOT SO GOOD AT OTHERS.

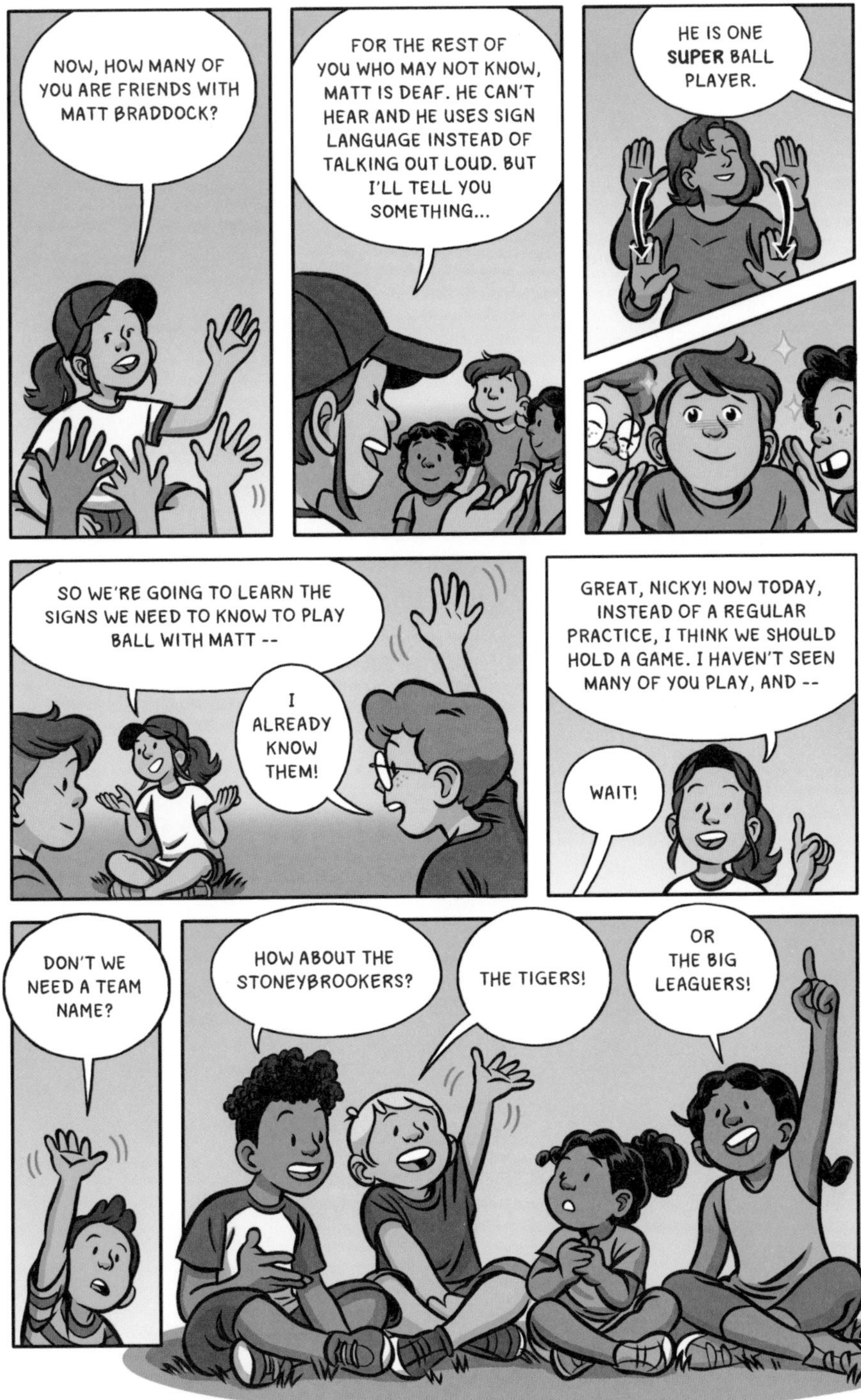
NOW, HOW MANY OF YOU ARE FRIENDS WITH MATT BRADDOCK?
FOR THE REST OF YOU WHO MAY NOT KNOW, MATT IS DEAF. HE CAN'T HEAR AND HE USES SIGN LANGUAGE INSTEAD OF TALKING OUT LOUD. BUT I'LL TELL YOU SOMETHING...
HE IS ONE **SUPER** BALL PLAYER.
SO WE'RE GOING TO LEARN THE SIGNS WE NEED TO KNOW TO PLAY BALL WITH MATT --
I ALREADY KNOW THEM!
GREAT, NICKY! NOW TODAY, INSTEAD OF A REGULAR PRACTICE, I THINK WE SHOULD HOLD A GAME. I HAVEN'T SEEN MANY OF YOU PLAY, AND --
WAIT!
DON'T WE NEED A TEAM NAME?
HOW ABOUT THE STONEYBROOKERS?
THE TIGERS!
OR THE BIG LEAGUERS!

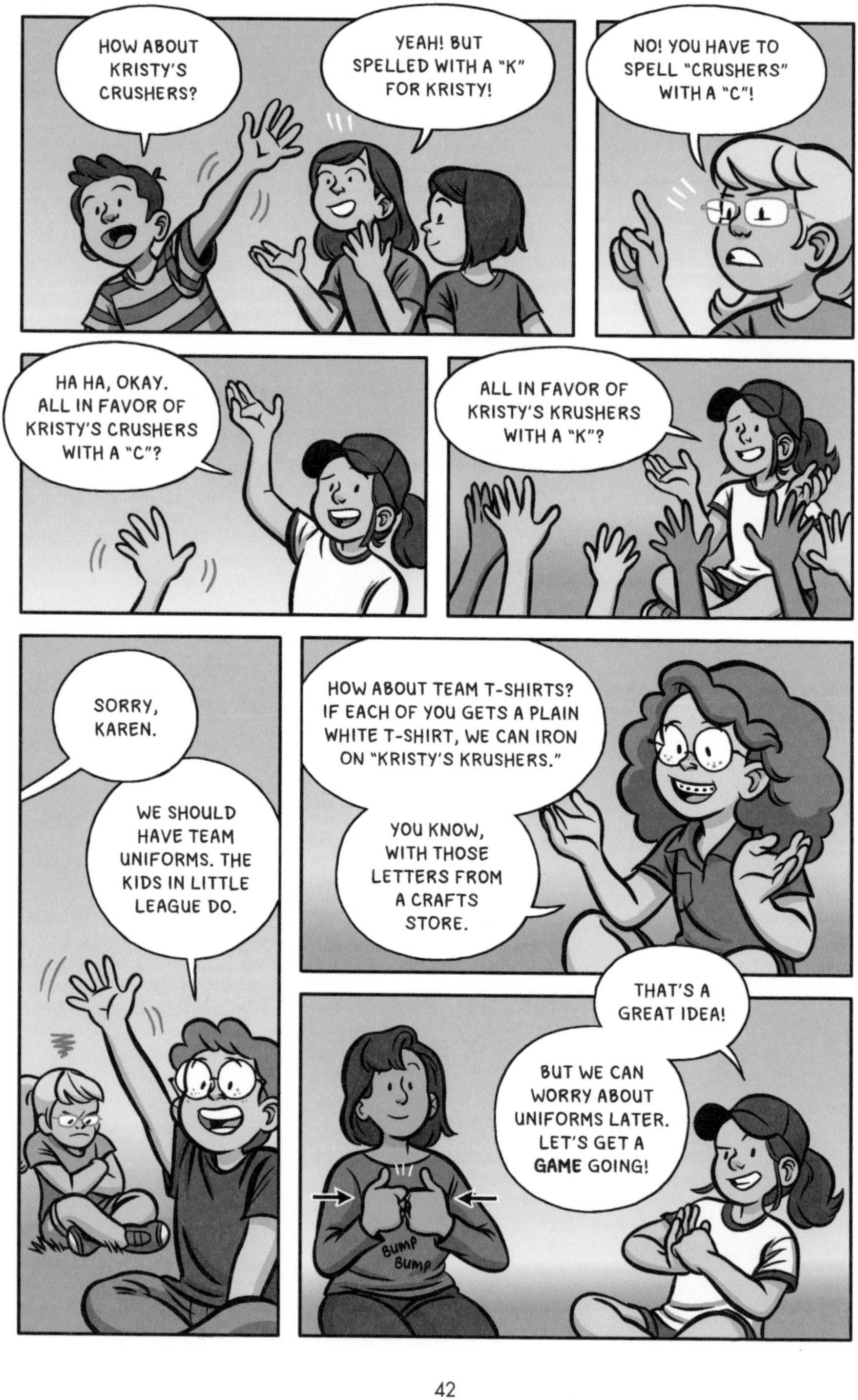
HOW ABOUT KRISTY'S CRUSHERS?
YEAH! BUT SPELLED WITH A "K" FOR KRISTY!
NO! YOU HAVE TO SPELL "CRUSHERS" WITH A "C"!
HA HA, OKAY. ALL IN FAVOR OF KRISTY'S CRUSHERS WITH A "C"?
ALL IN FAVOR OF KRISTY'S KRUSHERS WITH A "K"?
SORRY, KAREN.
WE SHOULD HAVE TEAM UNIFORMS. THE KIDS IN LITTLE LEAGUE DO.
HOW ABOUT TEAM T-SHIRTS? IF EACH OF YOU GETS A PLAIN WHITE T-SHIRT, WE CAN IRON ON "KRISTY'S KRUSHERS."
YOU KNOW, WITH THOSE LETTERS FROM A CRAFTS STORE.
BUMP BUMP
THAT'S A GREAT IDEA!
BUT WE CAN WORRY ABOUT UNIFORMS LATER. LET'S GET A **GAME** GOING!

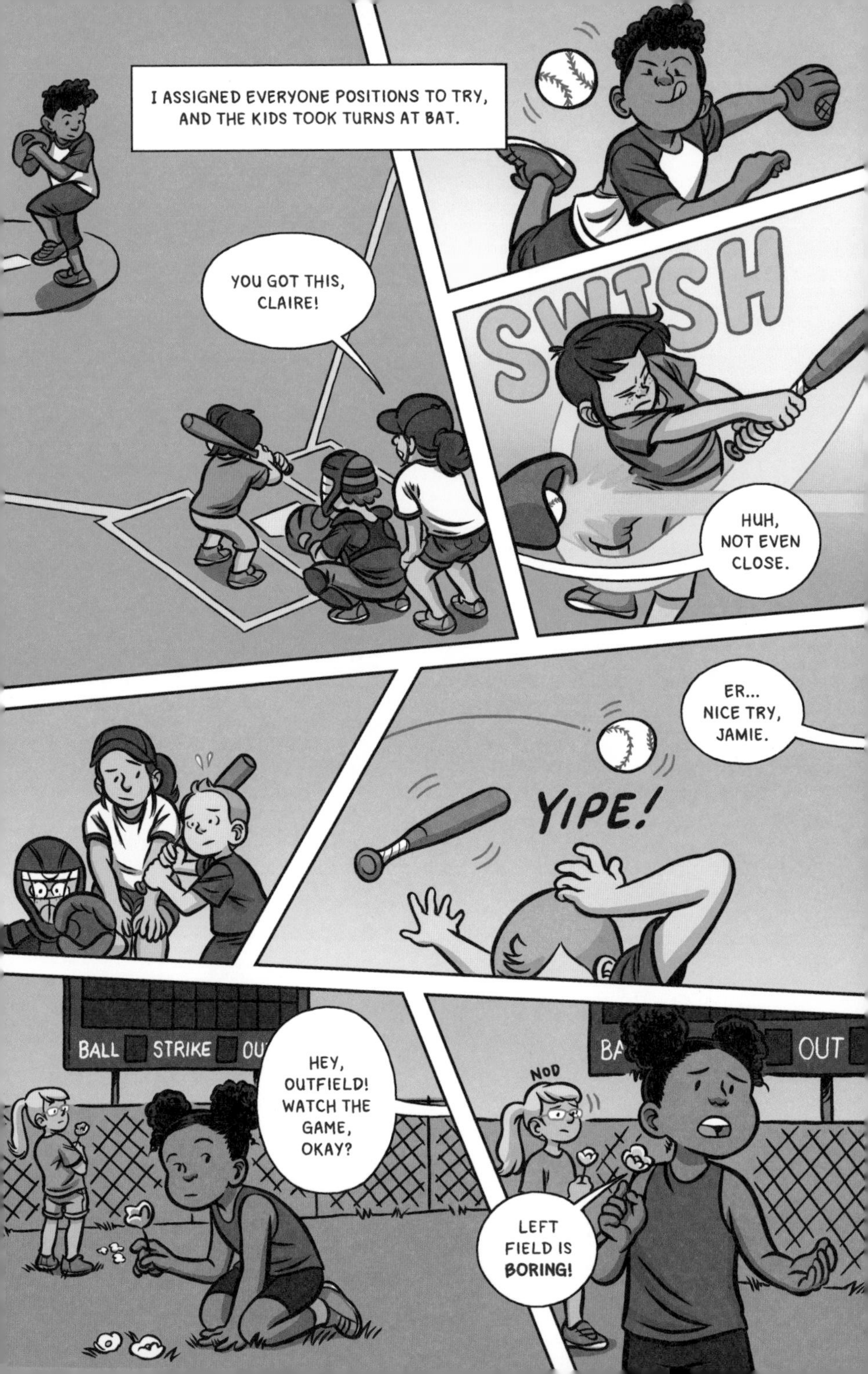
I ASSIGNED EVERYONE POSITIONS TO TRY, AND THE KIDS TOOK TURNS AT BAT.
YOU GOT THIS, CLAIRE!
SWISH
HUH, NOT EVEN CLOSE.
ER... NICE TRY, JAMIE.
YIPE!
BALL STRIKE OU
HEY, OUTFIELD! WATCH THE GAME, OKAY?
NOD
OUT
LEFT FIELD IS **BORING!**

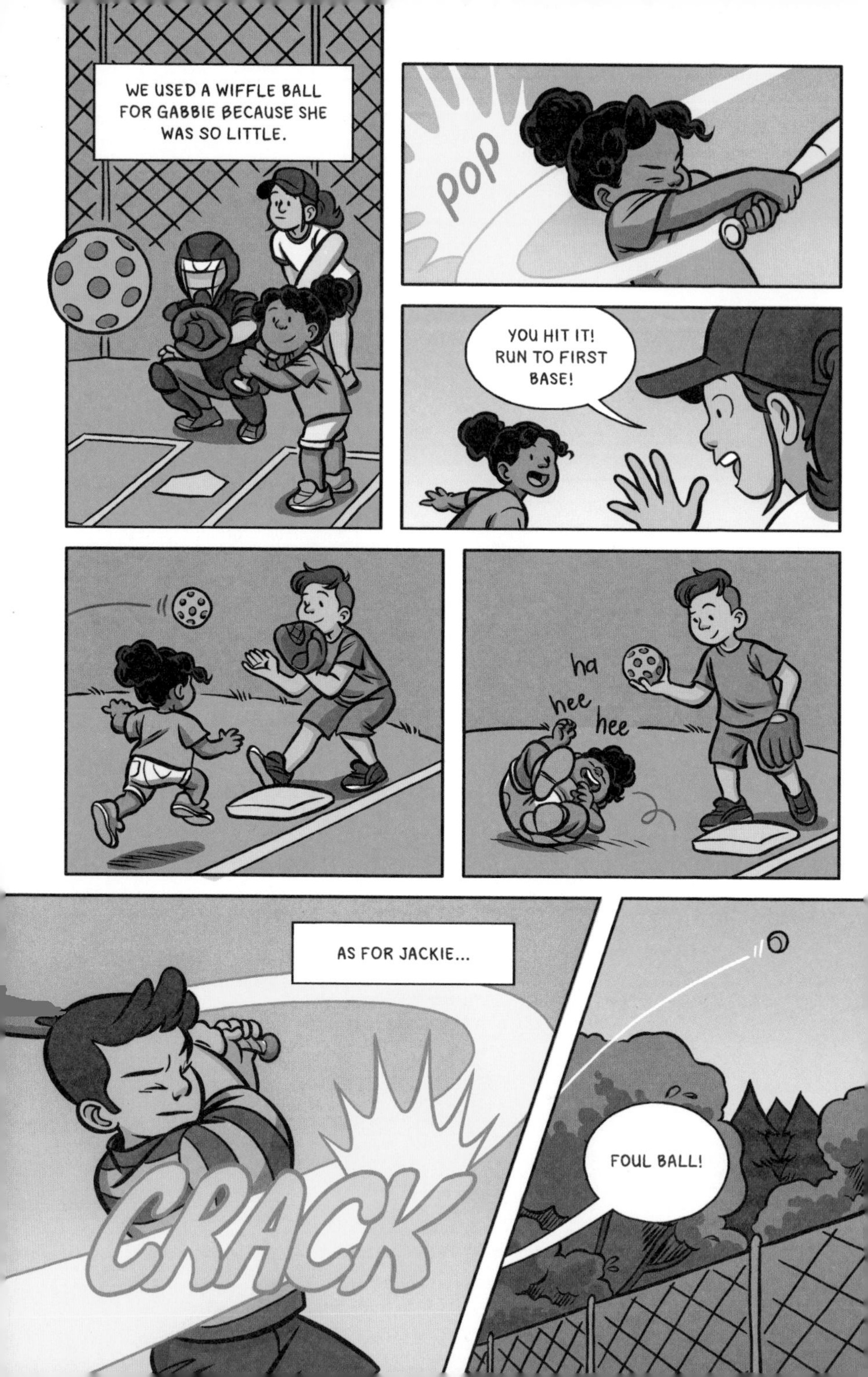
WE USED A WIFFLE BALL FOR GABBIE BECAUSE SHE WAS SO LITTLE.
pop
YOU HIT IT! RUN TO FIRST BASE!
ha
hee
hee
AS FOR JACKIE...
CRACK
FOUL BALL!

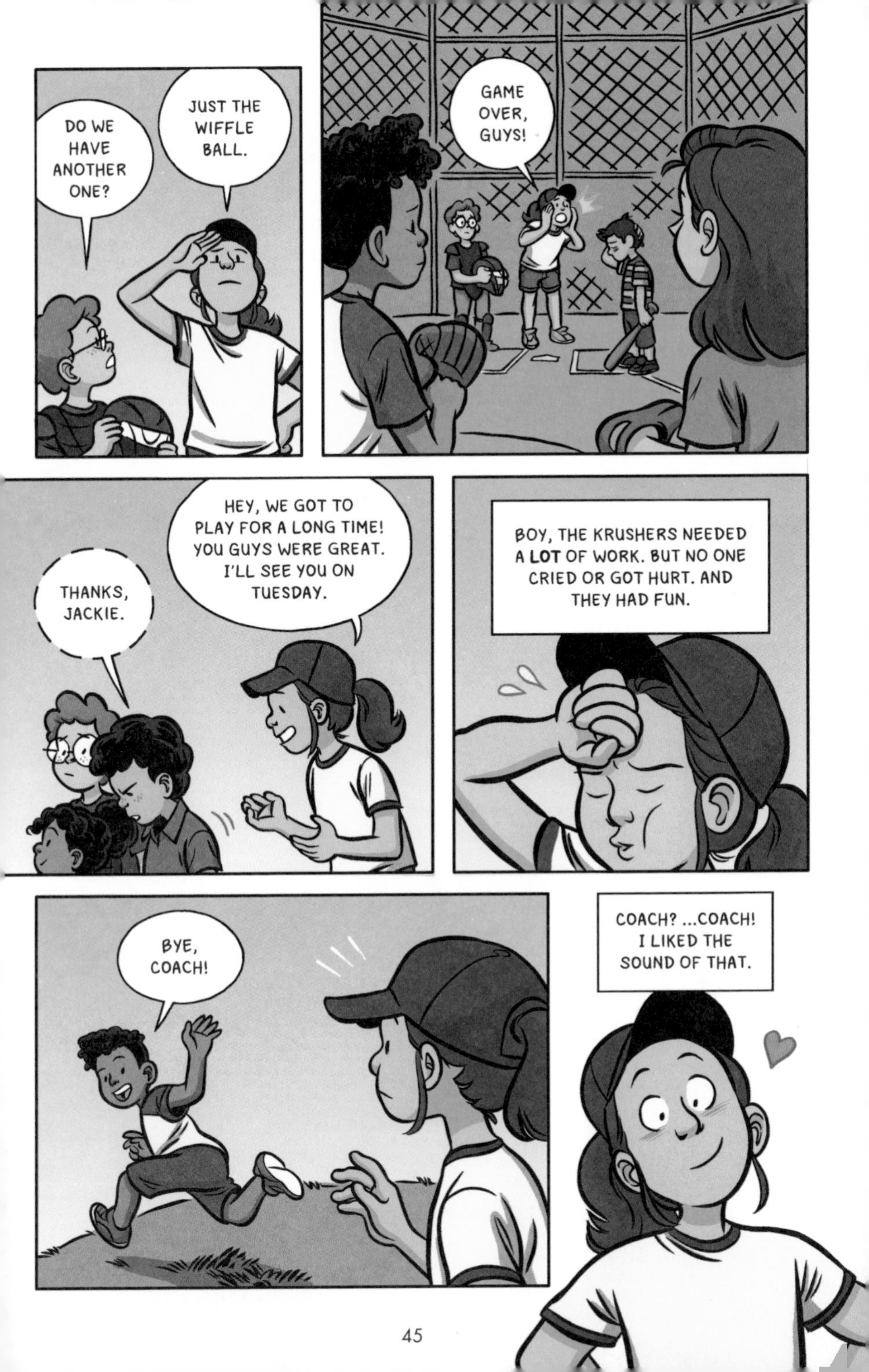
DO WE HAVE ANOTHER ONE?
JUST THE WIFFLE BALL.
GAME OVER, GUYS!
THANKS, JACKIE.
HEY, WE GOT TO PLAY FOR A LONG TIME! YOU GUYS WERE GREAT. I'LL SEE YOU ON TUESDAY.
BOY, THE KRUSHERS NEEDED A **LOT** OF WORK. BUT NO ONE CRIED OR GOT HURT. AND THEY HAD FUN.
BYE, COACH!
COACH? ...COACH! I LIKED THE SOUND OF THAT.

Monday

Mallory! What a game!

I'll say, Claud. Kristy's Krushers are terrific.

We hardly had to babbysit today.

Nope. We were fans instead.

Expect for that one tantrum.

Well, those are bound to happen every now and then.
I warned Kristy about them. Claire may be silly, but
she's also got a temper. Especially when she's doing
something, you know...

compertive?

Well, competitive. And only when it has to do with
baseball...

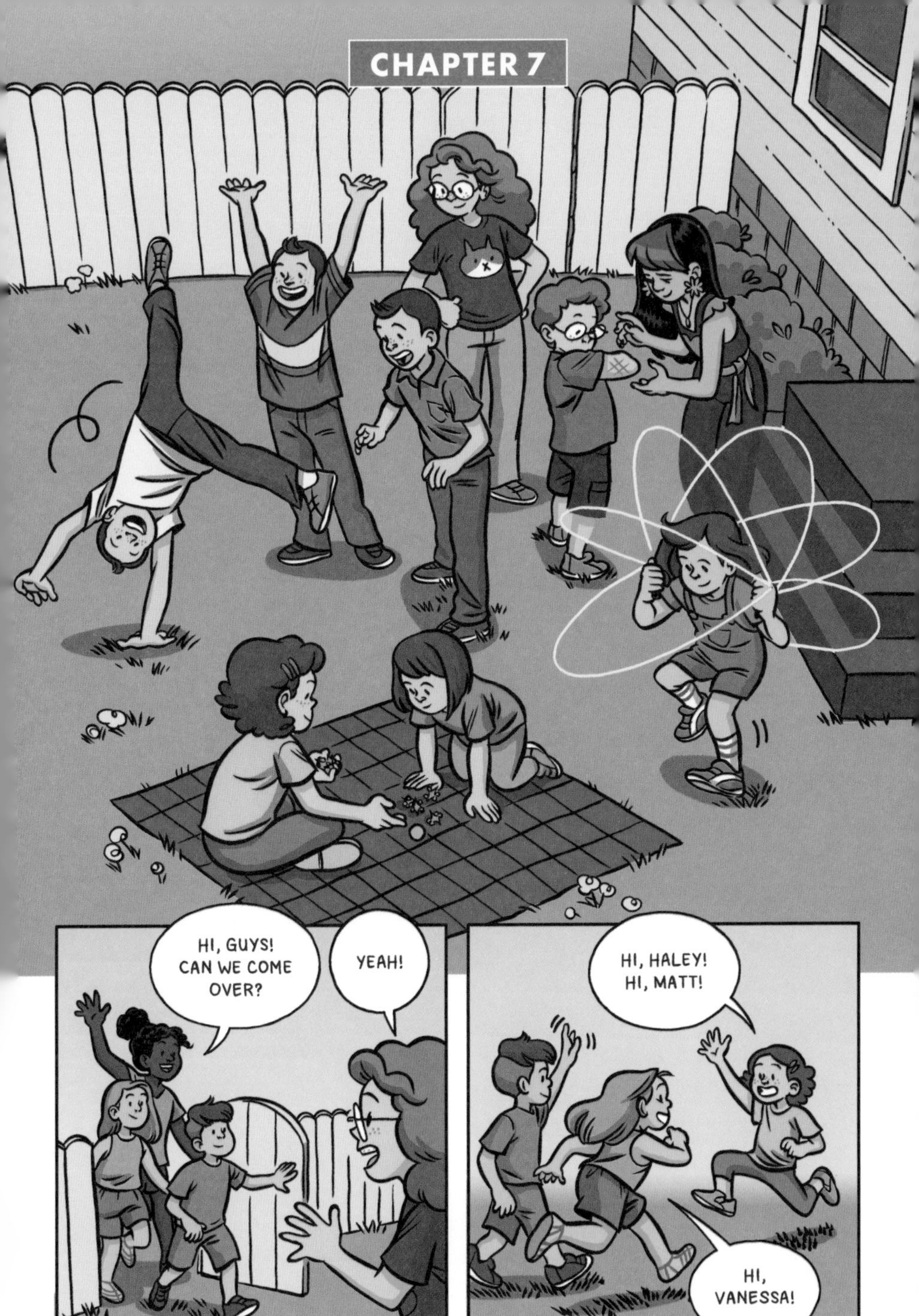
CHAPTER 7
HI, GUYS! CAN WE COME OVER?
YEAH!
HI, HALEY! HI, MATT!
HI, VANESSA!

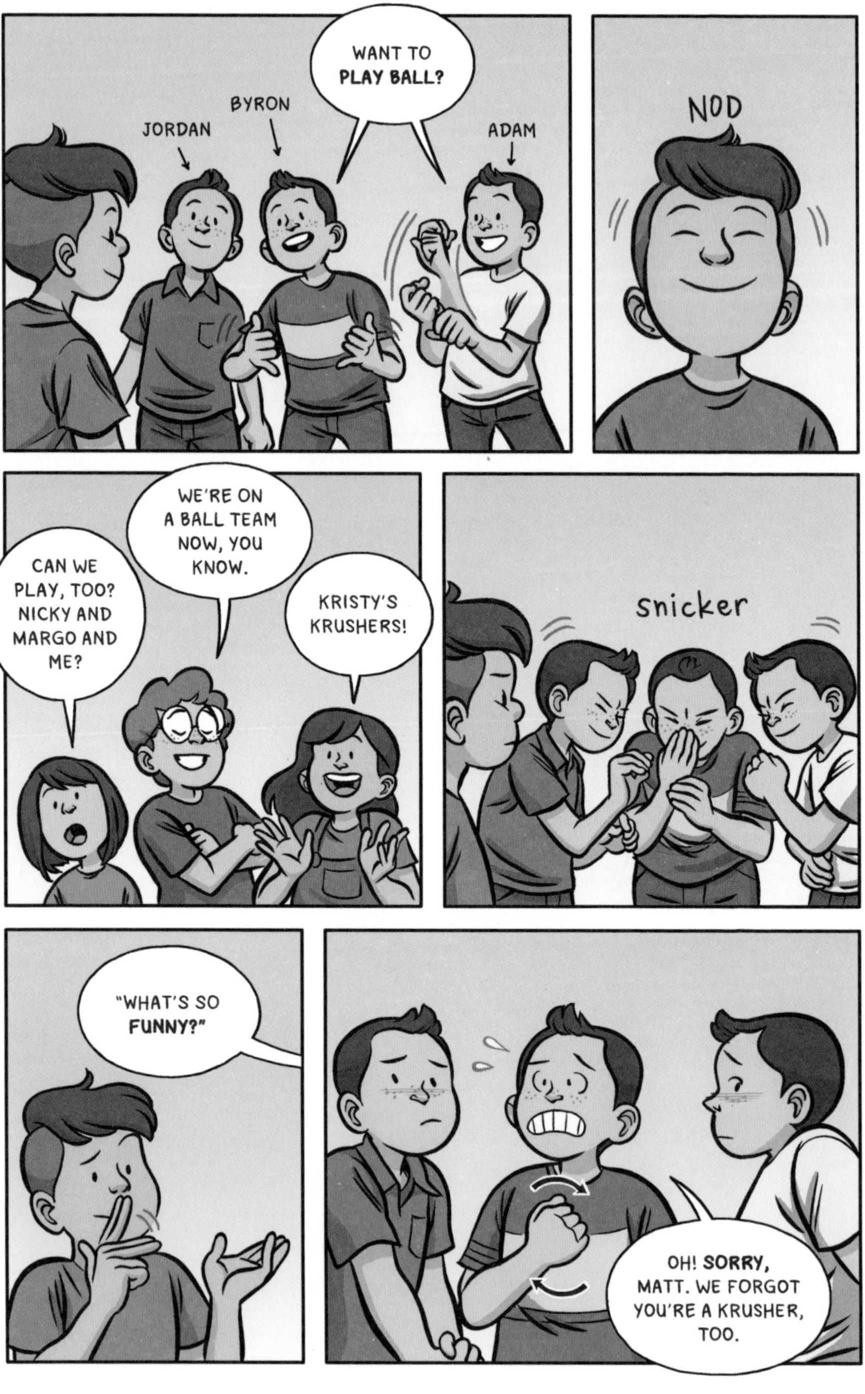
WANT TO PLAY BALL?
JORDAN
BYRON
ADAM
NOD
CAN WE PLAY, TOO? NICKY AND MARGO AND ME?
WE'RE ON A BALL TEAM NOW, YOU KNOW.
KRISTY'S KRUSHERS!
snicker
"WHAT'S SO FUNNY?"
OH! SORRY, MATT. WE FORGOT YOU'RE A KRUSHER, TOO.

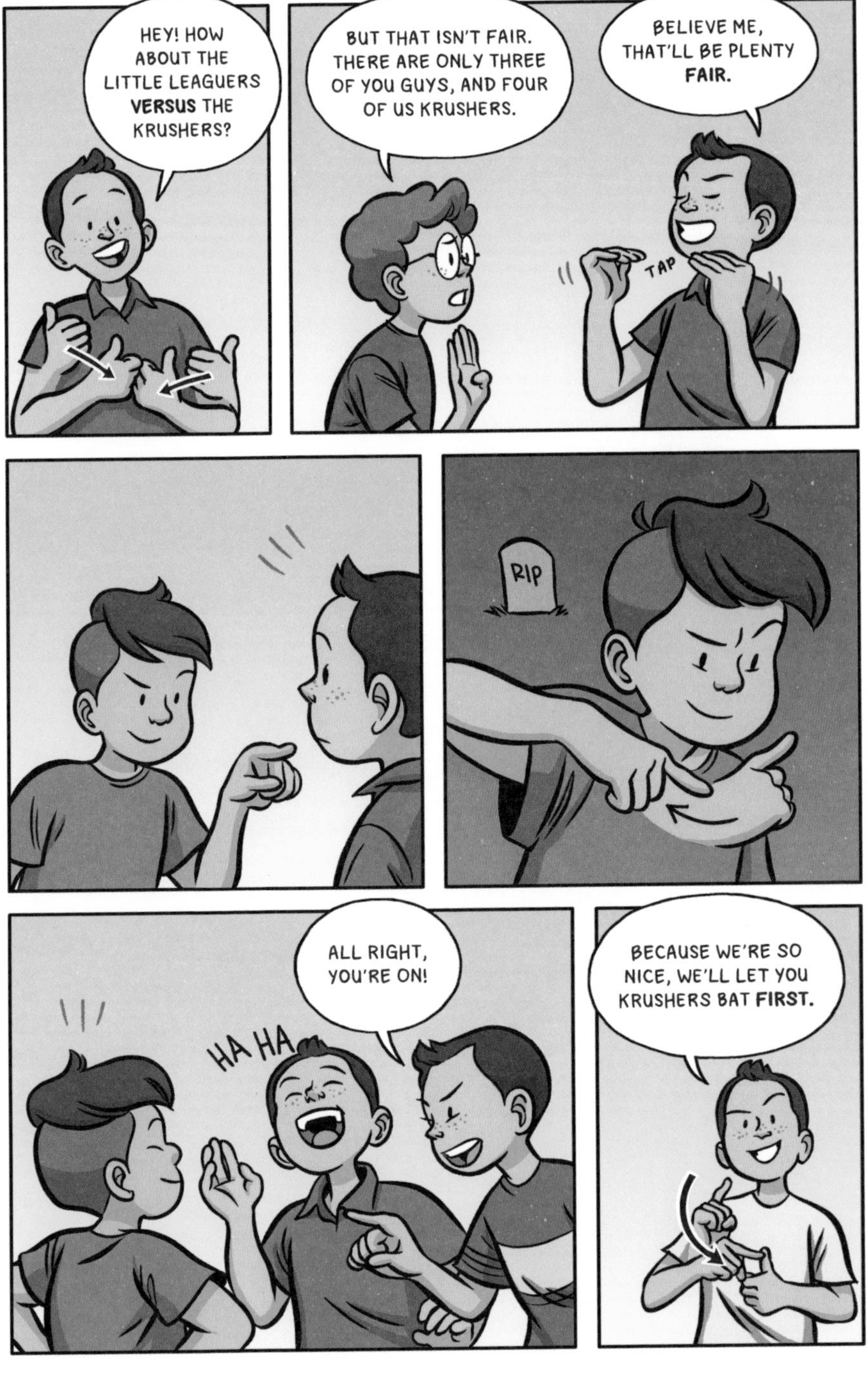
HEY! HOW ABOUT THE LITTLE LEAGUERS **VERSUS** THE KRUSHERS?
BUT THAT ISN'T FAIR. THERE ARE ONLY THREE OF YOU GUYS, AND FOUR OF US KRUSHERS.
BELIEVE ME, THAT'LL BE PLENTY **FAIR.**
TAP
RIP
HA HA
ALL RIGHT, YOU'RE ON!
BECAUSE WE'RE SO NICE, WE'LL LET YOU KRUSHERS BAT **FIRST.**

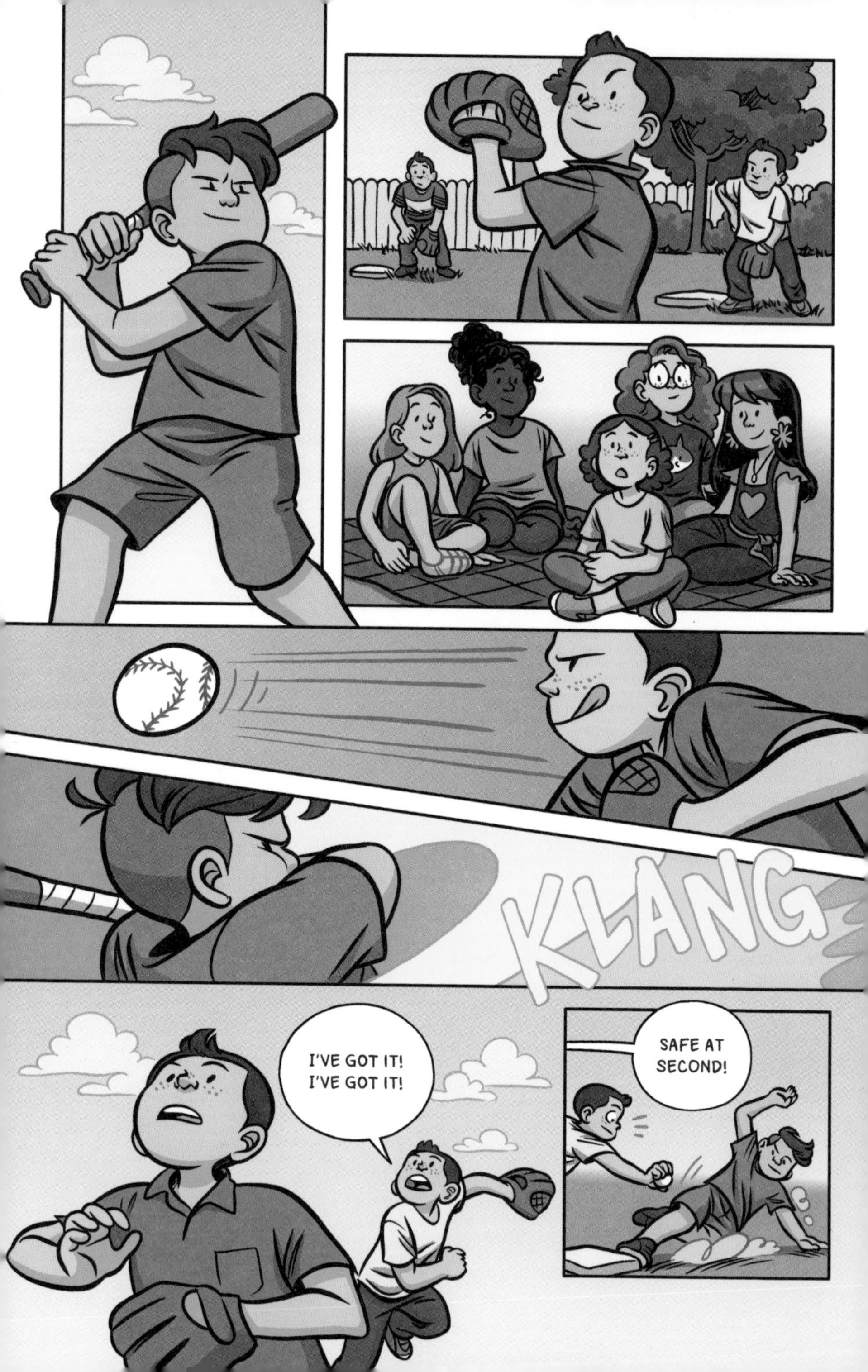
KLANG
I'VE GOT IT! I'VE GOT IT!
SAFE AT SECOND!

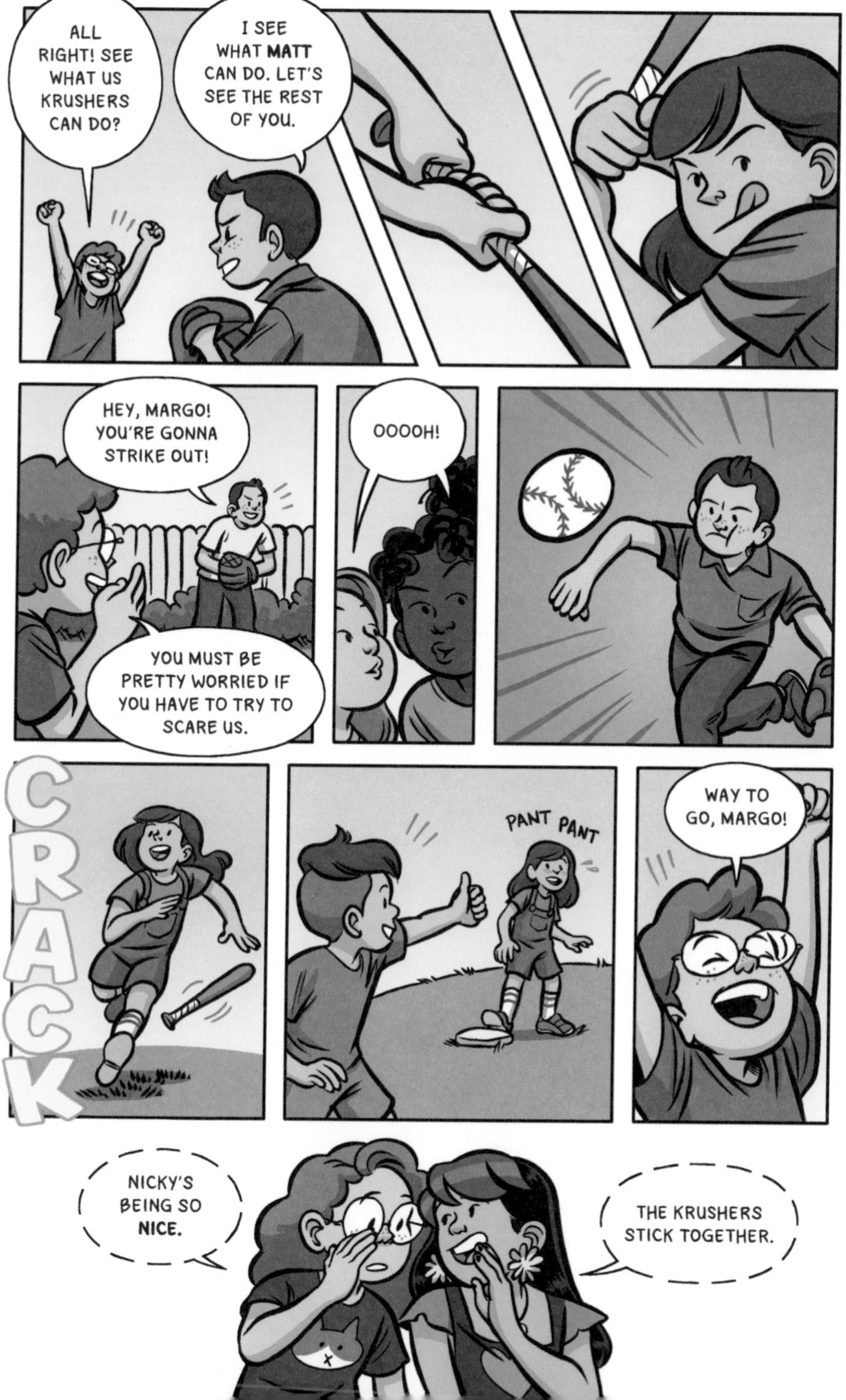
ALL RIGHT! SEE WHAT US KRUSHERS CAN DO?
I SEE WHAT **MATT** CAN DO. LET'S SEE THE REST OF YOU.
HEY, MARGO! YOU'RE GONNA STRIKE OUT!
YOU MUST BE PRETTY WORRIED IF YOU HAVE TO TRY TO SCARE US.
OOOOH!
CRACK
PANT PANT
WAY TO GO, MARGO!
NICKY'S BEING SO **NICE.**
THE KRUSHERS STICK TOGETHER.

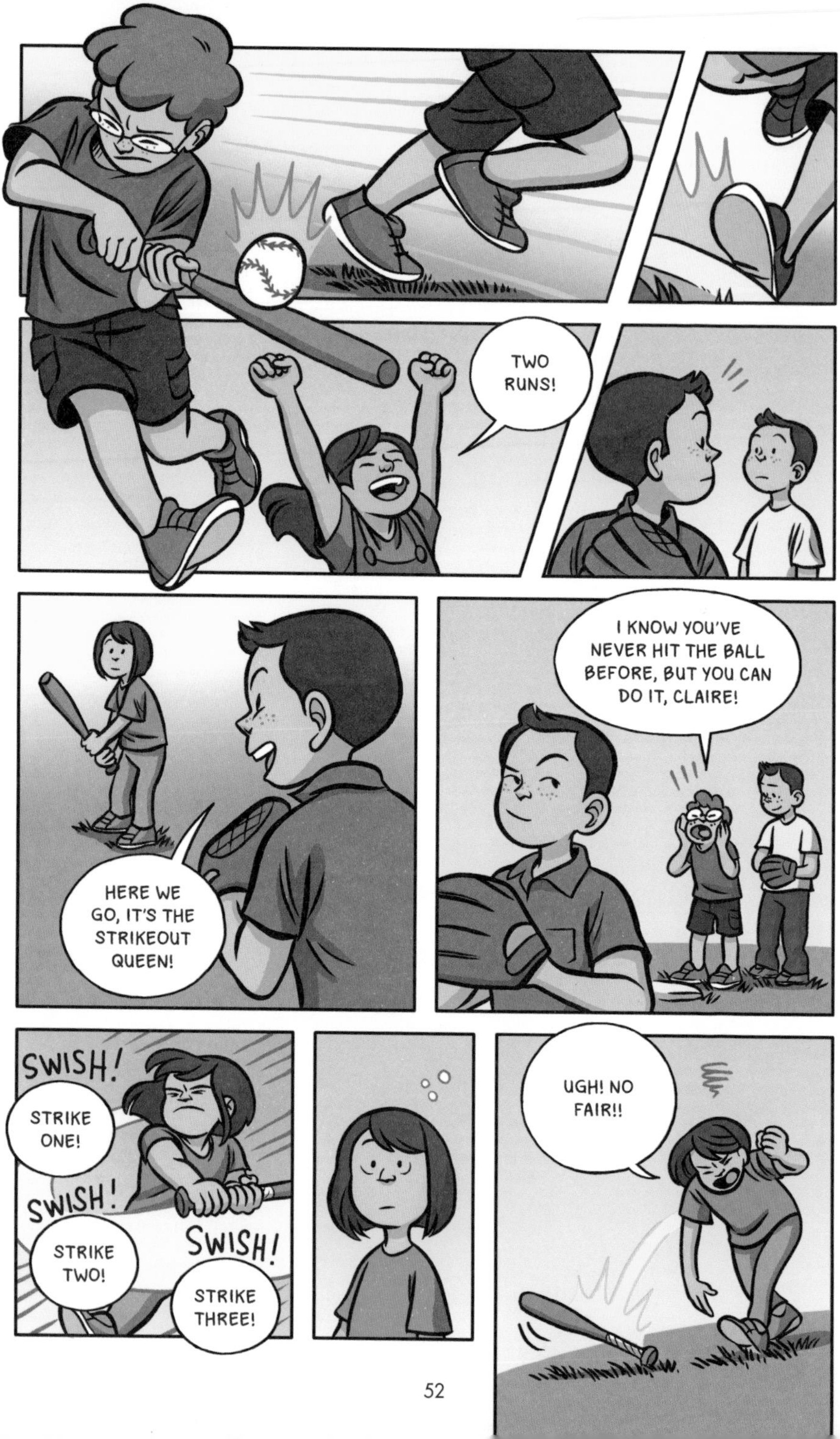
TWO RUNS!
HERE WE GO, IT'S THE STRIKEOUT QUEEN!
I KNOW YOU'VE NEVER HIT THE BALL BEFORE, BUT YOU CAN DO IT, CLAIRE!
SWISH!
STRIKE ONE!
SWISH!
STRIKE TWO!
SWISH!
STRIKE THREE!
UGH! NO FAIR!!

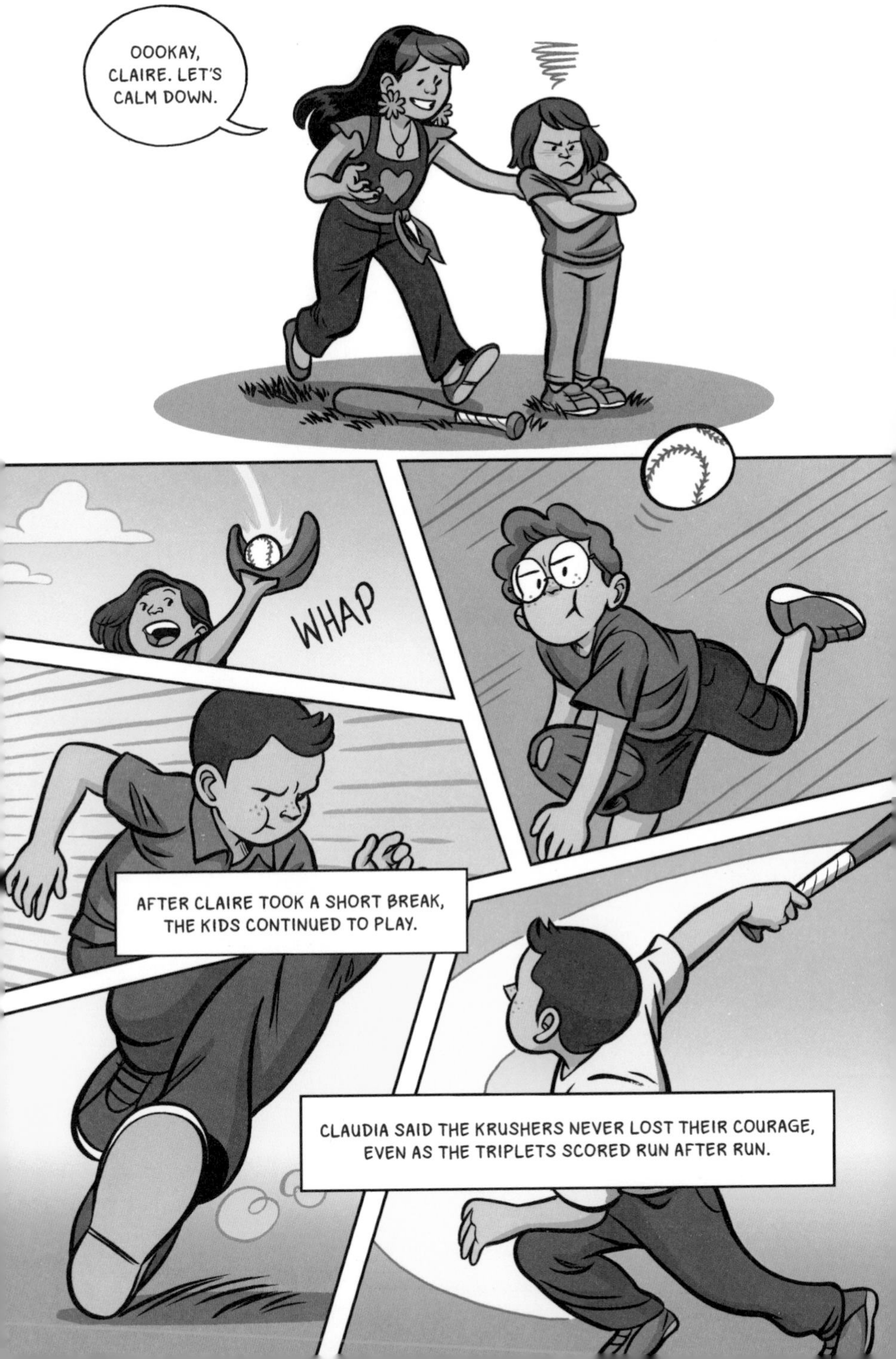
OOOKAY, CLAIRE. LET'S CALM DOWN.
WHAP
AFTER CLAIRE TOOK A SHORT BREAK, THE KIDS CONTINUED TO PLAY.
CLAUDIA SAID THE KRUSHERS NEVER LOST THEIR COURAGE, EVEN AS THE TRIPLETS SCORED RUN AFTER RUN.

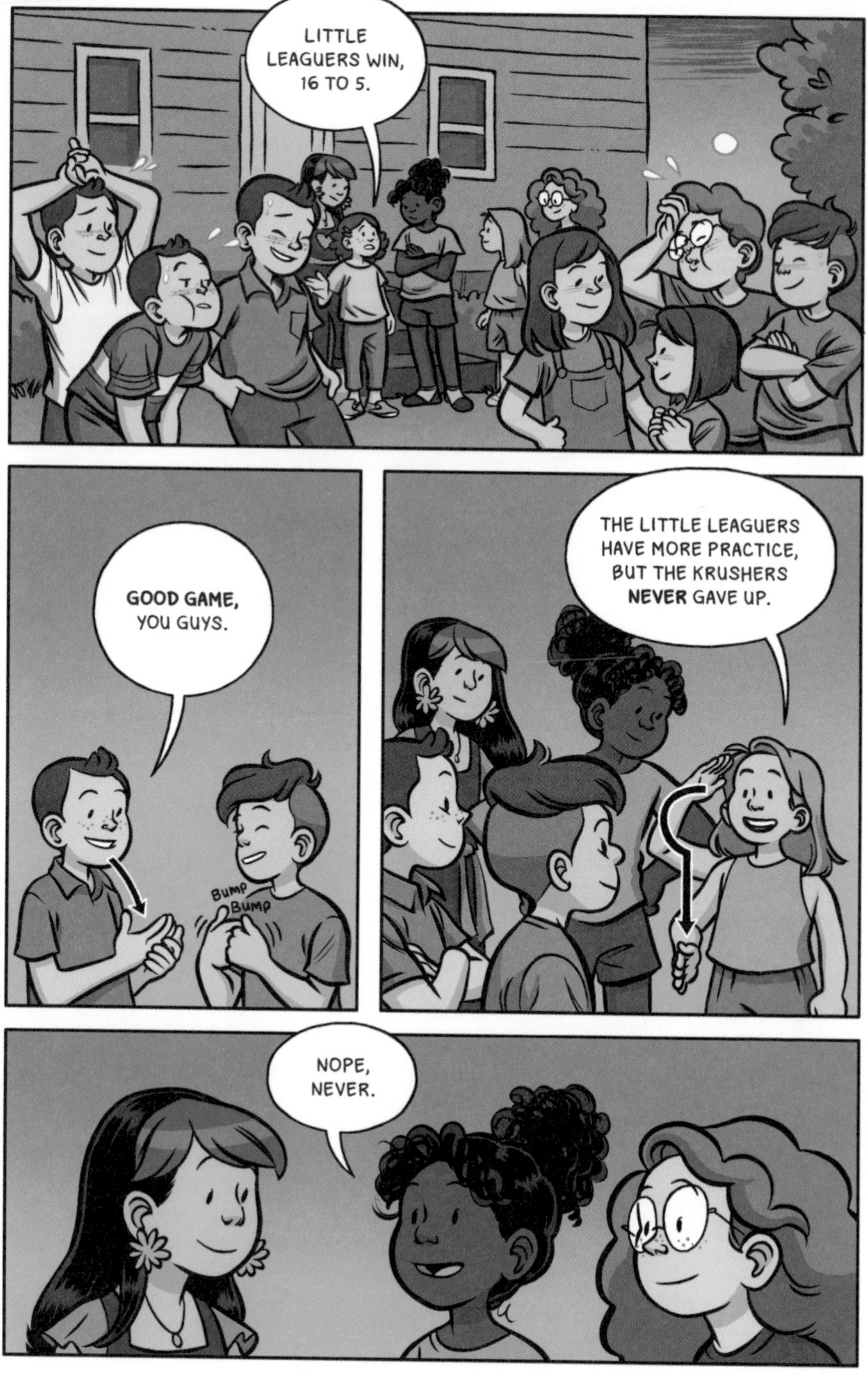
LITTLE LEAGUERS WIN, 16 TO 5.
GOOD GAME, YOU GUYS.
BUMP BUMP
THE LITTLE LEAGUERS HAVE MORE PRACTICE, BUT THE KRUSHERS NEVER GAVE UP.
NOPE, NEVER.

CHAPTER 8

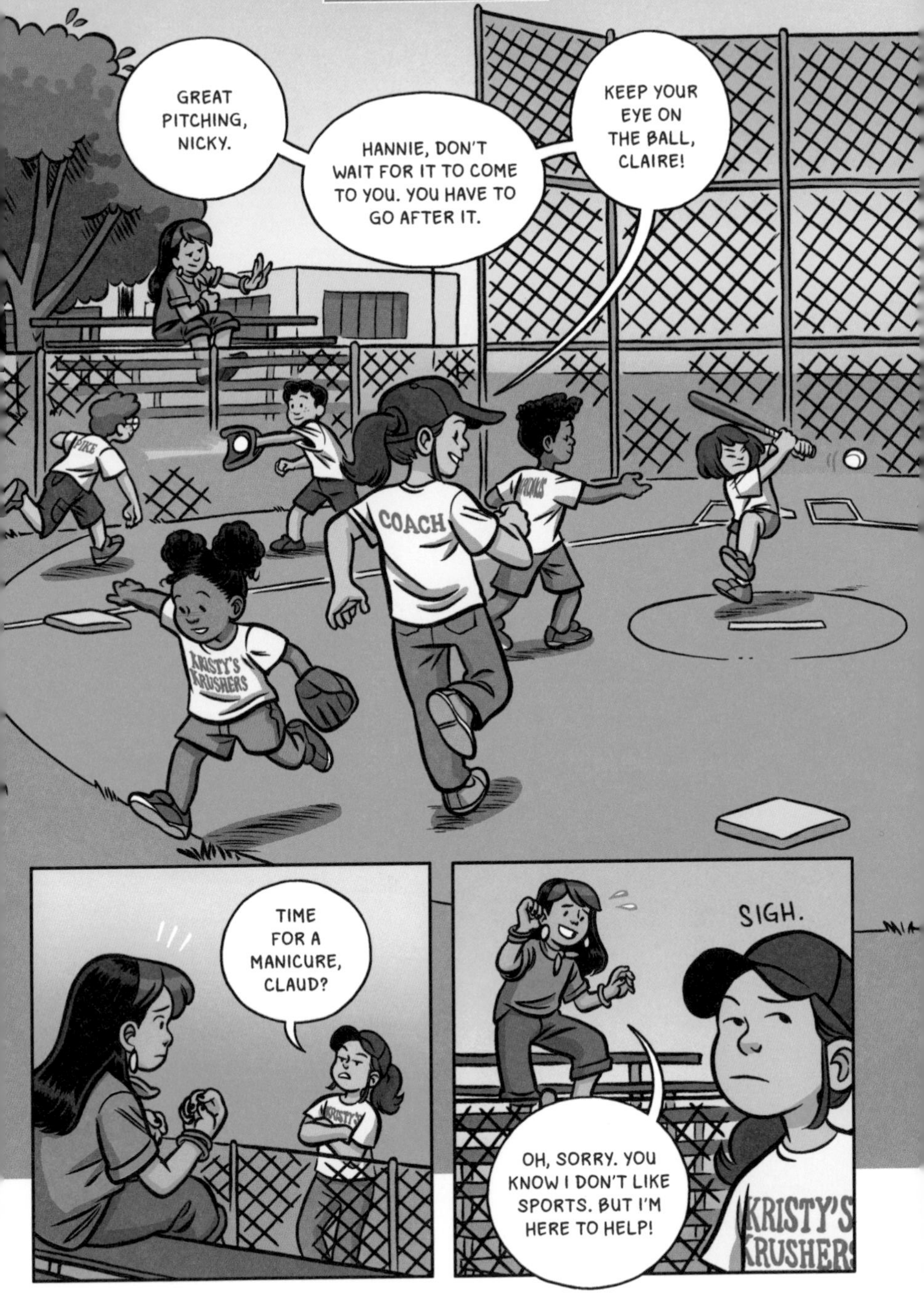
GREAT PITCHING, NICKY.
HANNIE, DON'T WAIT FOR IT TO COME TO YOU. YOU HAVE TO GO AFTER IT.
KEEP YOUR EYE ON THE BALL, CLAIRE!
COACH
KRISTY'S KRUSHERS
TIME FOR A MANICURE, CLAUD?
SIGH.
OH, SORRY. YOU KNOW I DON'T LIKE SPORTS. BUT I'M HERE TO HELP!
KRISTY'S KRUSHERS

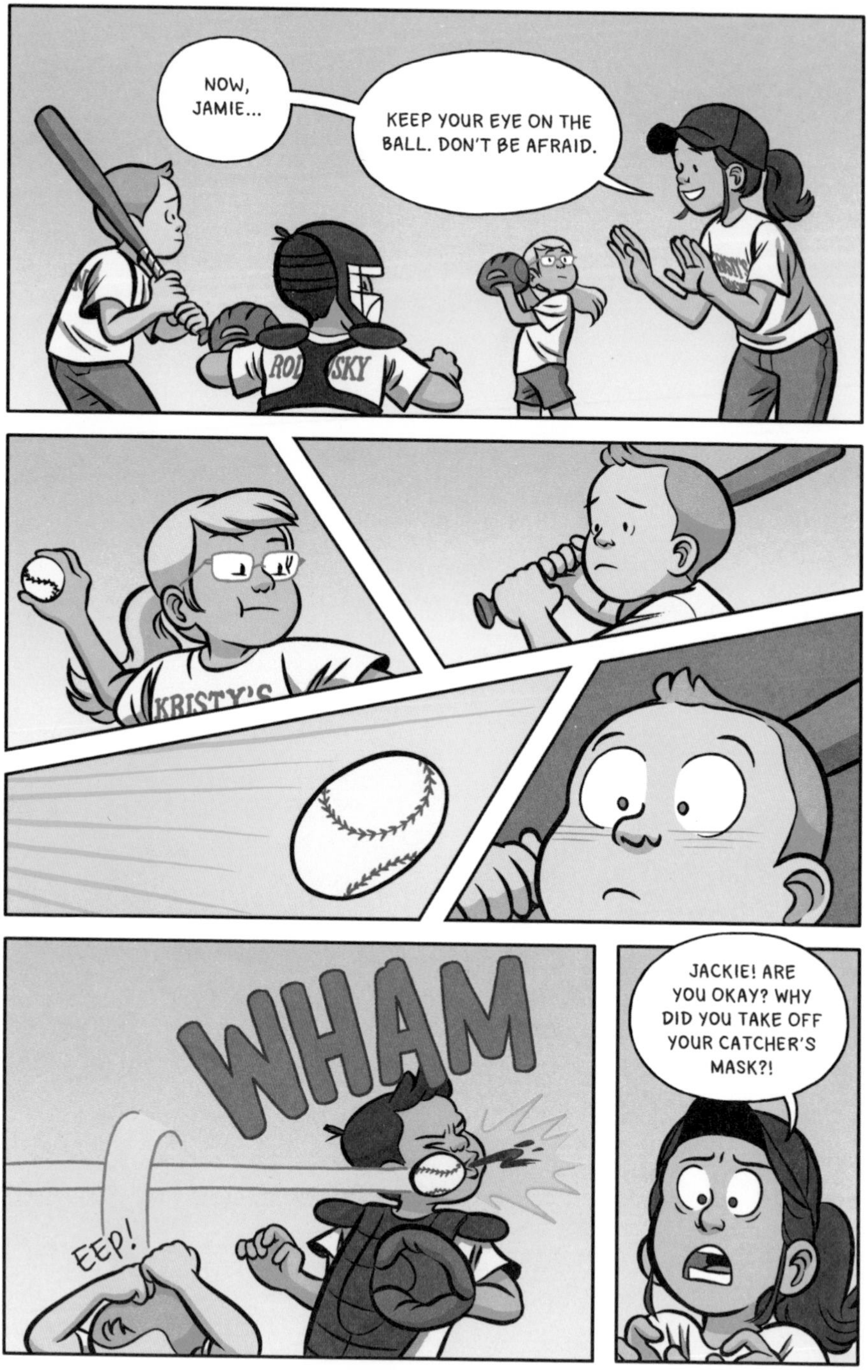
NOW, JAMIE...
KEEP YOUR EYE ON THE BALL. DON'T BE AFRAID.
KRISTY'S
WHAM
EEP!
JACKIE! ARE YOU OKAY? WHY DID YOU TAKE OFF YOUR CATCHER'S MASK?!

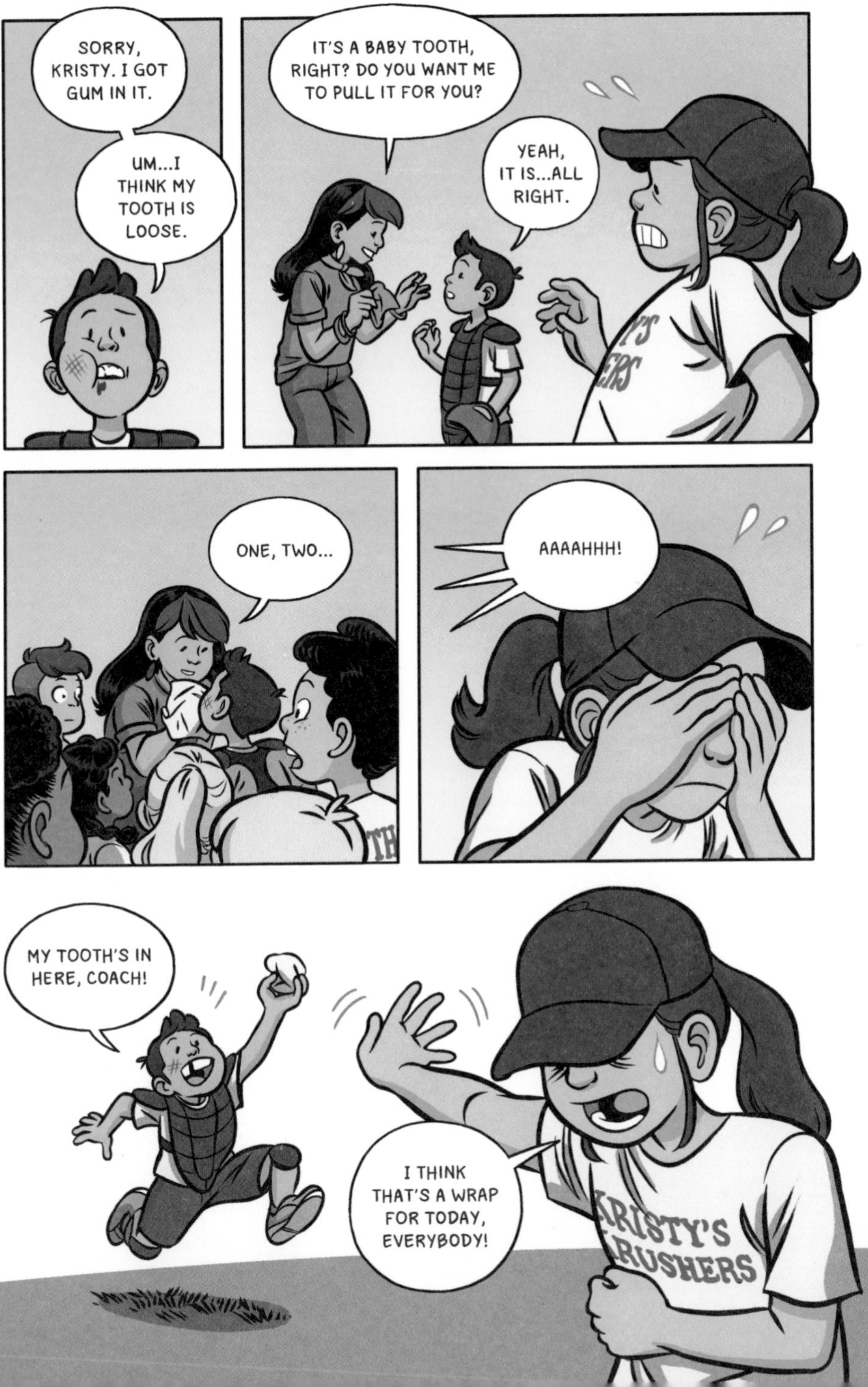
SORRY, KRISTY. I GOT GUM IN IT.
UM...I THINK MY TOOTH IS LOOSE.
IT'S A BABY TOOTH, RIGHT? DO YOU WANT ME TO PULL IT FOR YOU?
YEAH, IT IS...ALL RIGHT.
ONE, TWO...
AAAAHHH!
MY TOOTH'S IN HERE, COACH!
I THINK THAT'S A WRAP FOR TODAY, EVERYBODY!
KRISTY'S KRUSHERS

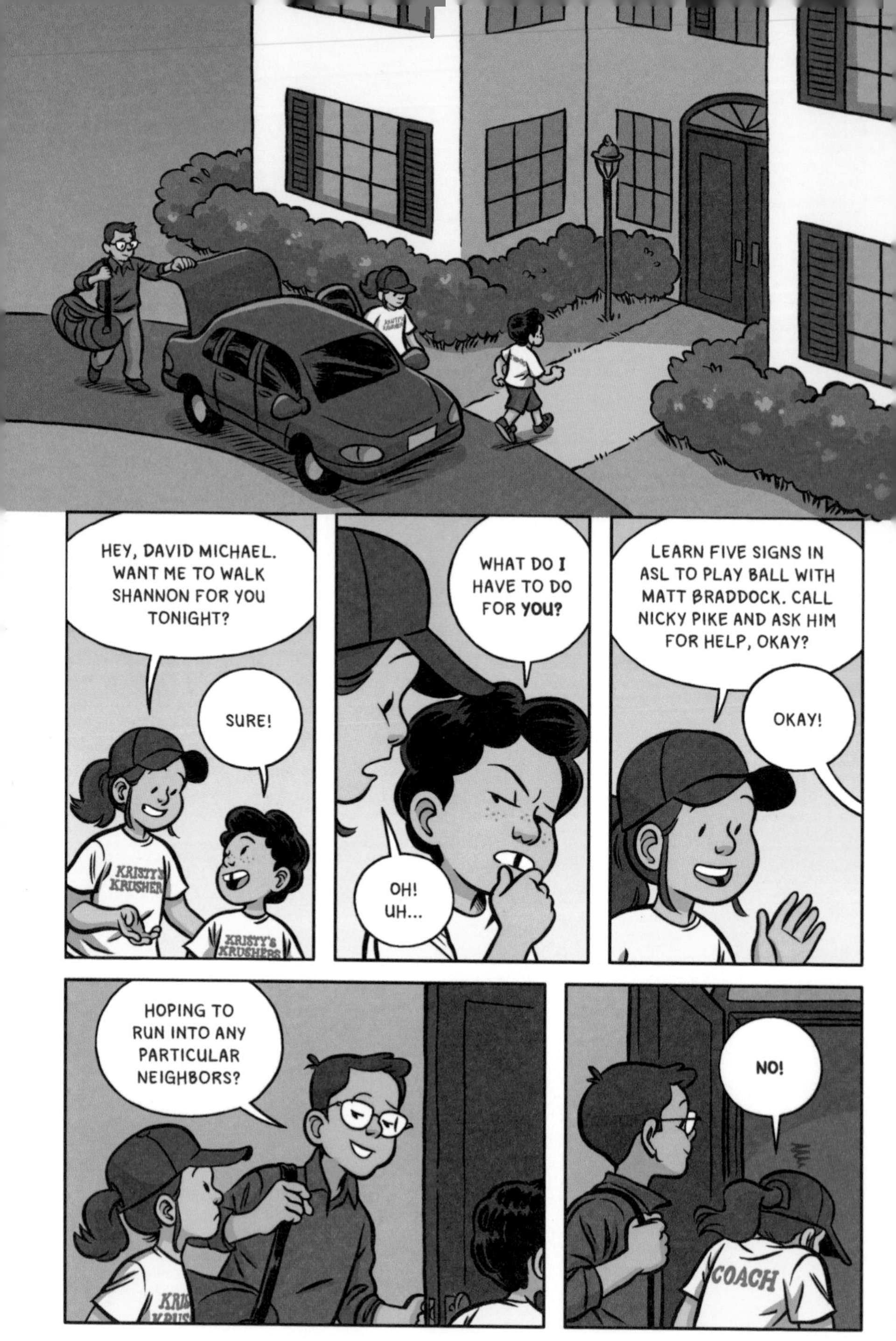
HEY, DAVID MICHAEL. WANT ME TO WALK SHANNON FOR YOU TONIGHT?
SURE!
KRISTY'S KRUSHERS
KRISTY'S KRUSHERS
WHAT DO I HAVE TO DO FOR **YOU?**
OH! UH...
LEARN FIVE SIGNS IN ASL TO PLAY BALL WITH MATT BRADDOCK. CALL NICKY PIKE AND ASK HIM FOR HELP, OKAY?
OKAY!
HOPING TO RUN INTO ANY PARTICULAR NEIGHBORS?
NO!
COACH

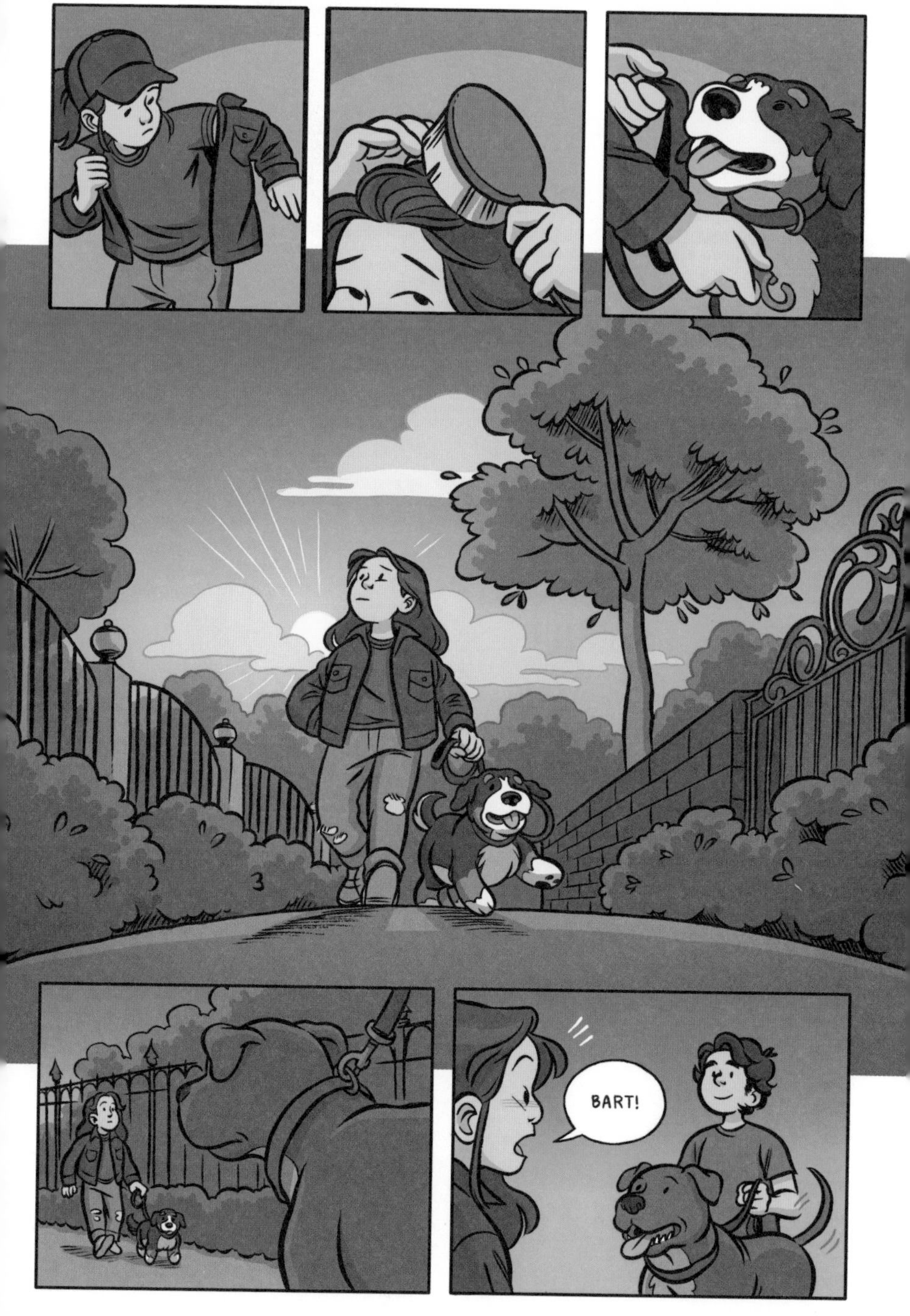
BART!

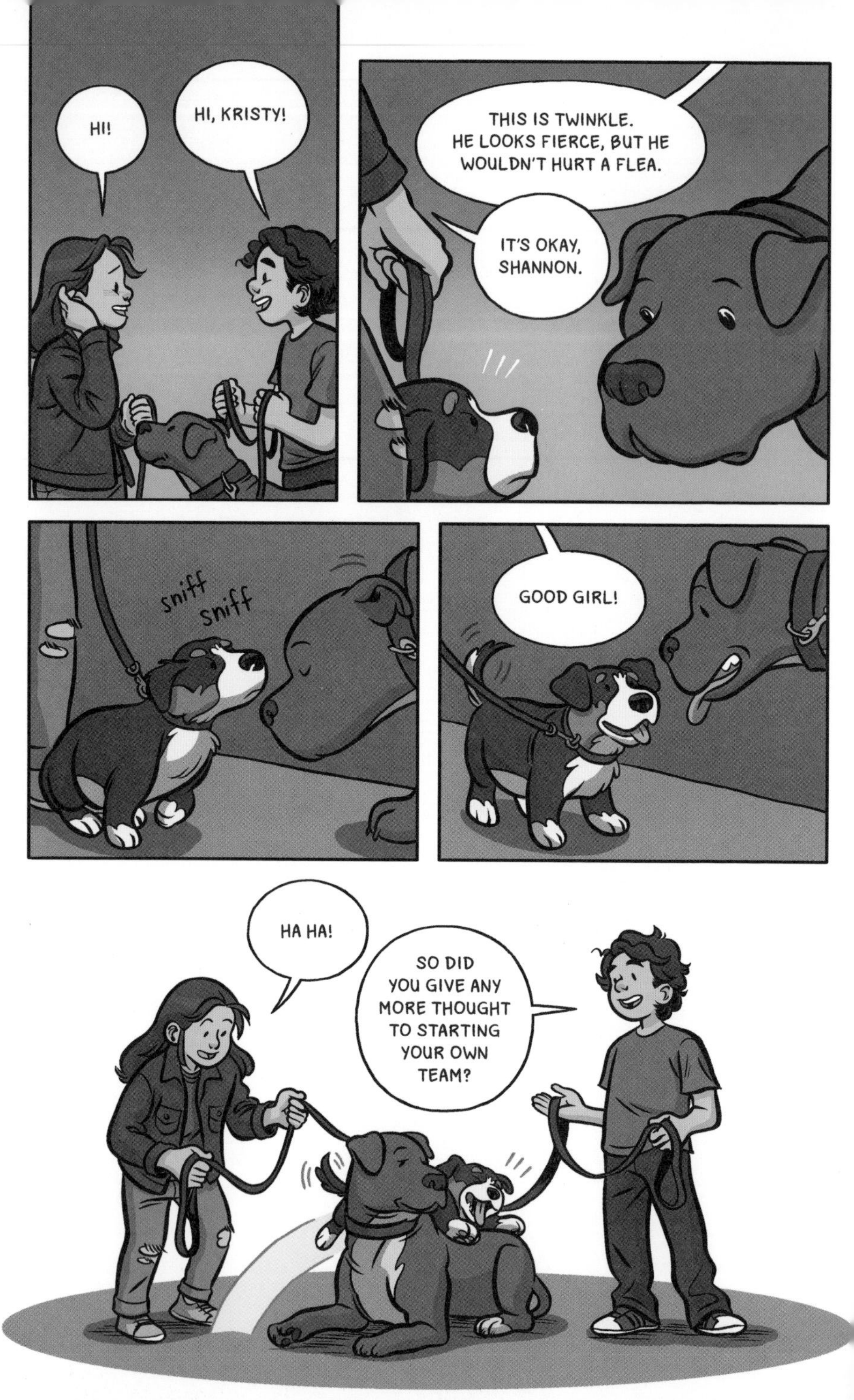
HI!
HI, KRISTY!
THIS IS TWINKLE. HE LOOKS FIERCE, BUT HE WOULDN'T HURT A FLEA.
IT'S OKAY, SHANNON.
sniff sniff
GOOD GIRL!
HA HA!
SO DID YOU GIVE ANY MORE THOUGHT TO STARTING YOUR OWN TEAM?

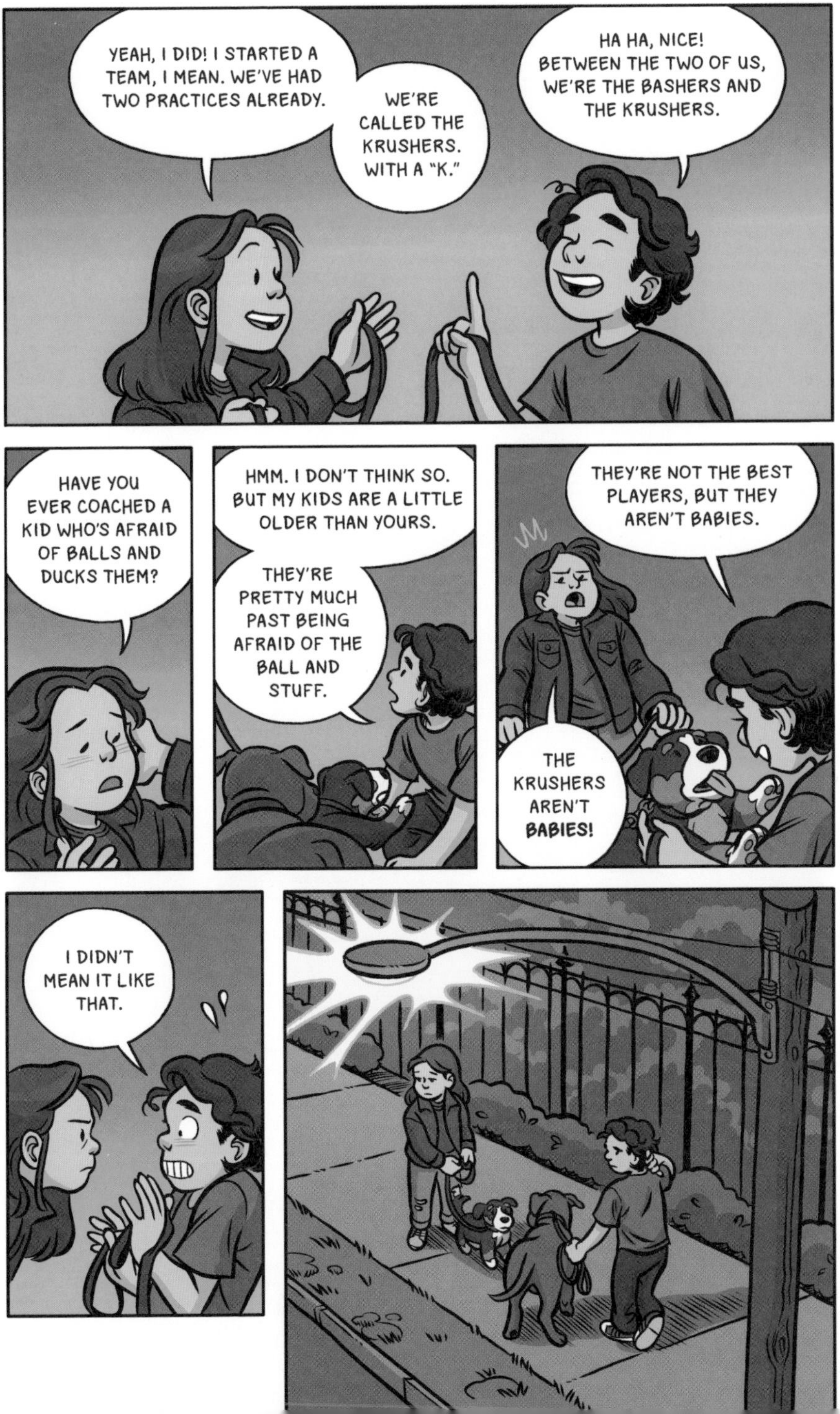
YEAH, I DID! I STARTED A TEAM, I MEAN. WE'VE HAD TWO PRACTICES ALREADY.
WE'RE CALLED THE KRUSHERS. WITH A "K."
HA HA, NICE! BETWEEN THE TWO OF US, WE'RE THE BASHERS AND THE KRUSHERS.
HAVE YOU EVER COACHED A KID WHO'S AFRAID OF BALLS AND DUCKS THEM?
HMM. I DON'T THINK SO. BUT MY KIDS ARE A LITTLE OLDER THAN YOURS.
THEY'RE PRETTY MUCH PAST BEING AFRAID OF THE BALL AND STUFF.
THEY'RE NOT THE BEST PLAYERS, BUT THEY AREN'T BABIES.
THE KRUSHERS AREN'T **BABIES!**
I DIDN'T MEAN IT LIKE THAT.

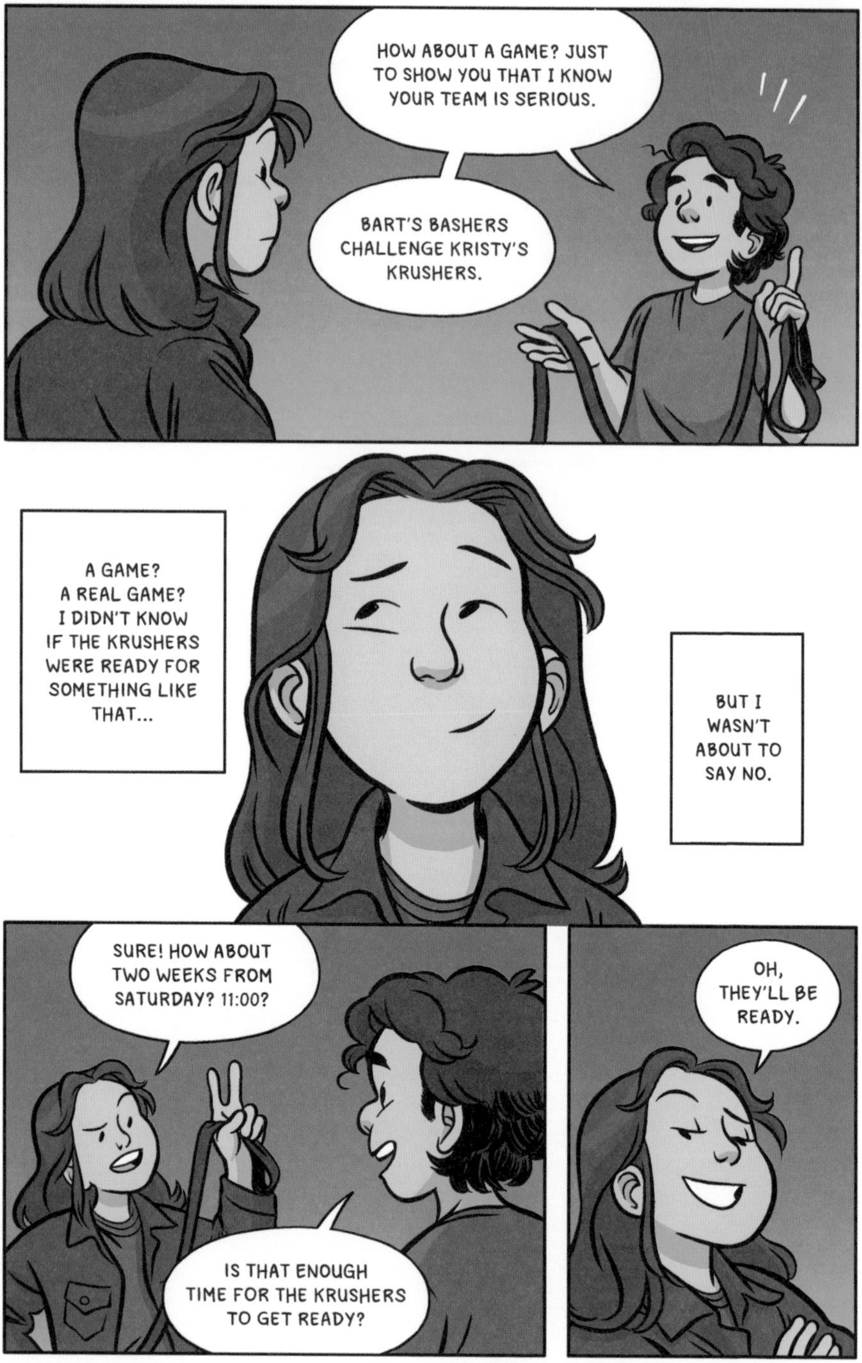
HOW ABOUT A GAME? JUST TO SHOW YOU THAT I KNOW YOUR TEAM IS SERIOUS.
BART'S BASHERS CHALLENGE KRISTY'S KRUSHERS.
A GAME? A REAL GAME? I DIDN'T KNOW IF THE KRUSHERS WERE READY FOR SOMETHING LIKE THAT...
BUT I WASN'T ABOUT TO SAY NO.
SURE! HOW ABOUT TWO WEEKS FROM SATURDAY? 11:00?
IS THAT ENOUGH TIME FOR THE KRUSHERS TO GET READY?
OH, THEY'LL BE READY.

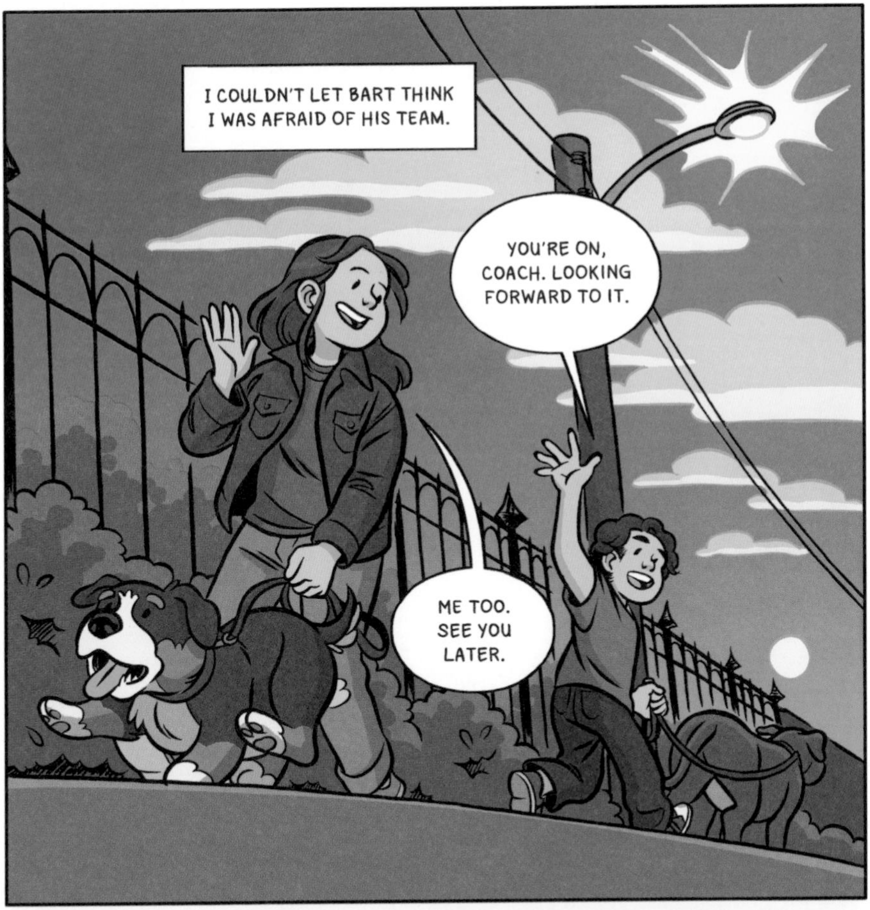
I COULDN'T LET BART THINK I WAS AFRAID OF HIS TEAM.
YOU'RE ON, COACH. LOOKING FORWARD TO IT.
ME TOO. SEE YOU LATER.

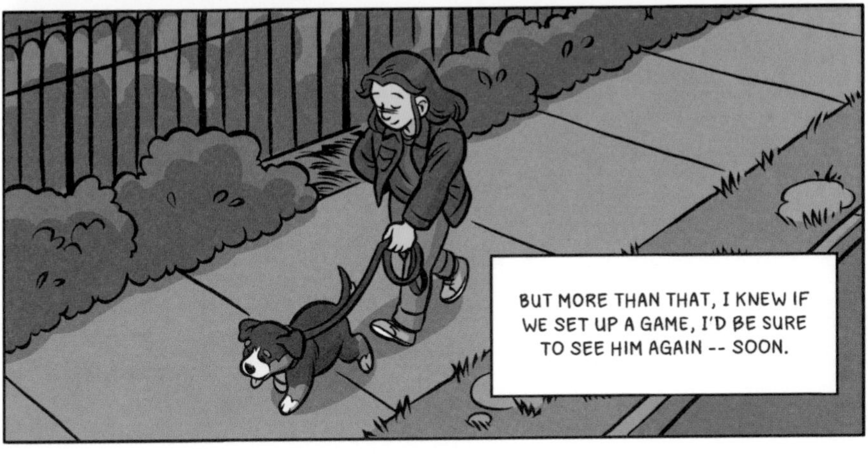
BUT MORE THAN THAT, I KNEW IF WE SET UP A GAME, I'D BE SURE TO SEE HIM AGAIN -- SOON.

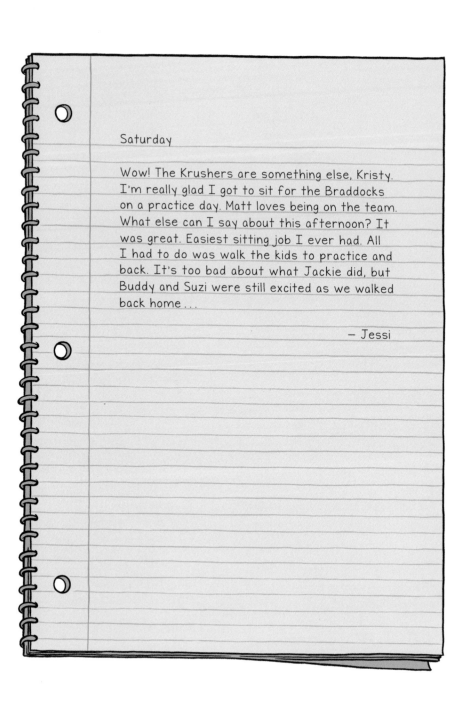

Saturday

Wow! The Krushers are something else, Kristy.
I'm really glad I got to sit for the Braddocks
on a practice day. Matt loves being on the team.
What else can I say about this afternoon? It
was great. Easiest sitting job I ever had. All
I had to do was walk the kids to practice and
back. It's too bad about what Jackie did, but
Buddy and Suzi were still excited as we walked
back home...

— Jessi

CHAPTER 9

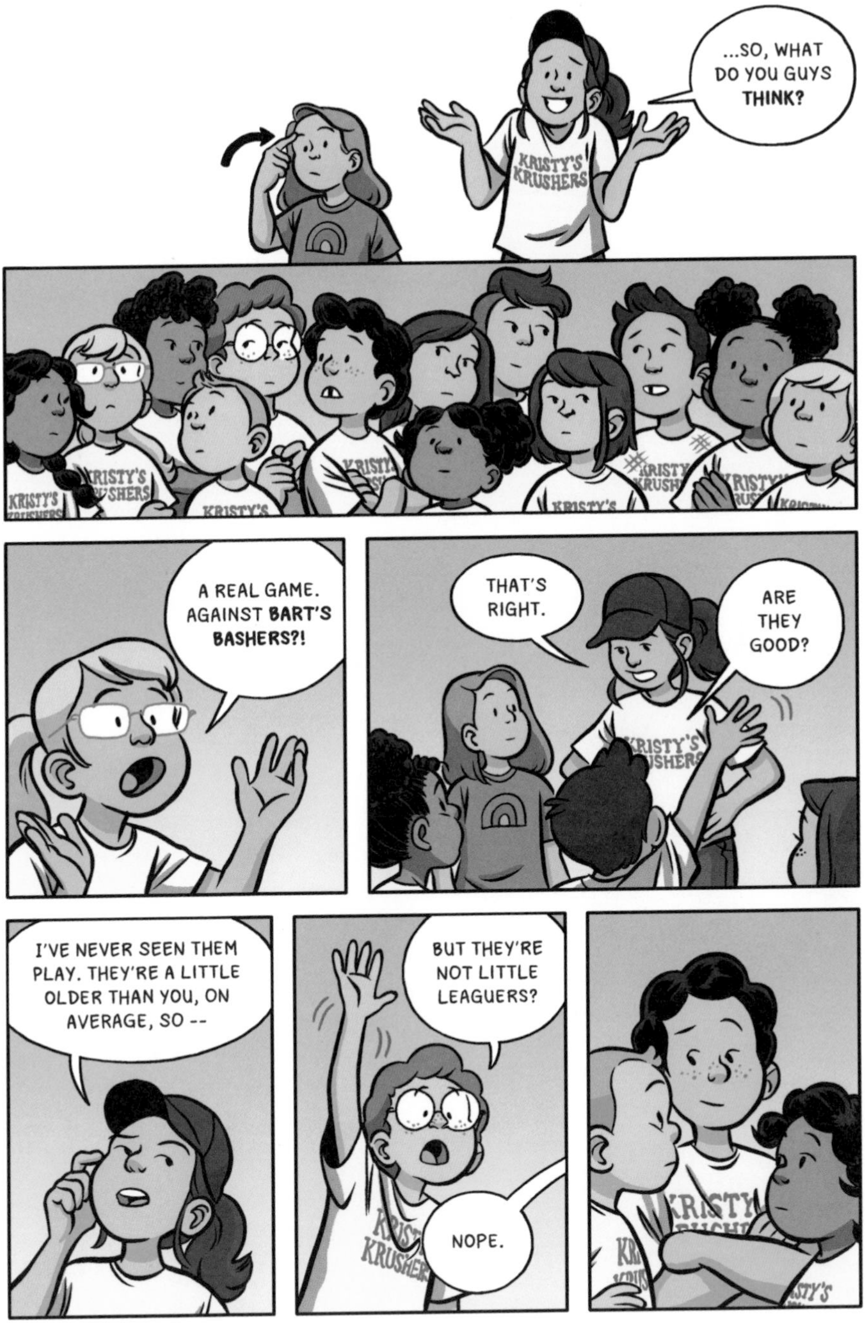
...SO, WHAT DO YOU GUYS THINK?
KRISTY'S KRUSHERS
A REAL GAME. AGAINST BART'S BASHERS?!
THAT'S RIGHT.
ARE THEY GOOD?
I'VE NEVER SEEN THEM PLAY. THEY'RE A LITTLE OLDER THAN YOU, ON AVERAGE, SO --
BUT THEY'RE NOT LITTLE LEAGUERS?
NOPE.

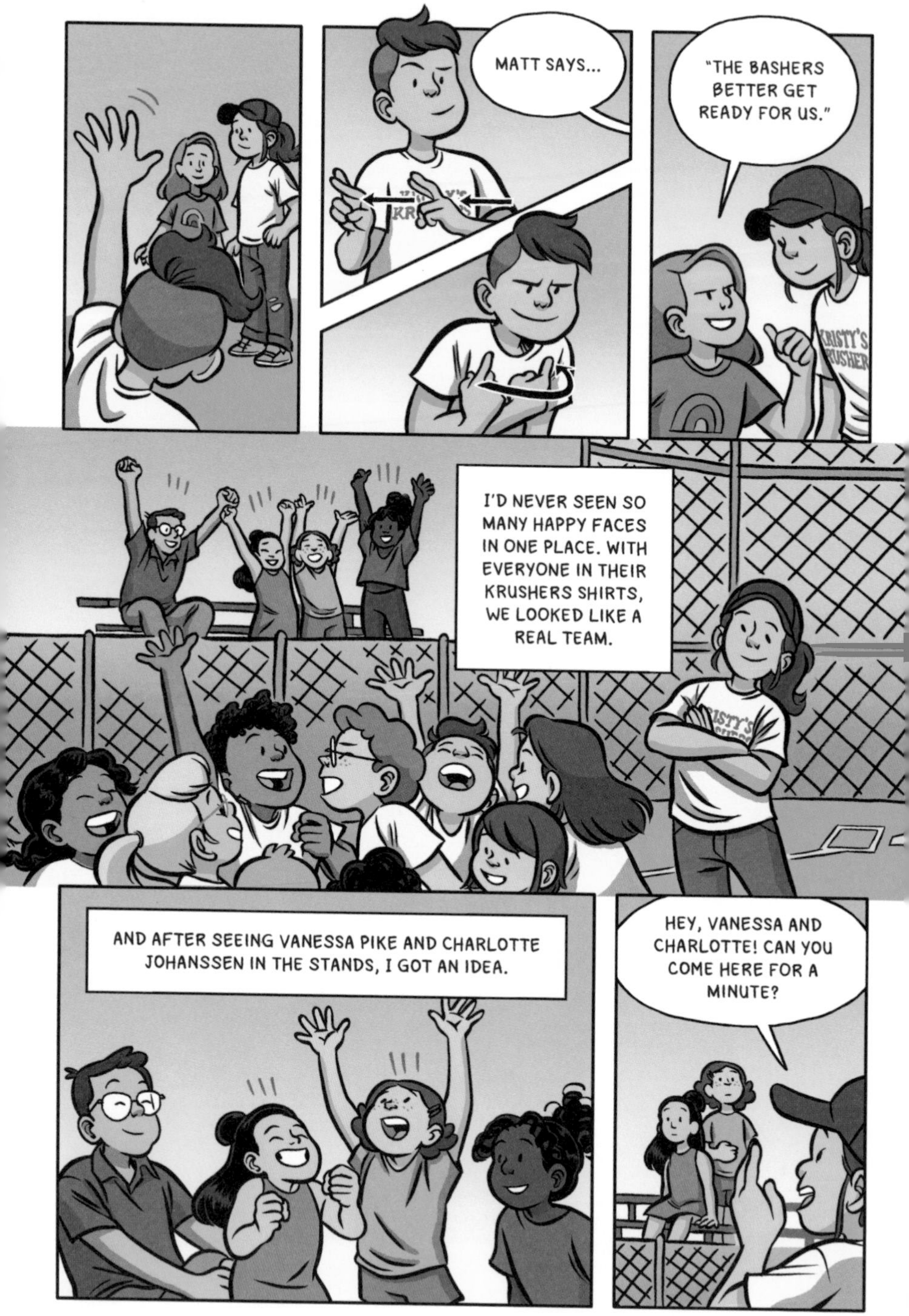
MATT SAYS...
"THE BASHERS BETTER GET READY FOR US."
KRISTY'S KRUSHERS
I'D NEVER SEEN SO MANY HAPPY FACES IN ONE PLACE. WITH EVERYONE IN THEIR KRUSHERS SHIRTS, WE LOOKED LIKE A REAL TEAM.
AND AFTER SEEING VANESSA PIKE AND CHARLOTTE JOHANSSEN IN THE STANDS, I GOT AN IDEA.
HEY, VANESSA AND CHARLOTTE! CAN YOU COME HERE FOR A MINUTE?

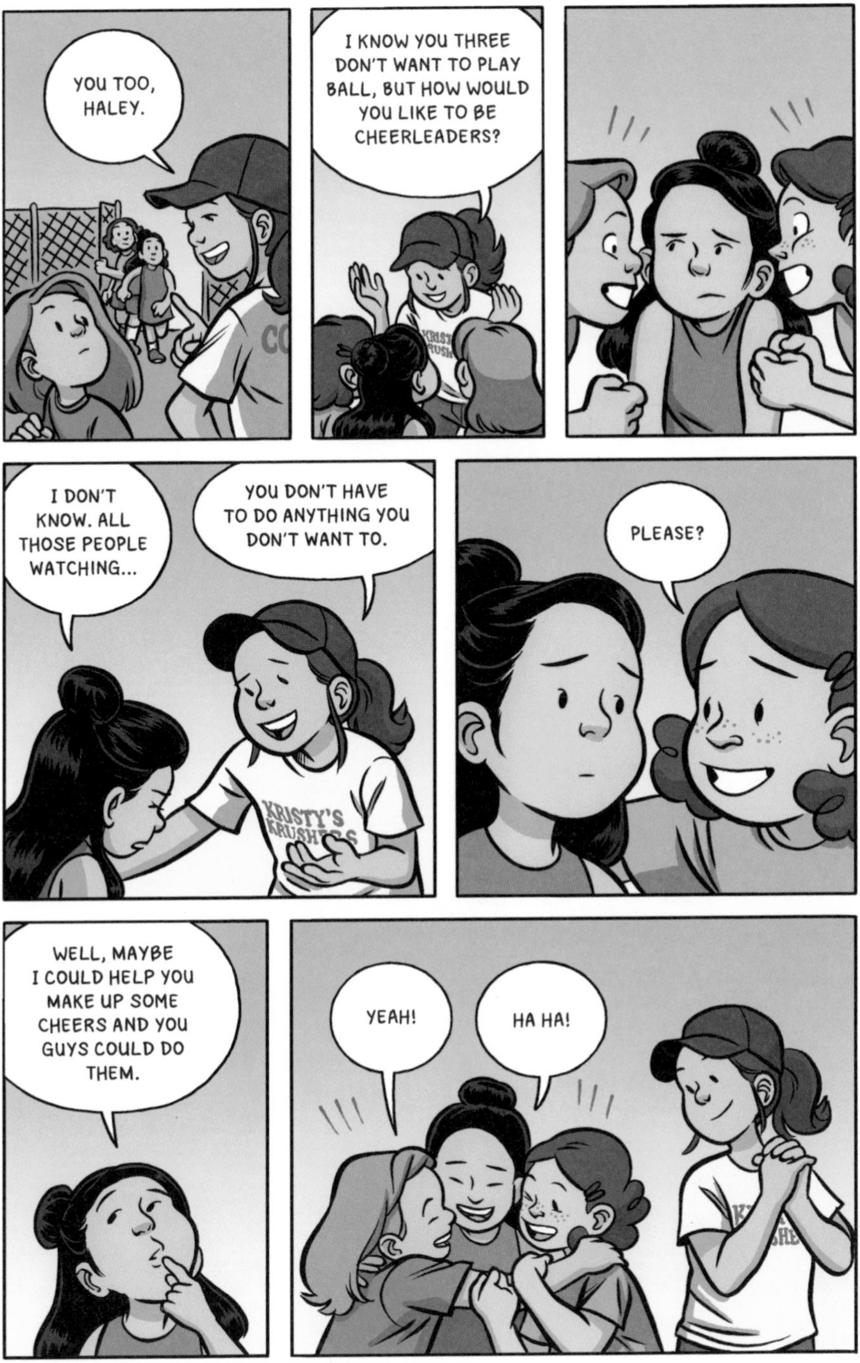
YOU TOO, HALEY.
I KNOW YOU THREE DON'T WANT TO PLAY BALL, BUT HOW WOULD YOU LIKE TO BE CHEERLEADERS?
I DON'T KNOW. ALL THOSE PEOPLE WATCHING...
YOU DON'T HAVE TO DO ANYTHING YOU DON'T WANT TO.
PLEASE?
WELL, MAYBE I COULD HELP YOU MAKE UP SOME CHEERS AND YOU GUYS COULD DO THEM.
YEAH!
HA HA!

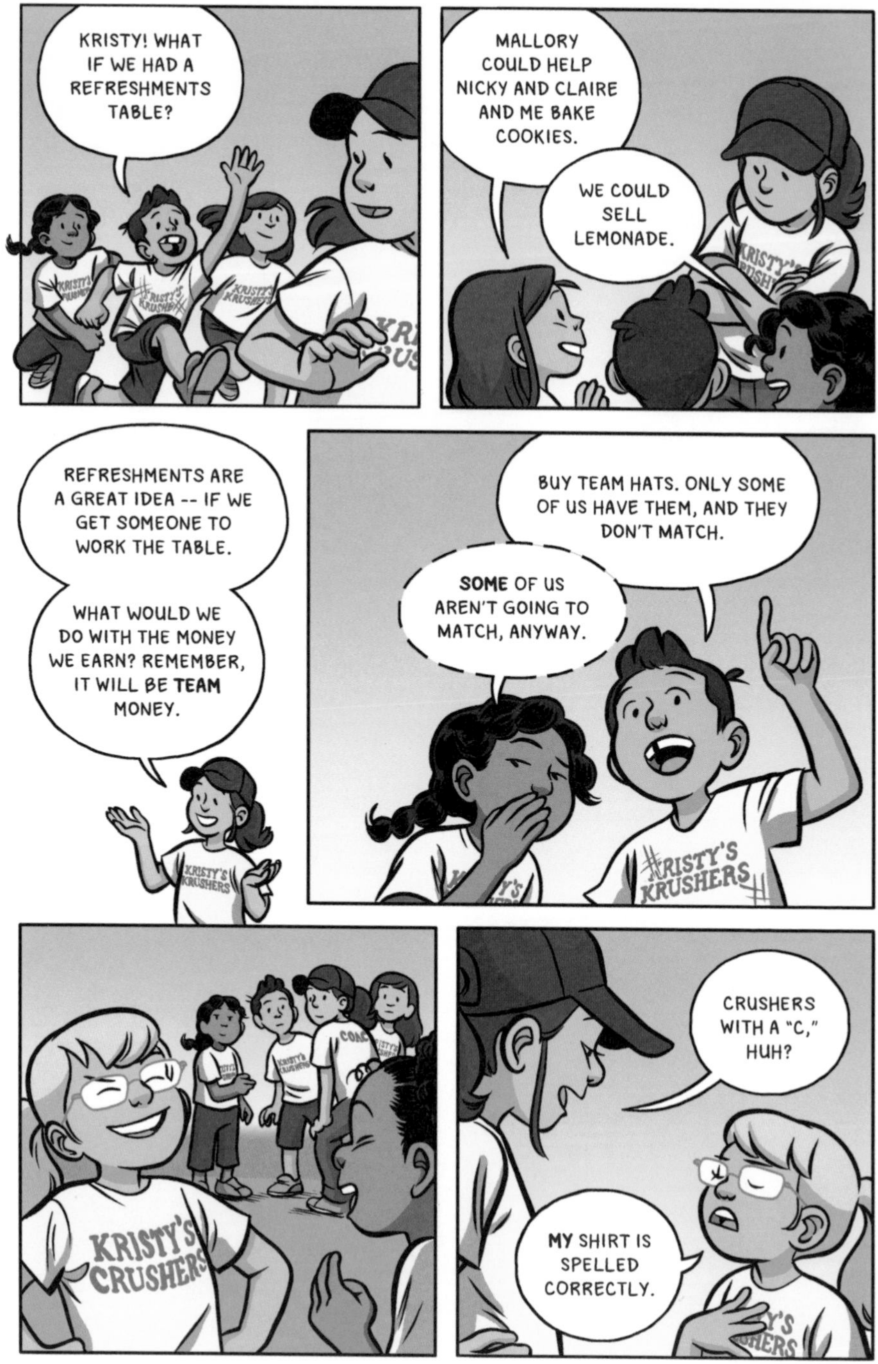
KRISTY! WHAT IF WE HAD A REFRESHMENTS TABLE?
KRISTY'S KRUSHERS
MALLORY COULD HELP NICKY AND CLAIRE AND ME BAKE COOKIES.
WE COULD SELL LEMONADE.
REFRESHMENTS ARE A GREAT IDEA -- IF WE GET SOMEONE TO WORK THE TABLE.
WHAT WOULD WE DO WITH THE MONEY WE EARN? REMEMBER, IT WILL BE **TEAM** MONEY.
KRISTY'S KRUSHERS
BUY TEAM HATS. ONLY SOME OF US HAVE THEM, AND THEY DON'T MATCH.
SOME OF US AREN'T GOING TO MATCH, ANYWAY.
KRISTY'S KRUSHERS
KRISTY'S CRUSHERS
CRUSHERS WITH A "C," HUH?
MY SHIRT IS SPELLED CORRECTLY.

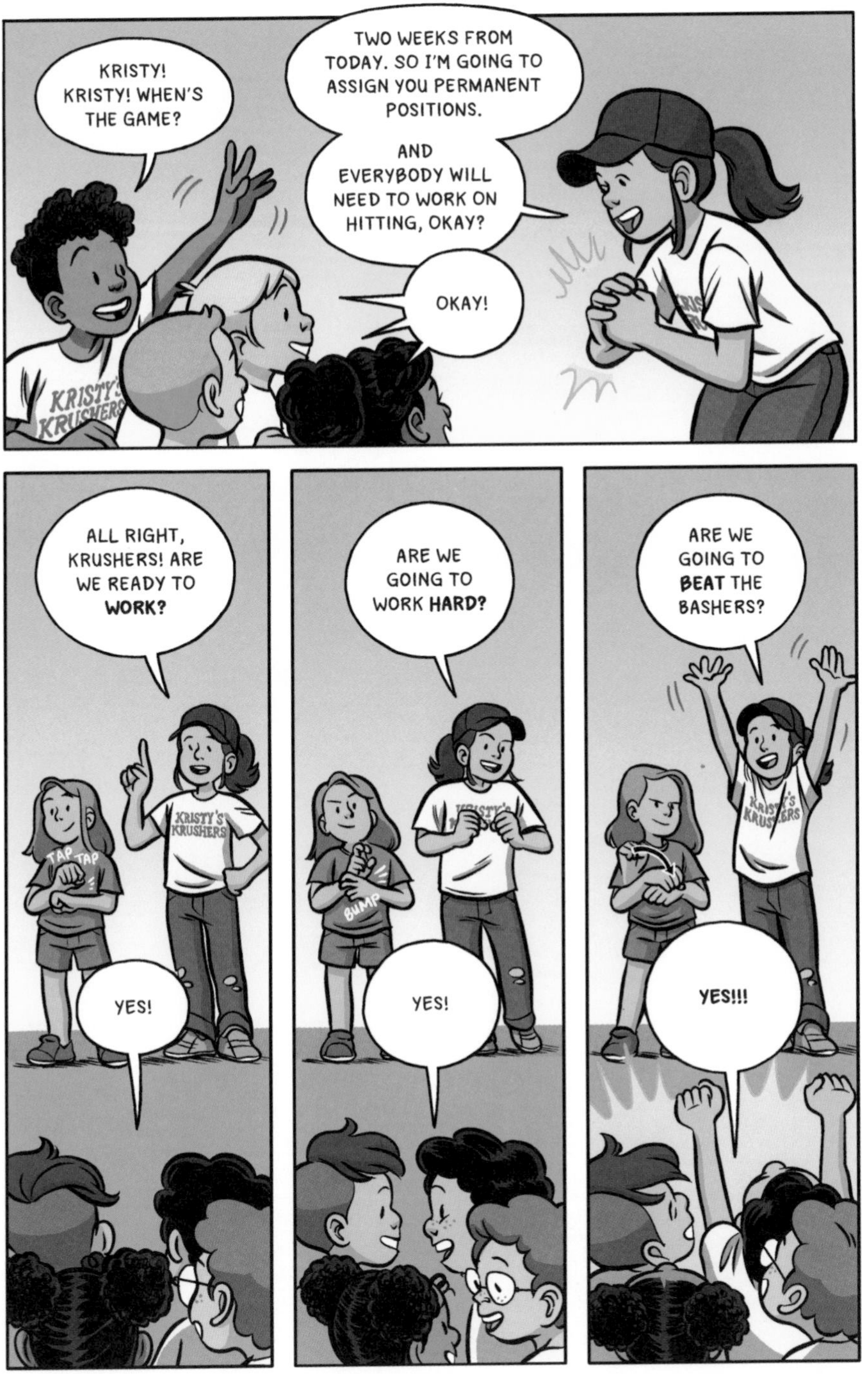
KRISTY! KRISTY! WHEN'S THE GAME?
TWO WEEKS FROM TODAY. SO I'M GOING TO ASSIGN YOU PERMANENT POSITIONS.
AND EVERYBODY WILL NEED TO WORK ON HITTING, OKAY?
OKAY!
KRISTY'S KRUSHERS
ALL RIGHT, KRUSHERS! ARE WE READY TO **WORK?**
TAP TAP
KRISTY'S KRUSHERS
YES!
ARE WE GOING TO WORK **HARD?**
BUMP
YES!
ARE WE GOING TO **BEAT** THE BASHERS?
KRISTY'S KRUSHERS
YES!!!

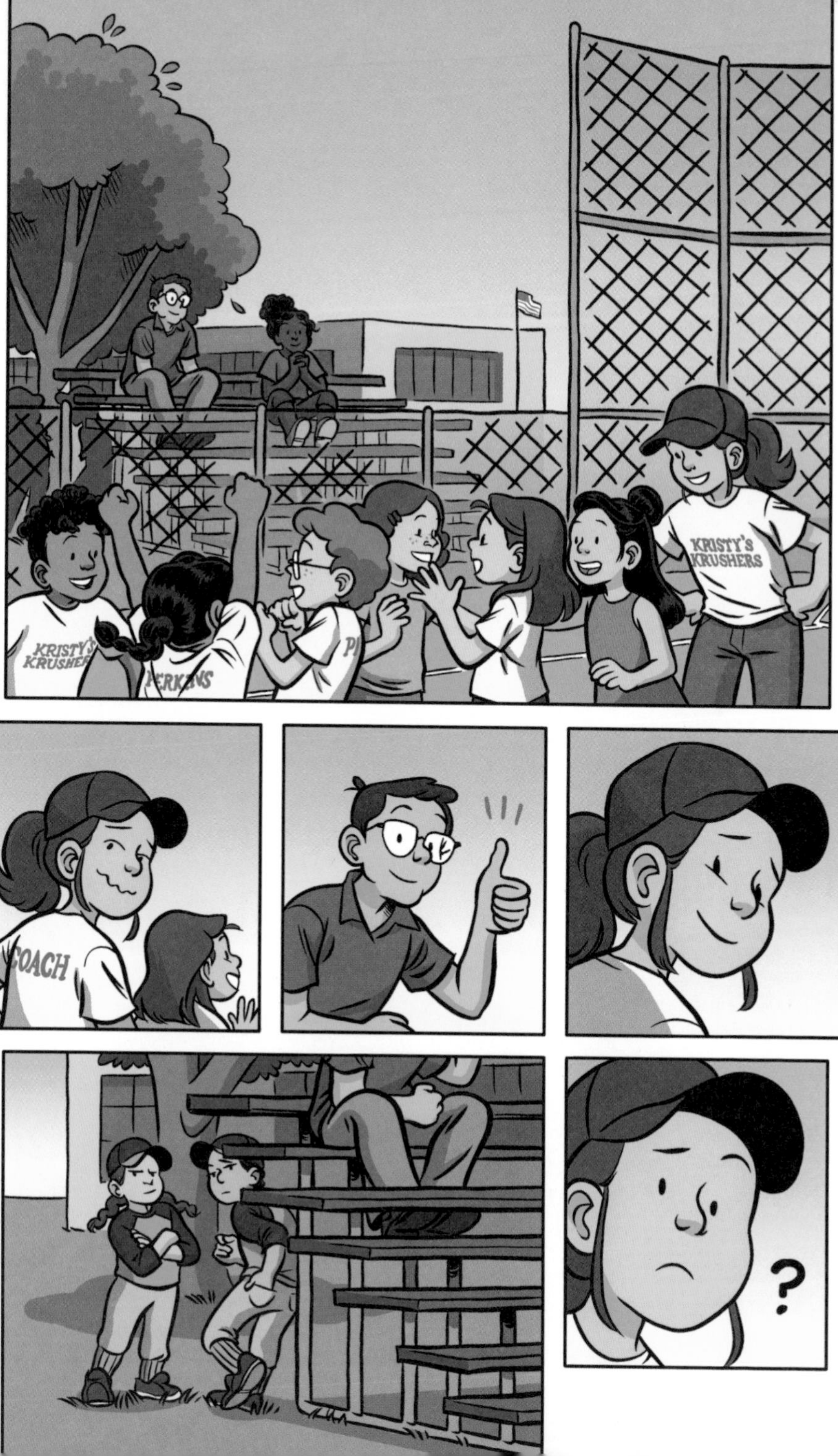

KRISTY'S KRUSHER
PERKINS
KRISTY'S KRUSHERS
COACH
?

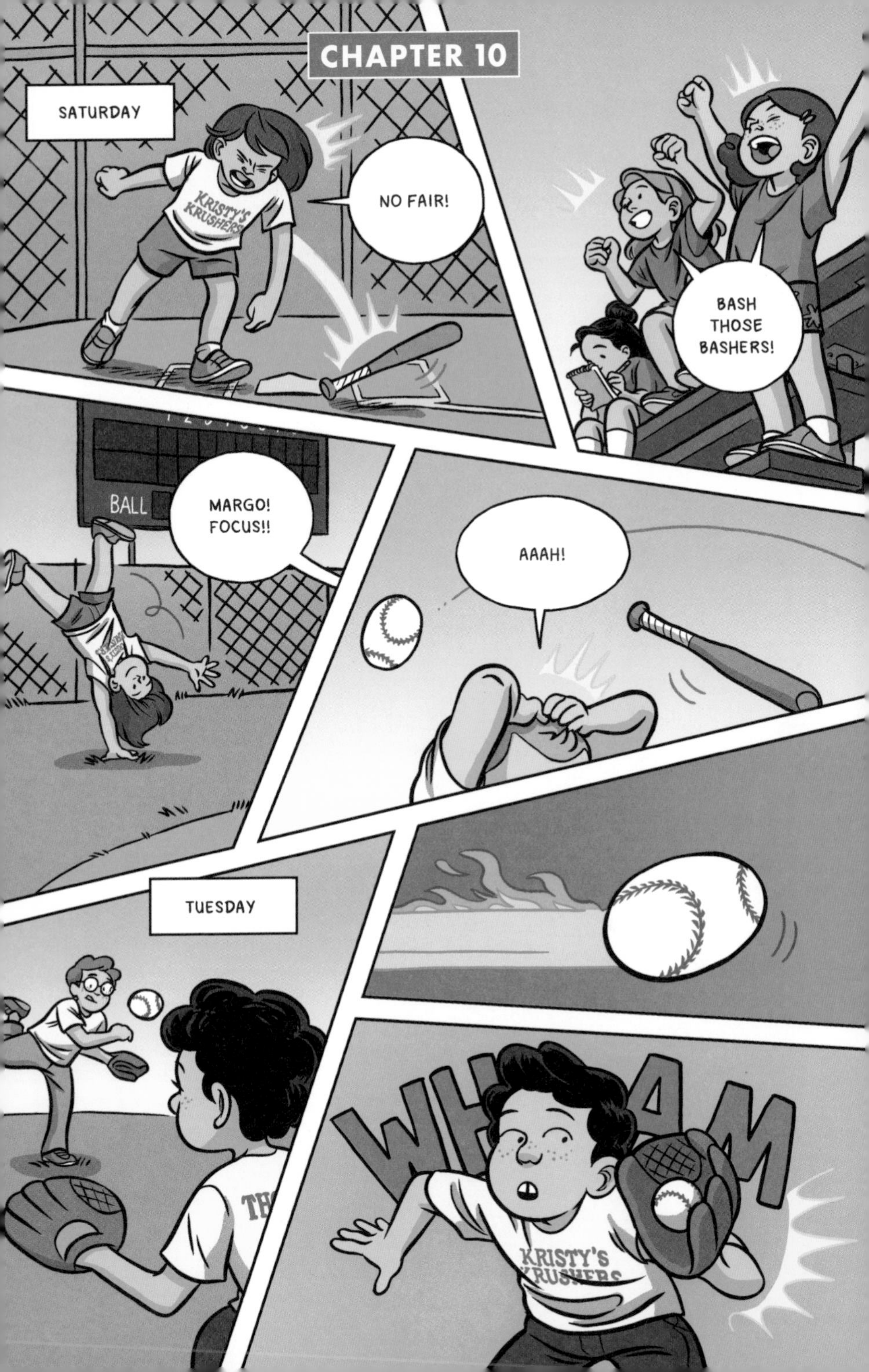
CHAPTER 10
SATURDAY
KRISTY'S KRUSHERS
NO FAIR!
BASH THOSE BASHERS!
BALL
MARGO! FOCUS!!
AAAH!
TUESDAY
WHAM
KRISTY'S

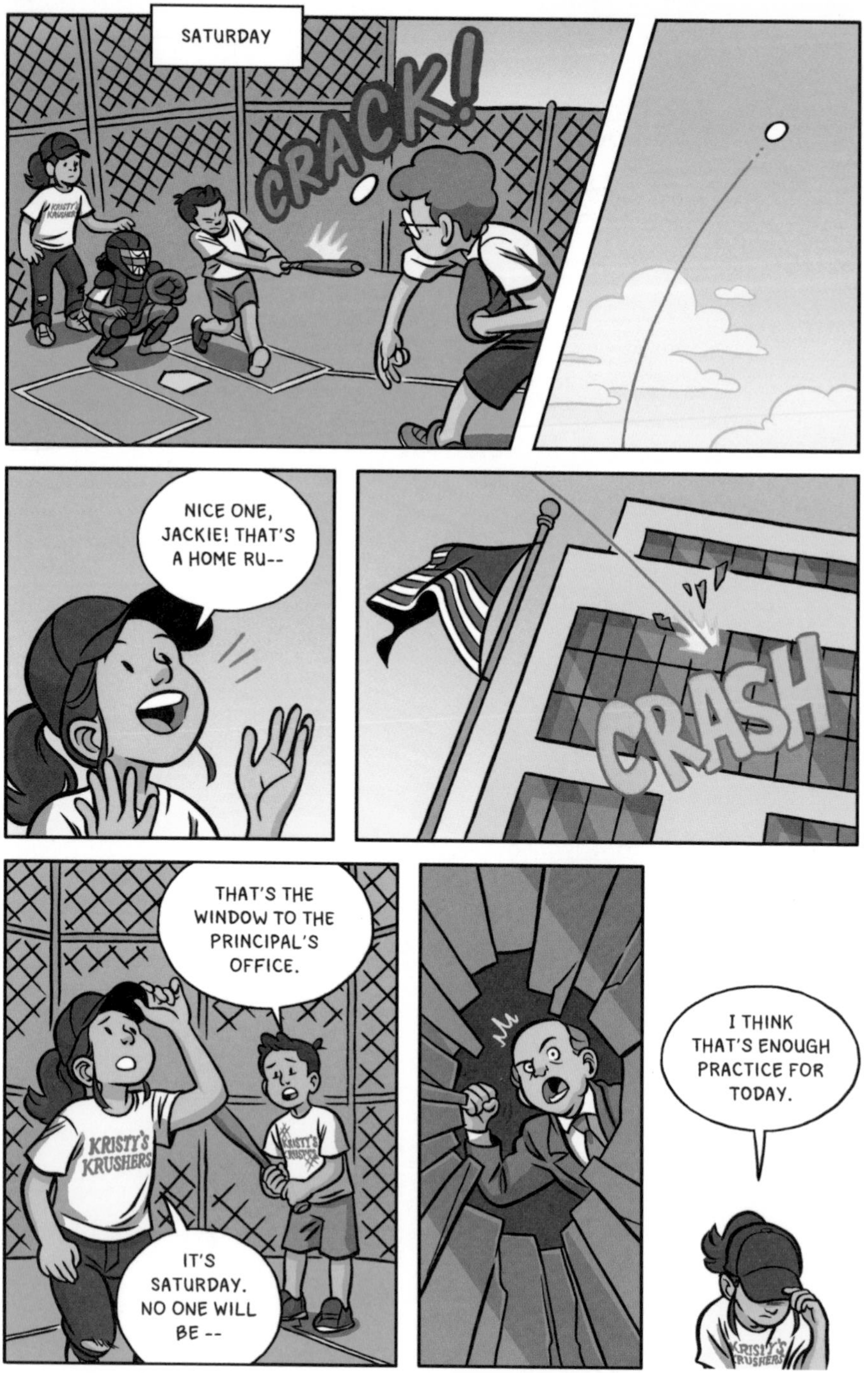
SATURDAY
CRACK!
NICE ONE, JACKIE! THAT'S A HOME RU--
CRASH
THAT'S THE WINDOW TO THE PRINCIPAL'S OFFICE.
IT'S SATURDAY. NO ONE WILL BE --
I THINK THAT'S ENOUGH PRACTICE FOR TODAY.

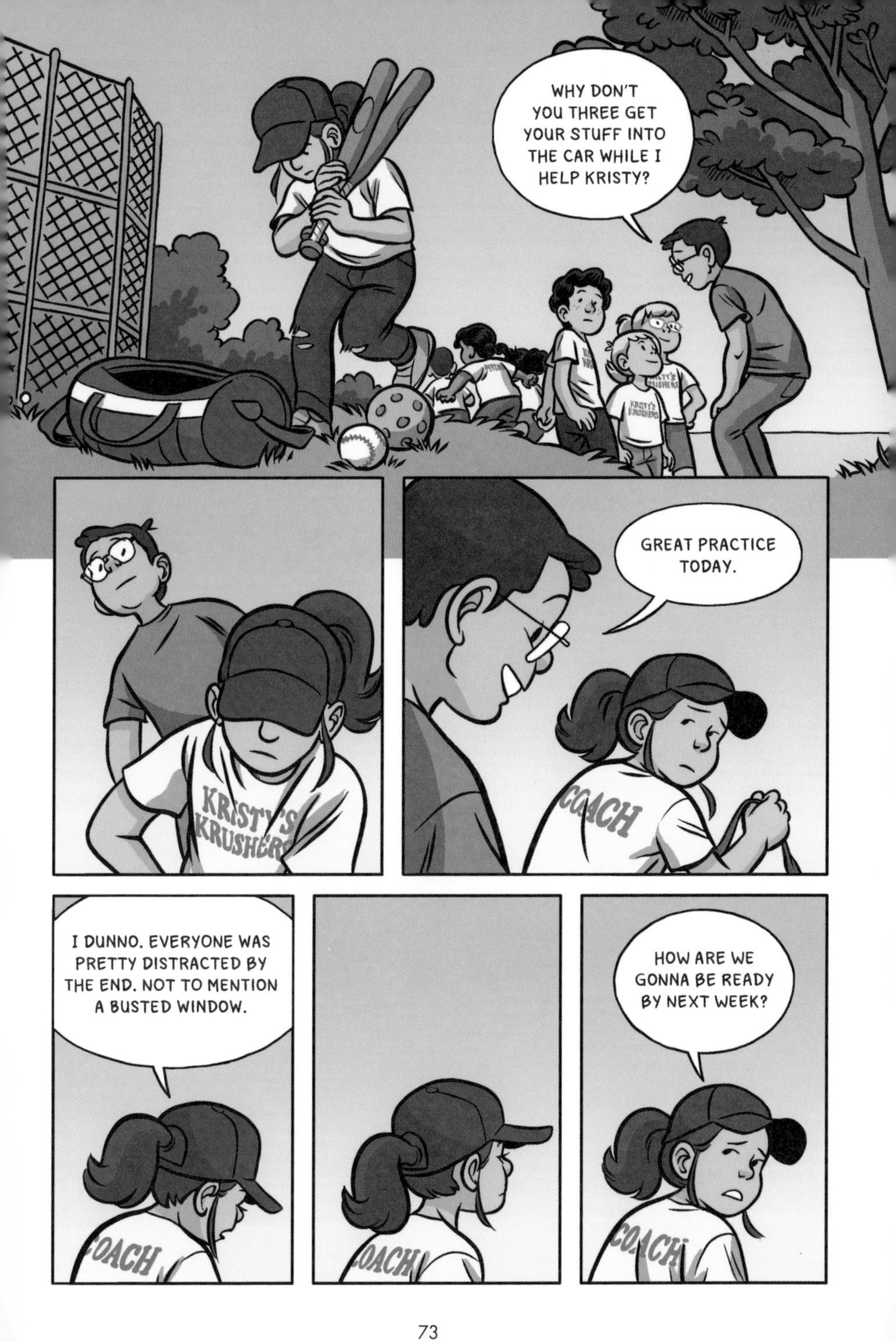
WHY DON'T YOU THREE GET YOUR STUFF INTO THE CAR WHILE I HELP KRISTY?
KRISTY'S KRUSHERS
KRISTY'S KRUSHERS
GREAT PRACTICE TODAY.
COACH
I DUNNO. EVERYONE WAS PRETTY DISTRACTED BY THE END. NOT TO MENTION A BUSTED WINDOW.
COACH
COACH
HOW ARE WE GONNA BE READY BY NEXT WEEK?
COACH

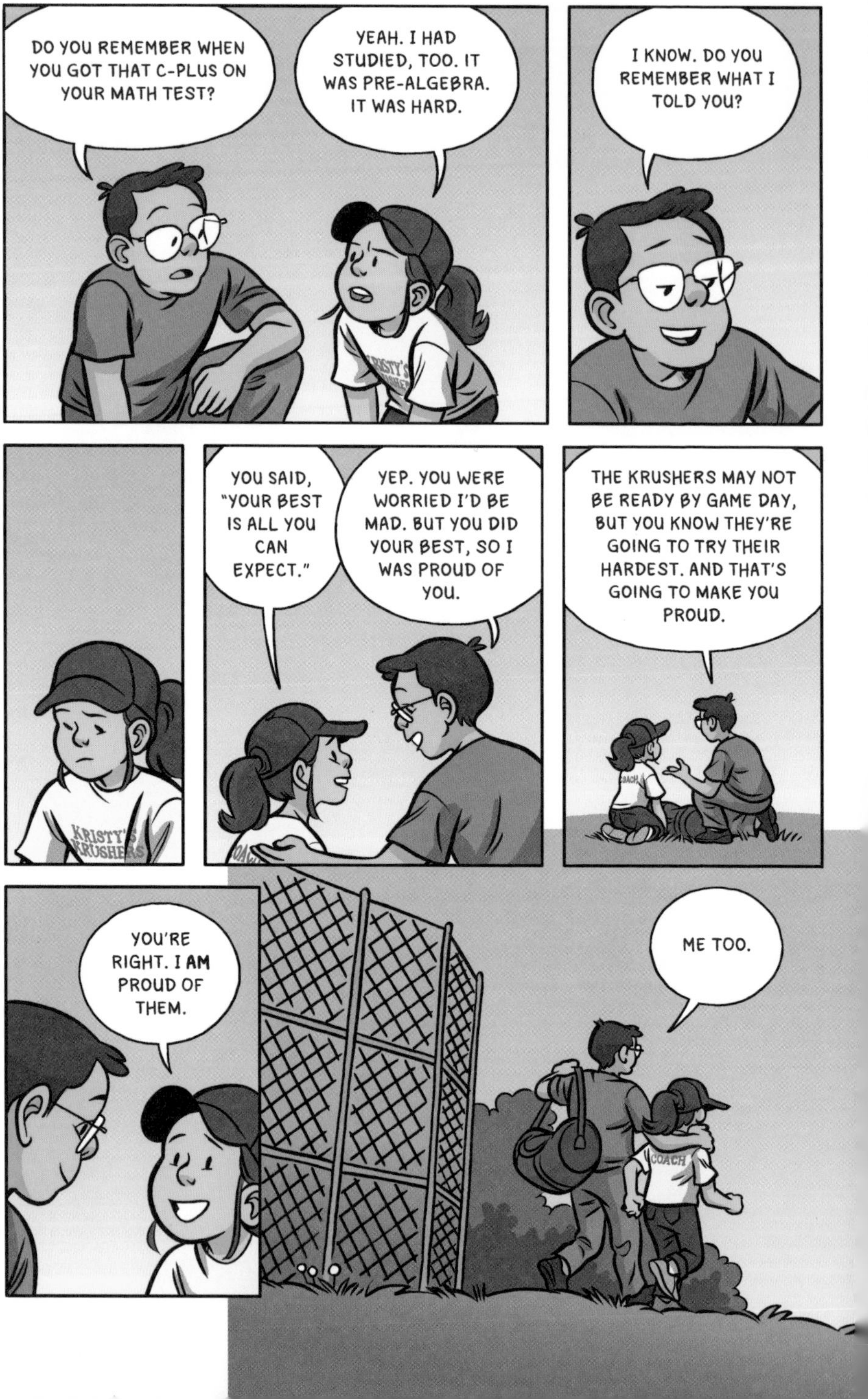
DO YOU REMEMBER WHEN YOU GOT THAT C-PLUS ON YOUR MATH TEST?
YEAH. I HAD STUDIED, TOO. IT WAS PRE-ALGEBRA. IT WAS HARD.
I KNOW. DO YOU REMEMBER WHAT I TOLD YOU?
KRISTY'S KRUSHERS
YOU SAID, "YOUR BEST IS ALL YOU CAN EXPECT."
YEP. YOU WERE WORRIED I'D BE MAD. BUT YOU DID YOUR BEST, SO I WAS PROUD OF YOU.
THE KRUSHERS MAY NOT BE READY BY GAME DAY, BUT YOU KNOW THEY'RE GOING TO TRY THEIR HARDEST. AND THAT'S GOING TO MAKE YOU PROUD.
COACH
YOU'RE RIGHT. I **AM** PROUD OF THEM.
ME TOO.
COACH

TUESDAY

WHOA! SOMETHING iS GOiNG ON. AND, KRiSTY, iT HAS
TO DO WiTH YOU AND THAT OTHER TEAM, THE BLASTERS
OR WHOEVER THEY ARE.

SEE, MRS. PERKiNS AND MRS. NEWTON ASKED ME TO
TAKE MYRiAH, GABBiE, AND JAMiE TO THE KRUSHERS
PRACTiCE. i WAS iN THE STANDS WATCHiNG THE GAME
WHEN THE BLASTERS CAME BY, AND KRiSTY, YOU KiND
OF GOT MAD AT THEiR COACH. BUT BEFORE YOU GOT
MAD, YOU GOT, OH . . . i BETTER STOP BEFORE i GET
MYSELF iN TROUBLE.

JUST ONE MORE THiNG. THE PERKiNS GiRLS AND
JAMiE WERE UPSET WHEN WE WALKED HOME THiS
AFTERNOON. THEY WERE REALLY ANNOYED WiTH WHAT
THE BLASTERS DiD, AND EMBARRASSED ABOUT iT,
TOO, i THiNK . . .

                                    - DAWN

CHAPTER 11

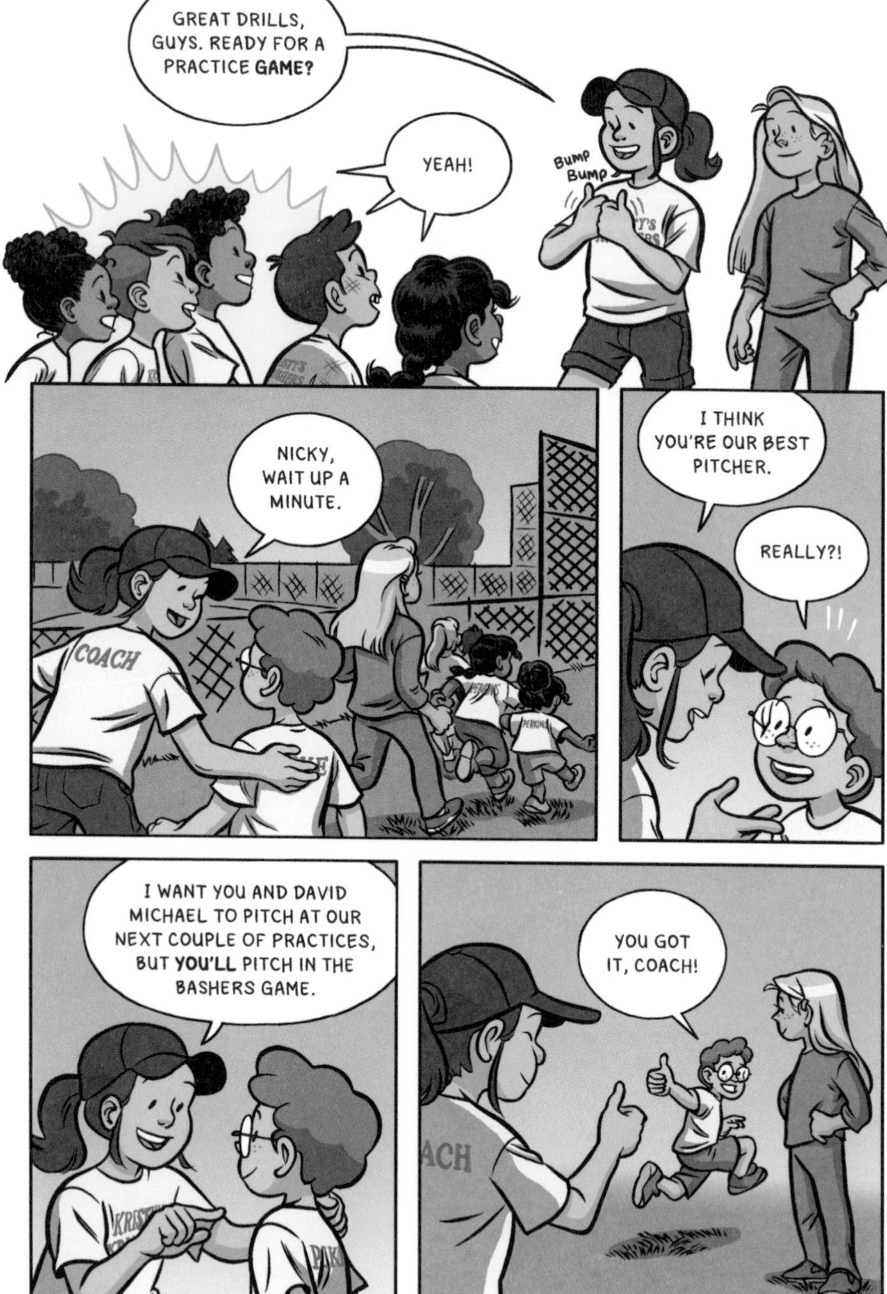
GREAT DRILLS, GUYS. READY FOR A PRACTICE **GAME?**
YEAH!
BUMP BUMP
NICKY, WAIT UP A MINUTE.
I THINK YOU'RE OUR BEST PITCHER.
REALLY?!
I WANT YOU AND DAVID MICHAEL TO PITCH AT OUR NEXT COUPLE OF PRACTICES, BUT **YOU'LL** PITCH IN THE BASHERS GAME.
YOU GOT IT, COACH!

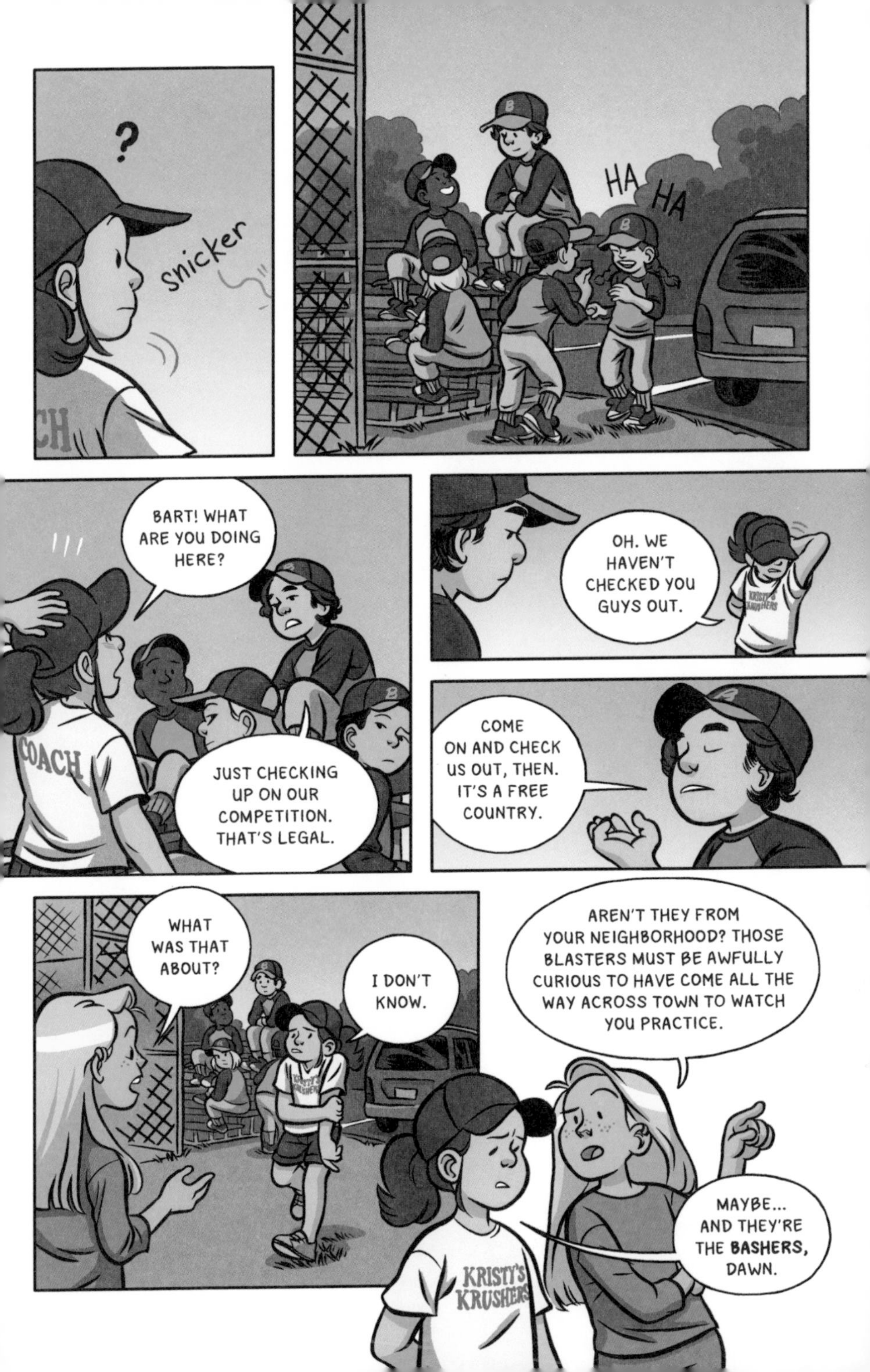
?
snicker
HA HA
BART! WHAT ARE YOU DOING HERE?
JUST CHECKING UP ON OUR COMPETITION. THAT'S LEGAL.
OH. WE HAVEN'T CHECKED YOU GUYS OUT.
COME ON AND CHECK US OUT, THEN. IT'S A FREE COUNTRY.
WHAT WAS THAT ABOUT?
I DON'T KNOW.
AREN'T THEY FROM YOUR NEIGHBORHOOD? THOSE BLASTERS MUST BE AWFULLY CURIOUS TO HAVE COME ALL THE WAY ACROSS TOWN TO WATCH YOU PRACTICE.
MAYBE... AND THEY'RE THE **BASHERS**, DAWN.
KRISTY'S KRUSHERS

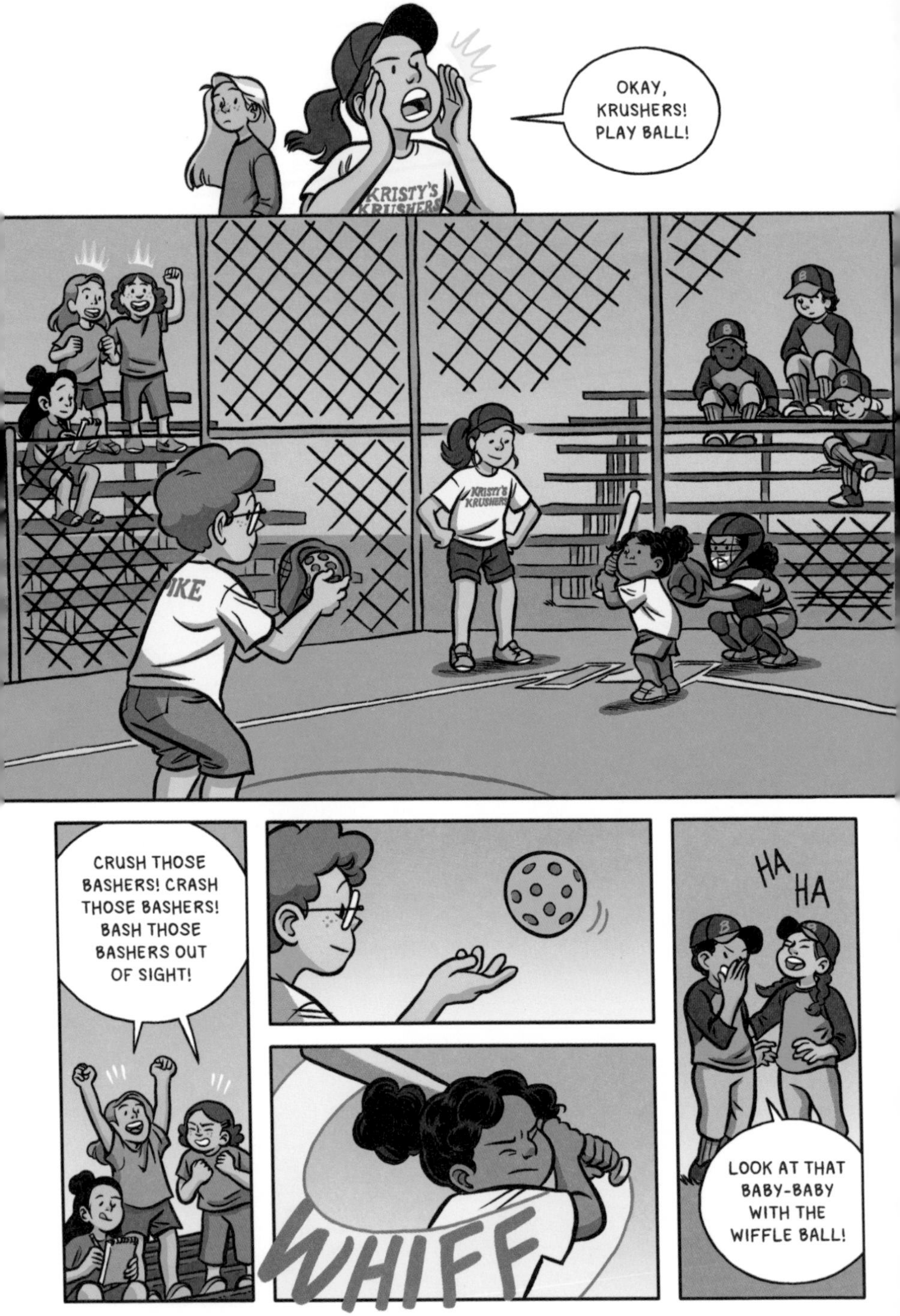
OKAY, KRUSHERS! PLAY BALL!
KRISTY'S KRUSHERS
KRISTY'S KRUSHERS
CRUSH THOSE BASHERS! CRASH THOSE BASHERS! BASH THOSE BASHERS OUT OF SIGHT!
WHIFF
HA HA
LOOK AT THAT BABY-BABY WITH THE WIFFLE BALL!

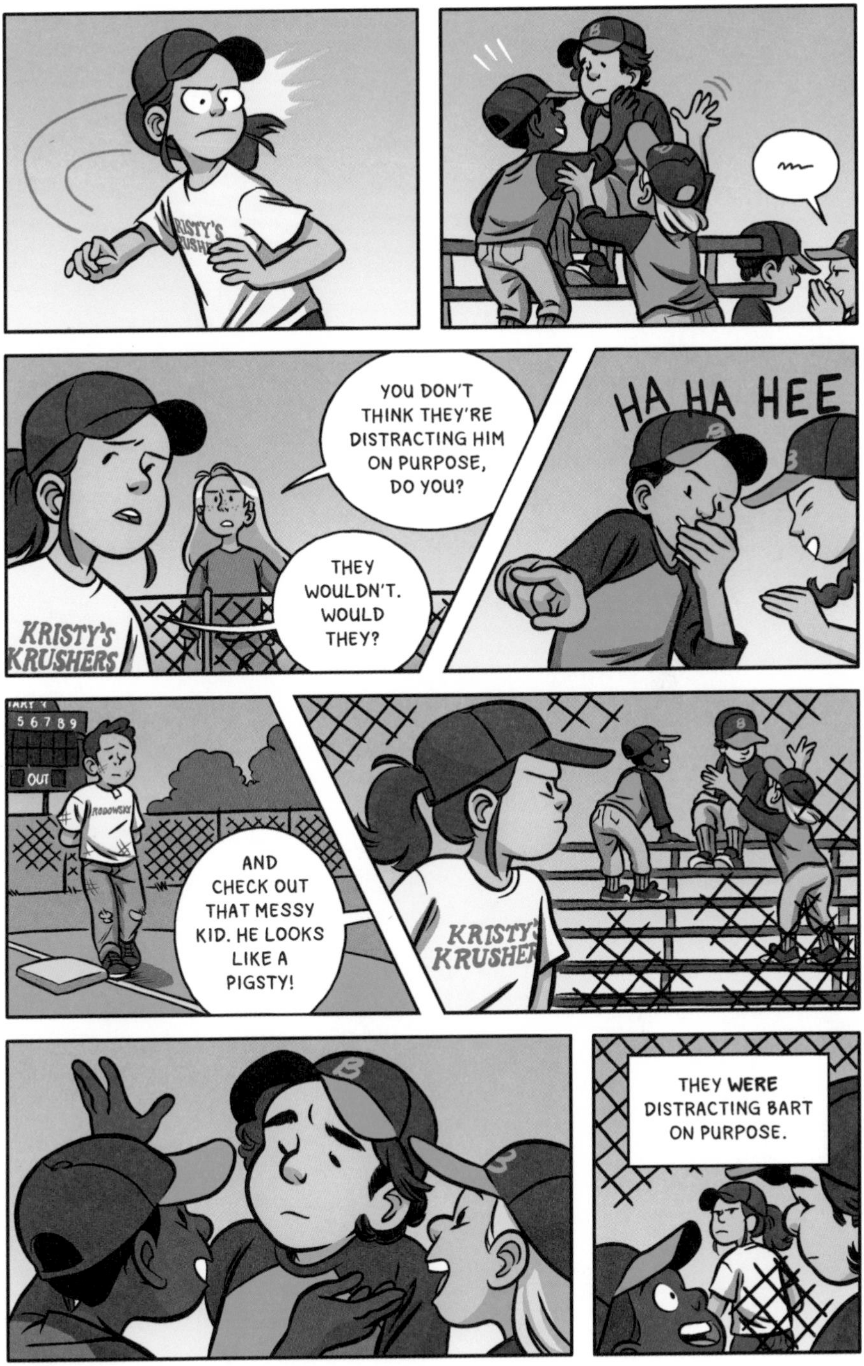
KRISTY'S KRUSHERS
YOU DON'T THINK THEY'RE DISTRACTING HIM ON PURPOSE, DO YOU?
THEY WOULDN'T. WOULD THEY?
KRISTY'S KRUSHERS
HA HA HEE
OUT
AND CHECK OUT THAT MESSY KID. HE LOOKS LIKE A PIGSTY!
KRISTY'S KRUSHERS
THEY WERE DISTRACTING BART ON PURPOSE.

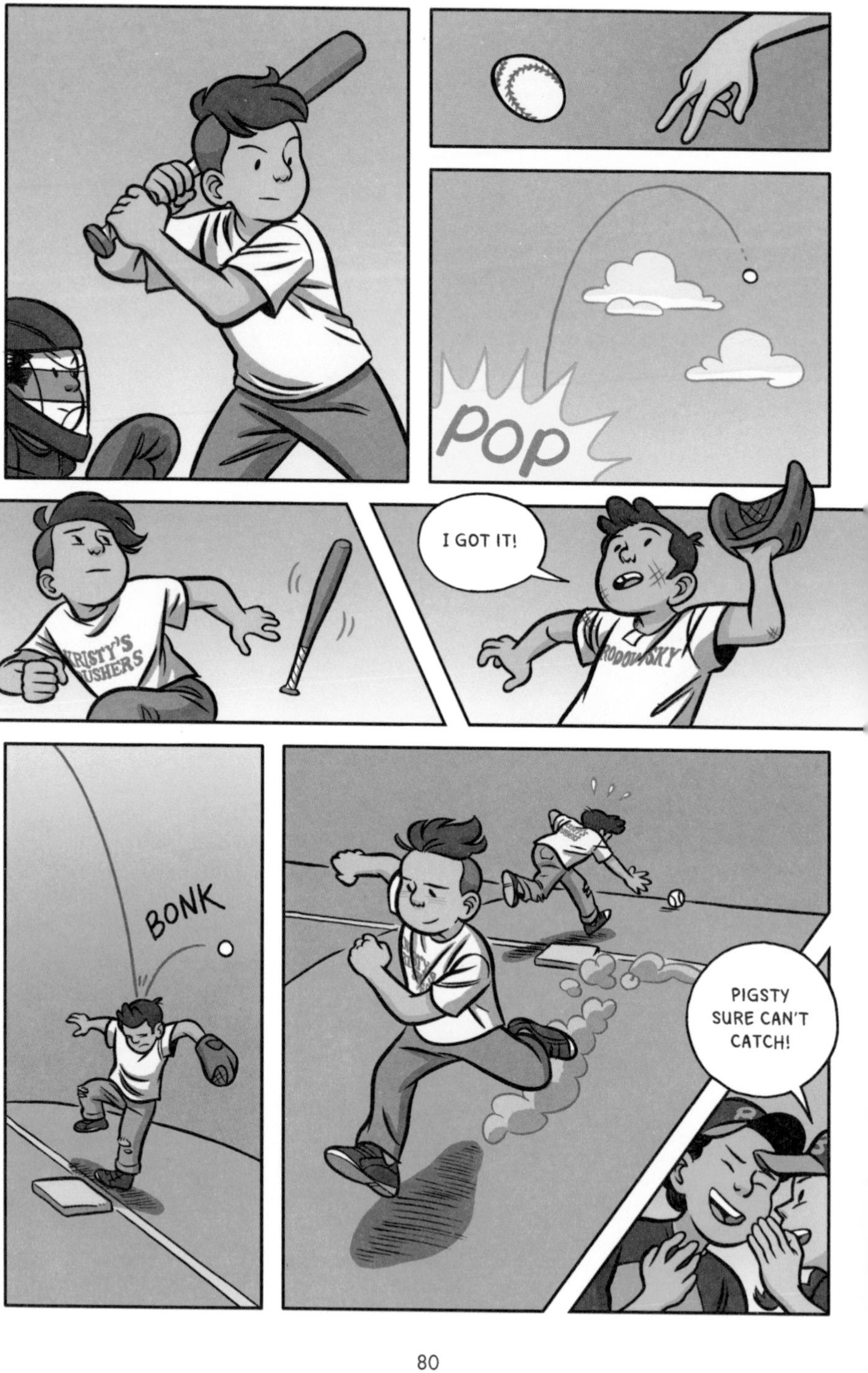
POP
I GOT IT!
KRISTY'S KRUSHERS
BRODOWSKY
BONK
PIGSTY SURE CAN'T CATCH!

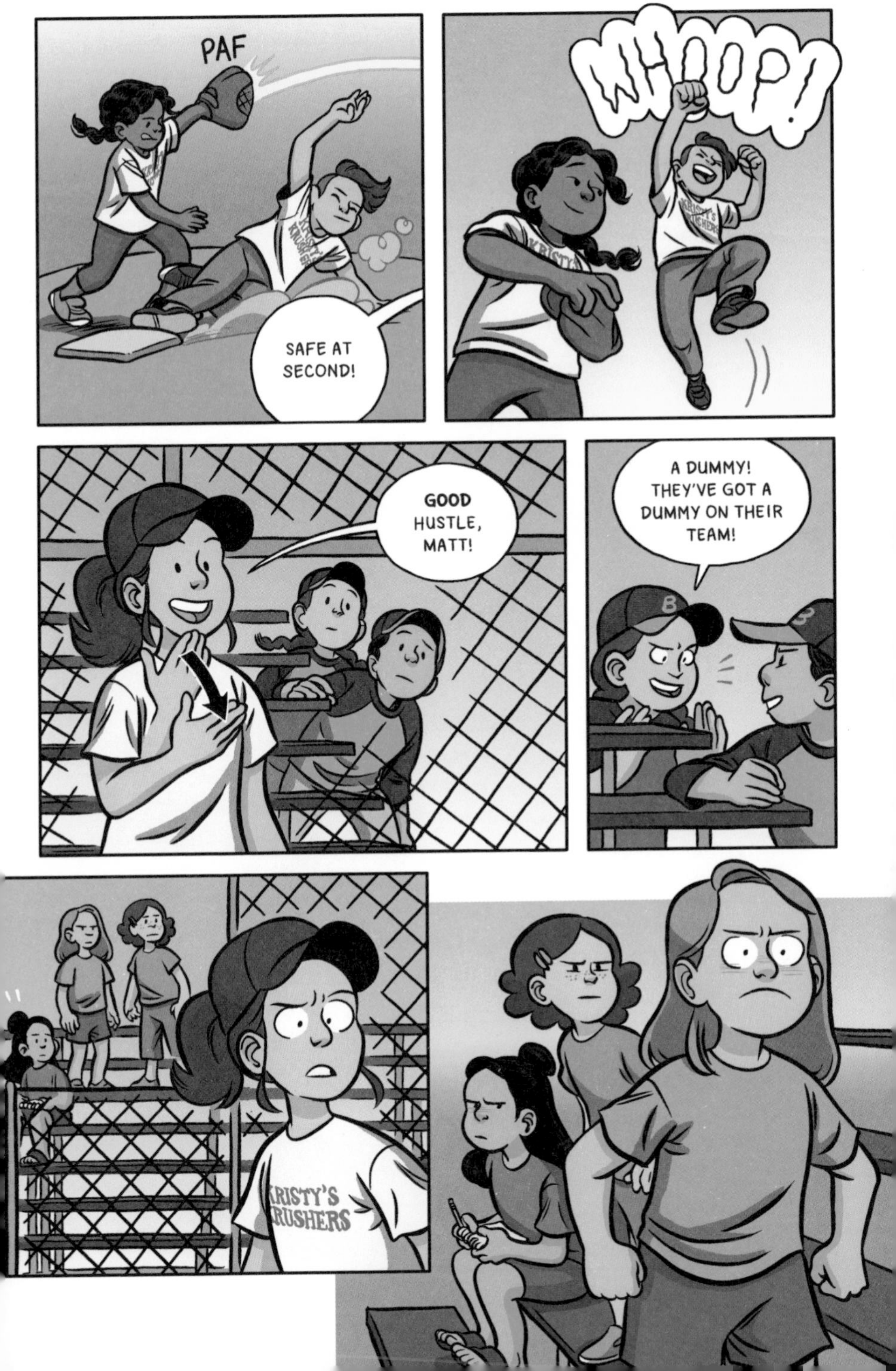
PAF
SAFE AT SECOND!
WHOOP!
GOOD HUSTLE, MATT!
A DUMMY! THEY'VE GOT A DUMMY ON THEIR TEAM!
KRISTY'S KRUSHERS

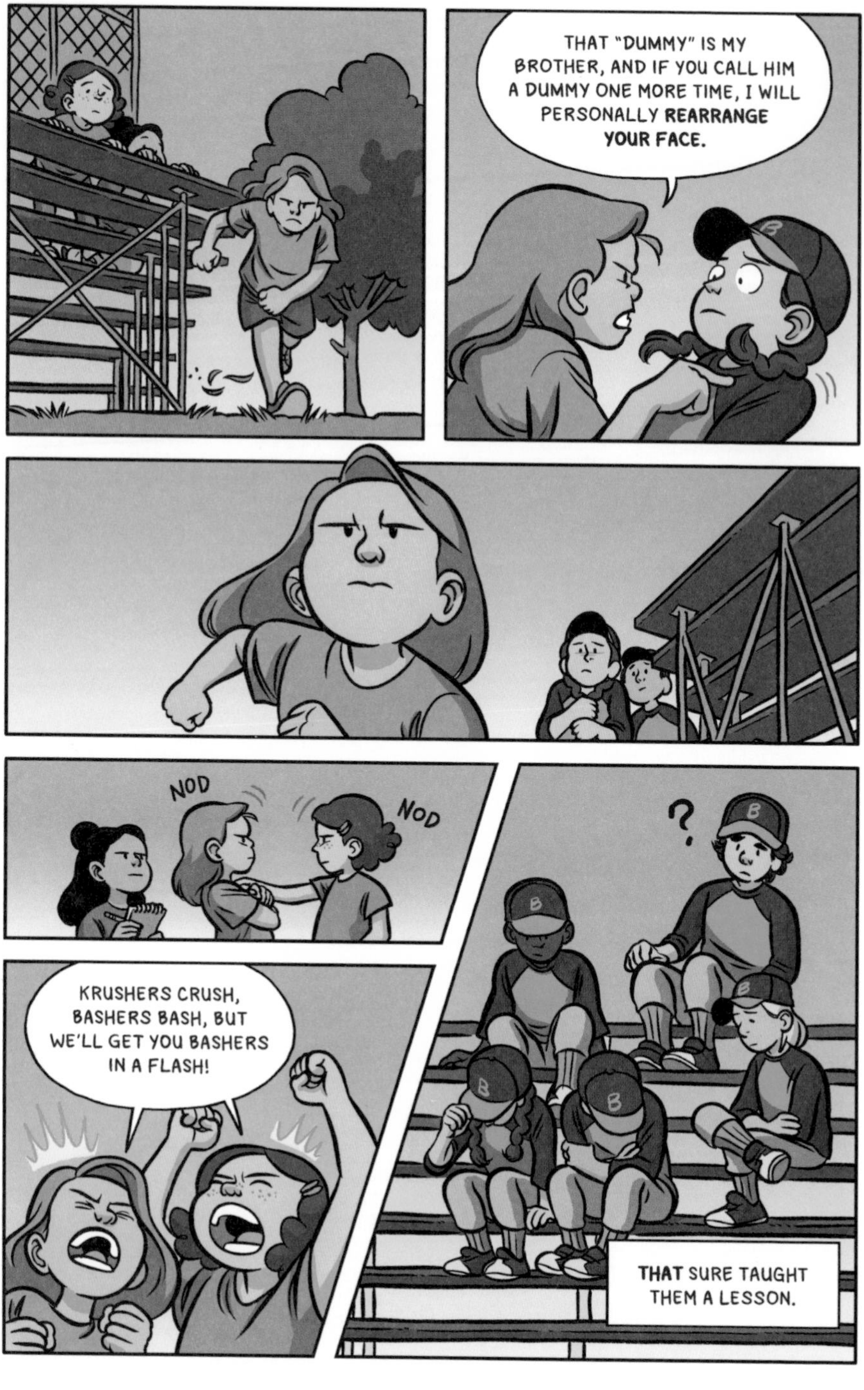
THAT "DUMMY" IS MY BROTHER, AND IF YOU CALL HIM A DUMMY ONE MORE TIME, I WILL PERSONALLY **REARRANGE YOUR FACE.**
NOD
NOD
?
KRUSHERS CRUSH, BASHERS BASH, BUT WE'LL GET YOU BASHERS IN A FLASH!
THAT SURE TAUGHT THEM A LESSON.

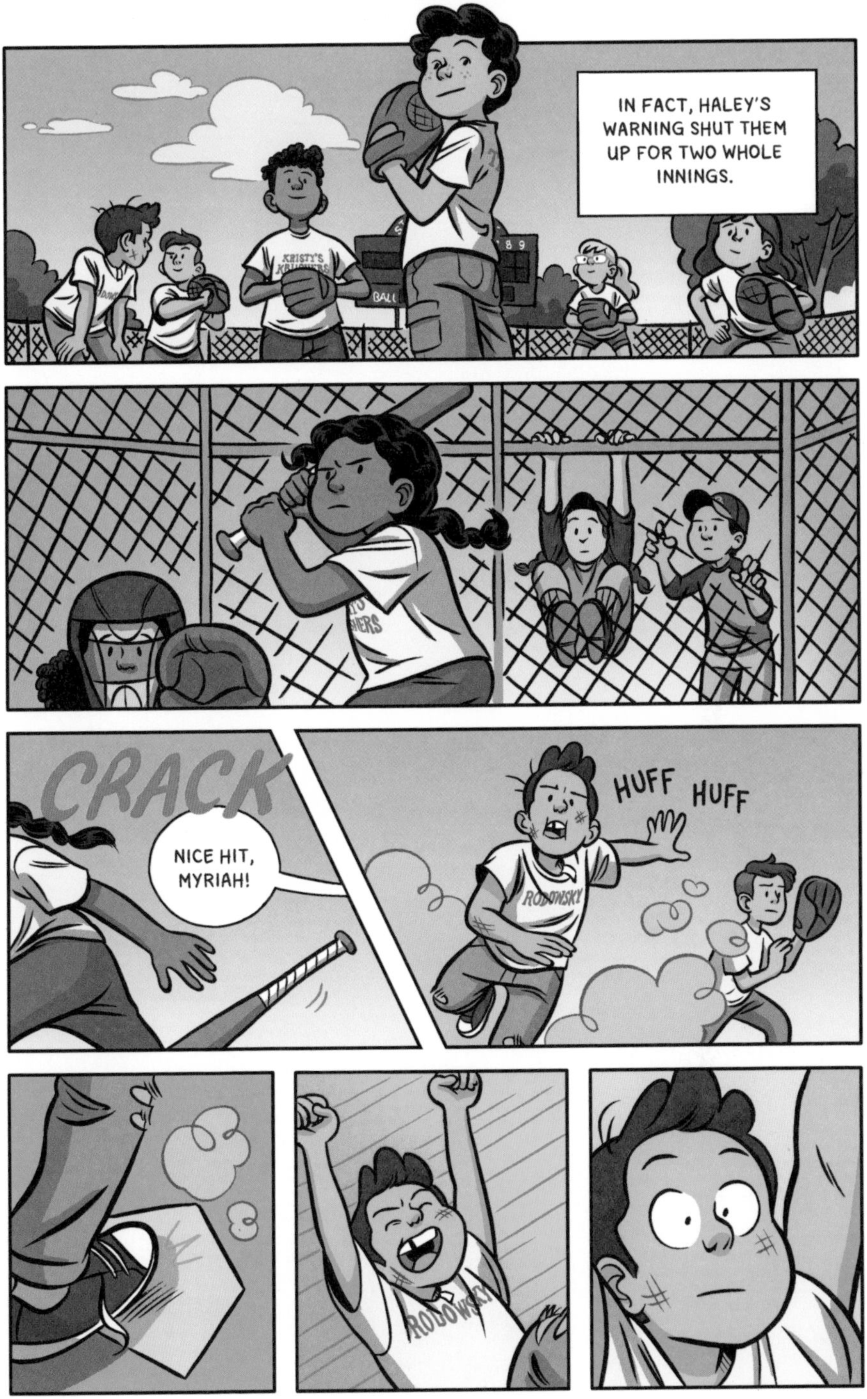
IN FACT, HALEY'S WARNING SHUT THEM UP FOR TWO WHOLE INNINGS.
KRISTY'S KRUSHERS
CRACK
NICE HIT, MYRIAH!
HUFF HUFF
RODOWSKY
RODOWSKY

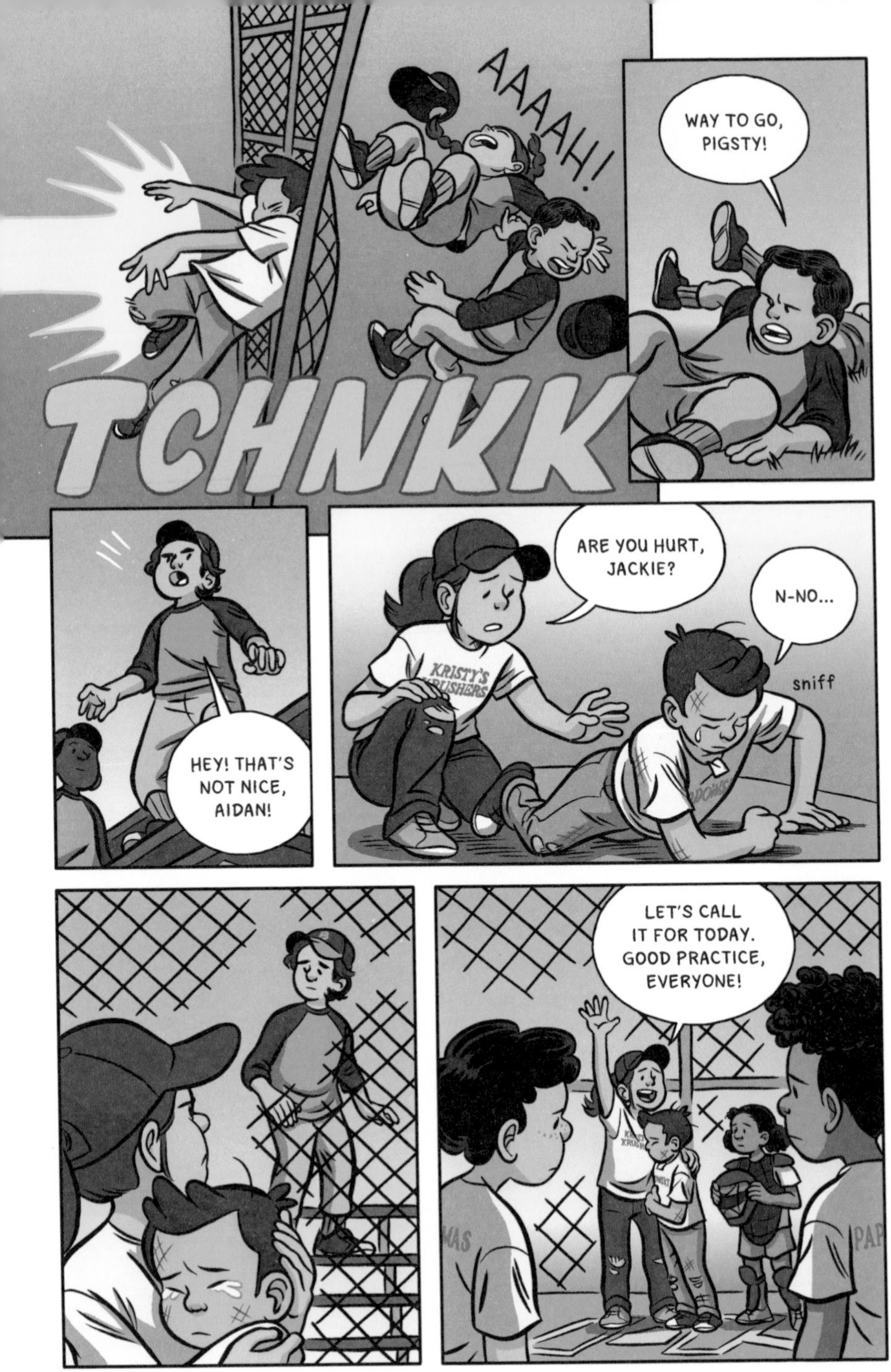
AAAAAH!
TCHNKK
WAY TO GO, PIGSTY!
HEY! THAT'S NOT NICE, AIDAN!
ARE YOU HURT, JACKIE?
N-NO...
sniff
KRISTY'S KRUSHERS
LET'S CALL IT FOR TODAY. GOOD PRACTICE, EVERYONE!

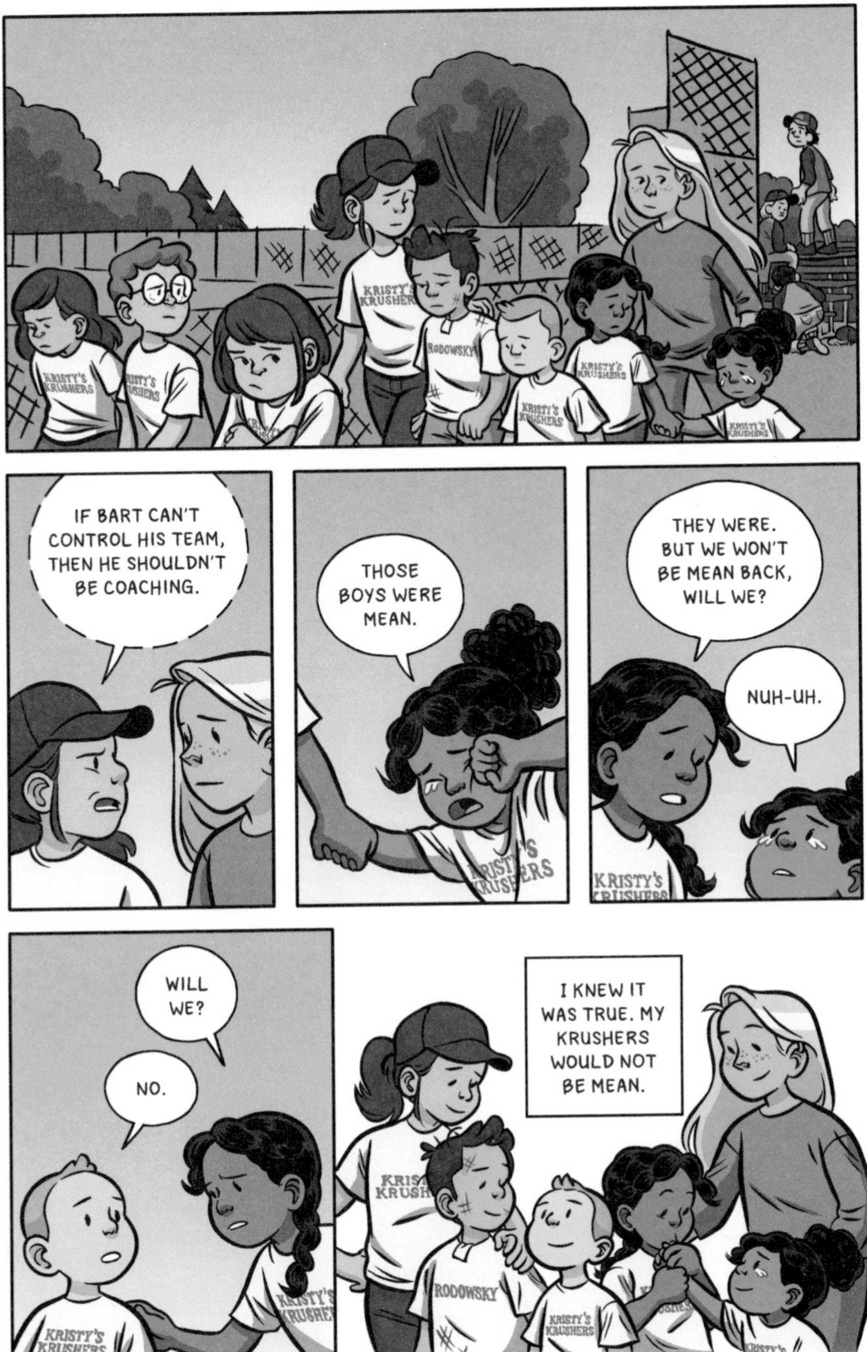
IF BART CAN'T CONTROL HIS TEAM, THEN HE SHOULDN'T BE COACHING.
THOSE BOYS WERE MEAN.
THEY WERE. BUT WE WON'T BE MEAN BACK, WILL WE?
NUH-UH.
WILL WE?
NO.
I KNEW IT WAS TRUE. MY KRUSHERS WOULD NOT BE MEAN.

CHAPTER 12

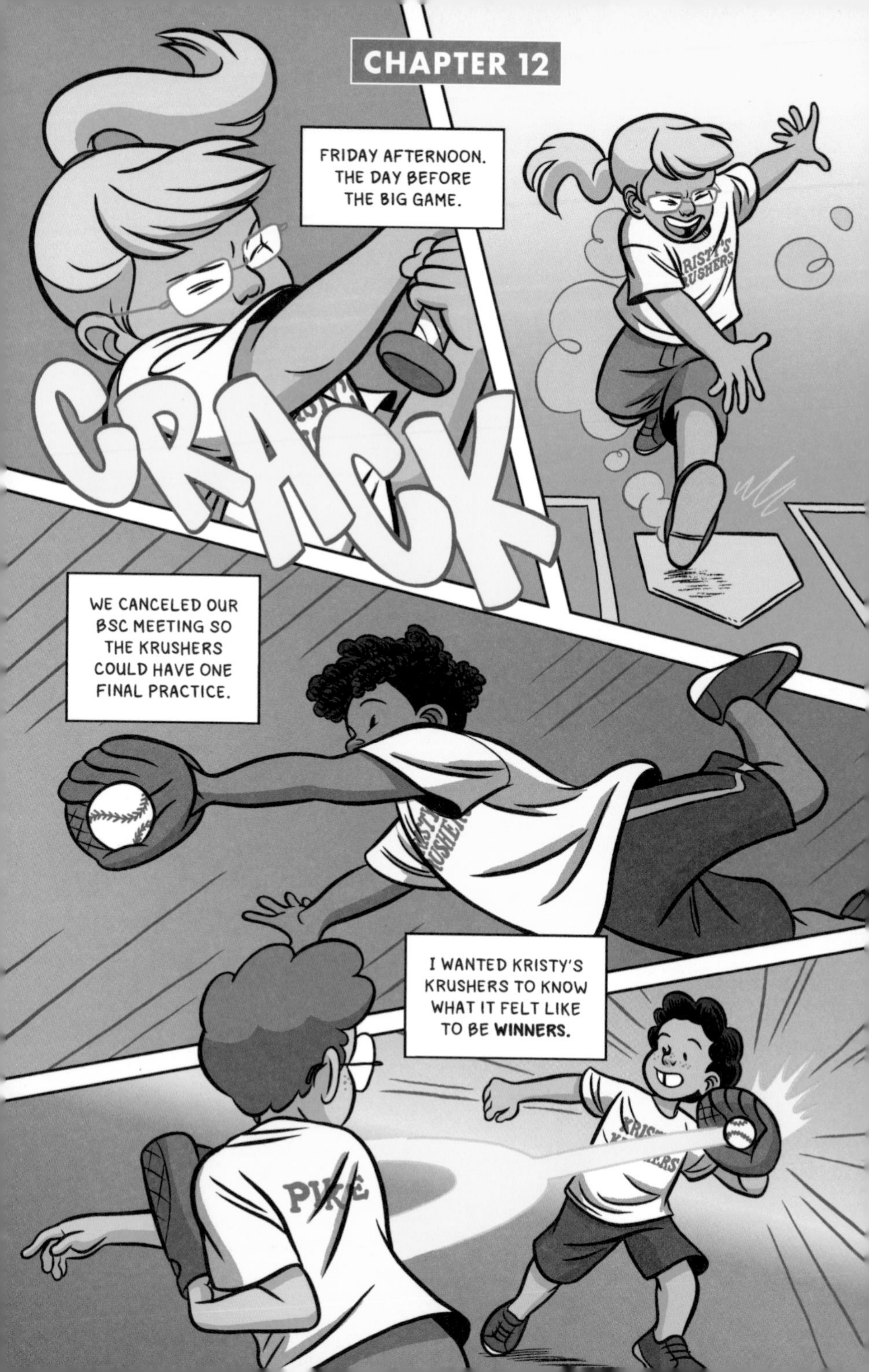
FRIDAY AFTERNOON. THE DAY BEFORE THE BIG GAME.
CRACK
KRISTY'S KRUSHERS
WE CANCELED OUR BSC MEETING SO THE KRUSHERS COULD HAVE ONE FINAL PRACTICE.
I WANTED KRISTY'S KRUSHERS TO KNOW WHAT IT FELT LIKE TO BE **WINNERS.**
PIKE

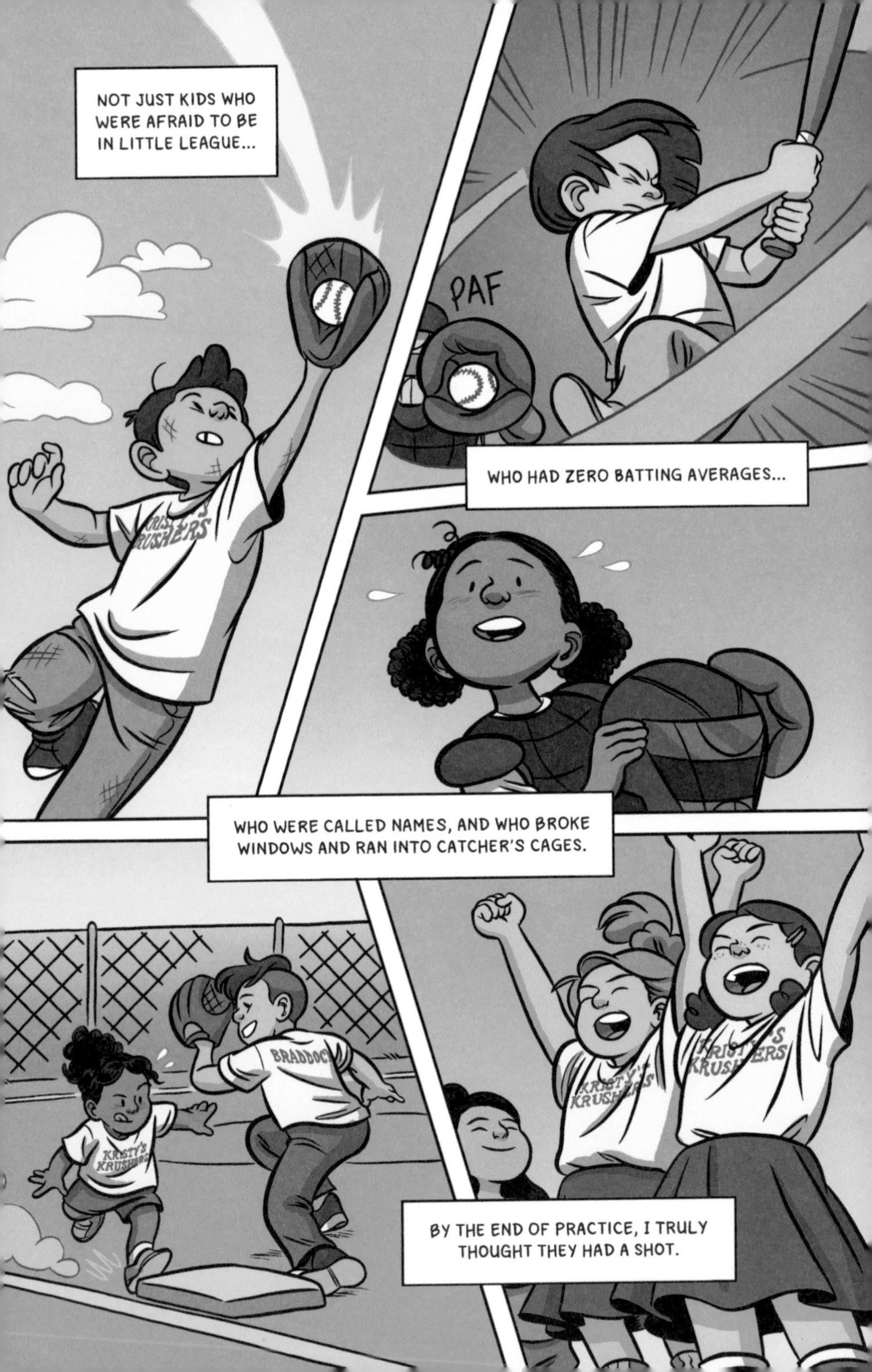
NOT JUST KIDS WHO WERE AFRAID TO BE IN LITTLE LEAGUE...
PAF
WHO HAD ZERO BATTING AVERAGES...
WHO WERE CALLED NAMES, AND WHO BROKE WINDOWS AND RAN INTO CATCHER'S CAGES.
BY THE END OF PRACTICE, I TRULY THOUGHT THEY HAD A SHOT.

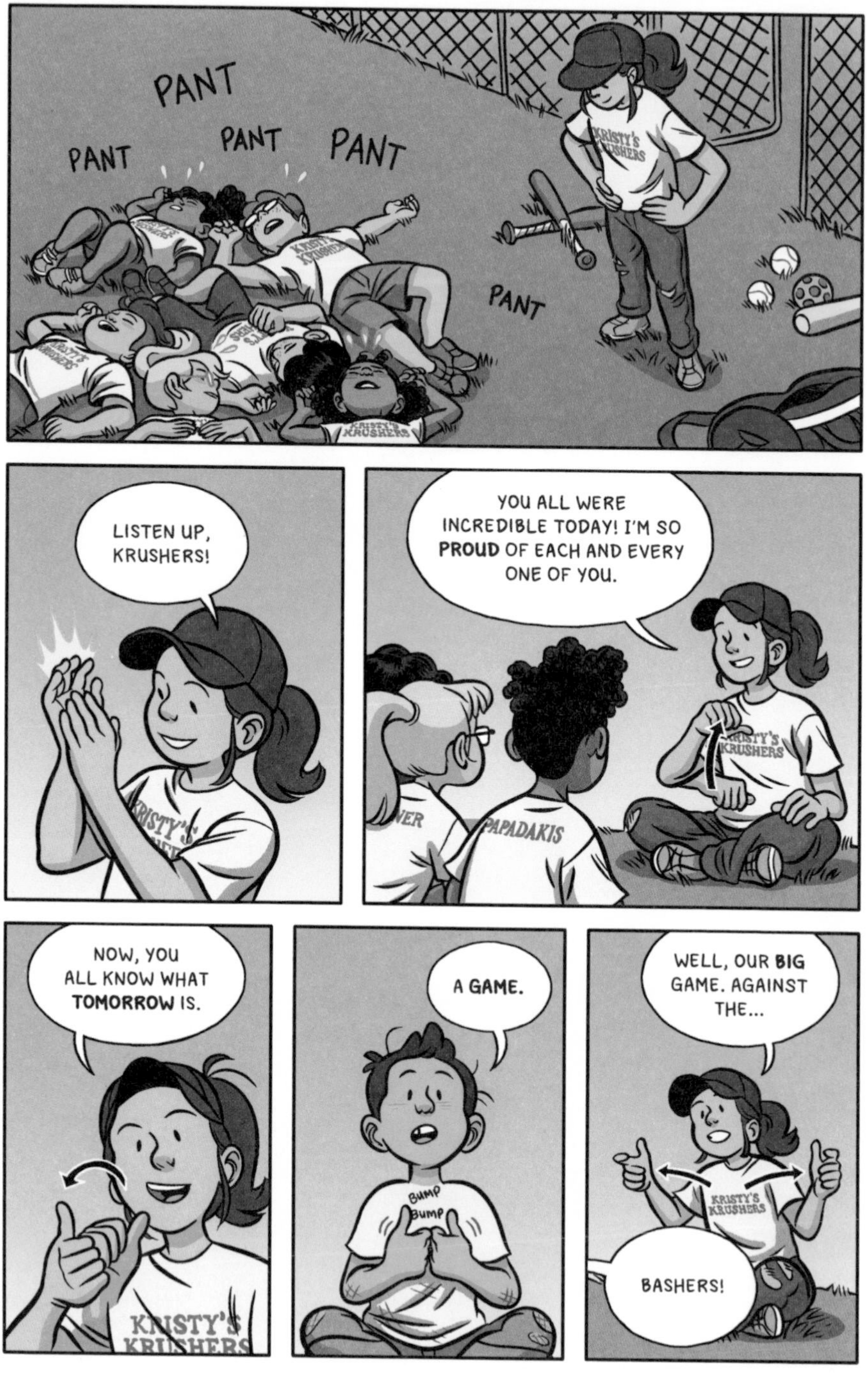
PANT
PANT
PANT
PANT
PANT
KRISTY'S KRUSHERS
LISTEN UP, KRUSHERS!
YOU ALL WERE INCREDIBLE TODAY! I'M SO **PROUD** OF EACH AND EVERY ONE OF YOU.
PAPADAKIS
NOW, YOU ALL KNOW WHAT **TOMORROW** IS.
A **GAME.**
BUMP
BUMP
WELL, OUR **BIG** GAME. AGAINST THE...
BASHERS!

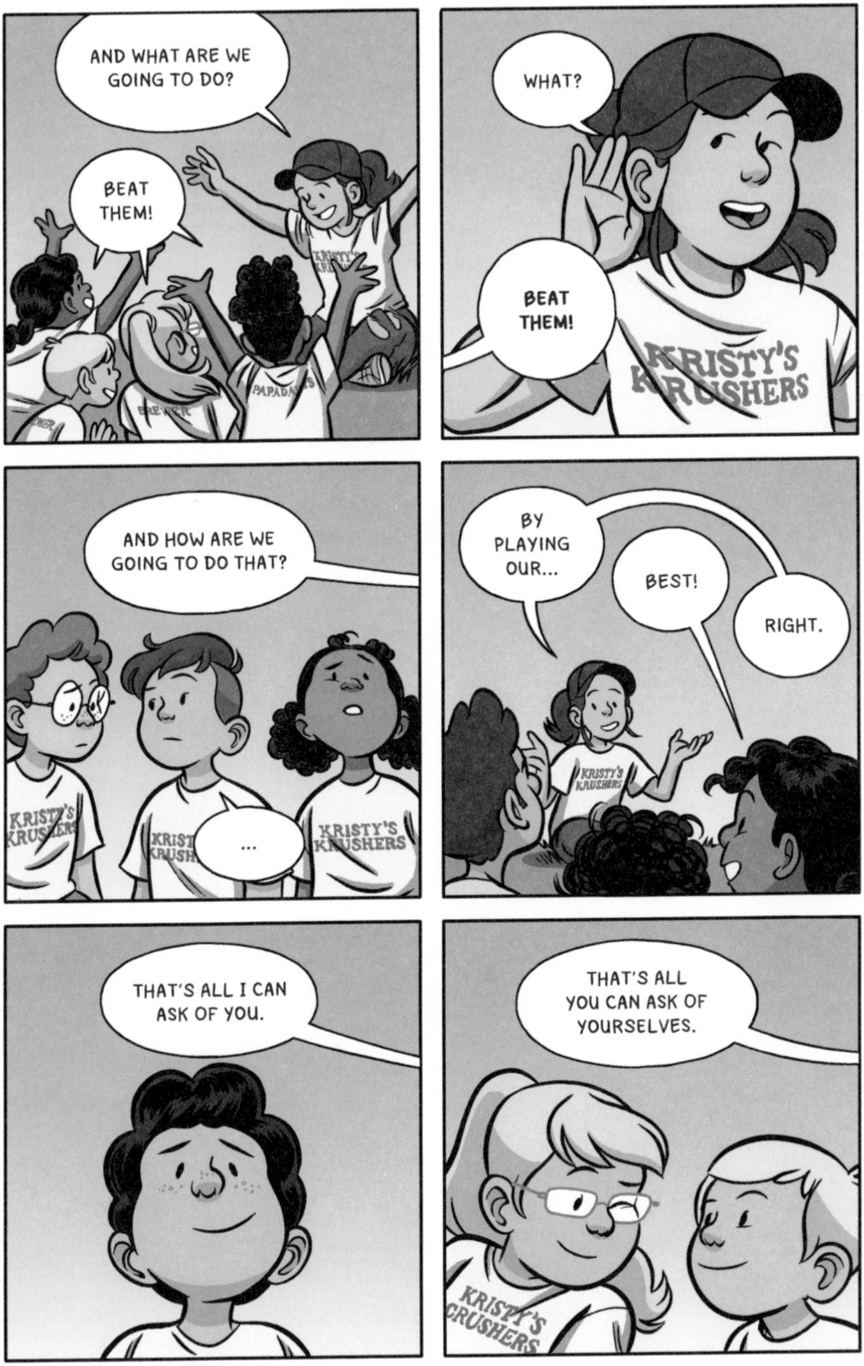
AND WHAT ARE WE GOING TO DO?
BEAT THEM!
KRISTY'S KRUSHERS
BREWER
PAPADAKIS
WHAT?
BEAT THEM!
KRISTY'S KRUSHERS
AND HOW ARE WE GOING TO DO THAT?
KRISTY'S KRUSHERS
...
KRISTY'S KRUSHERS
BY PLAYING OUR...
BEST!
RIGHT.
KRISTY'S KRUSHERS
THAT'S ALL I CAN ASK OF YOU.
THAT'S ALL YOU CAN ASK OF YOURSELVES.
KRISTY'S KRUSHERS

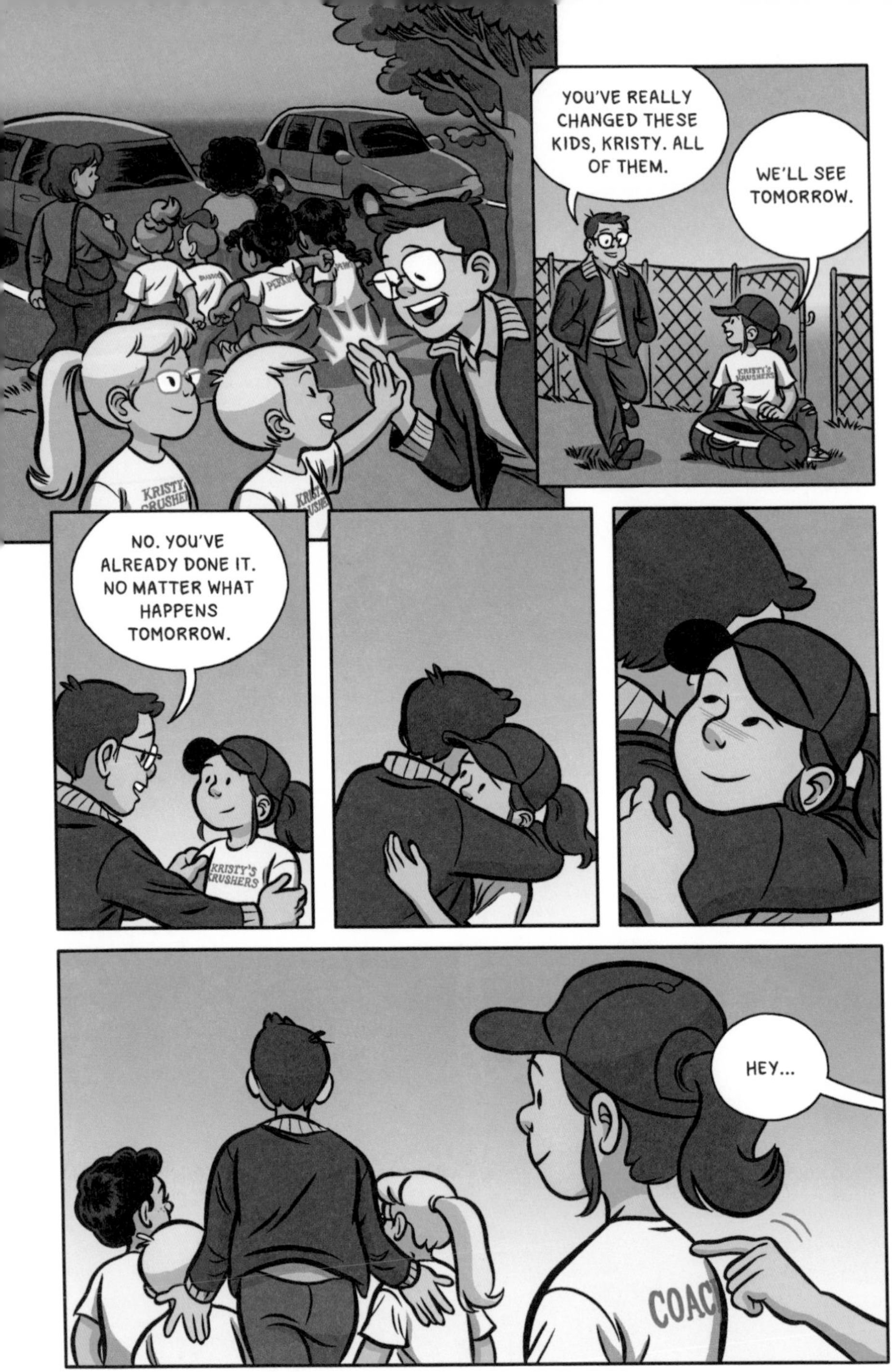

KRISTY'S CRUSHERS
YOU'VE REALLY CHANGED THESE KIDS, KRISTY. ALL OF THEM.
WE'LL SEE TOMORROW.
KRISTY'S KRUSHERS
NO. YOU'VE ALREADY DONE IT. NO MATTER WHAT HAPPENS TOMORROW.
KRISTY'S KRUSHERS
HEY...
COAC

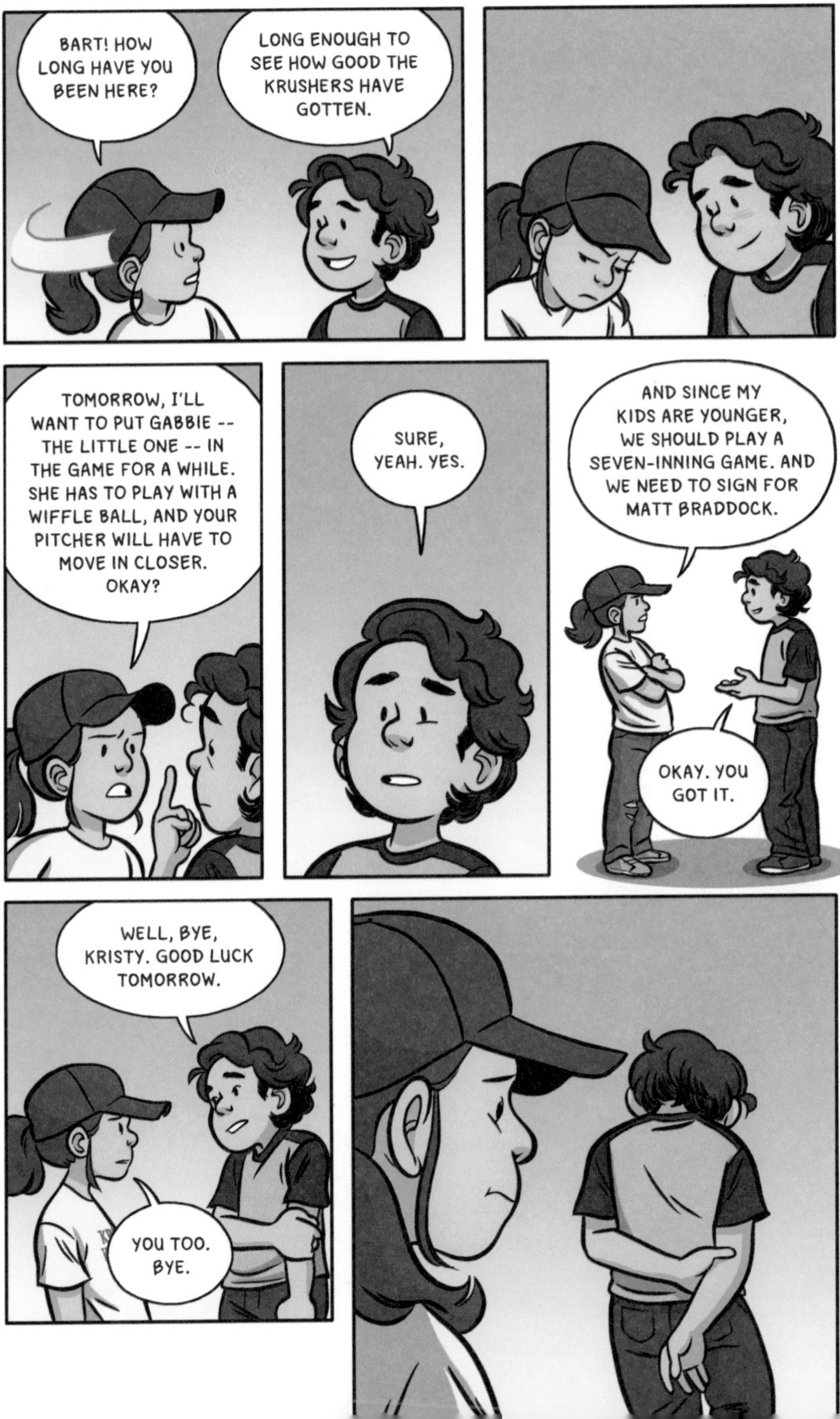
BART! HOW LONG HAVE YOU BEEN HERE?
LONG ENOUGH TO SEE HOW GOOD THE KRUSHERS HAVE GOTTEN.
TOMORROW, I'LL WANT TO PUT GABBIE -- THE LITTLE ONE -- IN THE GAME FOR A WHILE. SHE HAS TO PLAY WITH A WIFFLE BALL, AND YOUR PITCHER WILL HAVE TO MOVE IN CLOSER. OKAY?
SURE, YEAH. YES.
AND SINCE MY KIDS ARE YOUNGER, WE SHOULD PLAY A SEVEN-INNING GAME. AND WE NEED TO SIGN FOR MATT BRADDOCK.
OKAY. YOU GOT IT.
WELL, BYE, KRISTY. GOOD LUCK TOMORROW.
YOU TOO. BYE.

CHAPTER 13

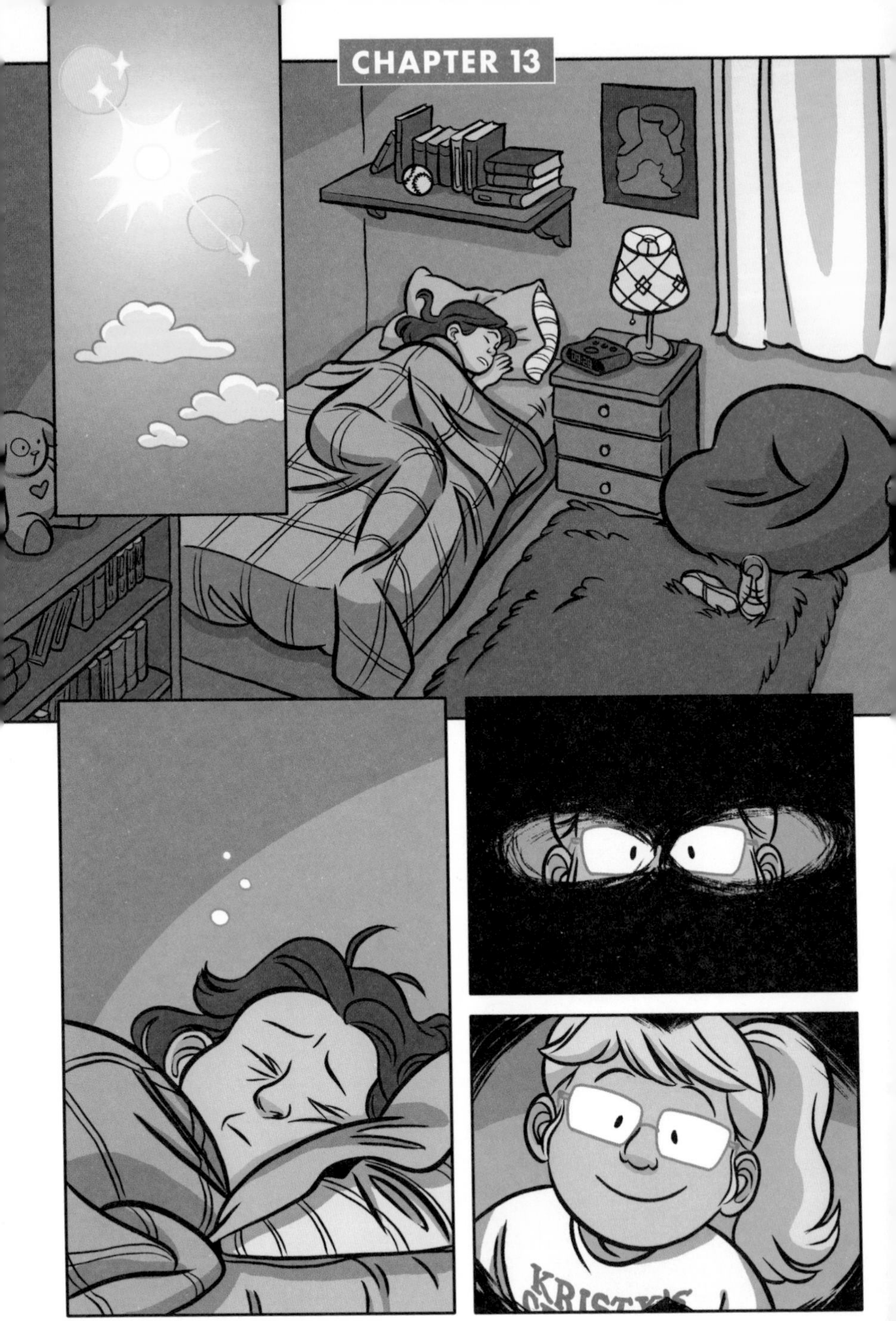

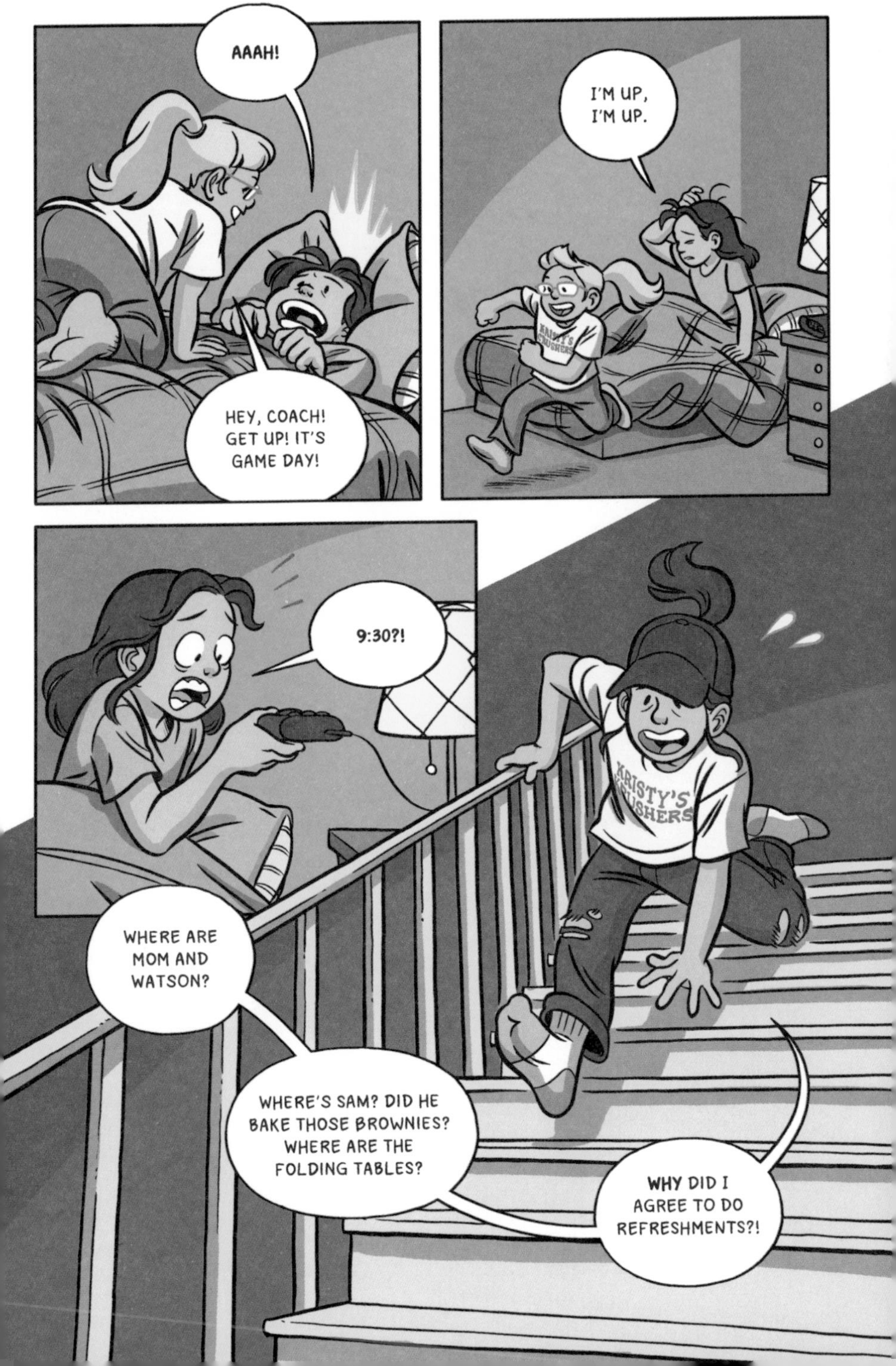
AAAH!
HEY, COACH! GET UP! IT'S GAME DAY!
I'M UP, I'M UP.
KRISTY'S KRUSHERS
9:30?!
KRISTY'S KRUSHERS
WHERE ARE MOM AND WATSON?
WHERE'S SAM? DID HE BAKE THOSE BROWNIES? WHERE ARE THE FOLDING TABLES?
WHY DID I AGREE TO DO REFRESHMENTS?!

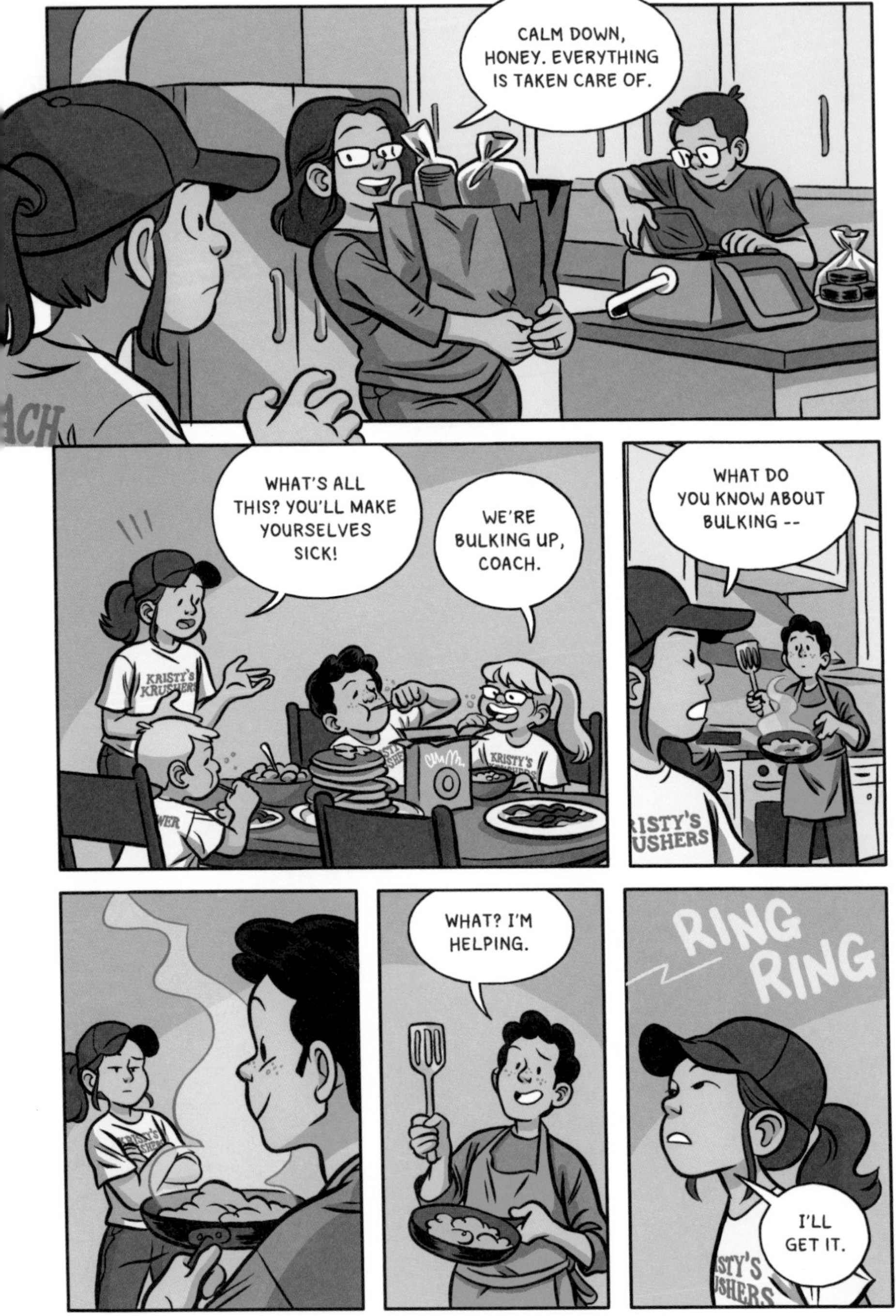
CALM DOWN, HONEY. EVERYTHING IS TAKEN CARE OF.
WHAT'S ALL THIS? YOU'LL MAKE YOURSELVES SICK!
WE'RE BULKING UP, COACH.
WHAT DO YOU KNOW ABOUT BULKING --
WHAT? I'M HELPING.
RING RING
I'LL GET IT.

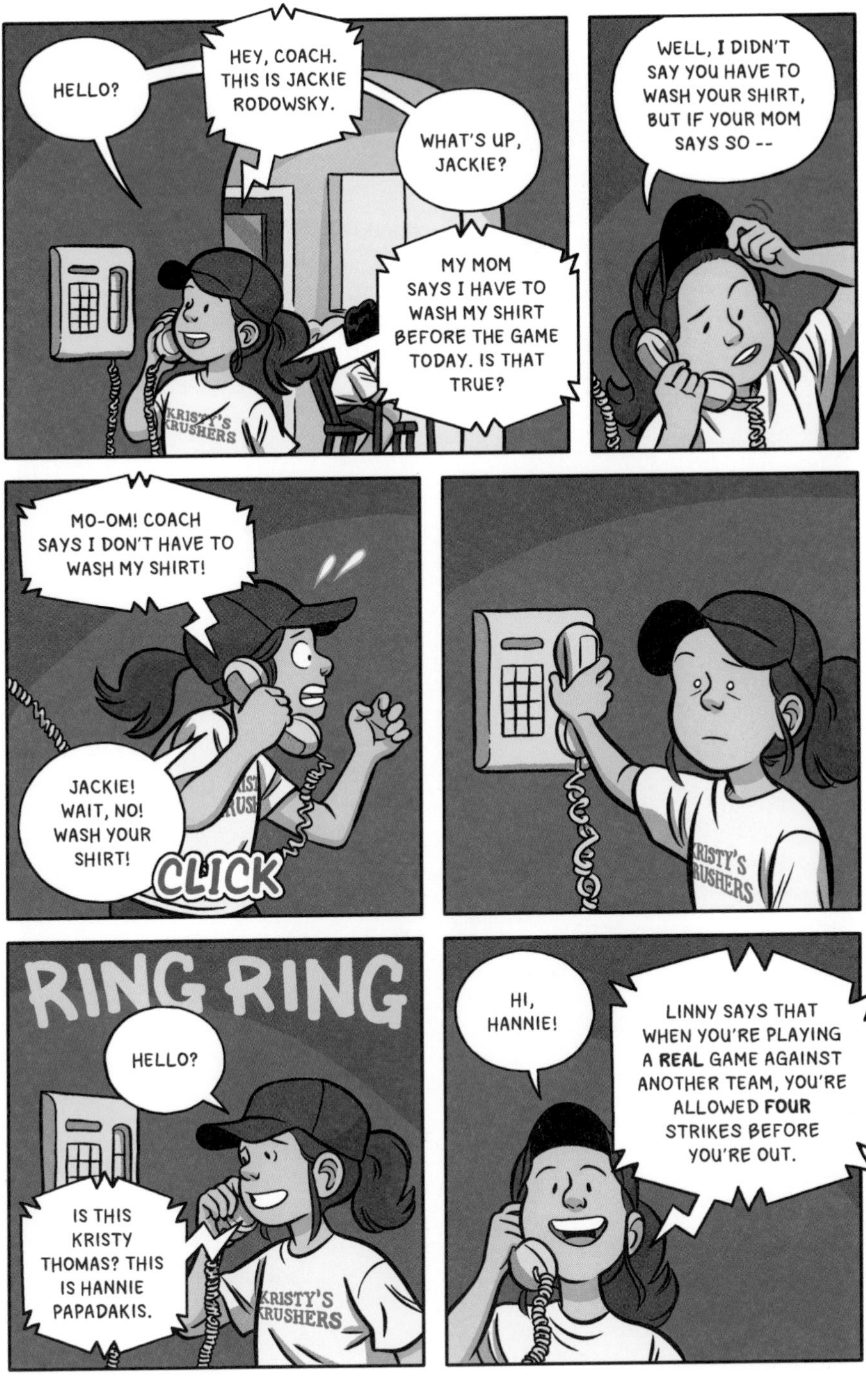
HELLO?
HEY, COACH. THIS IS JACKIE RODOWSKY.
WHAT'S UP, JACKIE?
MY MOM SAYS I HAVE TO WASH MY SHIRT BEFORE THE GAME TODAY. IS THAT TRUE?
KRISTY'S KRUSHERS
WELL, I DIDN'T SAY YOU HAVE TO WASH YOUR SHIRT, BUT IF YOUR MOM SAYS SO --
MO-OM! COACH SAYS I DON'T HAVE TO WASH MY SHIRT!
JACKIE! WAIT, NO! WASH YOUR SHIRT!
CLICK
KRISTY'S KRUSHERS
RING RING
HELLO?
IS THIS KRISTY THOMAS? THIS IS HANNIE PAPADAKIS.
KRISTY'S KRUSHERS
HI, HANNIE!
LINNY SAYS THAT WHEN YOU'RE PLAYING A **REAL** GAME AGAINST ANOTHER TEAM, YOU'RE ALLOWED **FOUR** STRIKES BEFORE YOU'RE OUT.

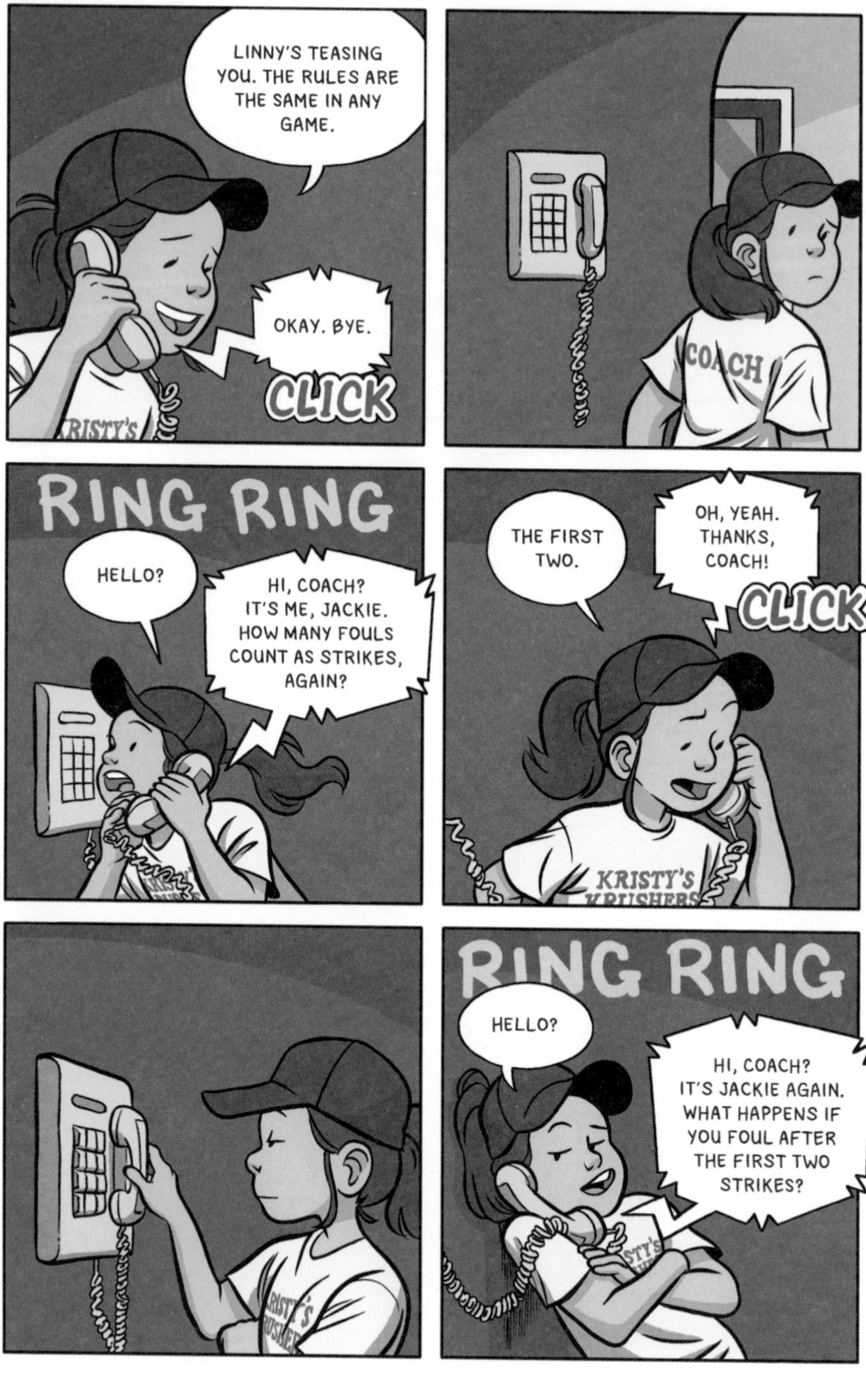
LINNY'S TEASING YOU. THE RULES ARE THE SAME IN ANY GAME.
OKAY. BYE.
CLICK
COACH
RING RING
HELLO?
HI, COACH? IT'S ME, JACKIE. HOW MANY FOULS COUNT AS STRIKES, AGAIN?
THE FIRST TWO.
OH, YEAH. THANKS, COACH!
CLICK
KRISTY'S
RING RING
HELLO?
HI, COACH? IT'S JACKIE AGAIN. WHAT HAPPENS IF YOU FOUL AFTER THE FIRST TWO STRIKES?

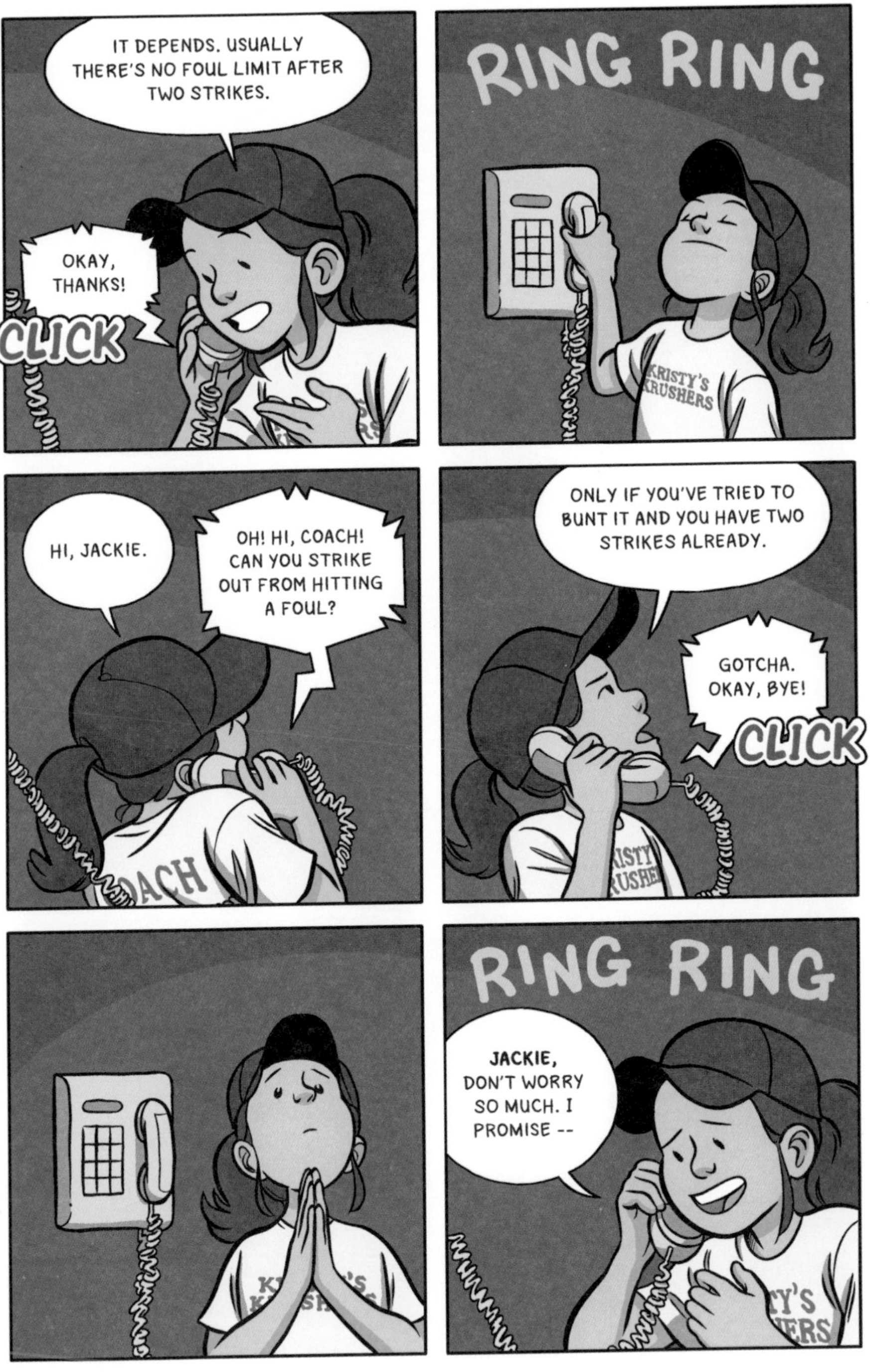
IT DEPENDS. USUALLY THERE'S NO FOUL LIMIT AFTER TWO STRIKES.
OKAY, THANKS!
CLICK
RING RING
KRISTY'S KRUSHERS
HI, JACKIE.
OH! HI, COACH! CAN YOU STRIKE OUT FROM HITTING A FOUL?
ONLY IF YOU'VE TRIED TO BUNT IT AND YOU HAVE TWO STRIKES ALREADY.
GOTCHA. OKAY, BYE!
CLICK
RING RING
JACKIE, DON'T WORRY SO MUCH. I PROMISE --

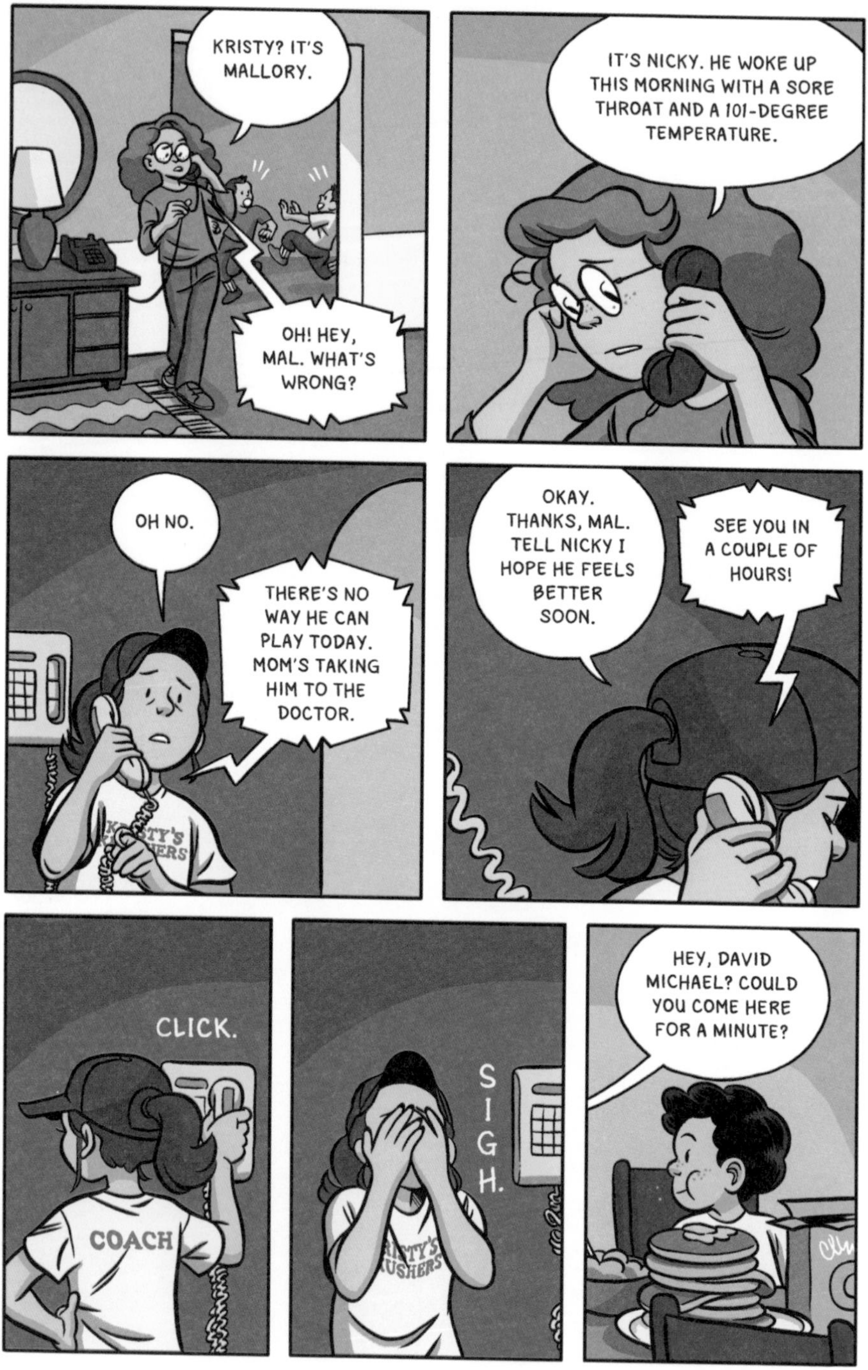
KRISTY? IT'S MALLORY.
OH! HEY, MAL. WHAT'S WRONG?
IT'S NICKY. HE WOKE UP THIS MORNING WITH A SORE THROAT AND A 101-DEGREE TEMPERATURE.
OH NO.
THERE'S NO WAY HE CAN PLAY TODAY. MOM'S TAKING HIM TO THE DOCTOR.
KRISTY'S KRUSHERS
OKAY. THANKS, MAL. TELL NICKY I HOPE HE FEELS BETTER SOON.
SEE YOU IN A COUPLE OF HOURS!
CLICK.
COACH
SIGH.
KRISTY'S KRUSHERS
HEY, DAVID MICHAEL? COULD YOU COME HERE FOR A MINUTE?

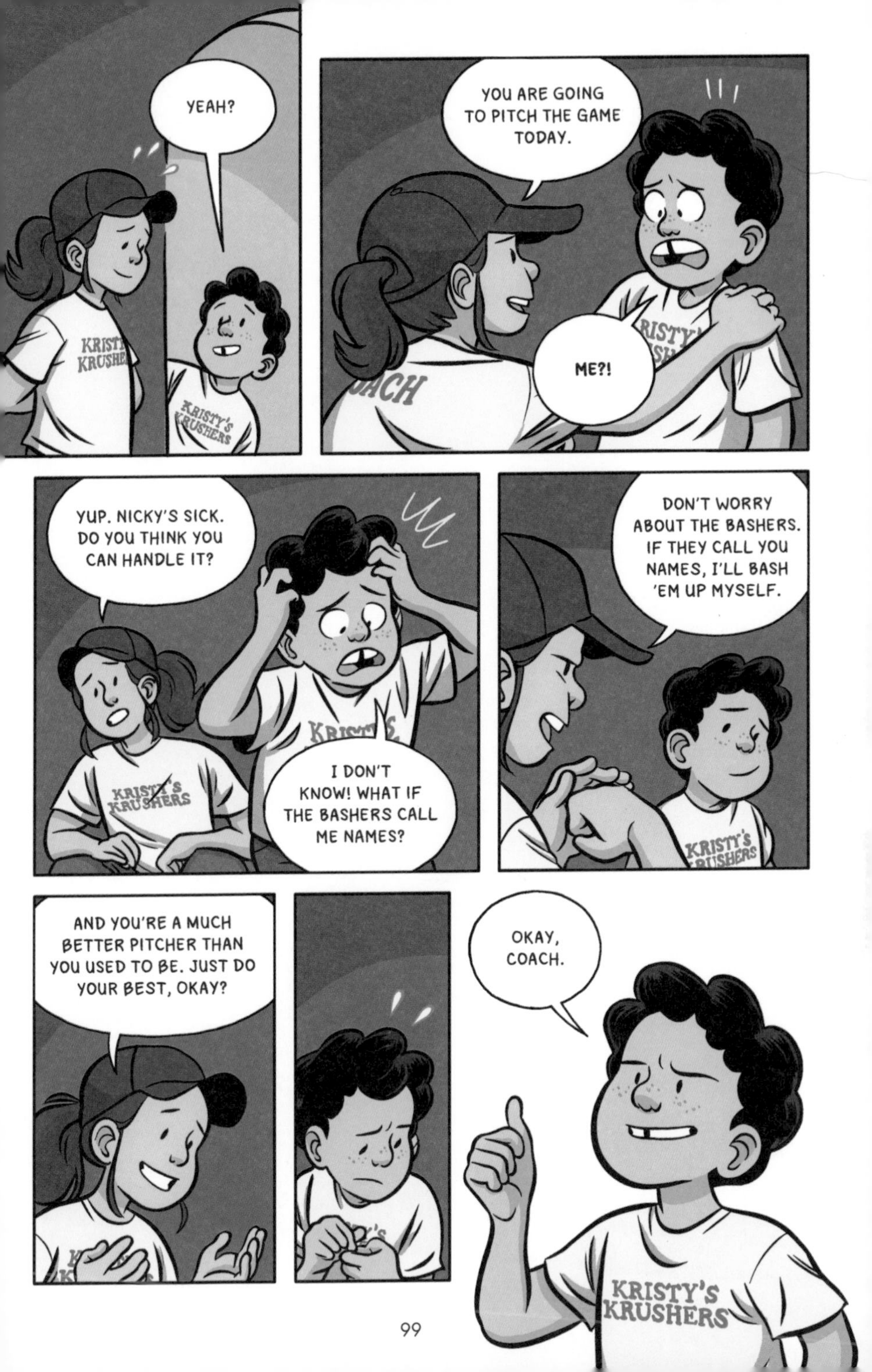
YEAH?
YOU ARE GOING TO PITCH THE GAME TODAY.
ME?!
YUP. NICKY'S SICK. DO YOU THINK YOU CAN HANDLE IT?
I DON'T KNOW! WHAT IF THE BASHERS CALL ME NAMES?
DON'T WORRY ABOUT THE BASHERS. IF THEY CALL YOU NAMES, I'LL BASH 'EM UP MYSELF.
AND YOU'RE A MUCH BETTER PITCHER THAN YOU USED TO BE. JUST DO YOUR BEST, OKAY?
OKAY, COACH.

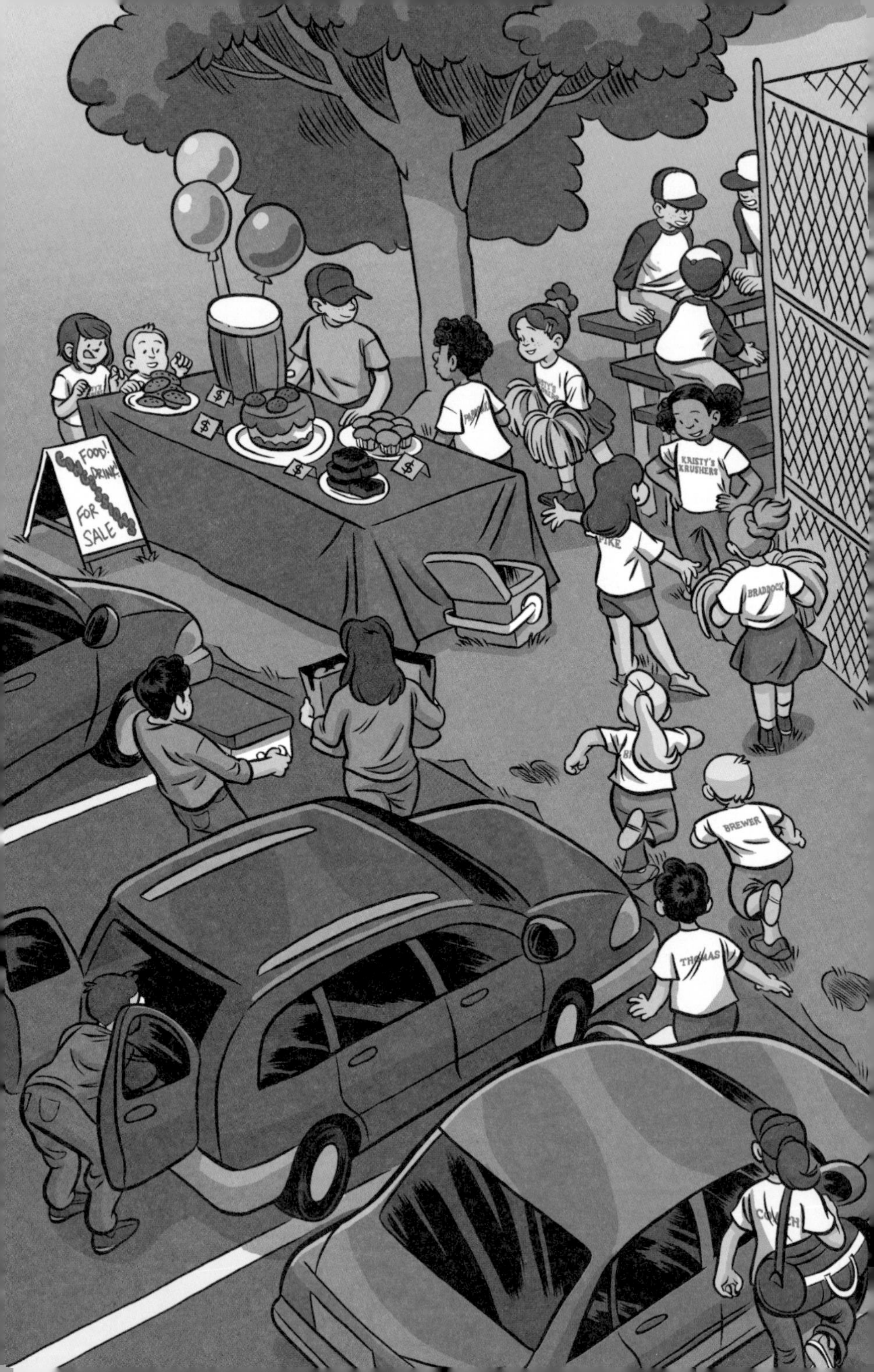
FOOD!
DRINKS!
FOR SALE
KRISTY'S KRUSHERS
PIKE
BRADDOCK
BREWER
THOMAS

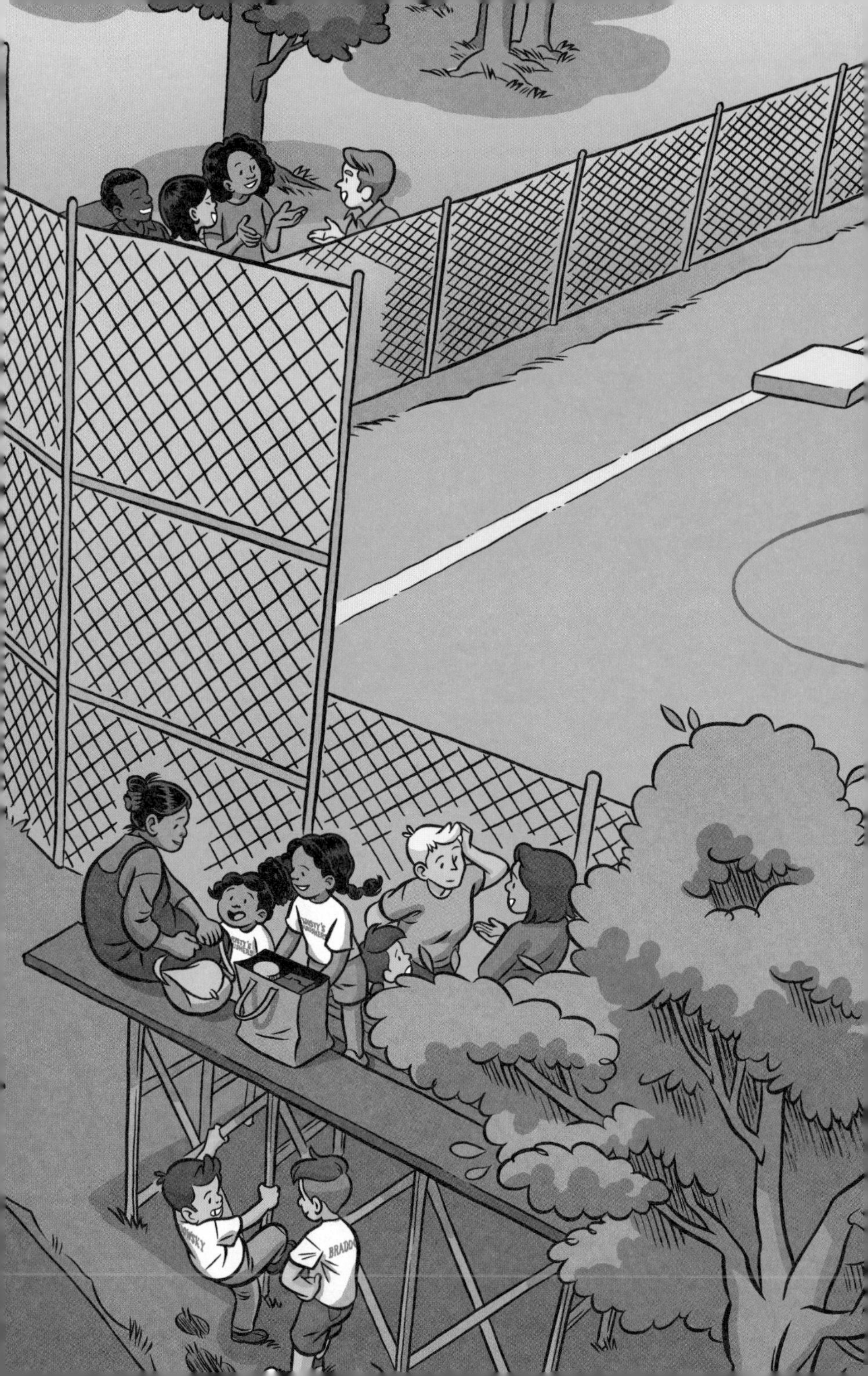

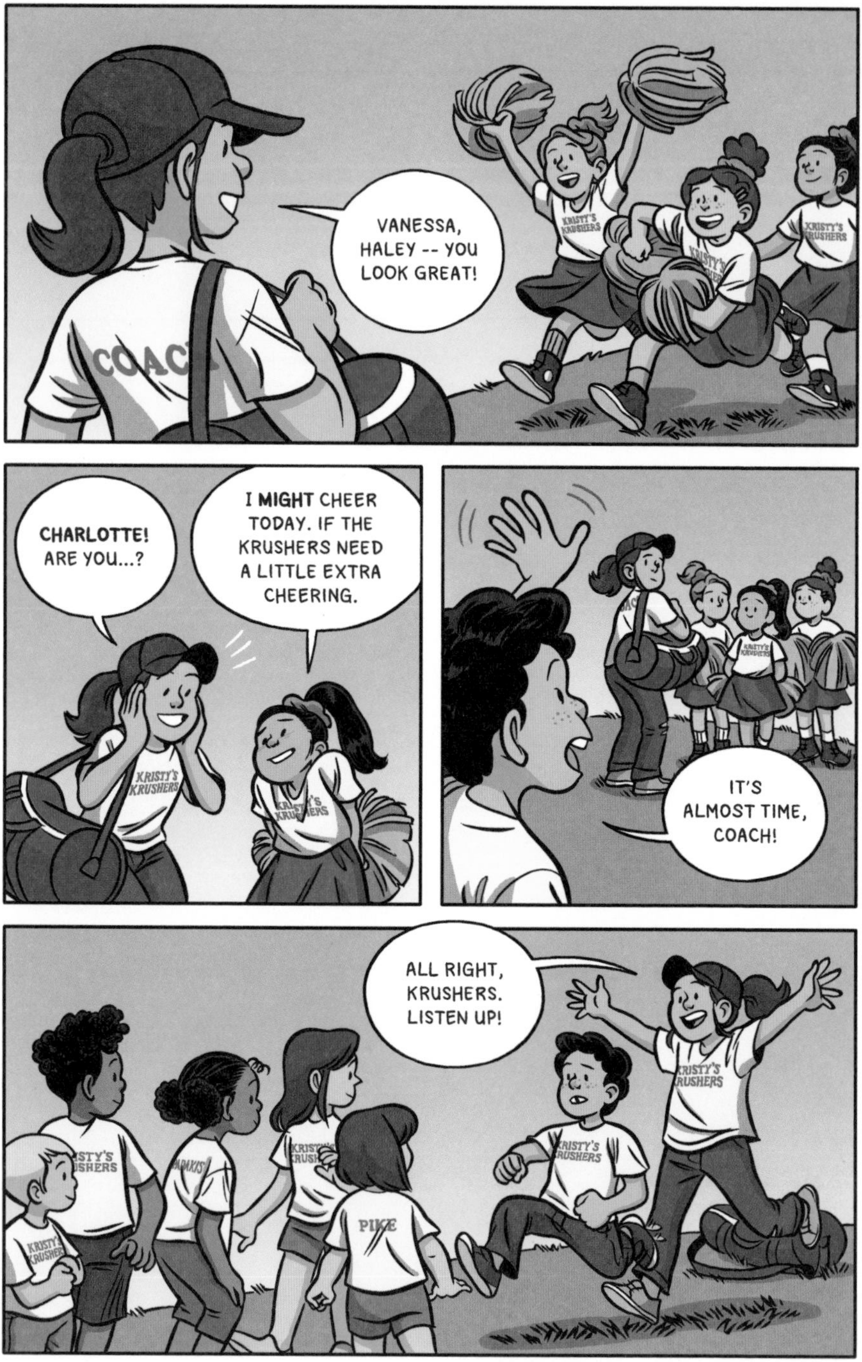
VANESSA, HALEY -- YOU LOOK GREAT!
COACH
KRISTY'S KRUSHERS
CHARLOTTE! ARE YOU...?
I MIGHT CHEER TODAY. IF THE KRUSHERS NEED A LITTLE EXTRA CHEERING.
IT'S ALMOST TIME, COACH!
ALL RIGHT, KRUSHERS. LISTEN UP!
PIKE

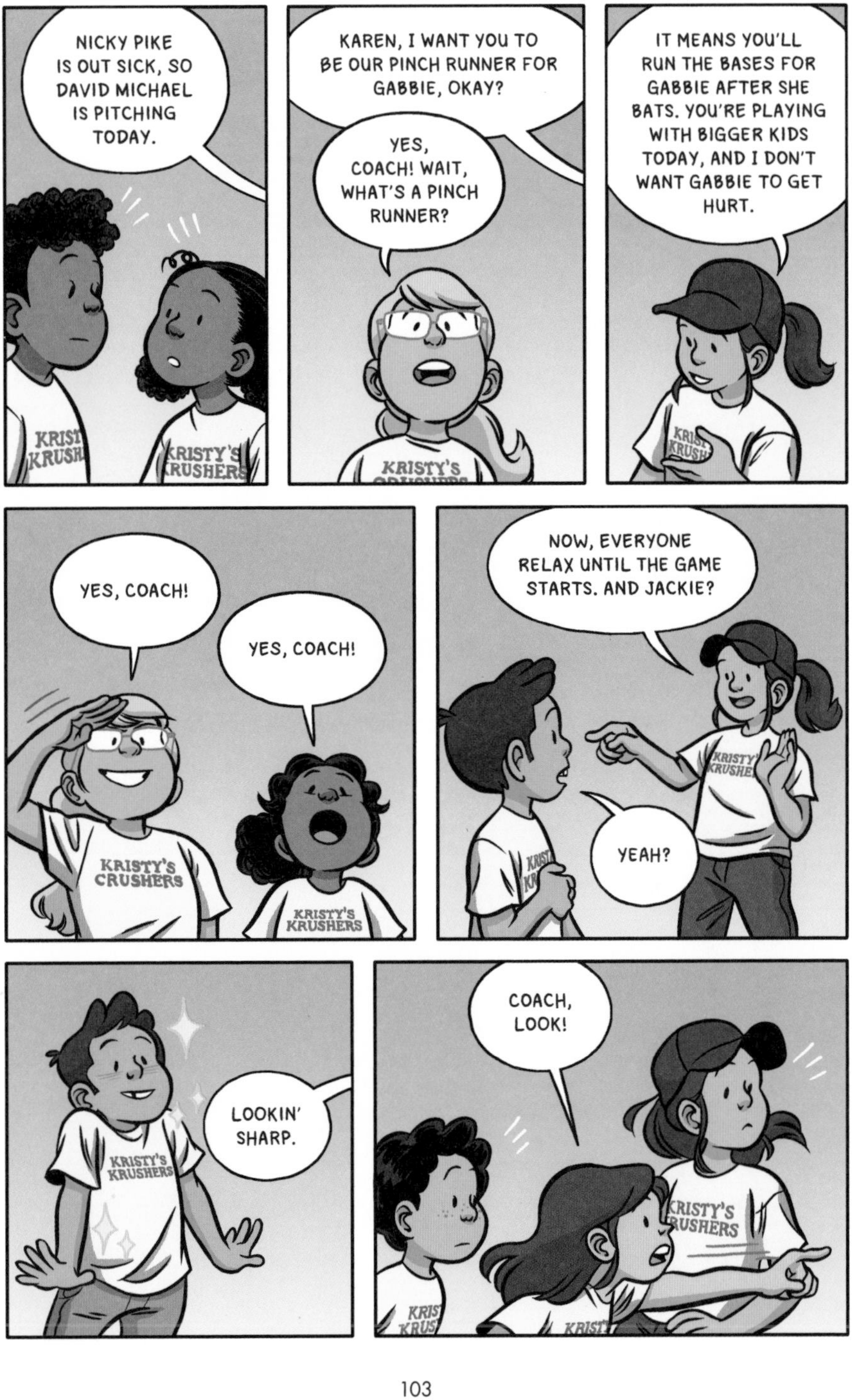

NICKY PIKE IS OUT SICK, SO DAVID MICHAEL IS PITCHING TODAY.
KRISTY'S KRUSHERS
KAREN, I WANT YOU TO BE OUR PINCH RUNNER FOR GABBIE, OKAY?
YES, COACH! WAIT, WHAT'S A PINCH RUNNER?
KRISTY'S
IT MEANS YOU'LL RUN THE BASES FOR GABBIE AFTER SHE BATS. YOU'RE PLAYING WITH BIGGER KIDS TODAY, AND I DON'T WANT GABBIE TO GET HURT.
YES, COACH!
YES, COACH!
KRISTY'S CRUSHERS
KRISTY'S KRUSHERS
NOW, EVERYONE RELAX UNTIL THE GAME STARTS. AND JACKIE?
YEAH?
KRISTY'S KRUSHERS
LOOKIN' SHARP.
COACH, LOOK!
KRISTY'S KRUSHERS

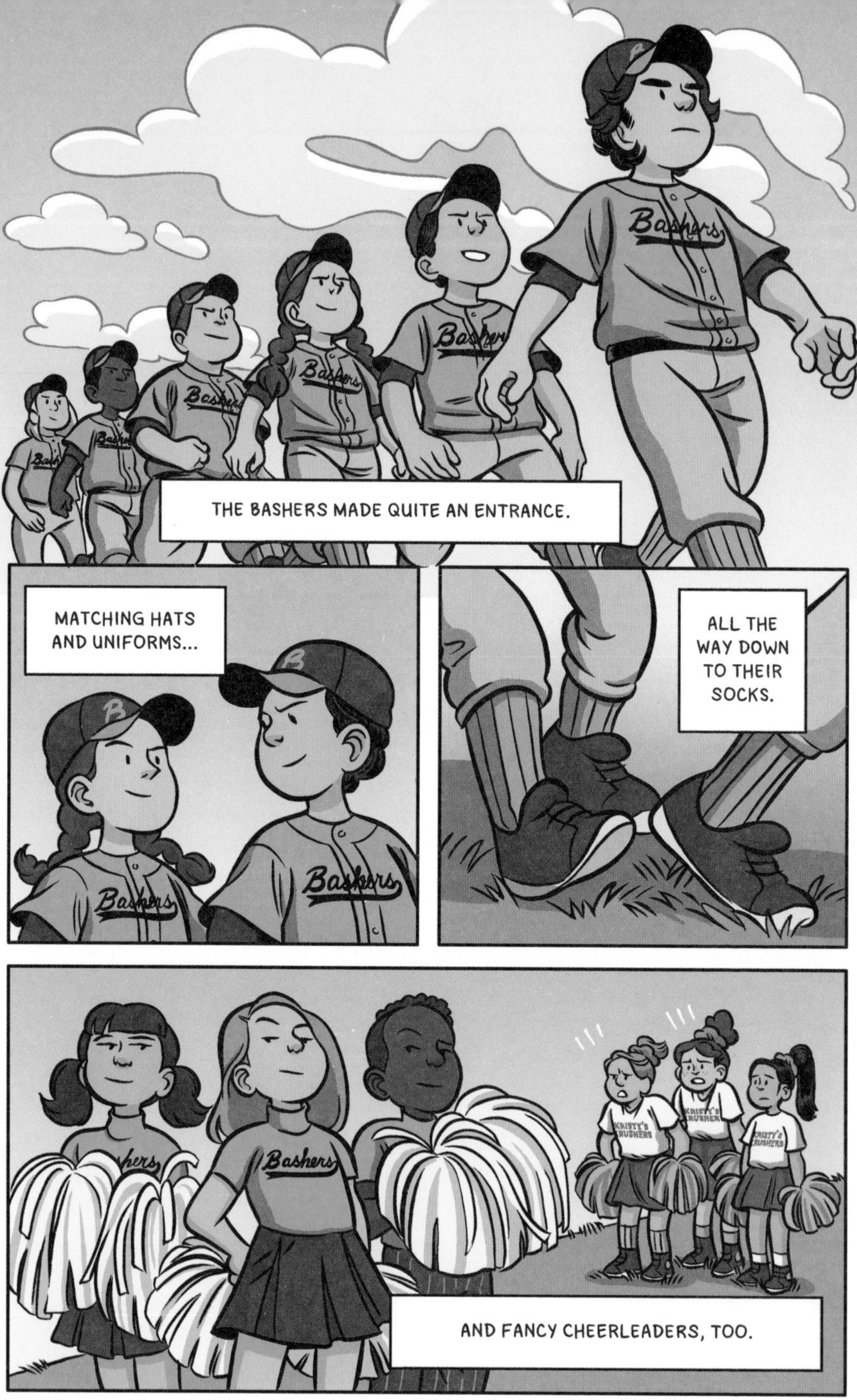

Bashers
THE BASHERS MADE QUITE AN ENTRANCE.
MATCHING HATS AND UNIFORMS...
Bashers
ALL THE WAY DOWN TO THEIR SOCKS.
Bashers
KRISTY'S KRUSHERS
AND FANCY CHEERLEADERS, TOO.

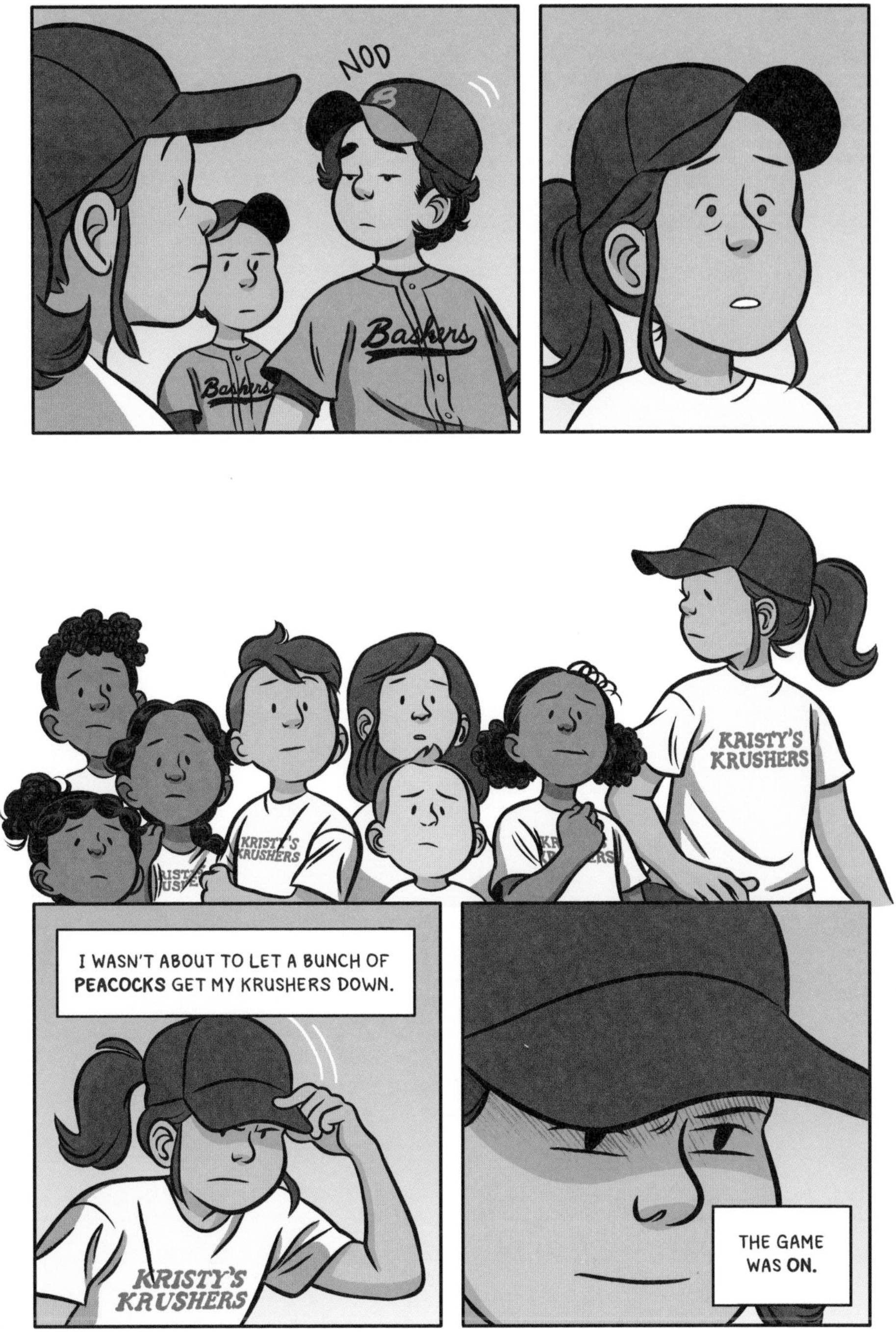
NOD
Bashers
Bashers
Bashers
KRISTY'S KRUSHERS
KRISTY'S KRUSHERS
I WASN'T ABOUT TO LET A BUNCH OF **PEACOCKS** GET MY KRUSHERS DOWN.
KRISTY'S KRUSHERS
THE GAME WAS **ON.**

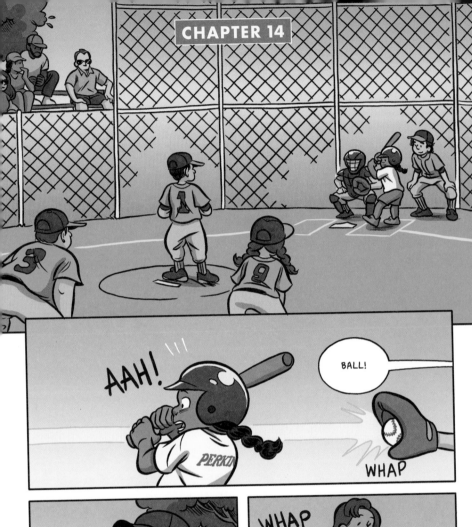

AAH!

BALL!

WHAP

WHAP

BALL!

GOOD EYE, MYRIAH!

B-A-L-L

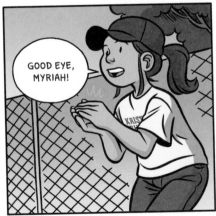

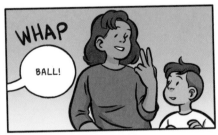

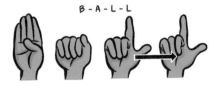

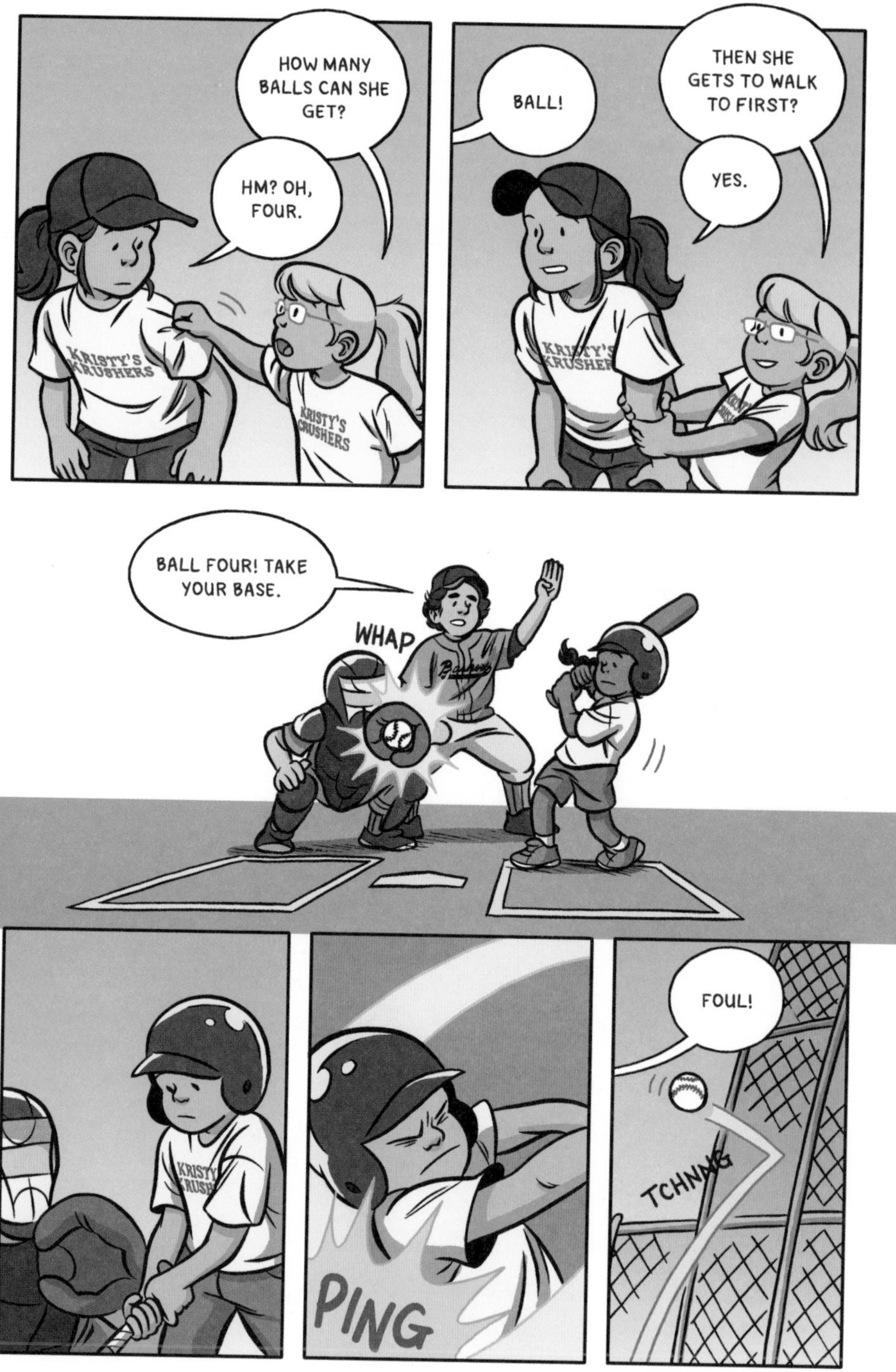
HOW MANY BALLS CAN SHE GET?
HM? OH, FOUR.
KRISTY'S KRUSHERS
KRISTY'S KRUSHERS
BALL!
THEN SHE GETS TO WALK TO FIRST?
YES.
BALL FOUR! TAKE YOUR BASE.
WHAP
PING
FOUL!
TCHNNG

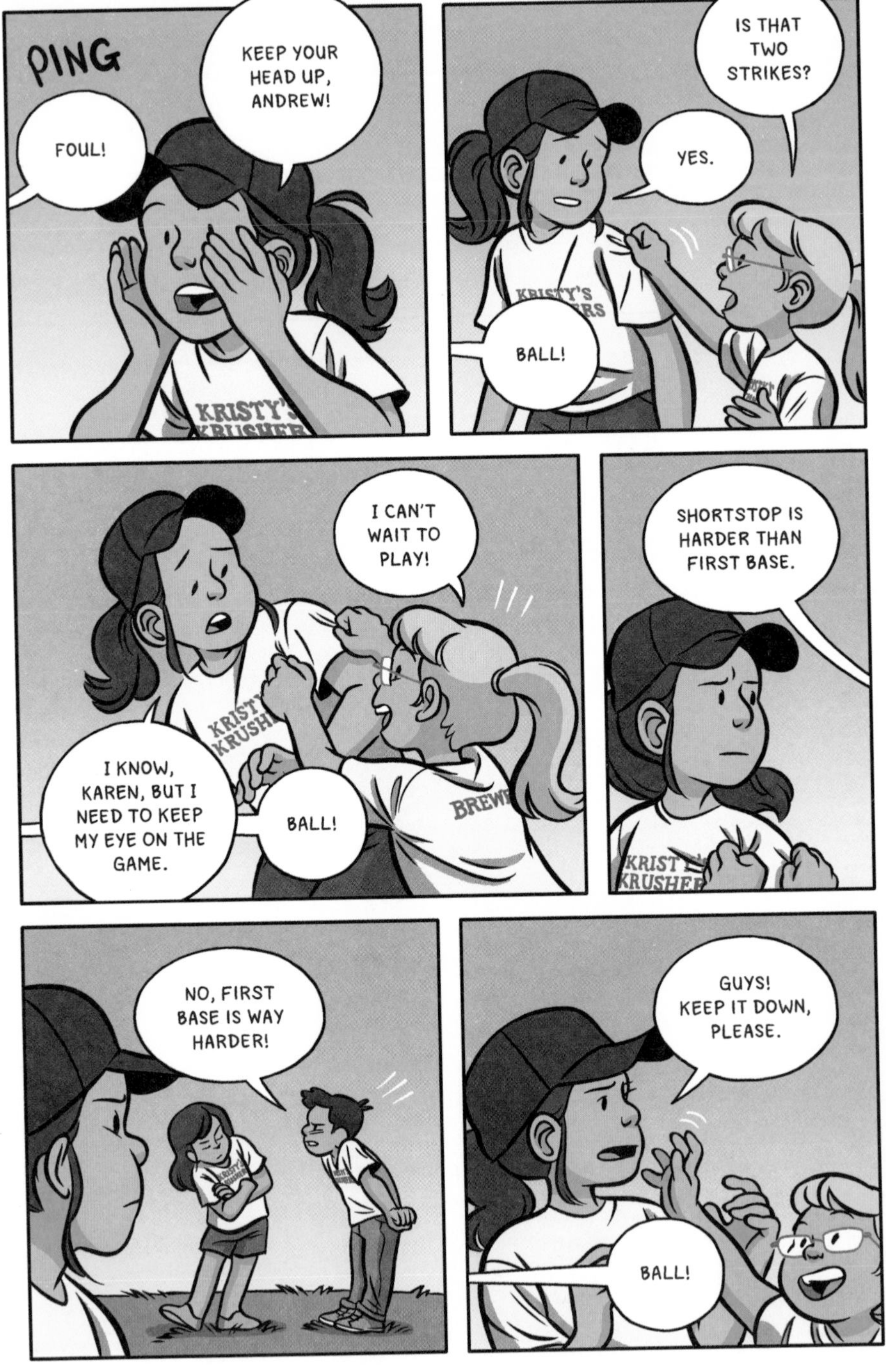
PING
FOUL!
KEEP YOUR HEAD UP, ANDREW!
KRISTY'S KRUSHERS
IS THAT TWO STRIKES?
YES.
BALL!
I CAN'T WAIT TO PLAY!
I KNOW, KAREN, BUT I NEED TO KEEP MY EYE ON THE GAME.
BALL!
SHORTSTOP IS HARDER THAN FIRST BASE.
NO, FIRST BASE IS WAY HARDER!
GUYS! KEEP IT DOWN, PLEASE.
BALL!

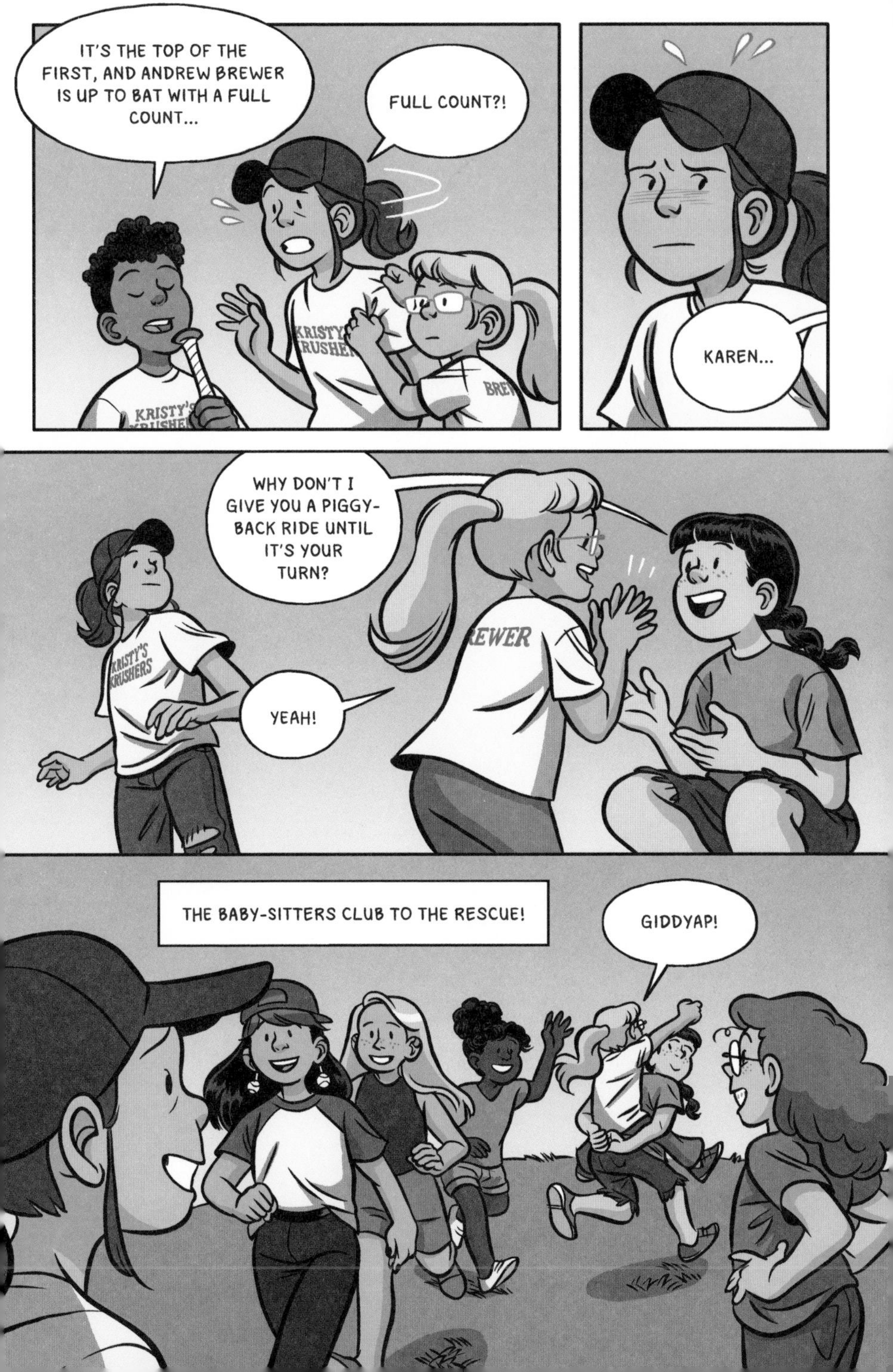
IT'S THE TOP OF THE FIRST, AND ANDREW BREWER IS UP TO BAT WITH A FULL COUNT...
FULL COUNT?!
KRISTY'S KRUSHERS
KAREN...
WHY DON'T I GIVE YOU A PIGGY-BACK RIDE UNTIL IT'S YOUR TURN?
KRISTY'S KRUSHERS
REWER
YEAH!
THE BABY-SITTERS CLUB TO THE RESCUE!
GIDDYAP!

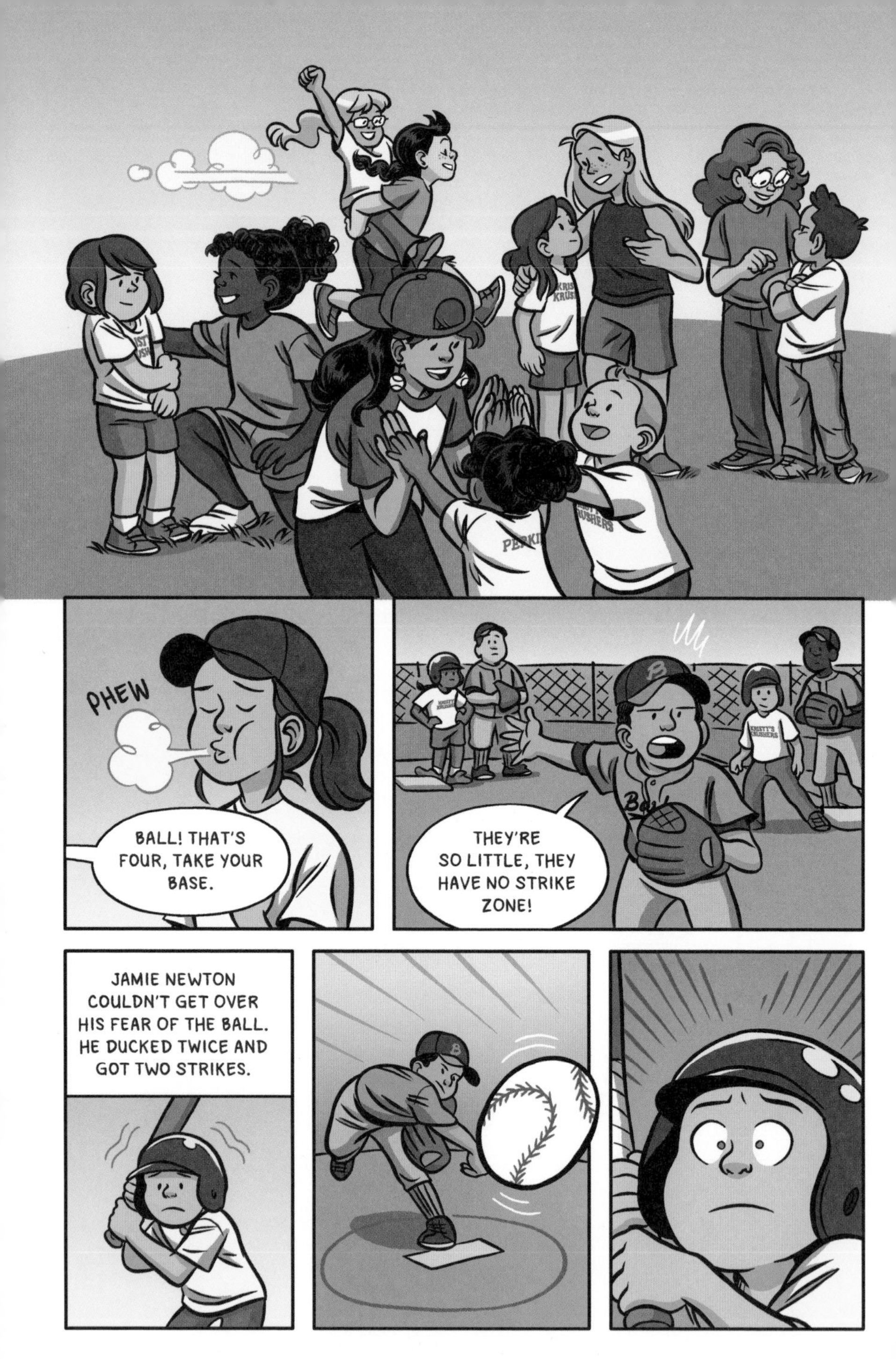
PHEW
BALL! THAT'S FOUR, TAKE YOUR BASE.
THEY'RE SO LITTLE, THEY HAVE NO STRIKE ZONE!
JAMIE NEWTON COULDN'T GET OVER HIS FEAR OF THE BALL. HE DUCKED TWICE AND GOT TWO STRIKES.

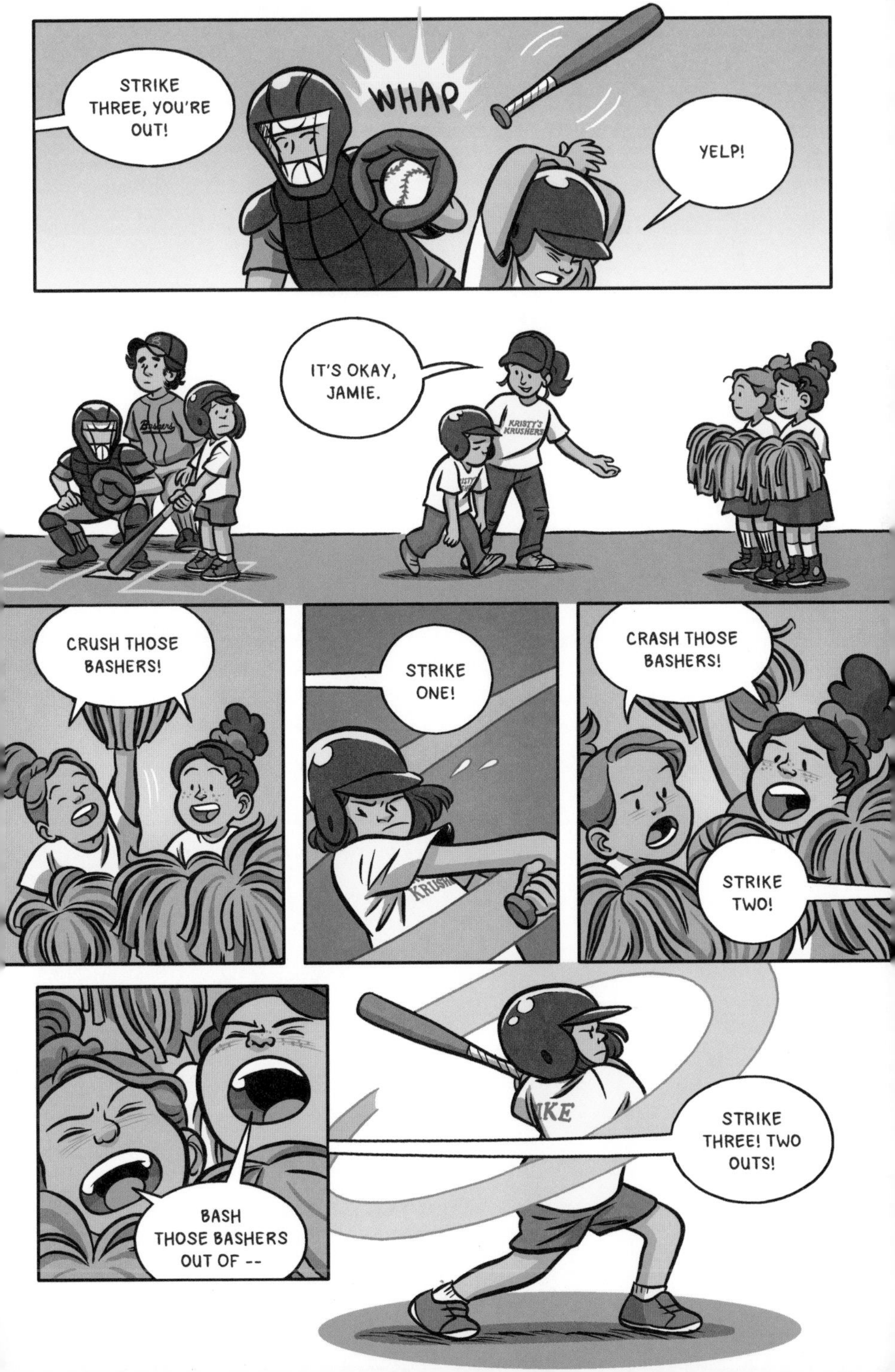
STRIKE THREE, YOU'RE OUT!
WHAP
YELP!
IT'S OKAY, JAMIE.
KRISTY'S KRUSHERS
CRUSH THOSE BASHERS!
STRIKE ONE!
CRASH THOSE BASHERS!
STRIKE TWO!
BASH THOSE BASHERS OUT OF --
STRIKE THREE! TWO OUTS!

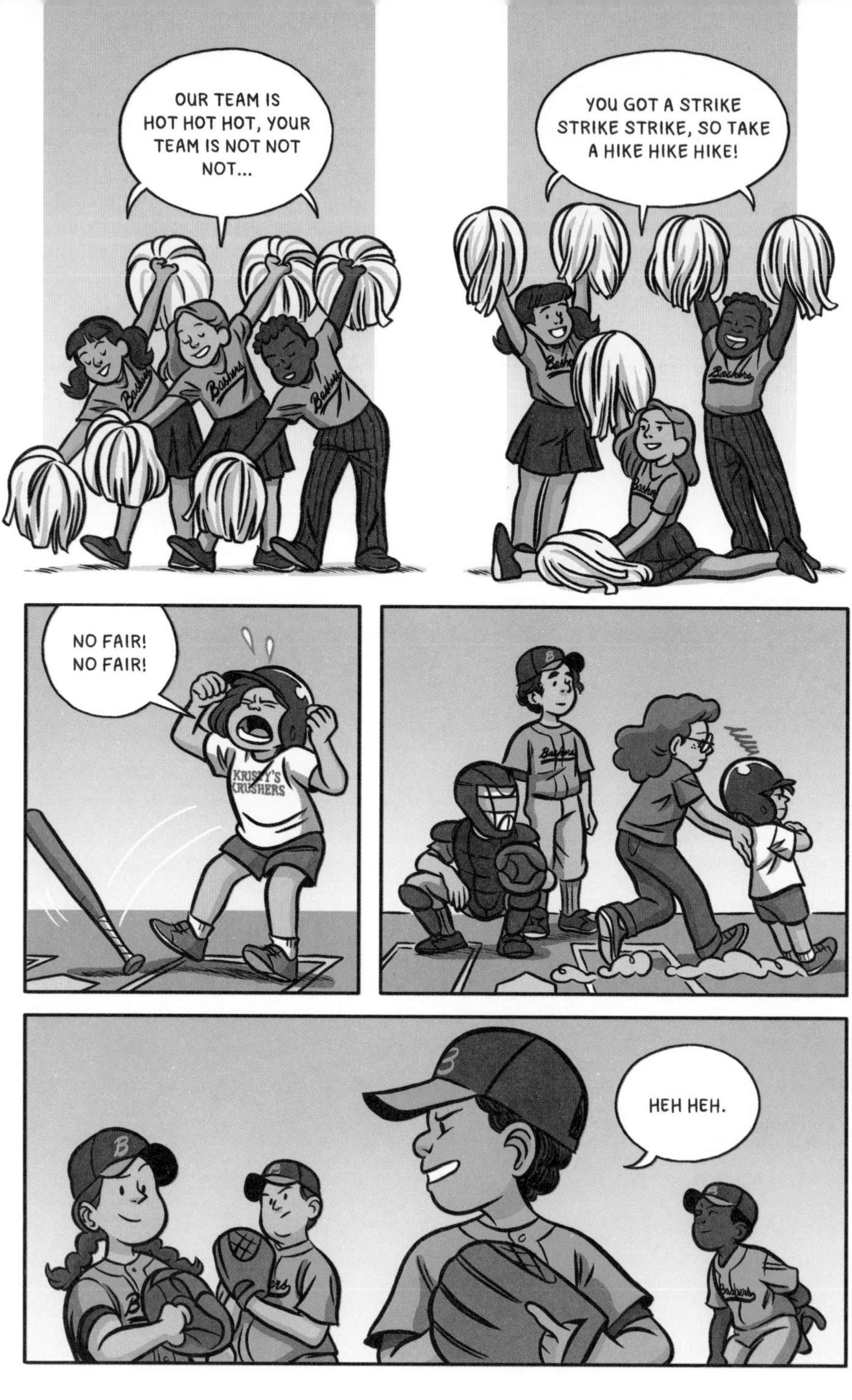
OUR TEAM IS HOT HOT HOT, YOUR TEAM IS NOT NOT NOT...
YOU GOT A STRIKE STRIKE STRIKE, SO TAKE A HIKE HIKE HIKE!
NO FAIR! NO FAIR!
HEH HEH.

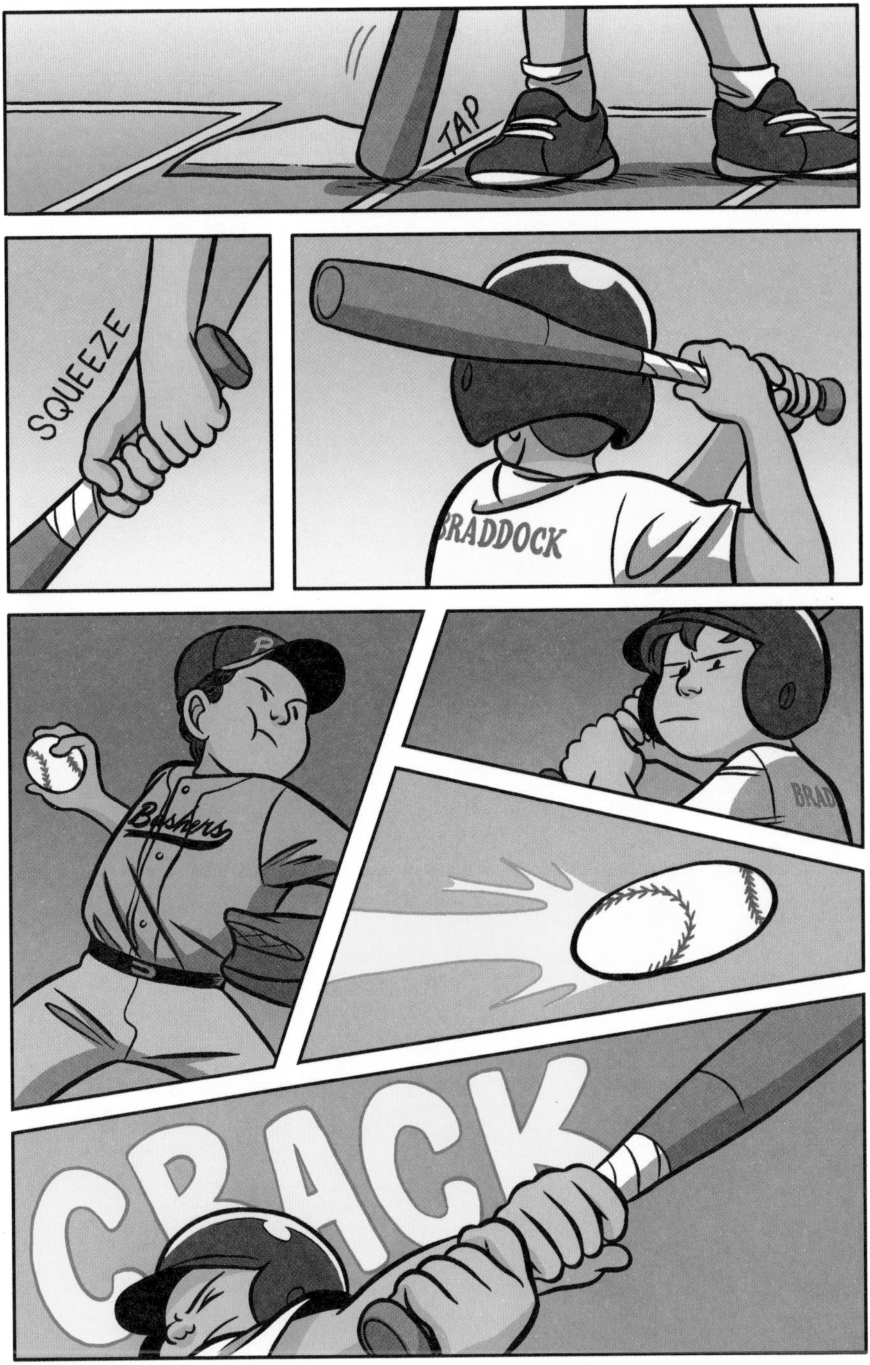
TAP
SQUEEZE
BRADDOCK
Bashers
BRAD
CRACK

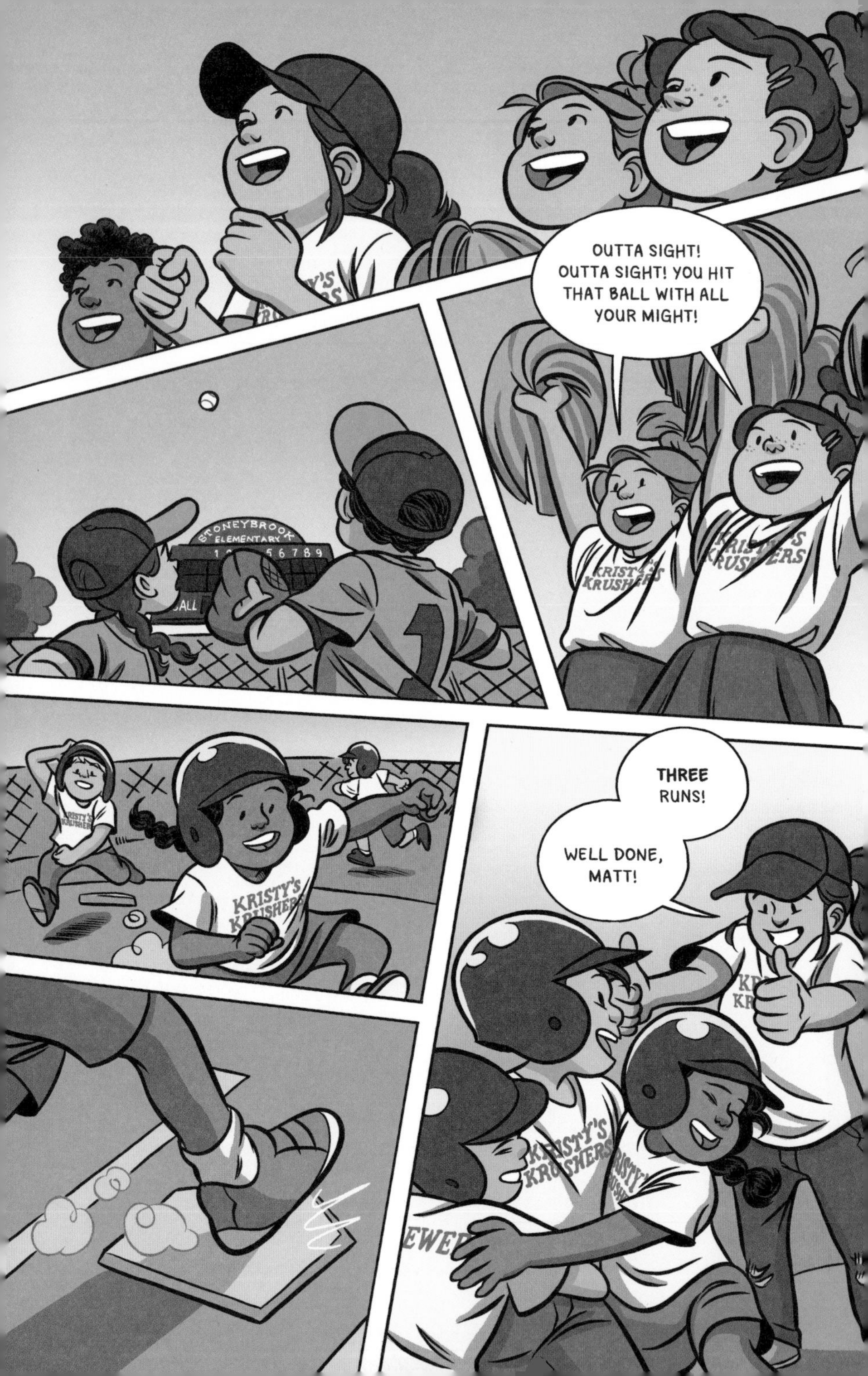
OUTTA SIGHT! OUTTA SIGHT! YOU HIT THAT BALL WITH ALL YOUR MIGHT!
STONEYBROOK ELEMENTARY
KRISTY'S KRUSHERS
THREE RUNS!
WELL DONE, MATT!

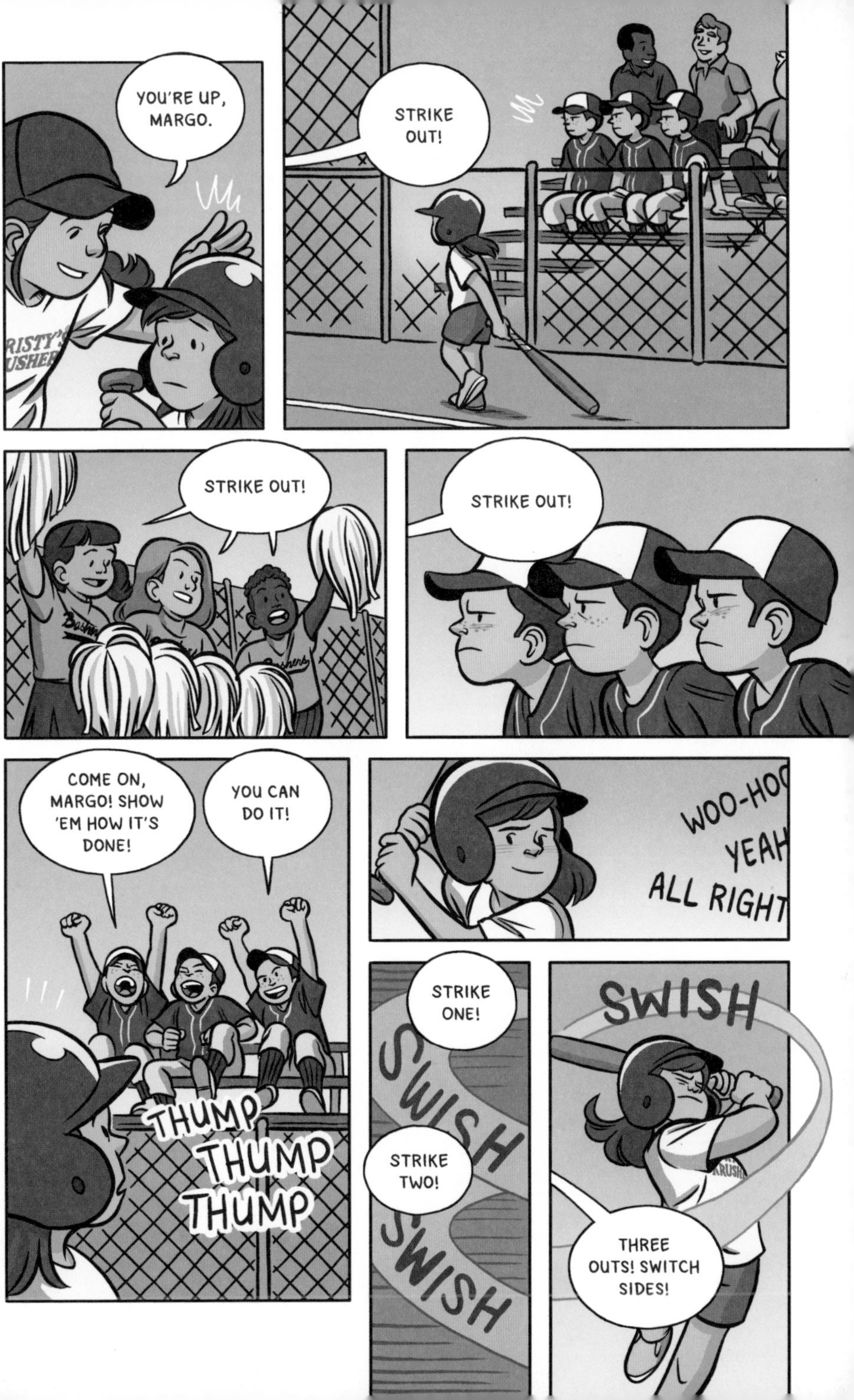
YOU'RE UP, MARGO.
STRIKE OUT!
STRIKE OUT!
STRIKE OUT!
COME ON, MARGO! SHOW 'EM HOW IT'S DONE!
YOU CAN DO IT!
THUMP
THUMP
THUMP
WOO-HO
YEAH
ALL RIGHT
STRIKE ONE!
SWISH
STRIKE TWO!
SWISH
SWISH
THREE OUTS! SWITCH SIDES!

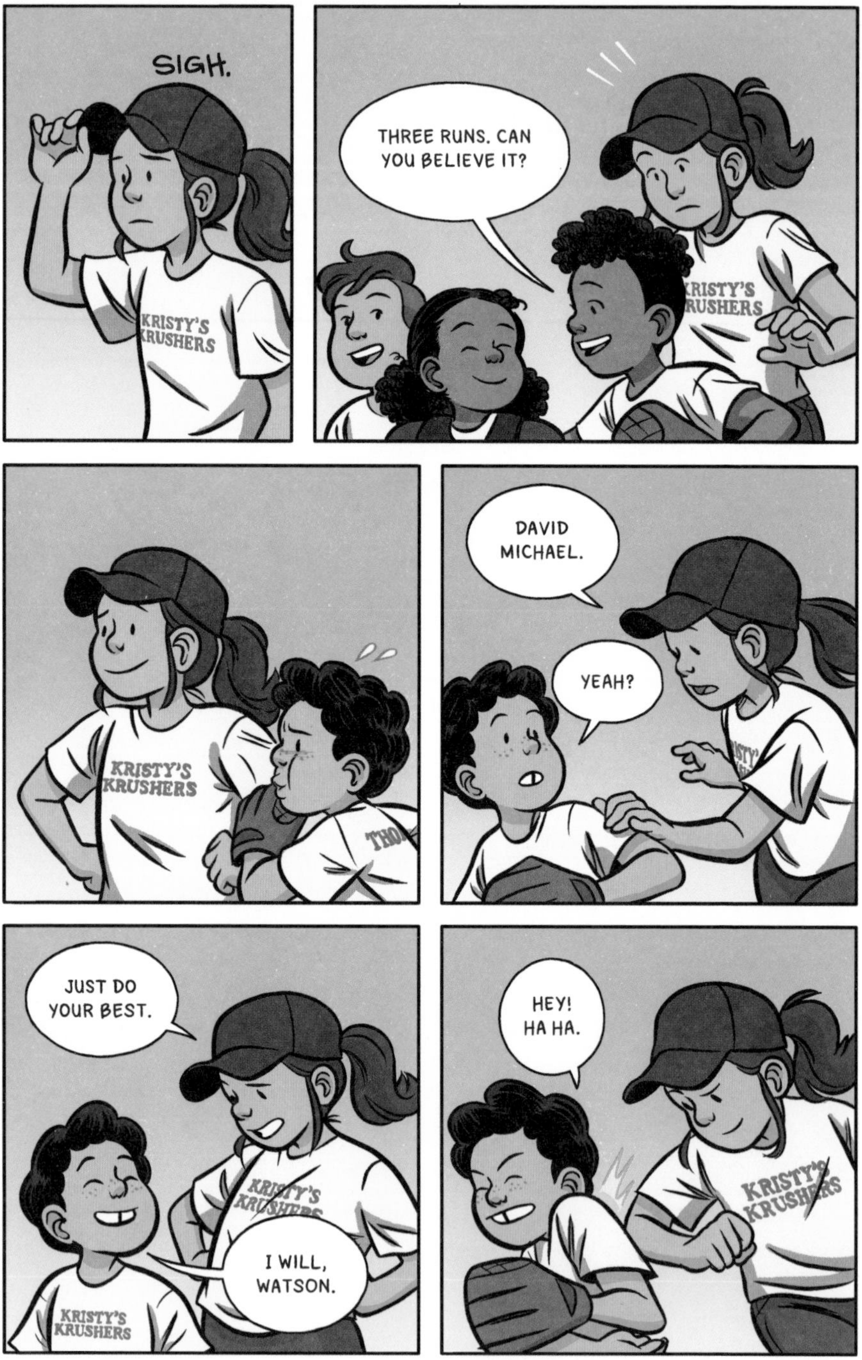
SIGH.
THREE RUNS. CAN YOU BELIEVE IT?
KRISTY'S KRUSHERS
DAVID MICHAEL.
YEAH?
JUST DO YOUR BEST.
I WILL, WATSON.
HEY! HA HA.

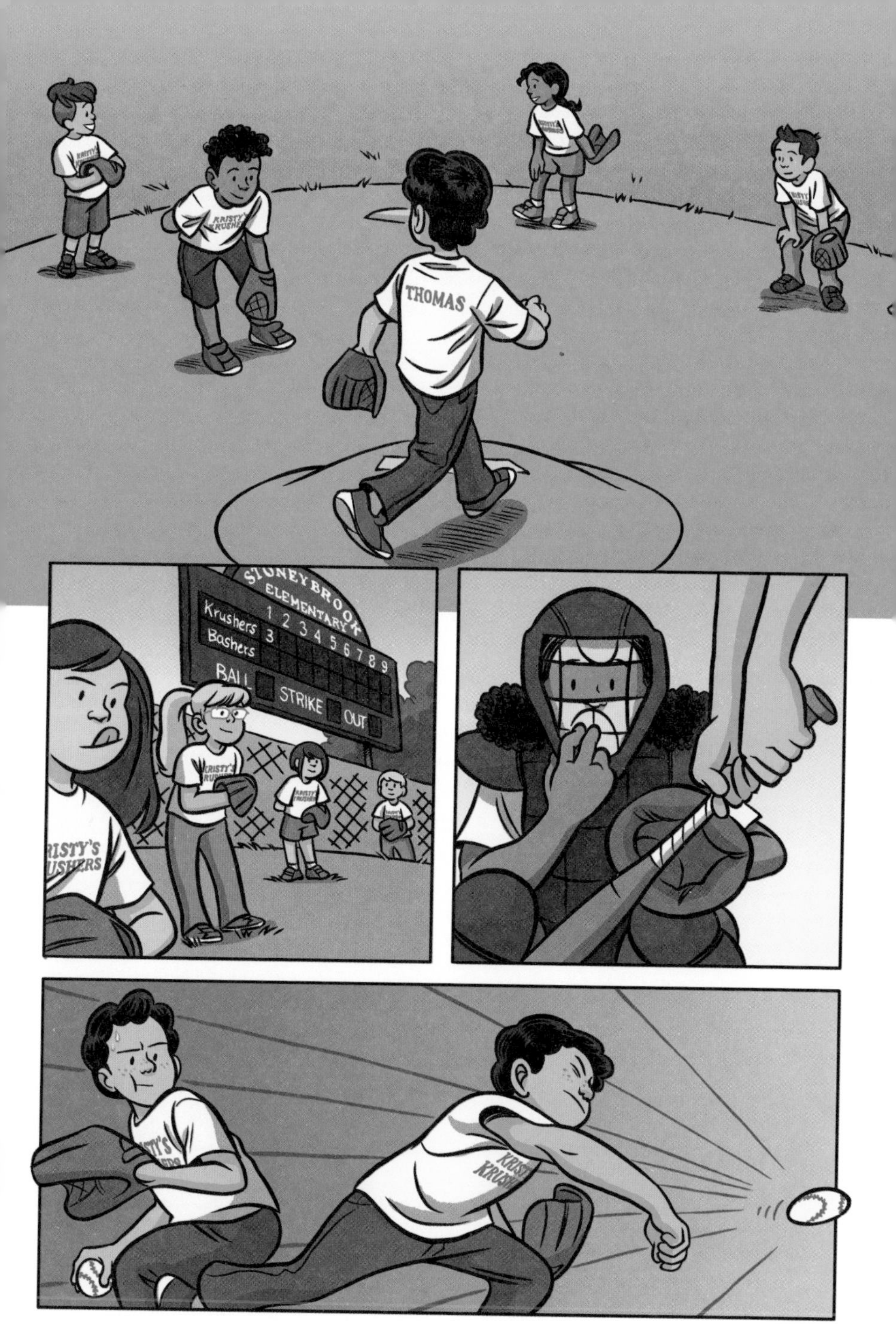
THOMAS
KRISTY'S KRUSHERS
STONEYBROOK ELEMENTARY
1 2 3 4 5 6 7 8 9
Krushers 3
Bashers
BALL
STRIKE
OUT

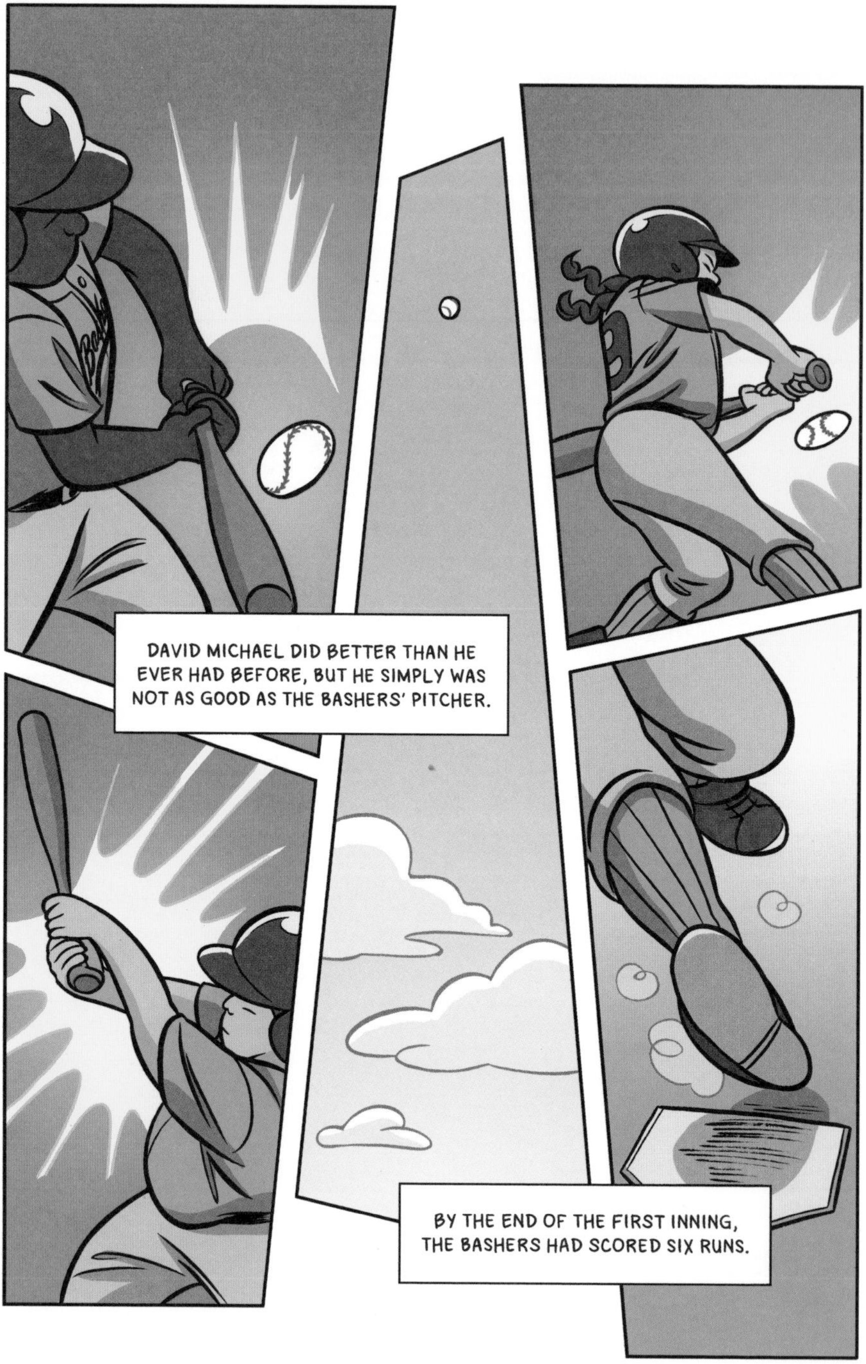
DAVID MICHAEL DID BETTER THAN HE EVER HAD BEFORE, BUT HE SIMPLY WAS NOT AS GOOD AS THE BASHERS' PITCHER.
BY THE END OF THE FIRST INNING, THE BASHERS HAD SCORED SIX RUNS.

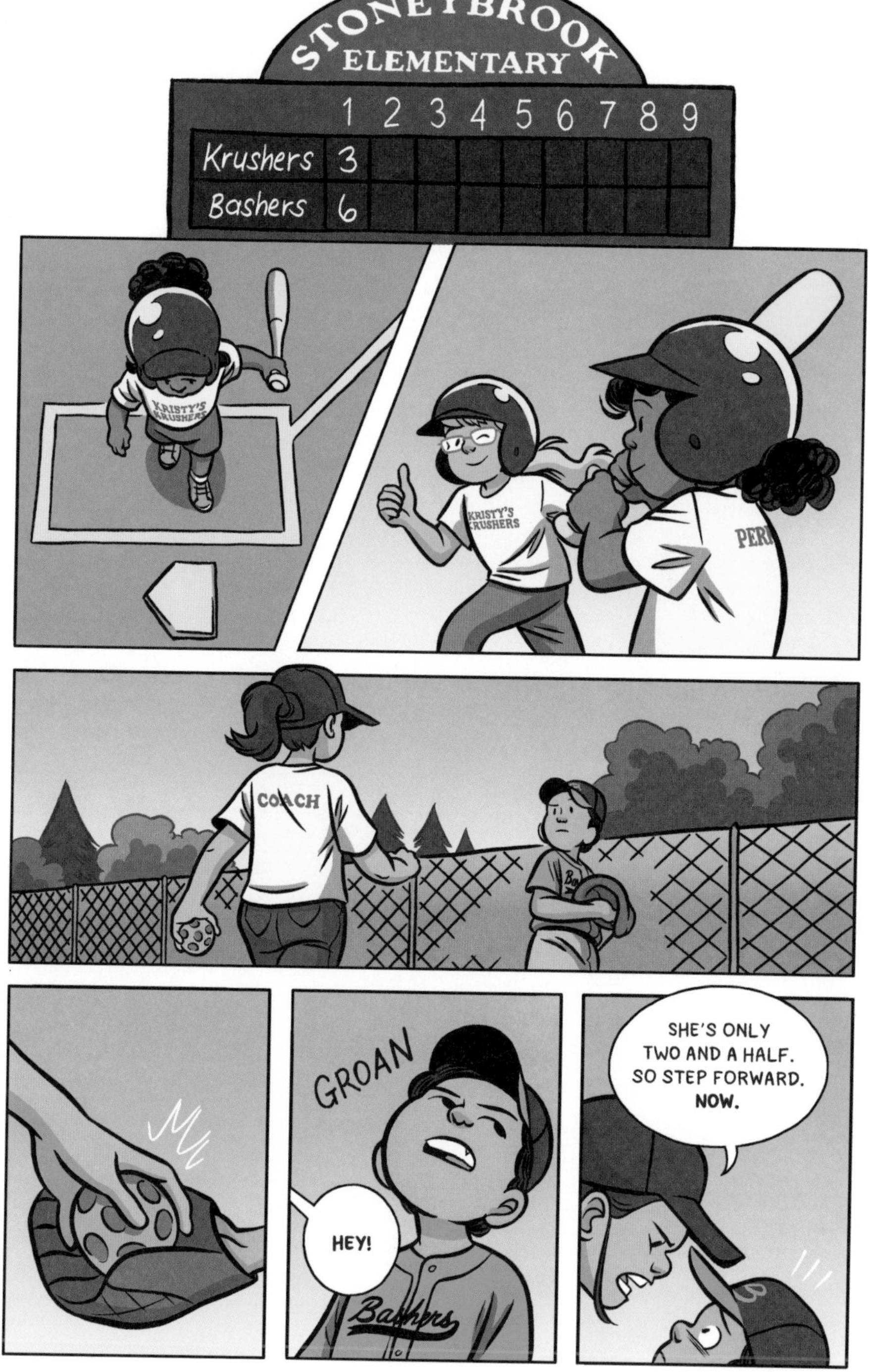
STONEYBROOK
ELEMENTARY
1 2 3 4 5 6 7 8 9
Krushers 3
Bashers 6
KRISTY'S KRUSHERS
KRISTY'S KRUSHERS
COACH
GROAN
HEY!
Bashers
SHE'S ONLY TWO AND A HALF. SO STEP FORWARD. **NOW.**

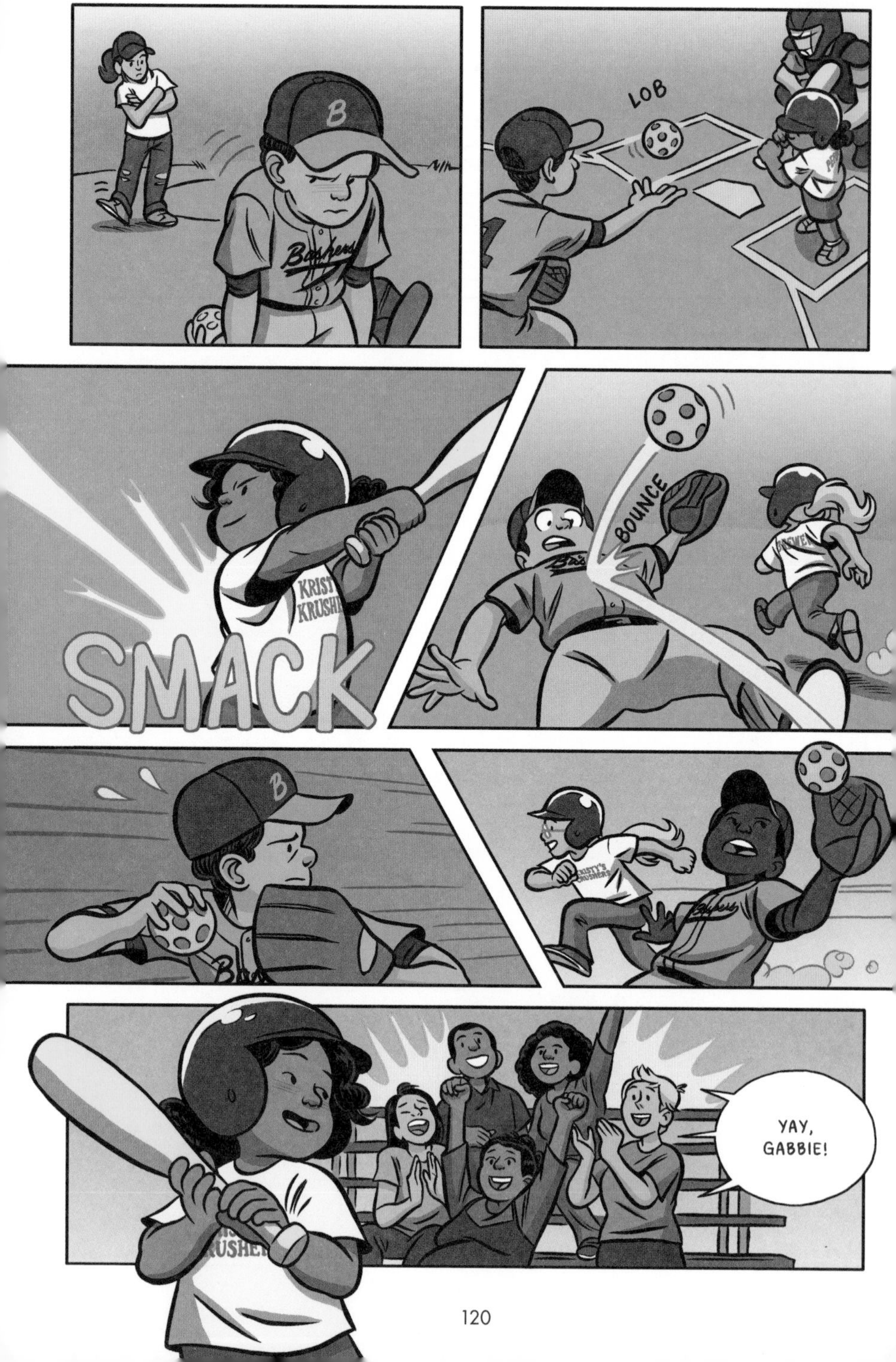
LOB
SMACK
BOUNCE
YAY, GABBIE!

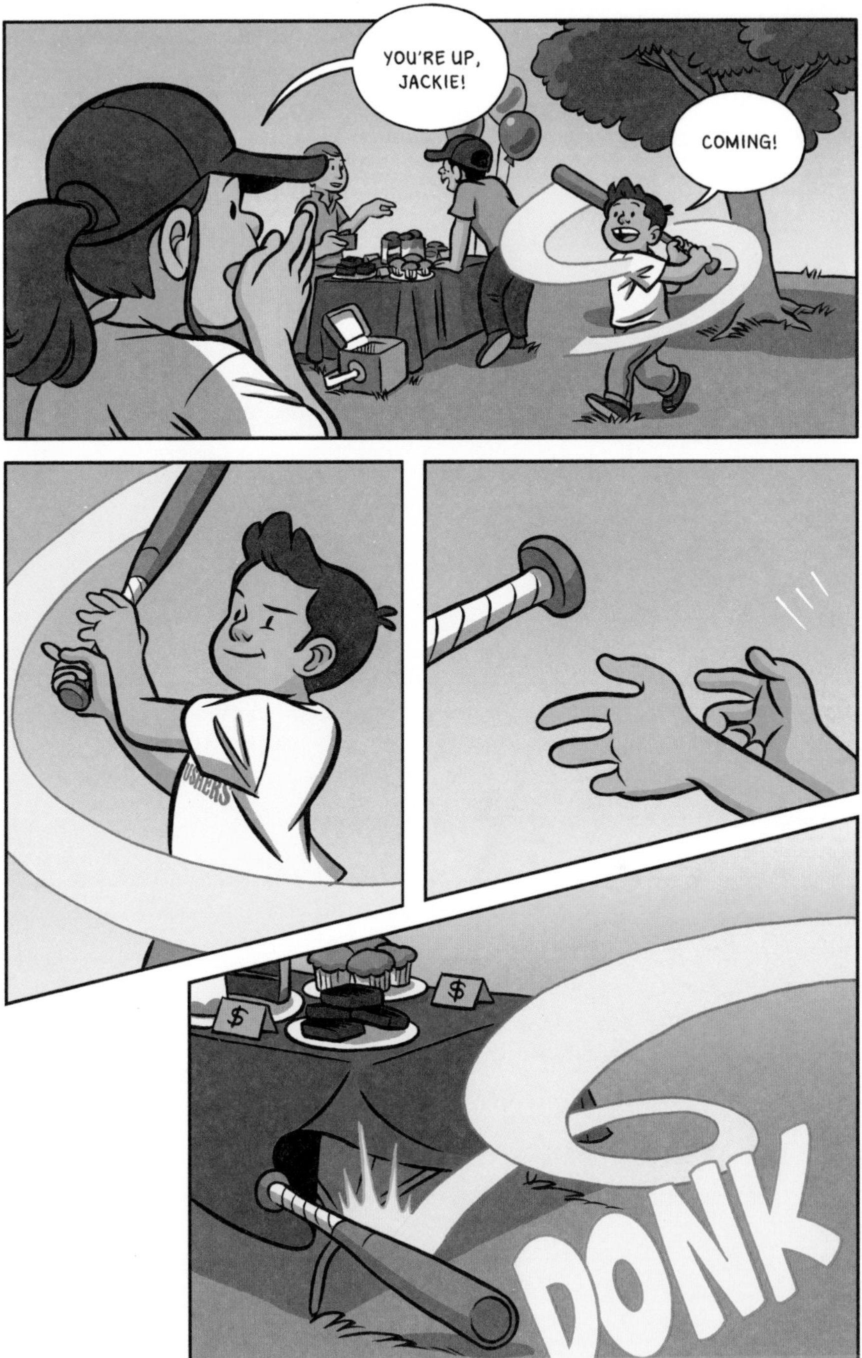
YOU'RE UP, JACKIE!
COMING!
DONK

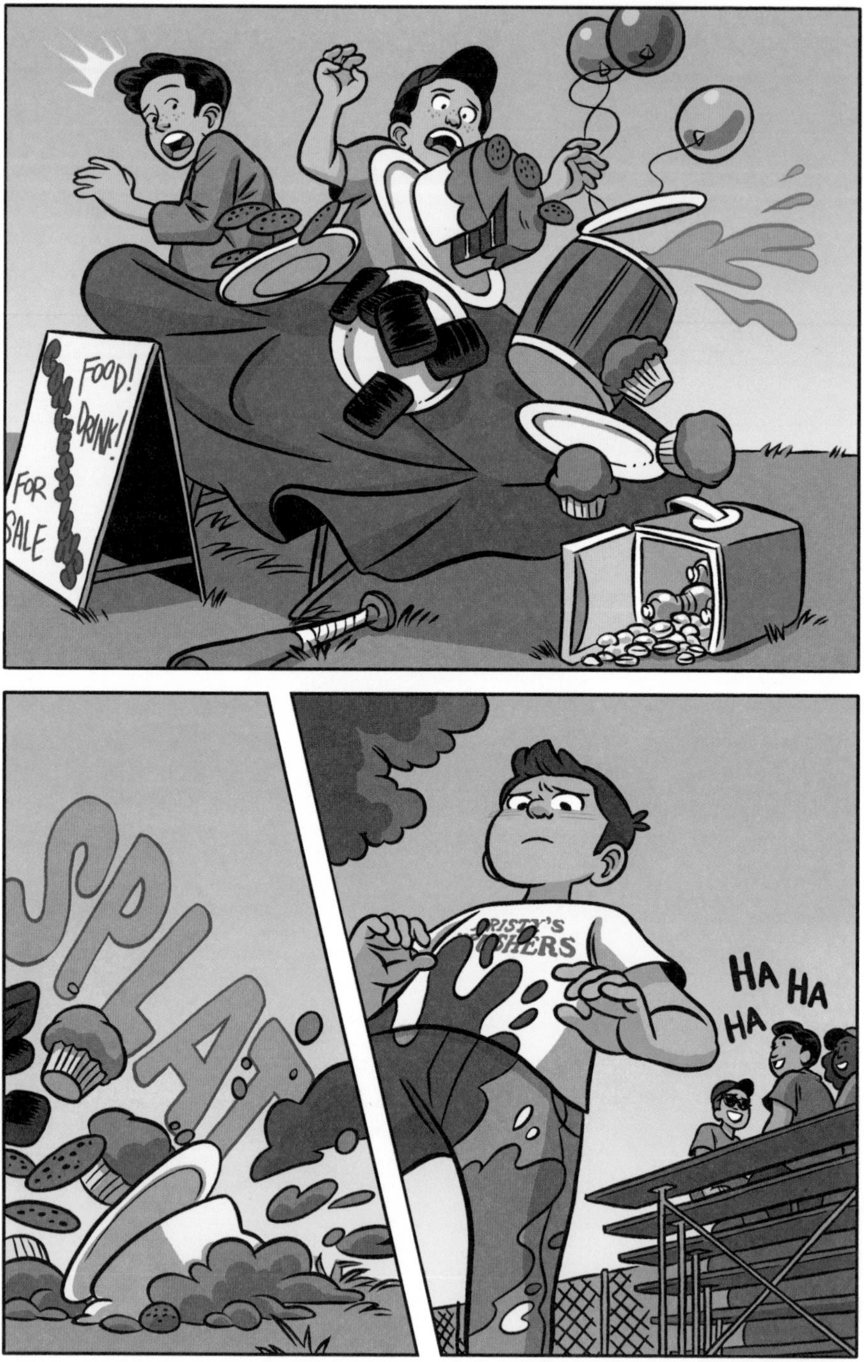
CONCESSIONS
FOOD!
DRINK!
FOR SALE
SPLAT
HA HA
HA

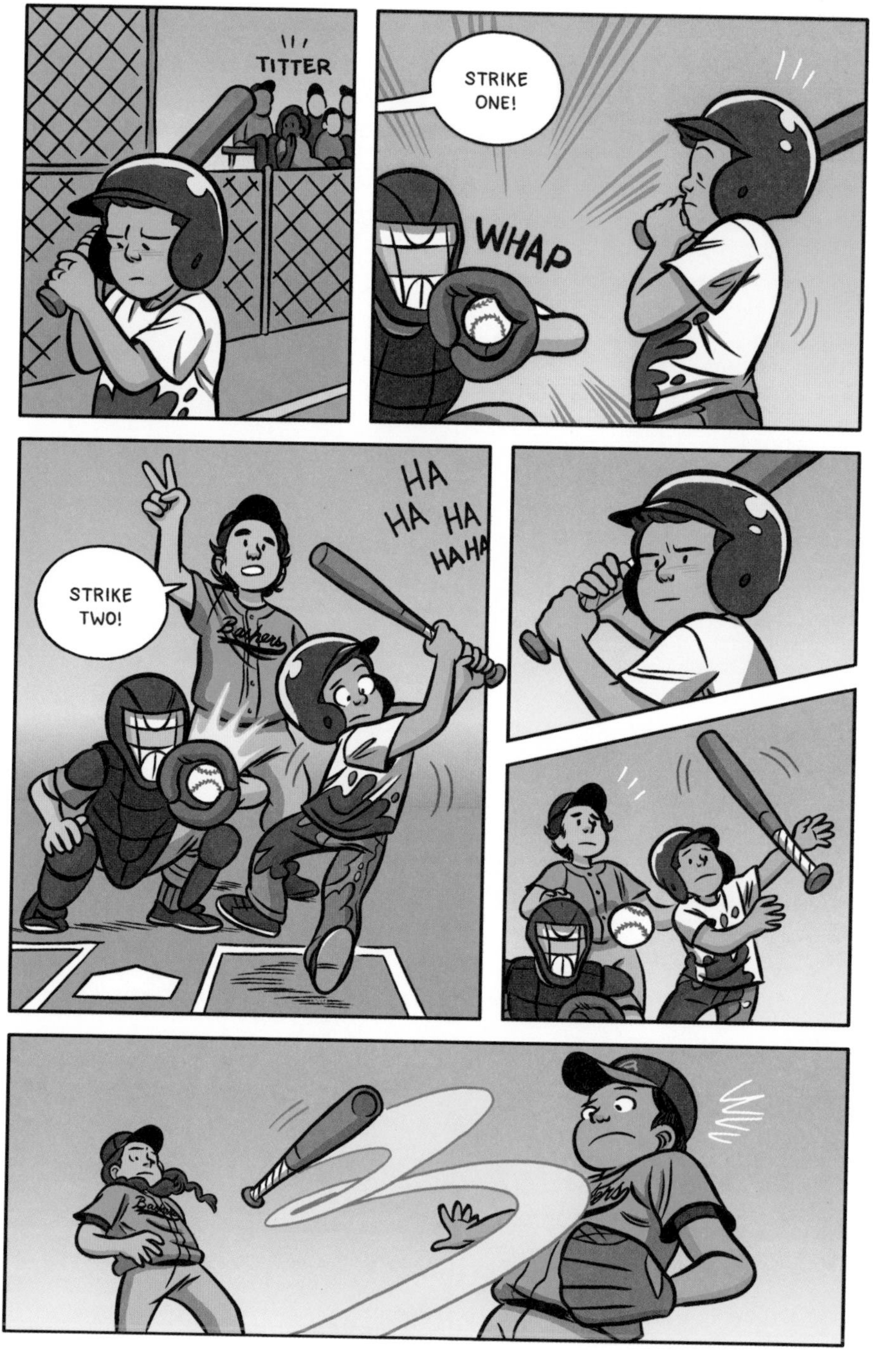
TITTER
STRIKE ONE!
WHAP
STRIKE TWO!
HA HA HA HAHA

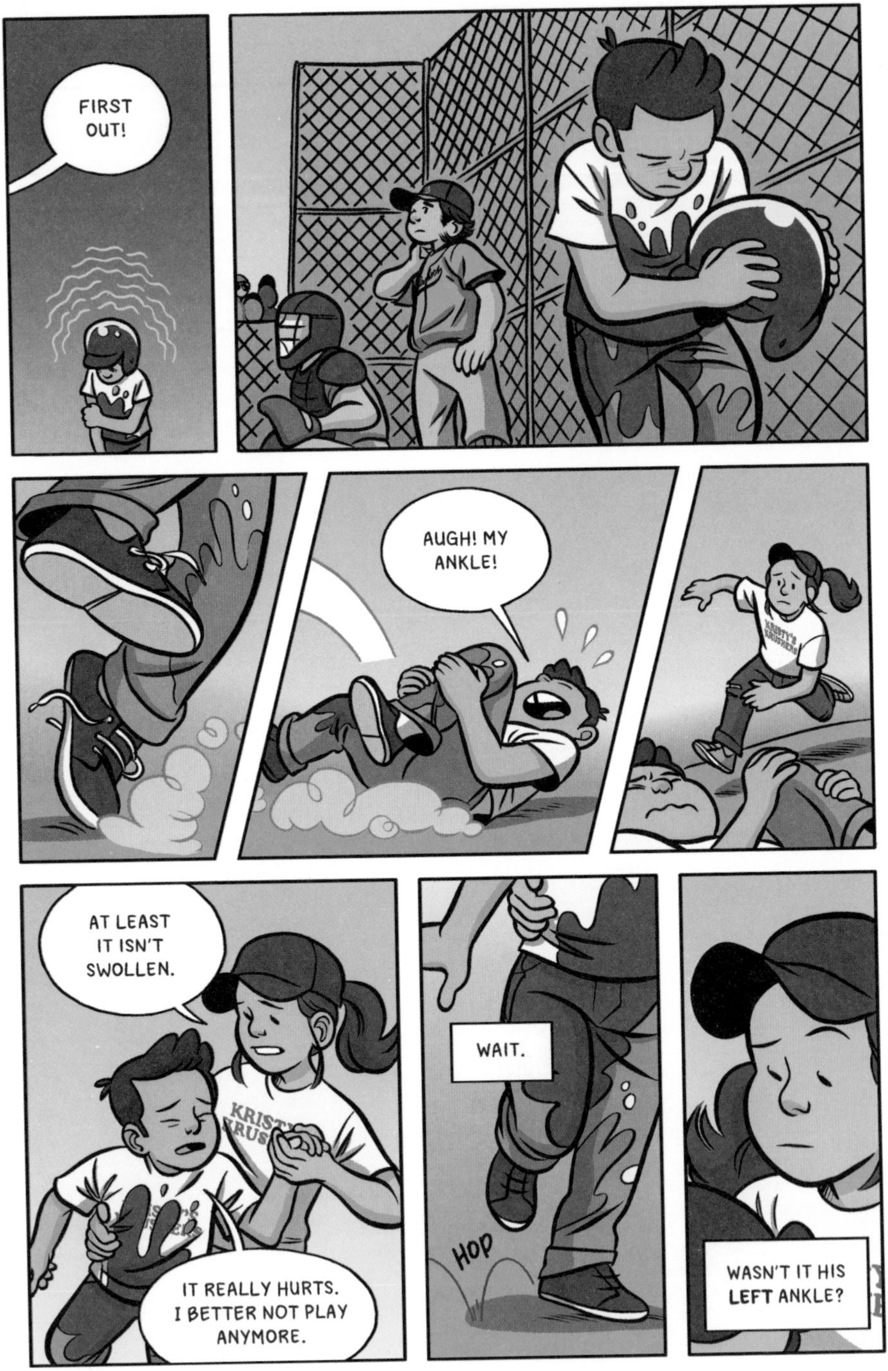
FIRST OUT!
AUGH! MY ANKLE!
KRISTY'S KRUSHERS
AT LEAST IT ISN'T SWOLLEN.
IT REALLY HURTS. I BETTER NOT PLAY ANYMORE.
WAIT.
HOP
WASN'T IT HIS **LEFT** ANKLE?

CHAPTER 15

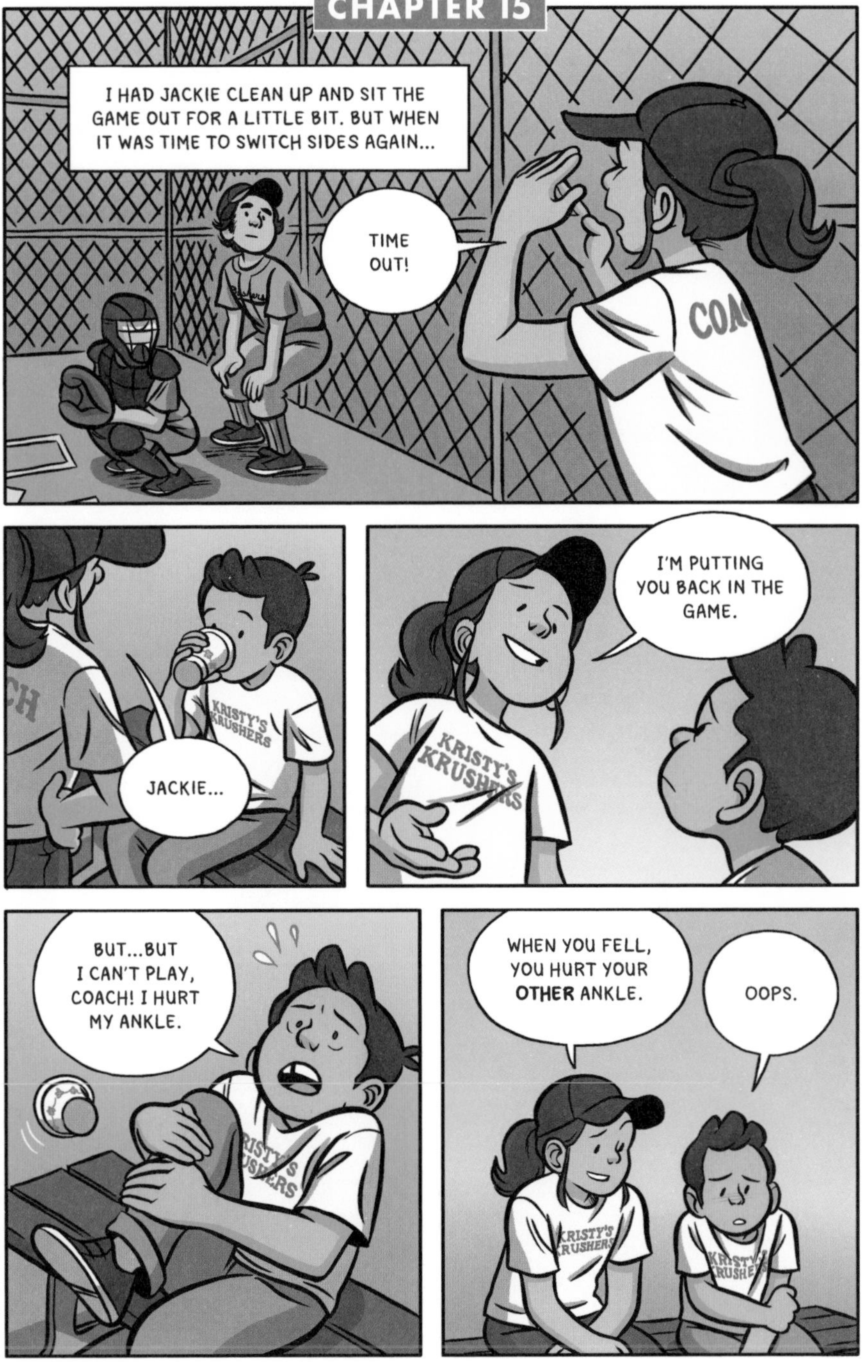

I HAD JACKIE CLEAN UP AND SIT THE GAME OUT FOR A LITTLE BIT. BUT WHEN IT WAS TIME TO SWITCH SIDES AGAIN...
TIME OUT!
COAC
CH
KRISTY'S KRUSHERS
JACKIE...
I'M PUTTING YOU BACK IN THE GAME.
KRISTY'S KRUSHERS
BUT...BUT I CAN'T PLAY, COACH! I HURT MY ANKLE.
WHEN YOU FELL, YOU HURT YOUR **OTHER** ANKLE.
OOPS.
KRISTY'S KRUSHERS

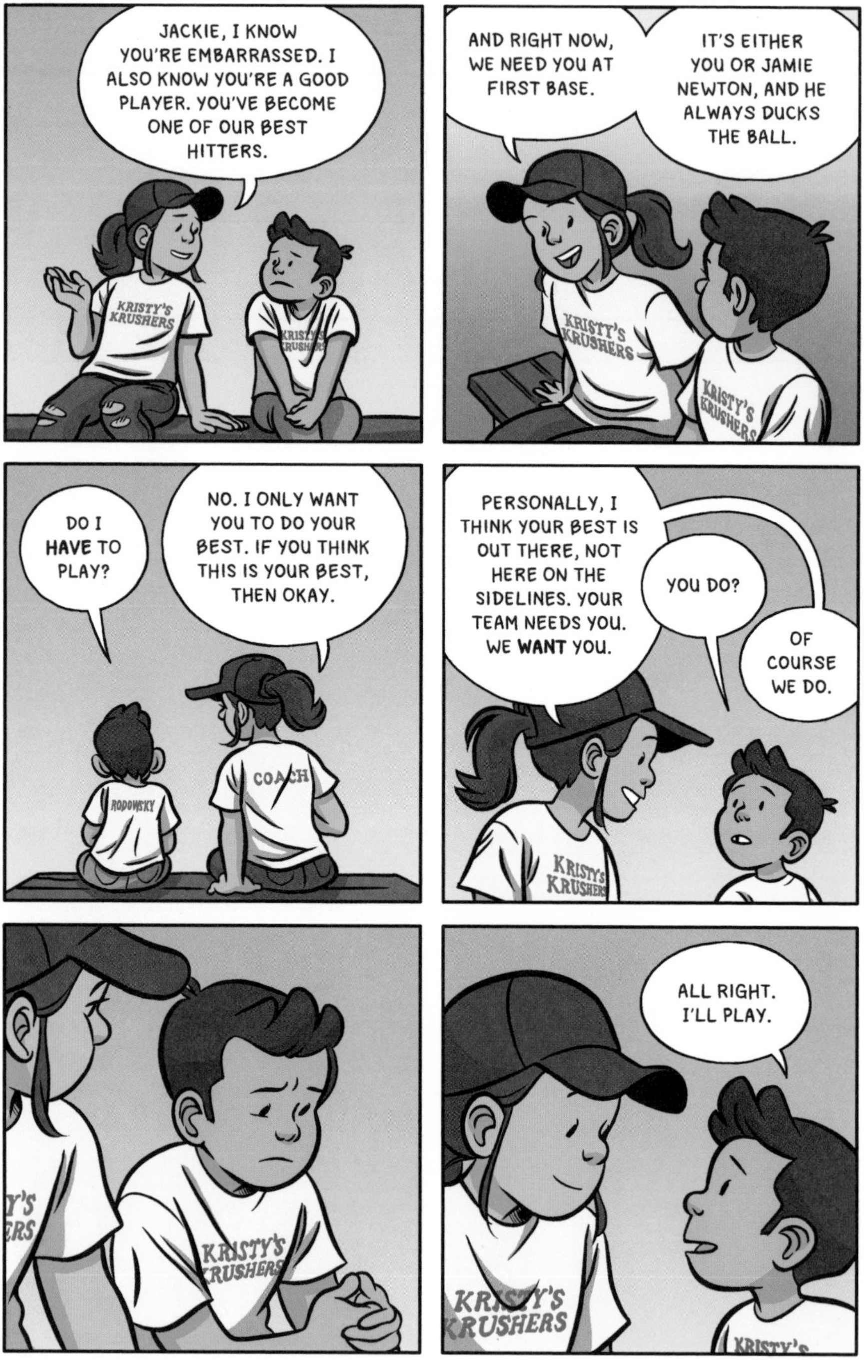
JACKIE, I KNOW YOU'RE EMBARRASSED. I ALSO KNOW YOU'RE A GOOD PLAYER. YOU'VE BECOME ONE OF OUR BEST HITTERS.
KRISTY'S KRUSHERS
AND RIGHT NOW, WE NEED YOU AT FIRST BASE.
IT'S EITHER YOU OR JAMIE NEWTON, AND HE ALWAYS DUCKS THE BALL.
KRISTY'S KRUSHERS
DO I **HAVE** TO PLAY?
NO. I ONLY WANT YOU TO DO YOUR BEST. IF YOU THINK THIS IS YOUR BEST, THEN OKAY.
RODOWSKY
COACH
PERSONALLY, I THINK YOUR BEST IS OUT THERE, NOT HERE ON THE SIDELINES. YOUR TEAM NEEDS YOU. WE **WANT** YOU.
YOU DO?
OF COURSE WE DO.
KRISTY'S KRUSHERS
KRISTY'S KRUSHERS
ALL RIGHT. I'LL PLAY.
KRISTY'S KRUSHERS

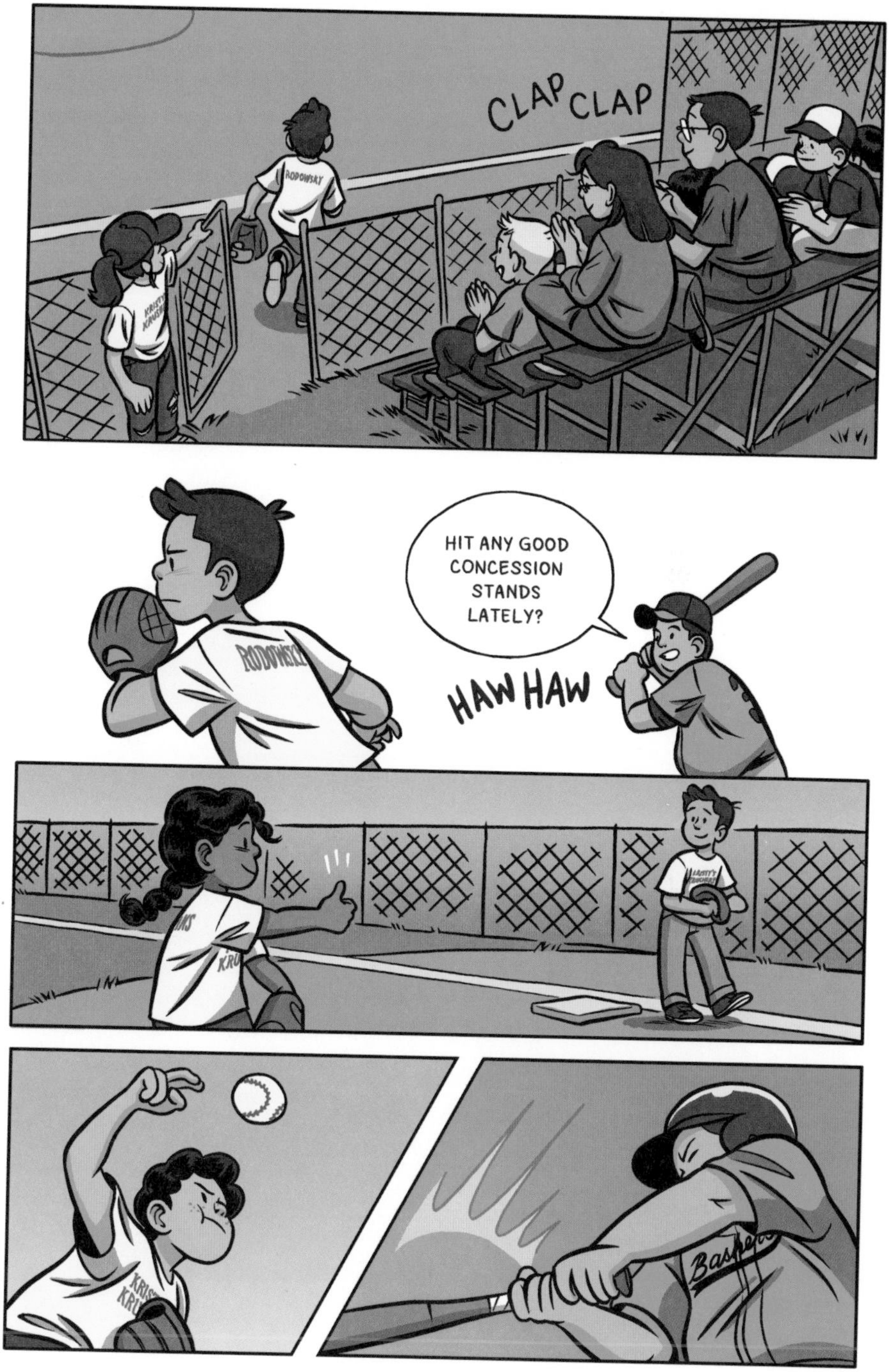
CLAP CLAP
HIT ANY GOOD CONCESSION STANDS LATELY?
HAW HAW

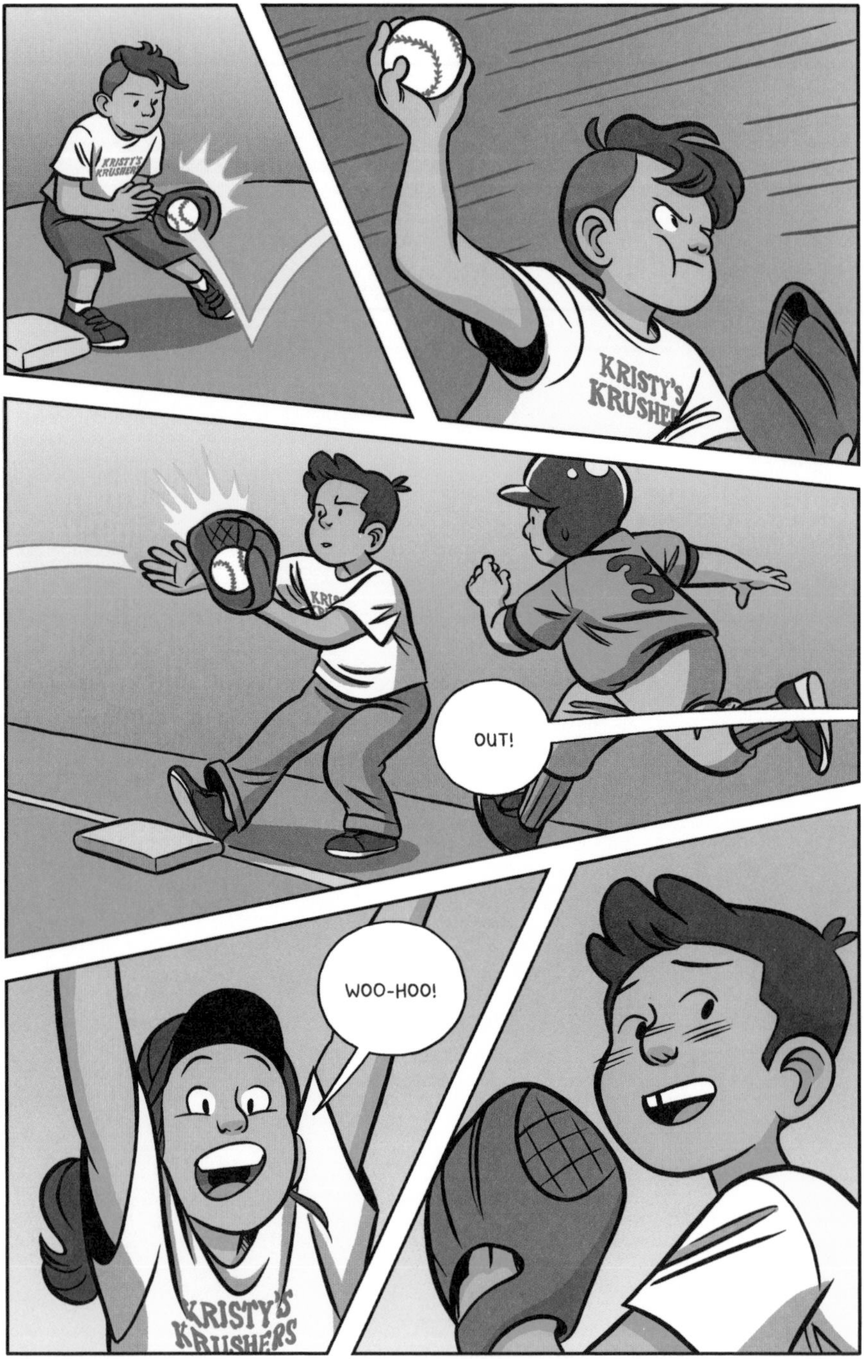
KRISTY'S KRUSHERS
KRISTY'S KRUSHERS
OUT!
WOO-HOO!
KRISTY'S KRUSHERS

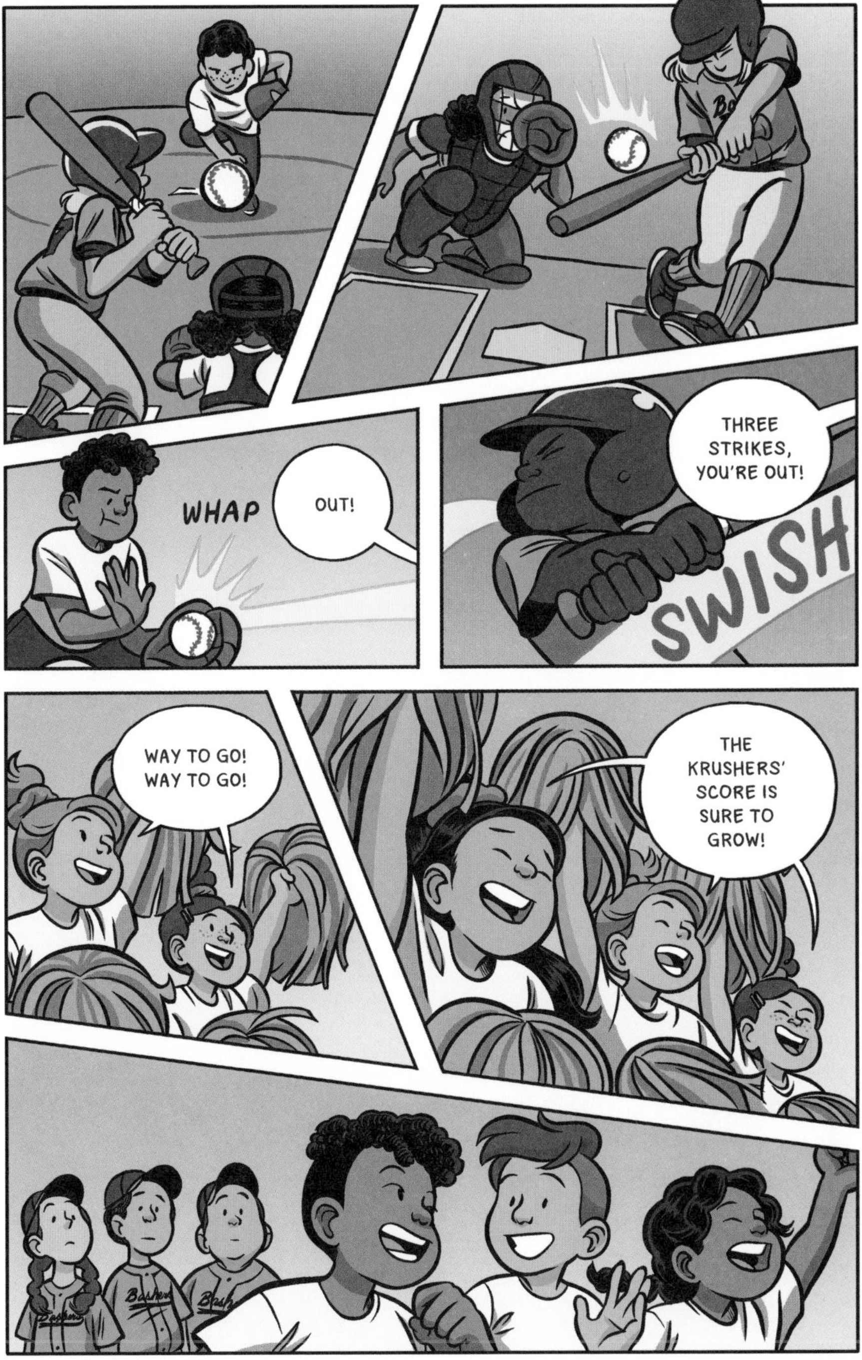
WHAP
OUT!
THREE STRIKES, YOU'RE OUT!
SWISH
WAY TO GO! WAY TO GO!
THE KRUSHERS' SCORE IS SURE TO GROW!

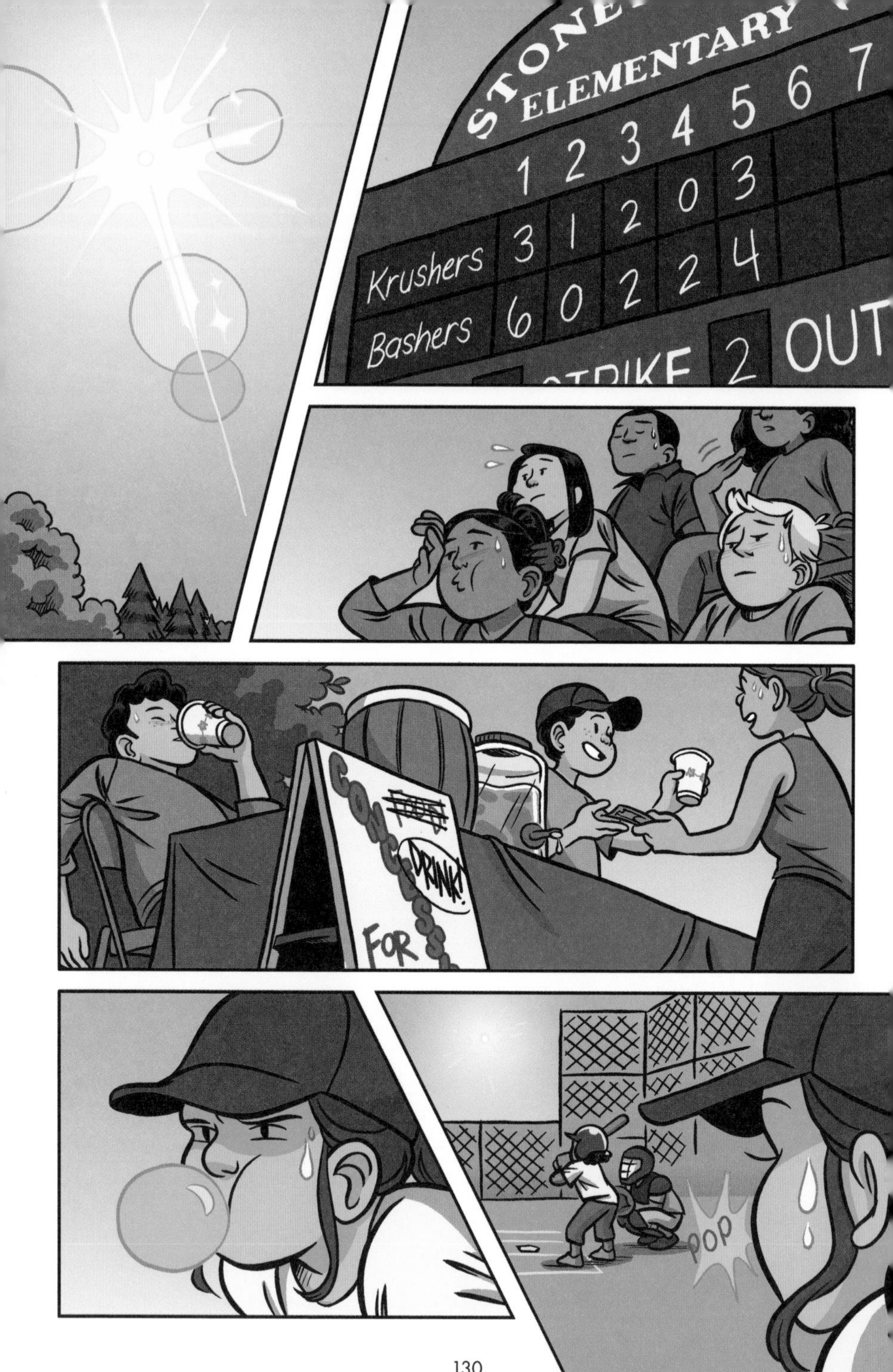
STONE
ELEMENTARY
1 2 3 4 5 6 7
Krushers 3 1 2 0 3
Bashers 6 0 2 2 4
STRIKE 2 OUT
CONCESSIONS
DRINK!
FOR
POP

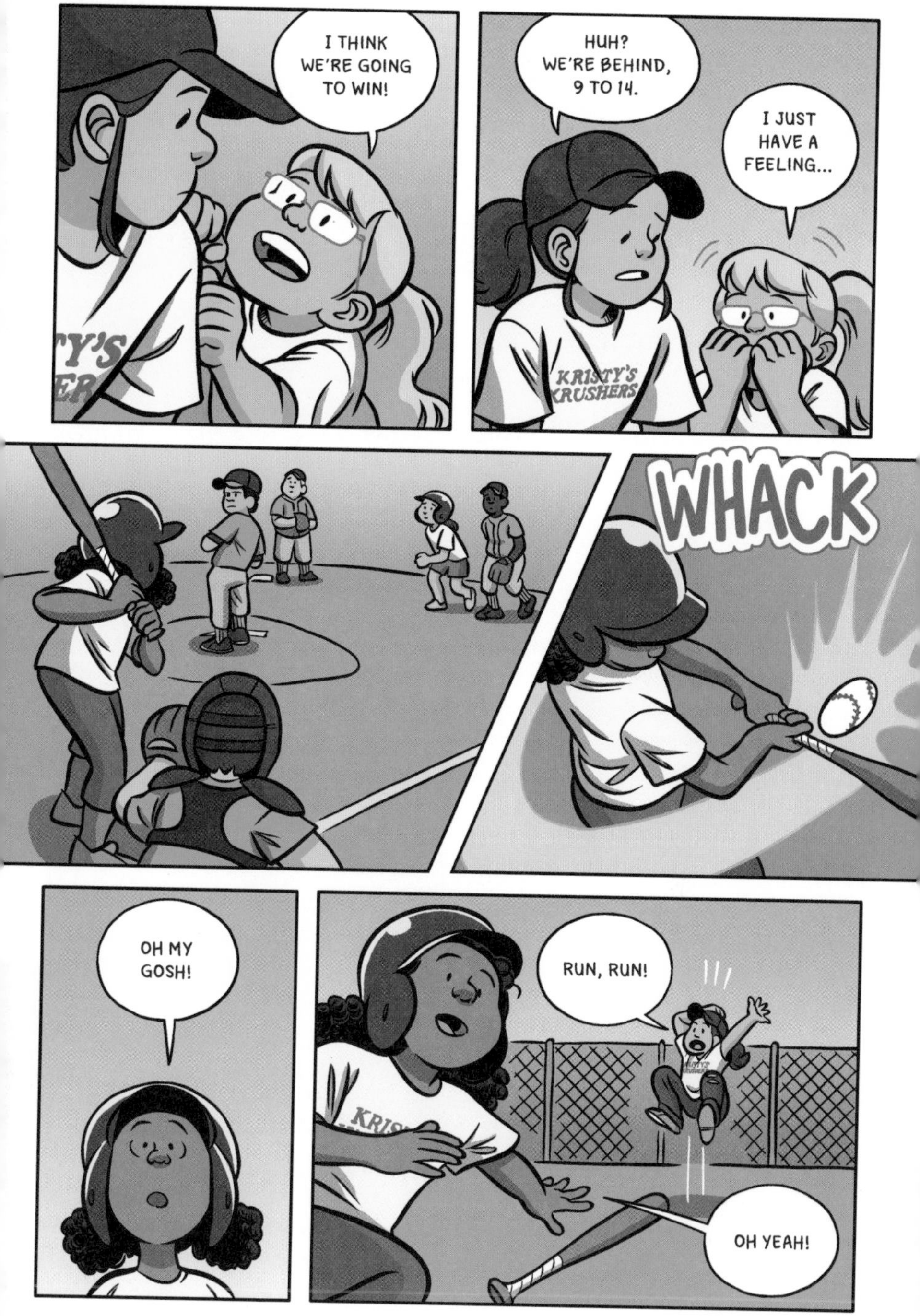
I THINK WE'RE GOING TO WIN!
HUH? WE'RE BEHIND, 9 TO 14.
I JUST HAVE A FEELING...
KRISTY'S KRUSHERS
WHACK
OH MY GOSH!
RUN, RUN!
OH YEAH!

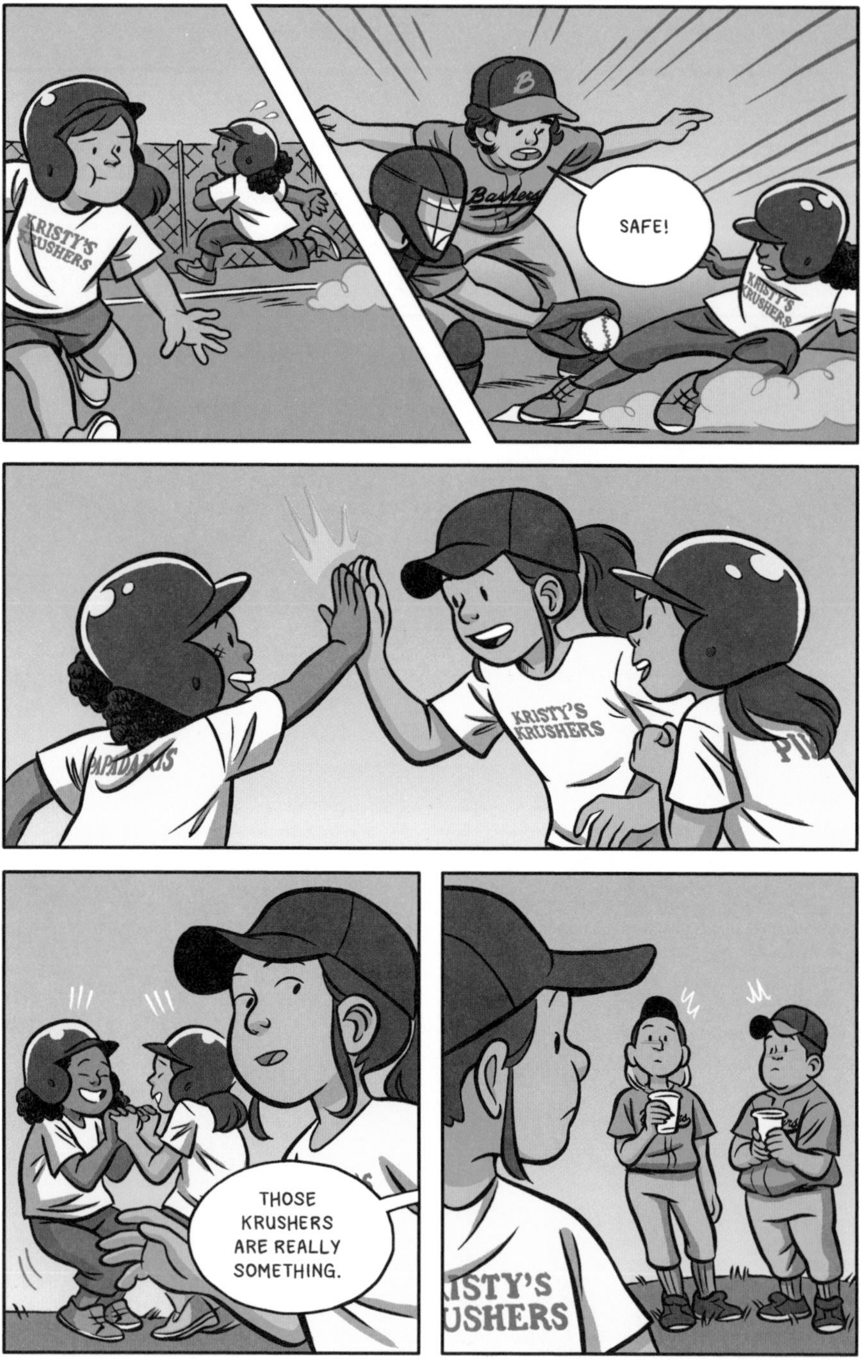
KRISTY'S KRUSHERS
SAFE!
KRISTY'S KRUSHERS
PAPADAKIS
KRISTY'S KRUSHERS
THOSE KRUSHERS ARE REALLY SOMETHING.
KRISTY'S KRUSHERS

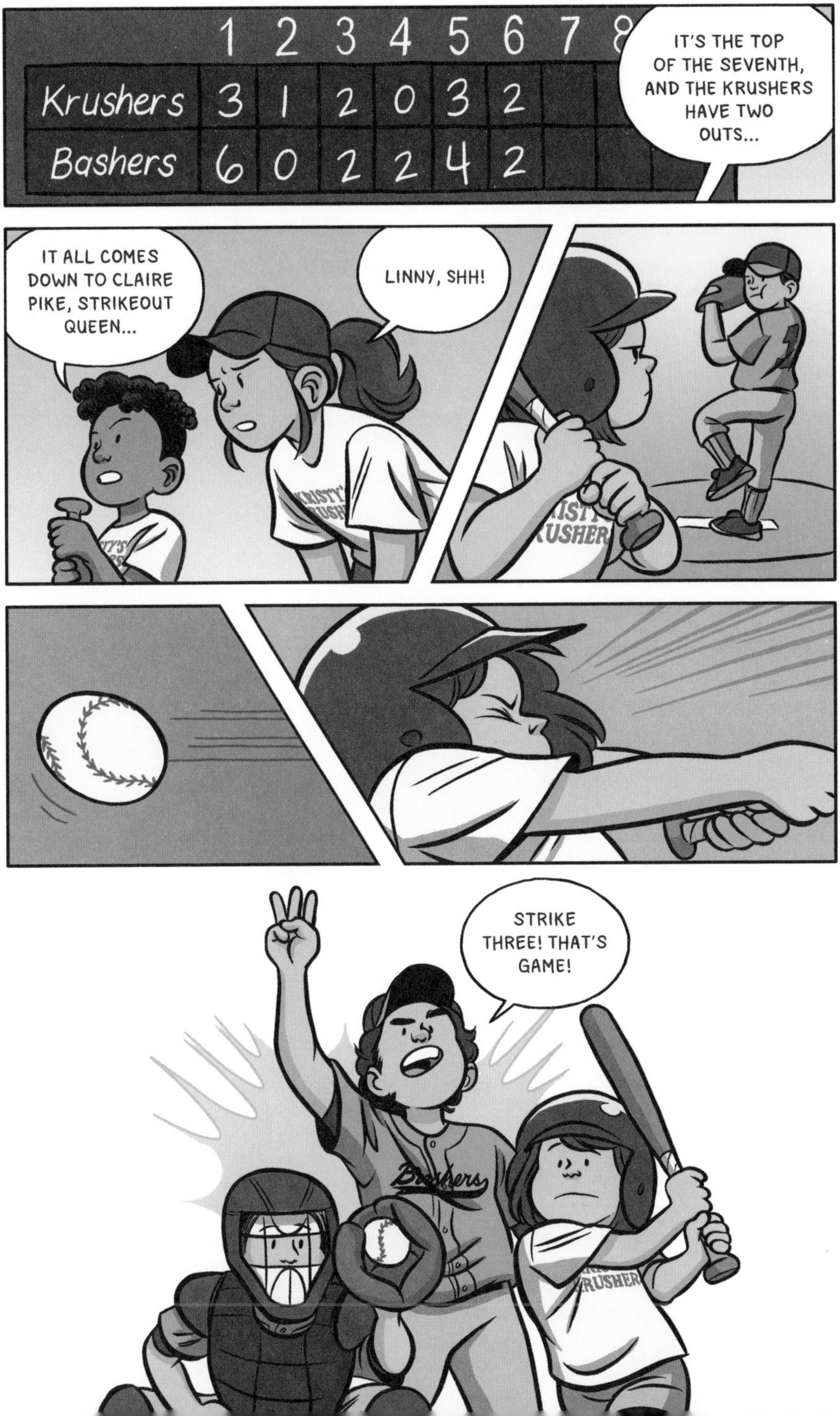
1 2 3 4 5 6 7
Krushers 3 1 2 0 3 2
Bashers 6 0 2 2 4 2
IT'S THE TOP OF THE SEVENTH, AND THE KRUSHERS HAVE TWO OUTS...
IT ALL COMES DOWN TO CLAIRE PIKE, STRIKEOUT QUEEN...
LINNY, SHH!
STRIKE THREE! THAT'S GAME!

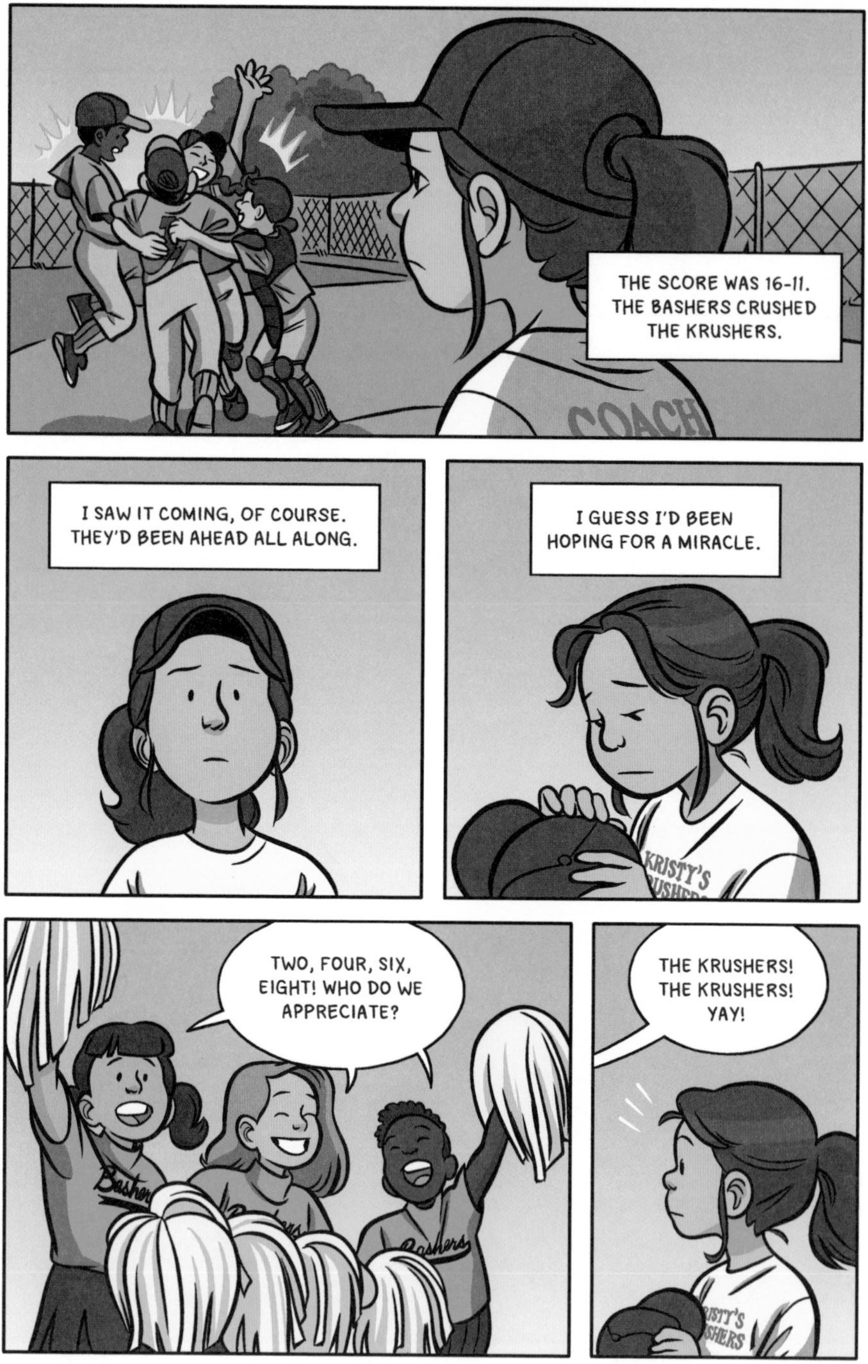
THE SCORE WAS 16-11. THE BASHERS CRUSHED THE KRUSHERS.
COACH
I SAW IT COMING, OF COURSE. THEY'D BEEN AHEAD ALL ALONG.
I GUESS I'D BEEN HOPING FOR A MIRACLE.
KRISTY'S
TWO, FOUR, SIX, EIGHT! WHO DO WE APPRECIATE?
Bashers
THE KRUSHERS! THE KRUSHERS! YAY!

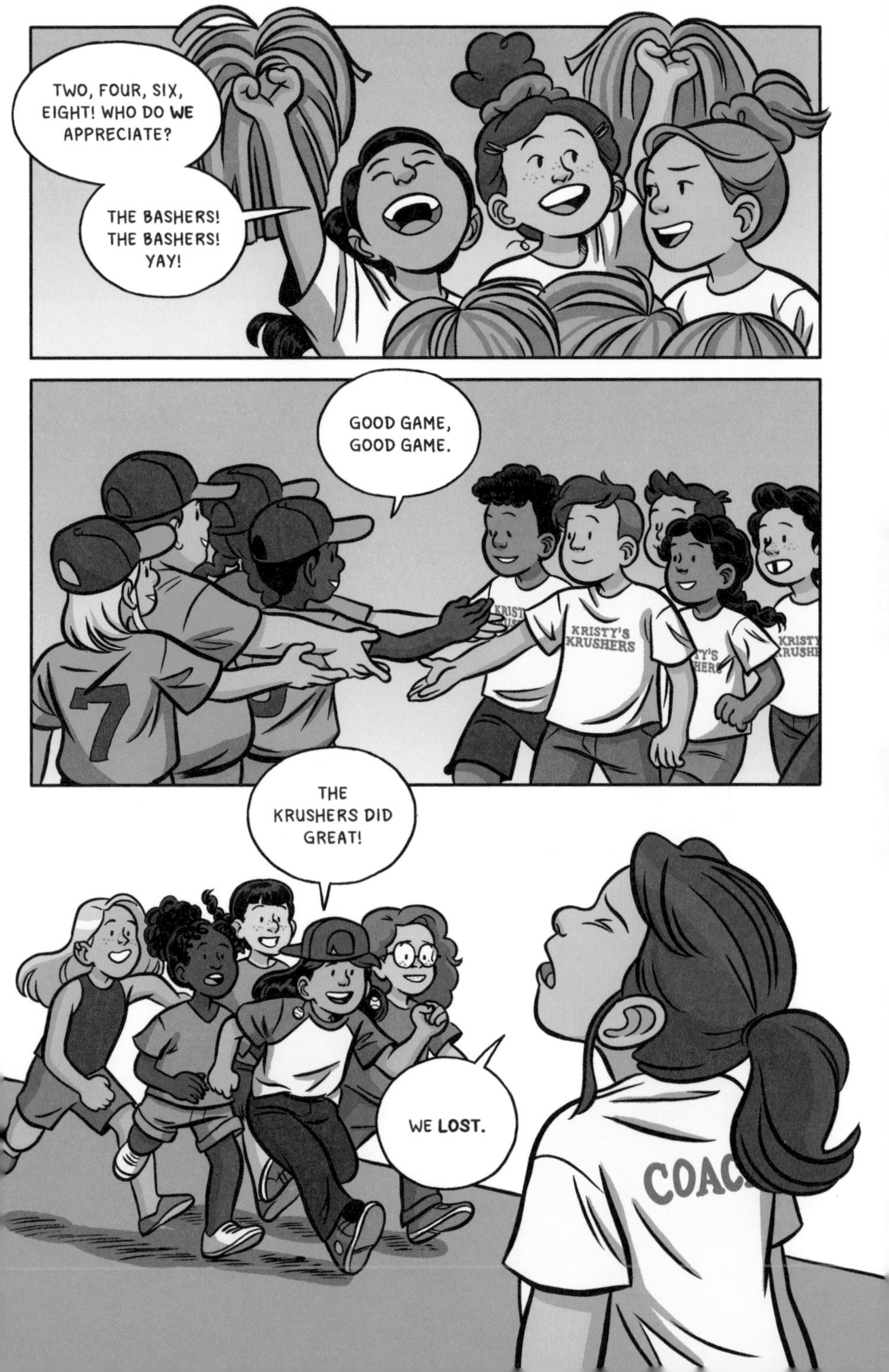
TWO, FOUR, SIX, EIGHT! WHO DO WE APPRECIATE?
THE BASHERS! THE BASHERS! YAY!
GOOD GAME, GOOD GAME.
KRISTY'S KRUSHERS
THE KRUSHERS DID GREAT!
WE LOST.
COAC

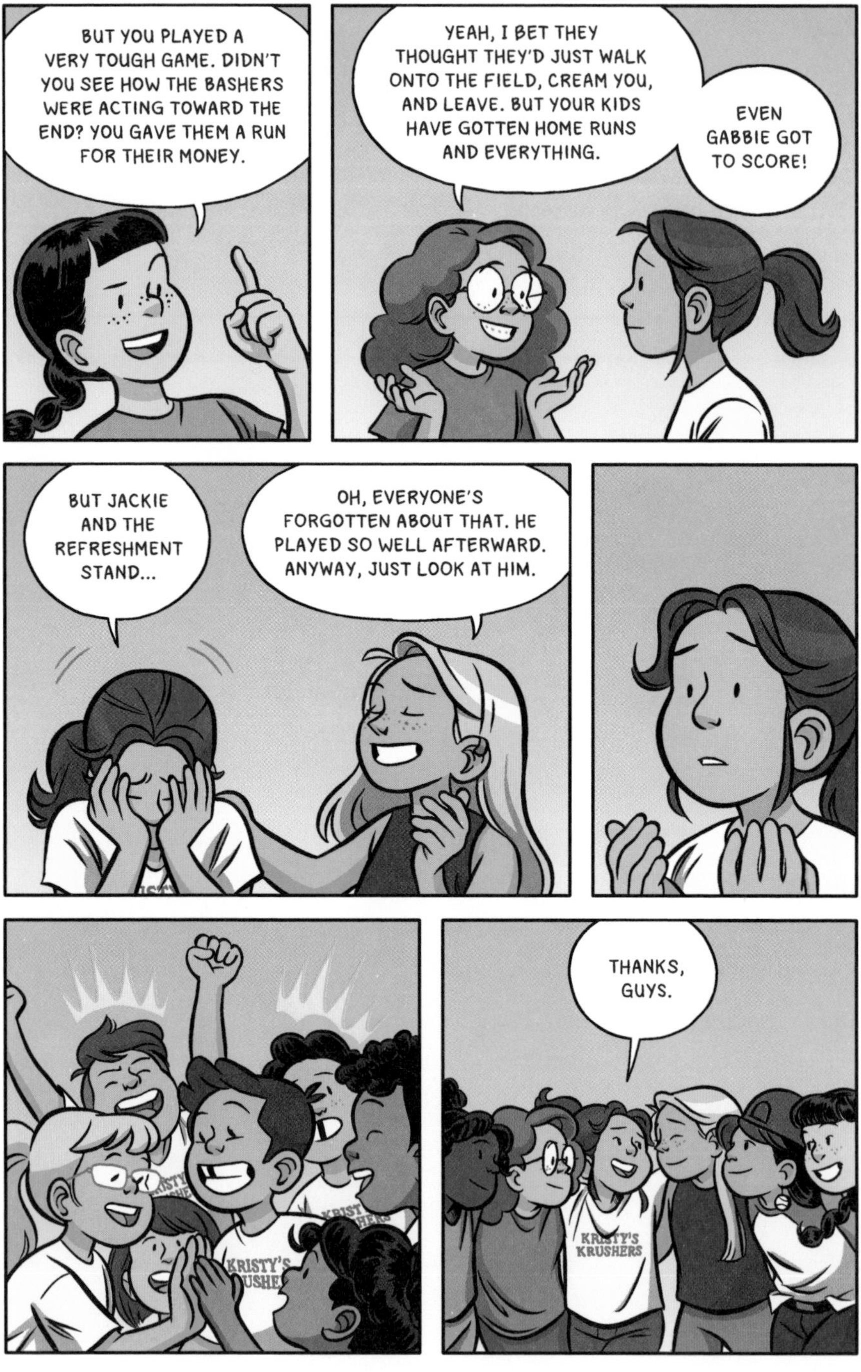
BUT YOU PLAYED A VERY TOUGH GAME. DIDN'T YOU SEE HOW THE BASHERS WERE ACTING TOWARD THE END? YOU GAVE THEM A RUN FOR THEIR MONEY.
YEAH, I BET THEY THOUGHT THEY'D JUST WALK ONTO THE FIELD, CREAM YOU, AND LEAVE. BUT YOUR KIDS HAVE GOTTEN HOME RUNS AND EVERYTHING.
EVEN GABBIE GOT TO SCORE!
BUT JACKIE AND THE REFRESHMENT STAND...
OH, EVERYONE'S FORGOTTEN ABOUT THAT. HE PLAYED SO WELL AFTERWARD. ANYWAY, JUST LOOK AT HIM.
KRISTY'S KRUSHERS
THANKS, GUYS.
KRISTY'S KRUSHERS

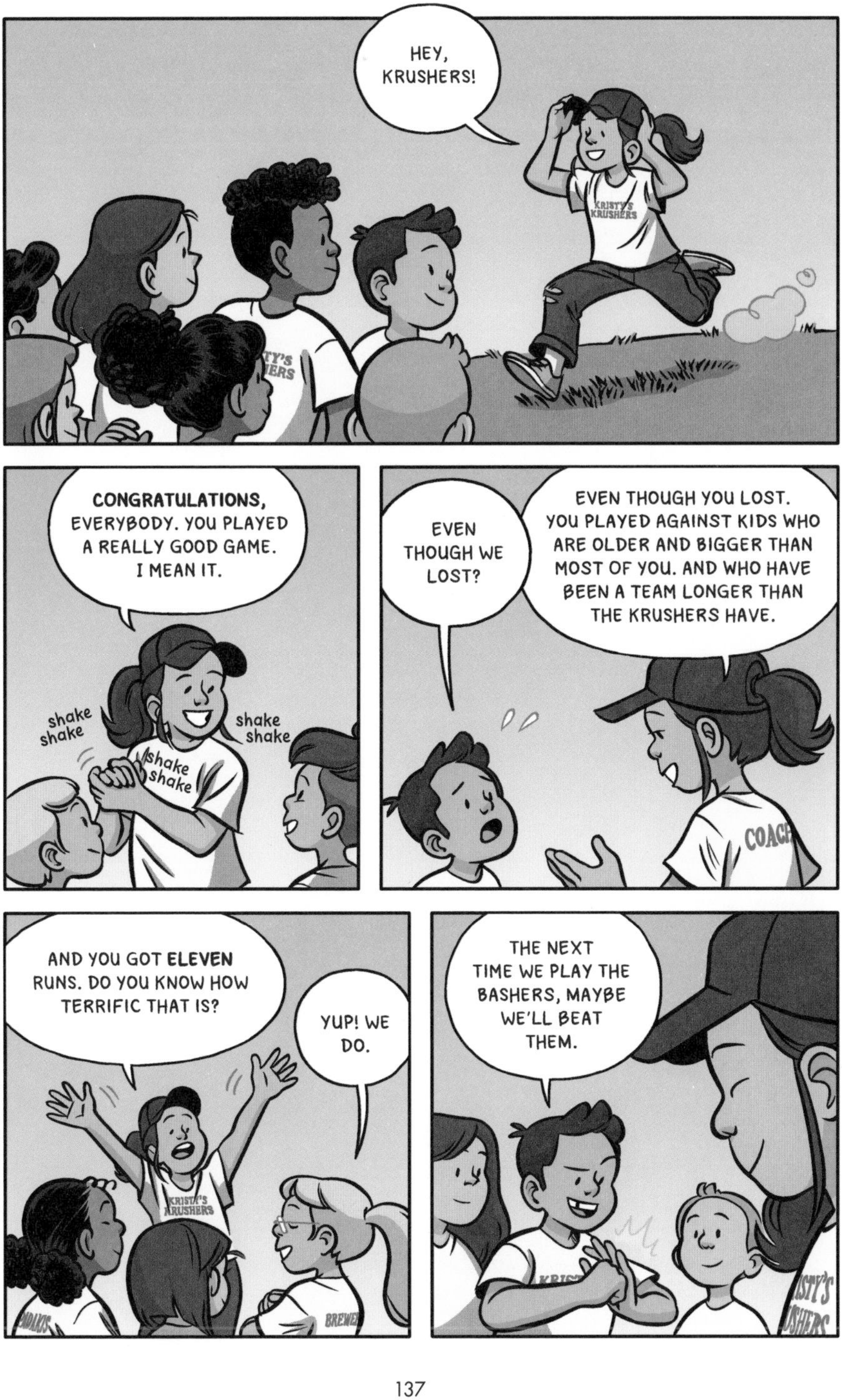
HEY, KRUSHERS!
KRISTY'S KRUSHERS
CONGRATULATIONS, EVERYBODY. YOU PLAYED A REALLY GOOD GAME. I MEAN IT.
shake shake
shake shake
shake shake
EVEN THOUGH WE LOST?
EVEN THOUGH YOU LOST. YOU PLAYED AGAINST KIDS WHO ARE OLDER AND BIGGER THAN MOST OF YOU. AND WHO HAVE BEEN A TEAM LONGER THAN THE KRUSHERS HAVE.
AND YOU GOT ELEVEN RUNS. DO YOU KNOW HOW TERRIFIC THAT IS?
YUP! WE DO.
KRISTY'S KRUSHERS
THE NEXT TIME WE PLAY THE BASHERS, MAYBE WE'LL BEAT THEM.

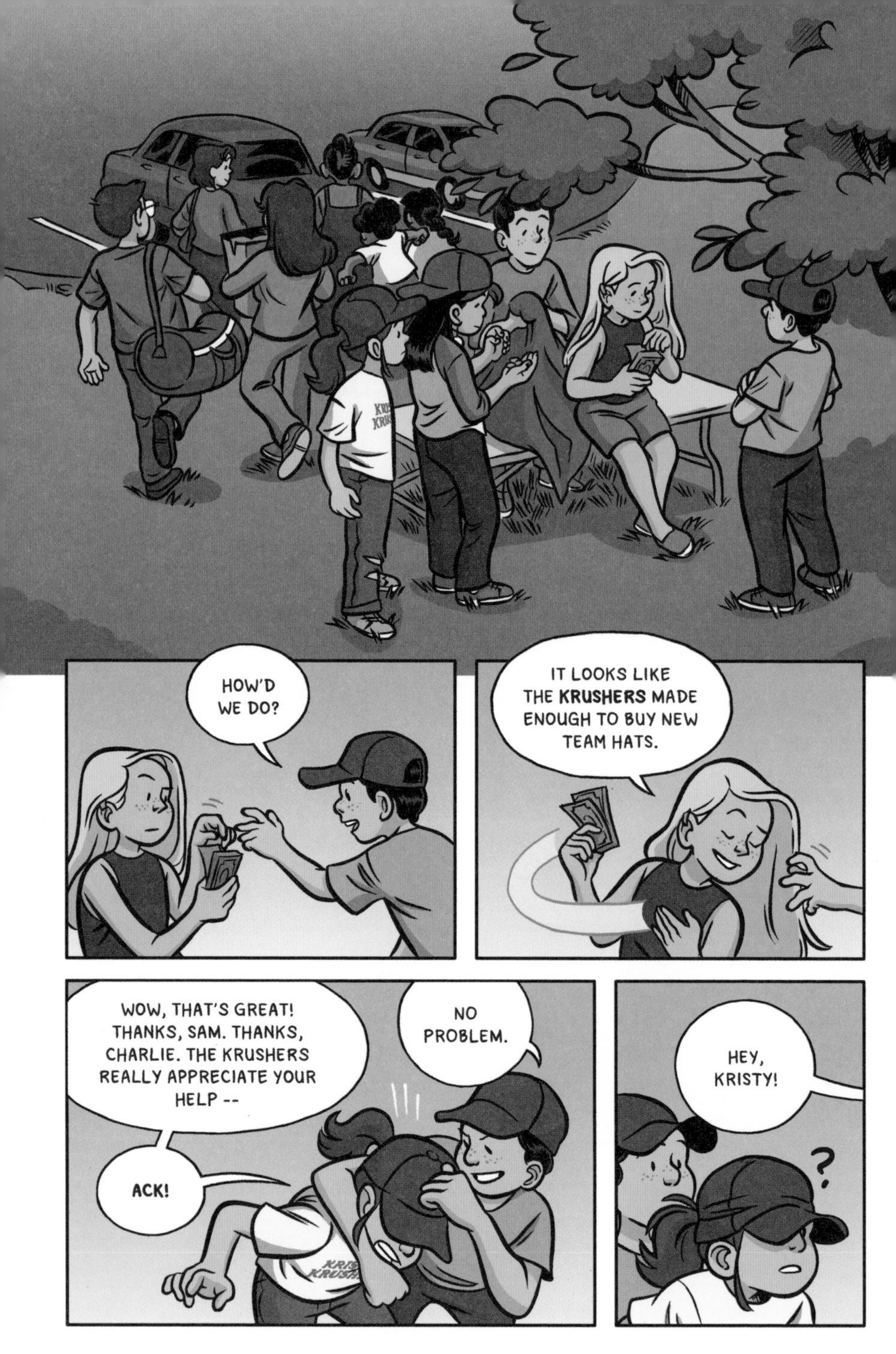
KRIS KRUSH
HOW'D WE DO?
IT LOOKS LIKE THE **KRUSHERS** MADE ENOUGH TO BUY NEW TEAM HATS.
WOW, THAT'S GREAT! THANKS, SAM. THANKS, CHARLIE. THE KRUSHERS REALLY APPRECIATE YOUR HELP --
NO PROBLEM.
ACK!
KRIS KRUSH
HEY, KRISTY!
?

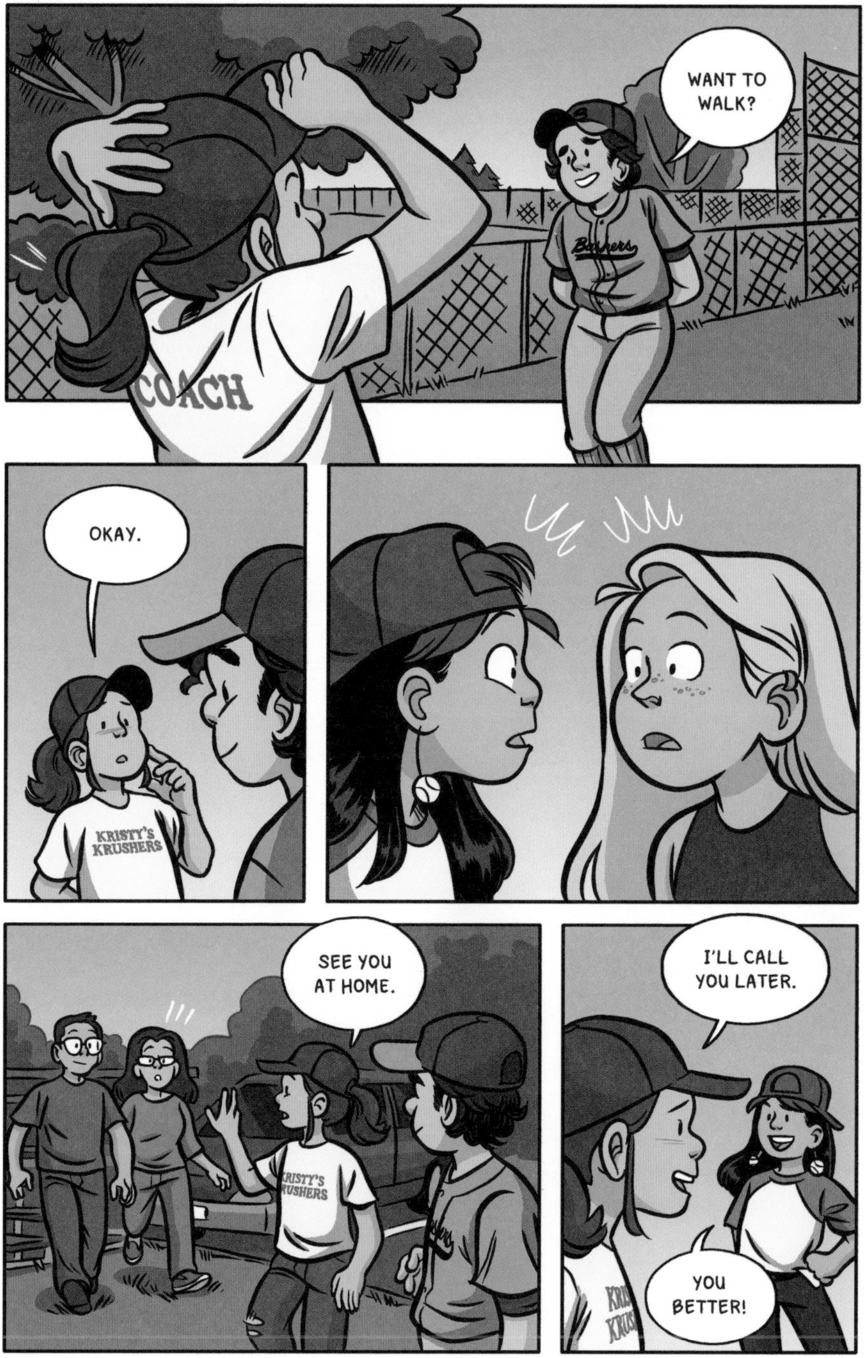
COACH
WANT TO WALK?
Bashers
OKAY.
KRISTY'S KRUSHERS
SEE YOU AT HOME.
KRISTY'S KRUSHERS
I'LL CALL YOU LATER.
YOU BETTER!

CHAPTER 16

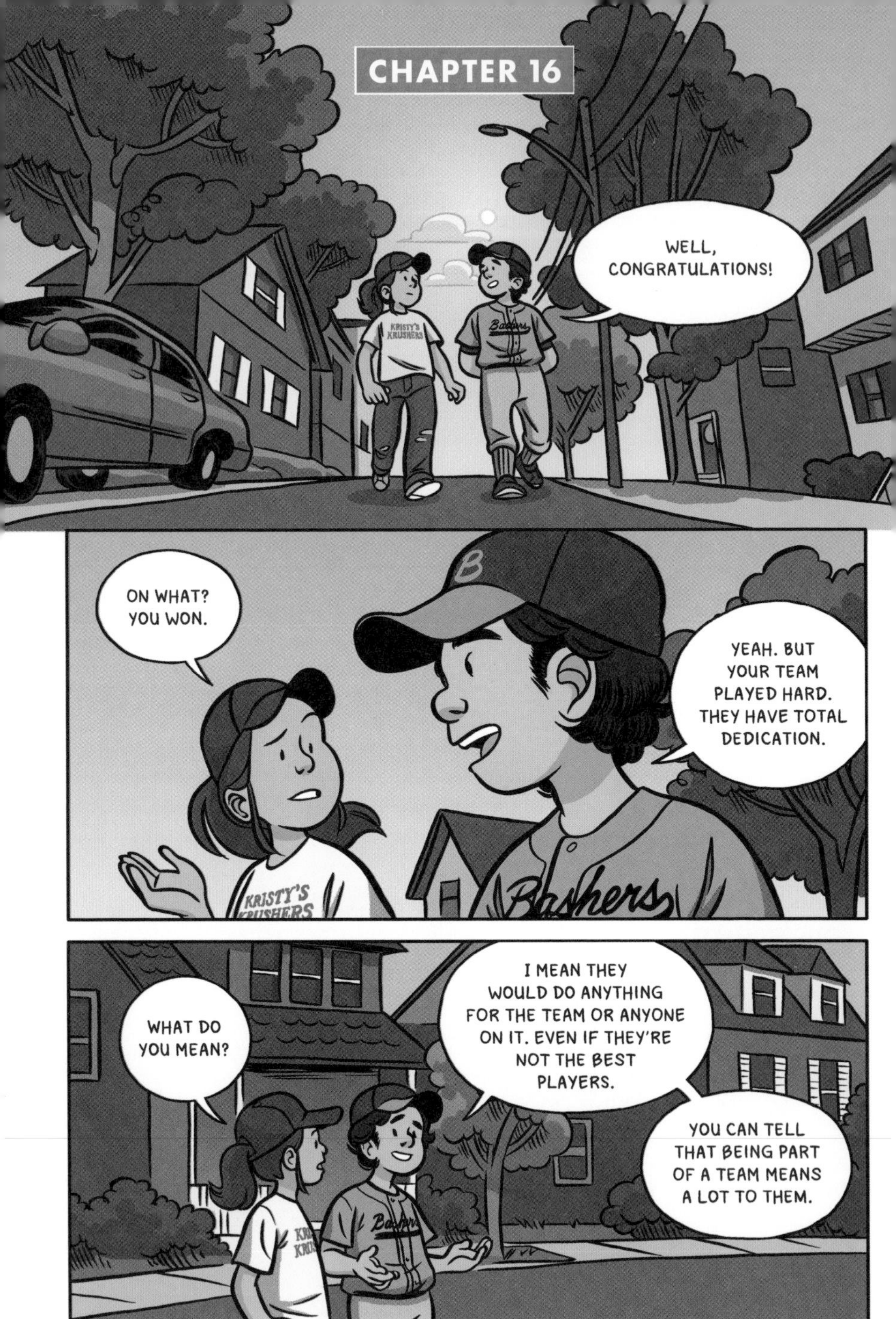
WELL, CONGRATULATIONS!
ON WHAT? YOU WON.
YEAH. BUT YOUR TEAM PLAYED HARD. THEY HAVE TOTAL DEDICATION.
KRISTY'S KRUSHERS
Bashers
WHAT DO YOU MEAN?
I MEAN THEY WOULD DO ANYTHING FOR THE TEAM OR ANYONE ON IT. EVEN IF THEY'RE NOT THE BEST PLAYERS.
YOU CAN TELL THAT BEING PART OF A TEAM MEANS A LOT TO THEM.

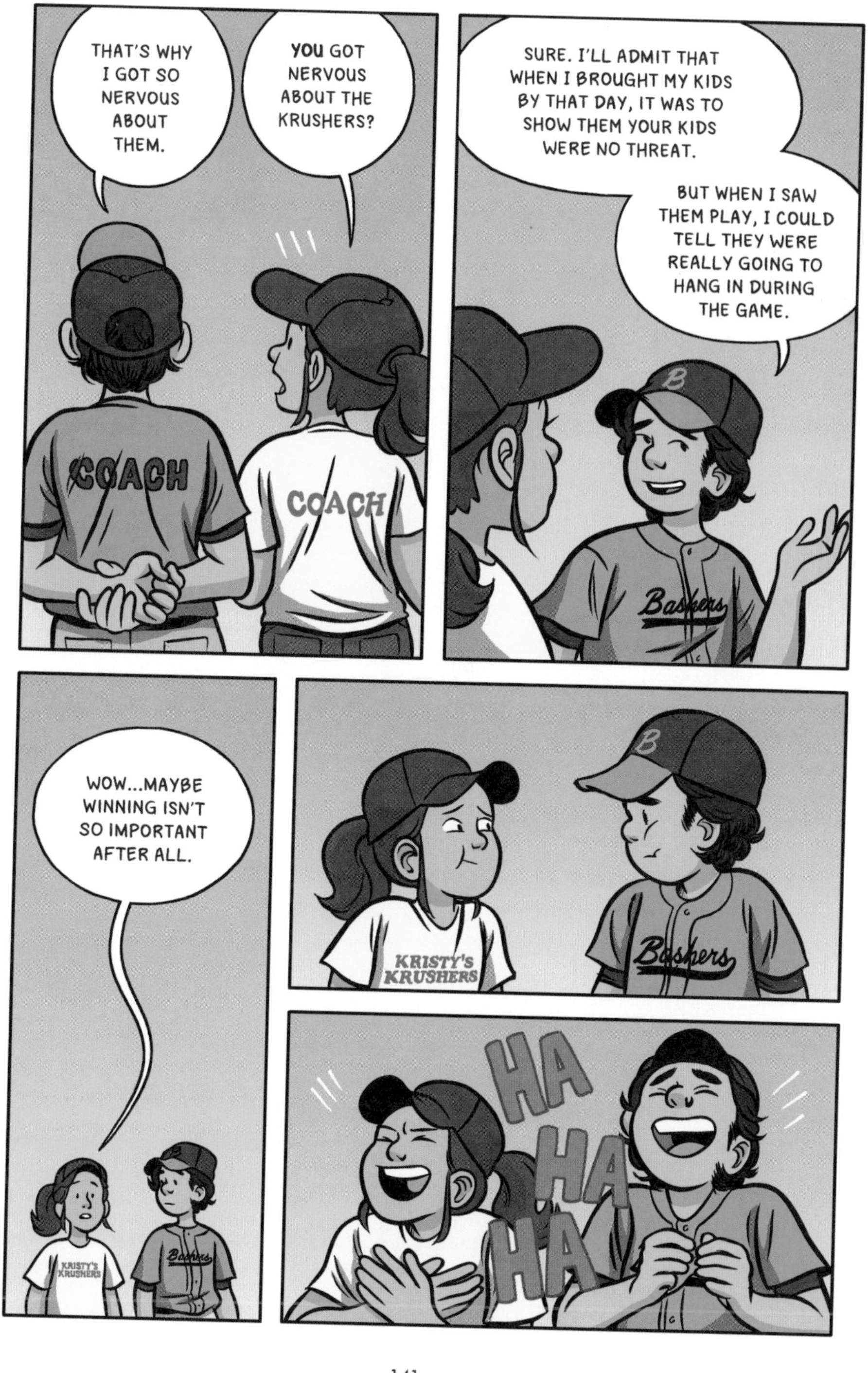
THAT'S WHY I GOT SO NERVOUS ABOUT THEM.
YOU GOT NERVOUS ABOUT THE KRUSHERS?
COACH
COACH
SURE. I'LL ADMIT THAT WHEN I BROUGHT MY KIDS BY THAT DAY, IT WAS TO SHOW THEM YOUR KIDS WERE NO THREAT.
BUT WHEN I SAW THEM PLAY, I COULD TELL THEY WERE REALLY GOING TO HANG IN DURING THE GAME.
Bashers
WOW...MAYBE WINNING ISN'T SO IMPORTANT AFTER ALL.
KRISTY'S KRUSHERS
Bashers
HA HA HA

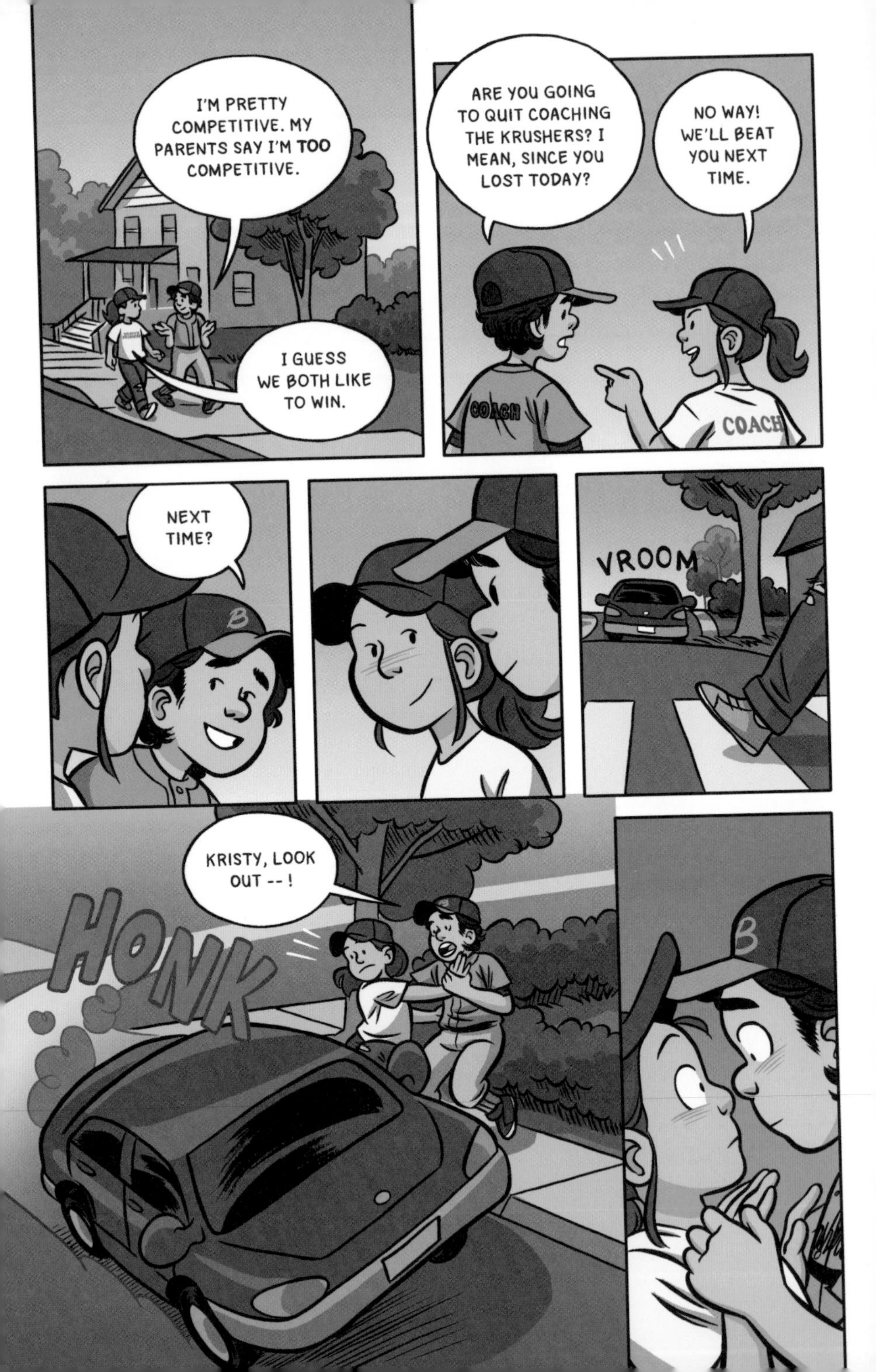
I'M PRETTY COMPETITIVE. MY PARENTS SAY I'M **TOO** COMPETITIVE.
I GUESS WE BOTH LIKE TO WIN.
ARE YOU GOING TO QUIT COACHING THE KRUSHERS? I MEAN, SINCE YOU LOST TODAY?
NO WAY! WE'LL BEAT YOU NEXT TIME.
COACH
COACH
NEXT TIME?
VROOM
KRISTY, LOOK OUT -- !
HONK

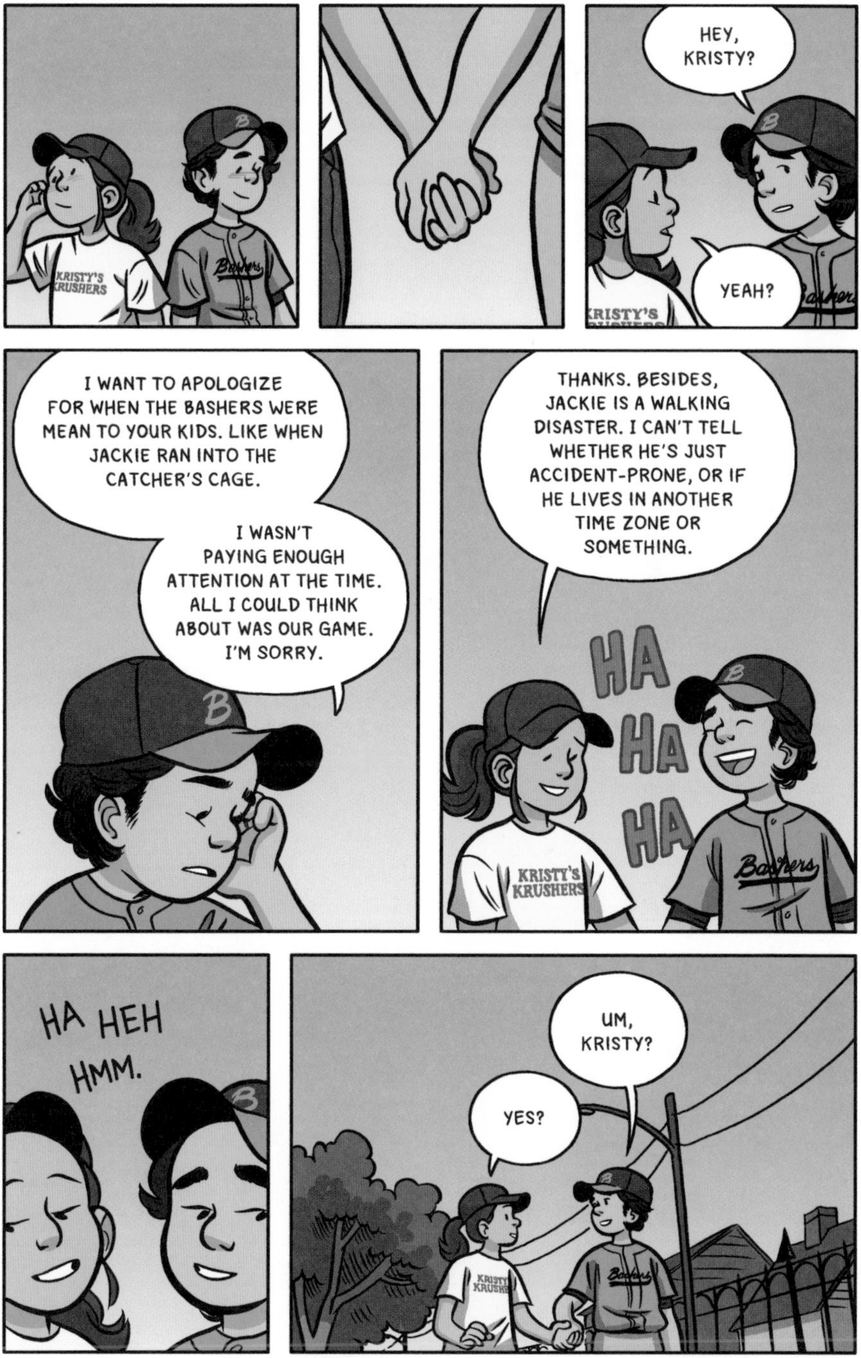
HEY, KRISTY?
YEAH?
I WANT TO APOLOGIZE FOR WHEN THE BASHERS WERE MEAN TO YOUR KIDS. LIKE WHEN JACKIE RAN INTO THE CATCHER'S CAGE.
I WASN'T PAYING ENOUGH ATTENTION AT THE TIME. ALL I COULD THINK ABOUT WAS OUR GAME. I'M SORRY.
THANKS. BESIDES, JACKIE IS A WALKING DISASTER. I CAN'T TELL WHETHER HE'S JUST ACCIDENT-PRONE, OR IF HE LIVES IN ANOTHER TIME ZONE OR SOMETHING.
HA HA HA
HA HEH HMM.
UM, KRISTY?
YES?

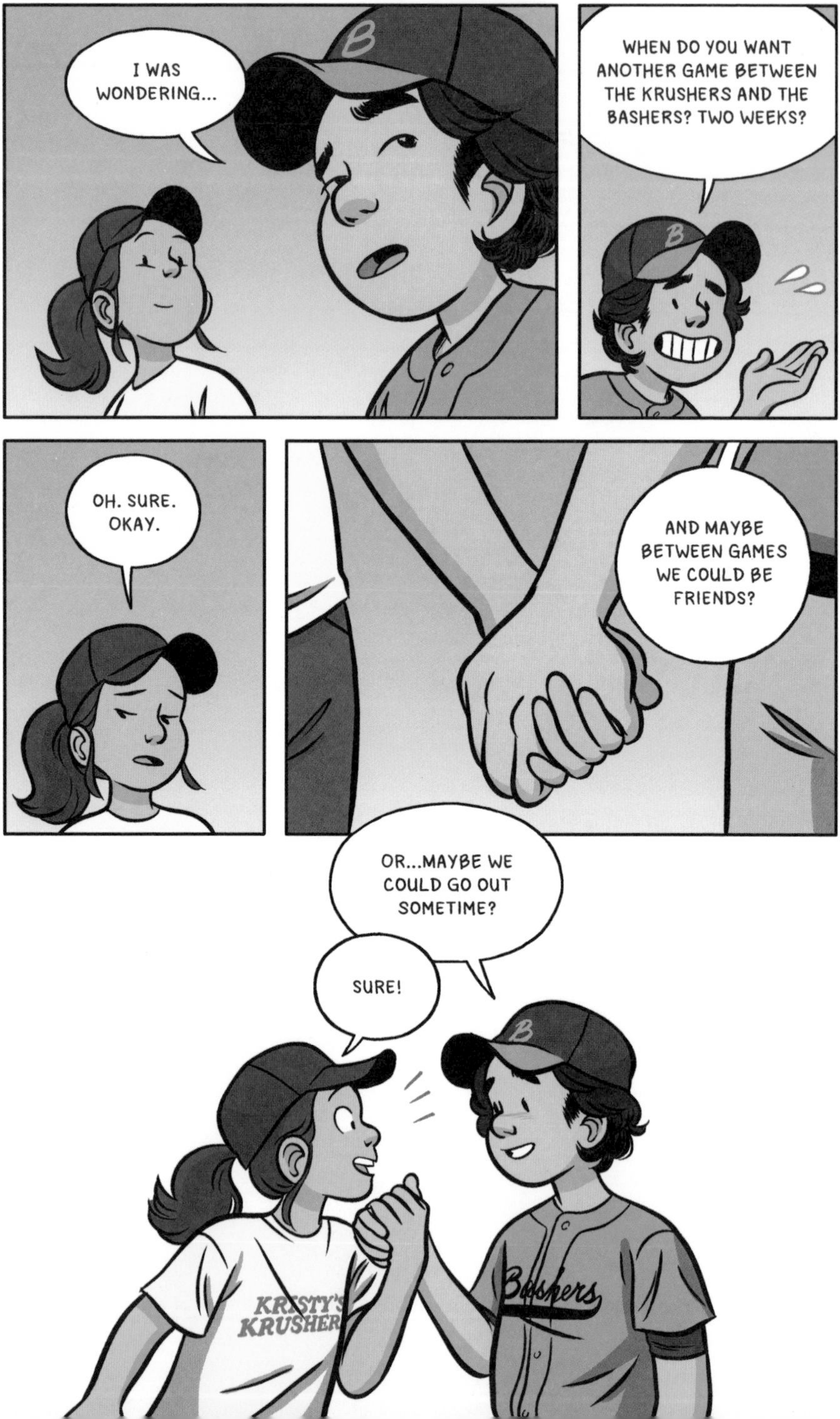
I WAS WONDERING...
WHEN DO YOU WANT ANOTHER GAME BETWEEN THE KRUSHERS AND THE BASHERS? TWO WEEKS?
OH. SURE. OKAY.
AND MAYBE BETWEEN GAMES WE COULD BE FRIENDS?
OR...MAYBE WE COULD GO OUT SOMETIME?
SURE!
Bashers

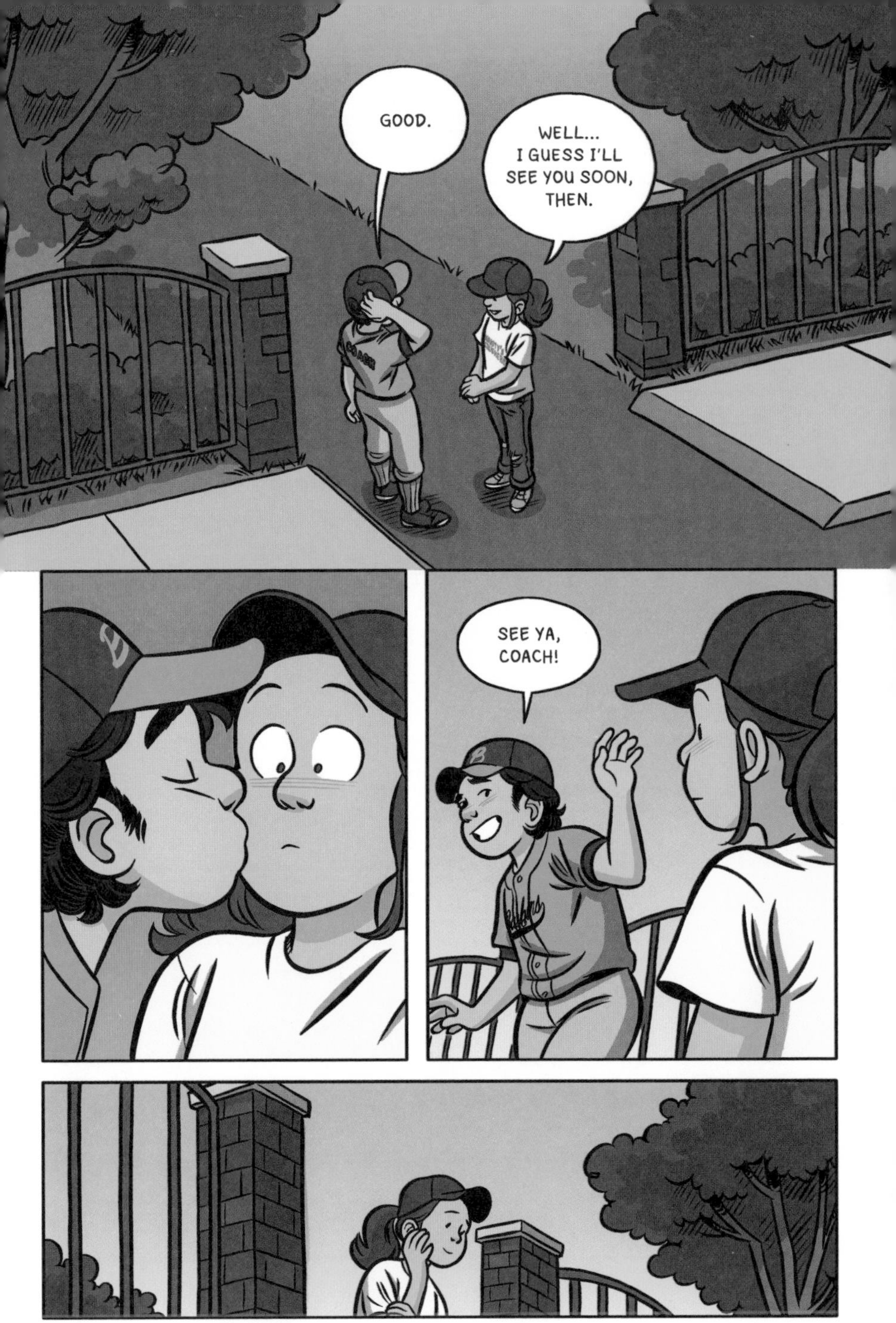
GOOD.
WELL... I GUESS I'LL SEE YOU SOON, THEN.
SEE YA, COACH!

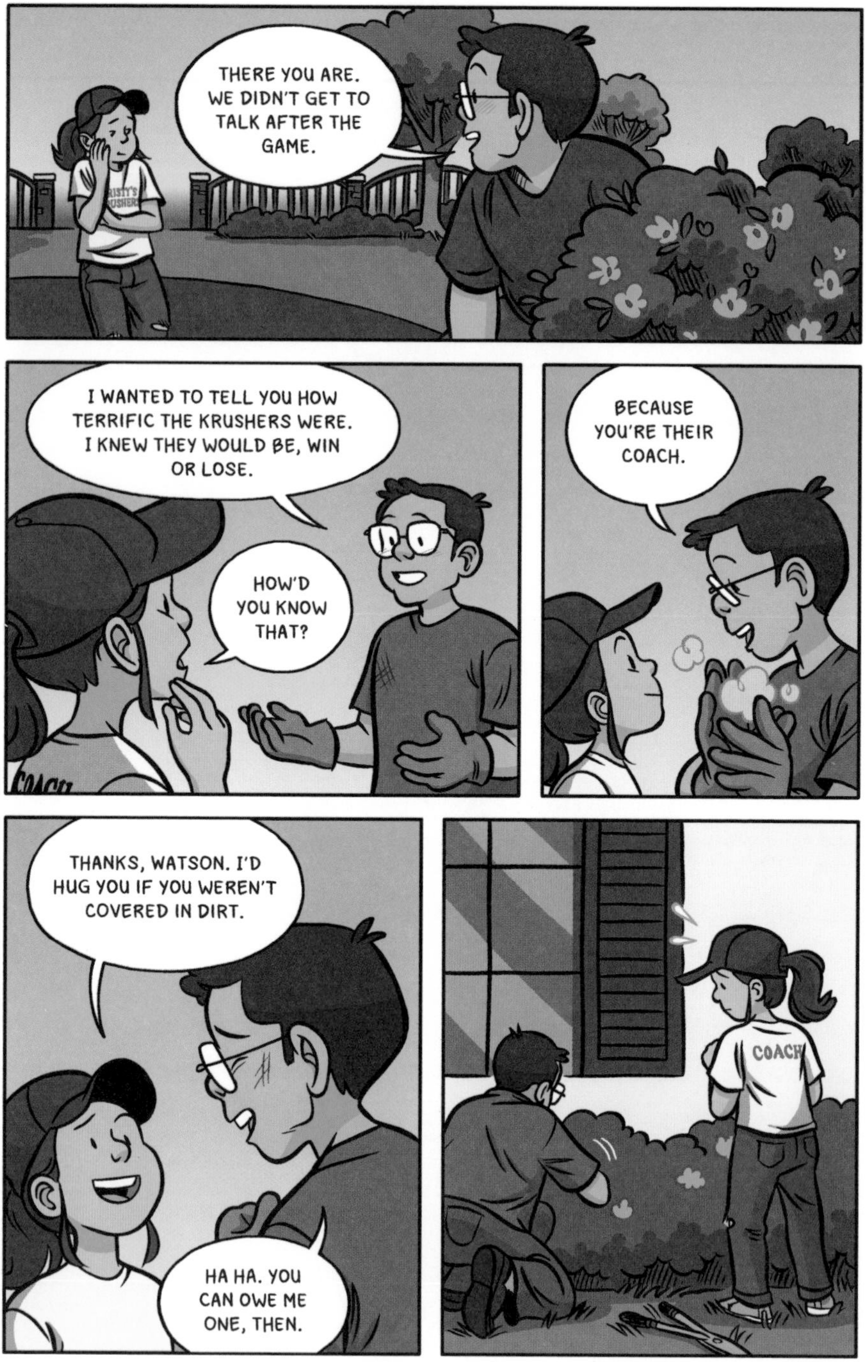
THERE YOU ARE. WE DIDN'T GET TO TALK AFTER THE GAME.
I WANTED TO TELL YOU HOW TERRIFIC THE KRUSHERS WERE. I KNEW THEY WOULD BE, WIN OR LOSE.
HOW'D YOU KNOW THAT?
BECAUSE YOU'RE THEIR COACH.
THANKS, WATSON. I'D HUG YOU IF YOU WEREN'T COVERED IN DIRT.
HA HA. YOU CAN OWE ME ONE, THEN.
COACH

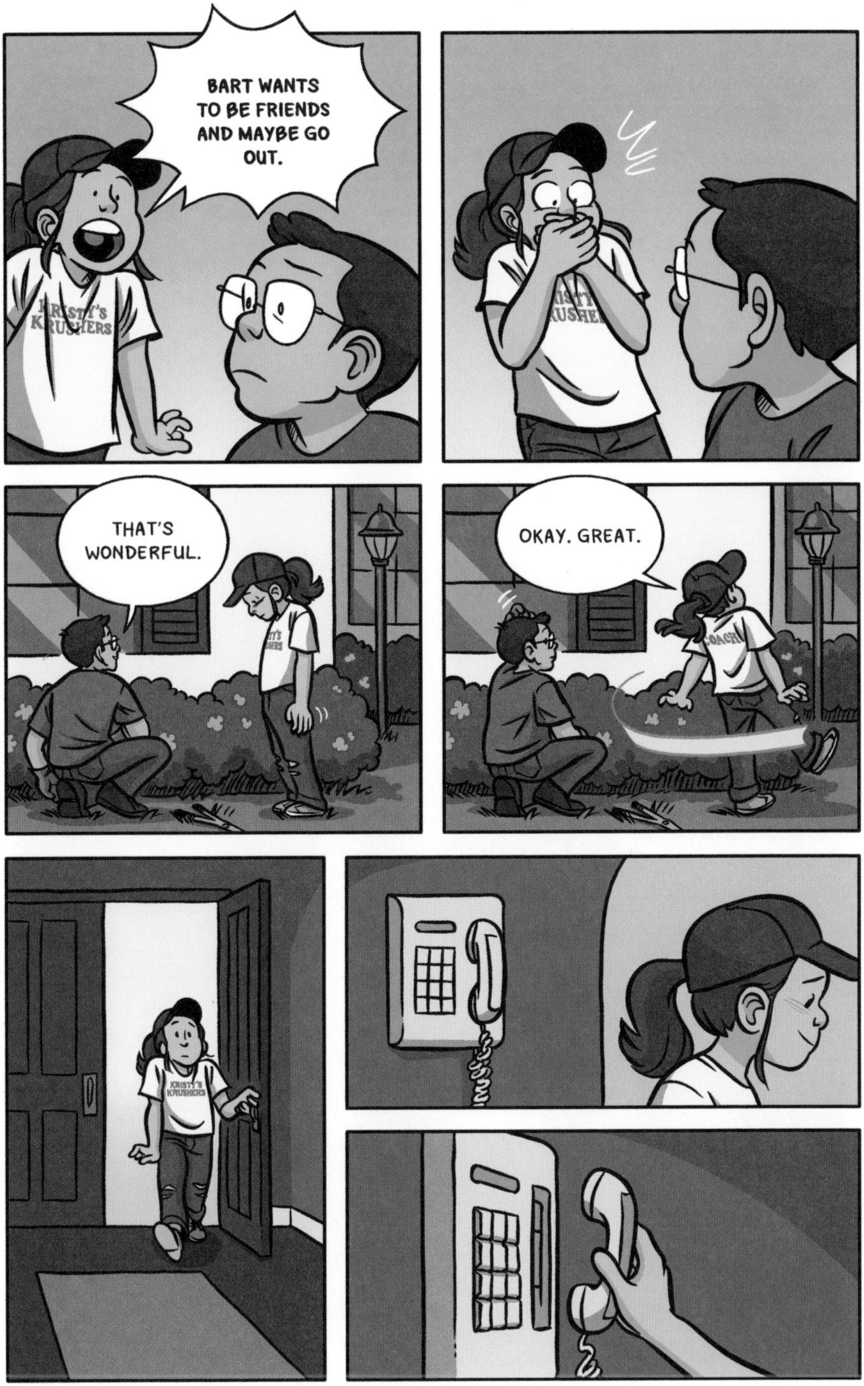
BART WANTS TO BE FRIENDS AND MAYBE GO OUT.
KRISTY'S KRUSHERS
THAT'S WONDERFUL.
OKAY. GREAT.
COACH
KRISTY'S KRUSHERS

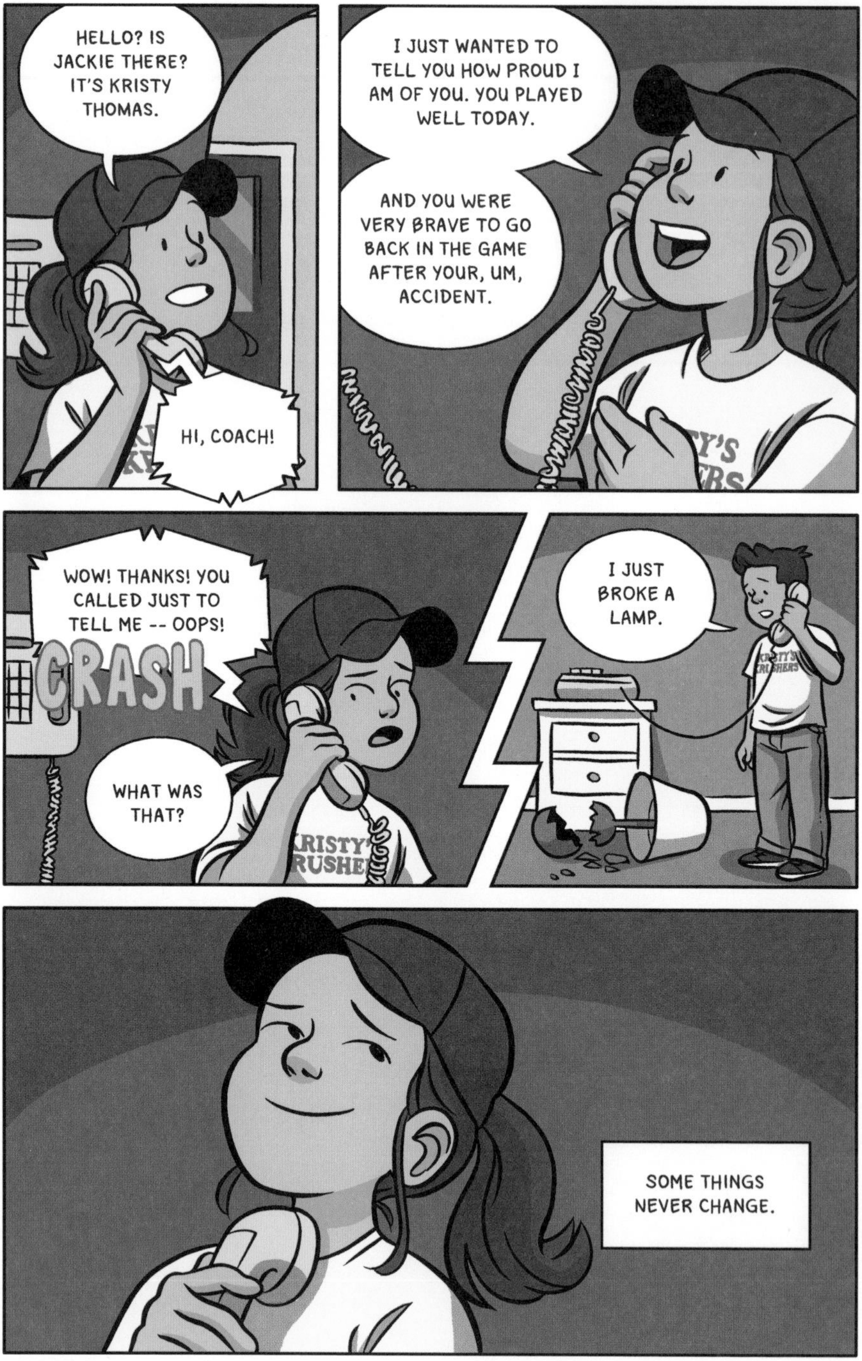
HELLO? IS JACKIE THERE? IT'S KRISTY THOMAS.
HI, COACH!
I JUST WANTED TO TELL YOU HOW PROUD I AM OF YOU. YOU PLAYED WELL TODAY.
AND YOU WERE VERY BRAVE TO GO BACK IN THE GAME AFTER YOUR, UM, ACCIDENT.
WOW! THANKS! YOU CALLED JUST TO TELL ME -- OOPS!
CRASH
WHAT WAS THAT?
I JUST BROKE A LAMP.
SOME THINGS NEVER CHANGE.

ANN M. MARTIN'S The Baby-sitters Club is one of the most popular series in the history of publishing — with more than 190 million books in print worldwide — and inspired a generation of young readers. Her novels include *Belle Teal*, *A Corner of the Universe* (a Newbery Honor Book), *Here Today*, *A Dog's Life*, and *On Christmas Eve*, as well as the much loved collaborations, *P.S. Longer Letter Later* and *Snail Mail No More* with Paula Danziger, and *The Doll People* and *The Meanest Doll in the World*, written with Laura Godwin and illustrated by Brian Selznick. Ann lives in upstate New York.